■ ONE MAN'S MEAT... ■

Abruptly there was a flash of green light on the enormous sphere, green lights winked in the array below the humans. The aliens came to life, limbs snaking out to hit buttons, adjust control knobs.

A bewildering mass of screen windows lit up. In a central band, a solar system schematic flickered. But there was no single primary, just five points of intense white light performing a complex orbital dance, a blinding design of pure light.

"Abernatha's Knot!" Nathan had an expression of stunned joy on his face. "Neutron stars in orbital lock. I think the ship will head for the knot's midpoint."

"Why?" Cracka asked as he stared at the thing on the screen. The small suns seemed virtually one, a hot little blaze of cold white light.

"At the midpoint the fabric of the universe itself is weak."

Cracka was startled. "So this ship could be going somewhere else? Maybe another galaxy?"

"Yeah, something like that."

By Christopher Rowley
Published by Ballantine Books:

THE BLACK SHIP

GOLDEN SUNLANDS

STARHAMMER

THE WAR FOR ETERNITY

GOLDEN SUNLANDS

Christopher Rowley

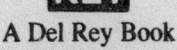

A Del Rey Book

BALLANTINE BOOKS • NEW YORK

A Del Rey Book
Published by Ballantine Books
Copyright © 1987 by Christopher B. Rowley

Library of Congress Catalog Card Number: 87-91137

ISBN 0-345-33174-5

Manufactured in the United States of America

First Edition: July 1987

Cover Art by Ralph McQuarrie

■ PROLOGUE

From Dyxman's *Encyclopedia of the Inexplicable: Phenomena of the Human/Nonhuman Interface*.

Diaden Cluster (Calabel's World colony)

This globular cluster consists primarily of 6,000 small red stars and a halo of gas, and younger, hotter stars collected during the globular's most recent orbital pass through the galactic disk.

For many millennia the Diadem Cluster has enjoyed an ominous reputation in the Human Milieu . . .

■ CHAPTER ONE

The surface of the pond was perfectly smooth, except where a jagged dendron jutted up, bearing a single eye flower.

A small airfish, with iridescent skin, fluttered to the flower and sipped the nectar.

Clouds had gathered in the lee of the skyreef and had thickened to a dark mass. Far off, lightning flashed down into the forest of hand palms. The clouds covered the small golden sun, and the air cooled.

The small airfish flew away. Raindrops began to fall, and under cover of the rain, tadpoles rose from the bottom of the pond and began to climb out into the air. Metamorphosis overtook them, and their smooth, slimy skins cracked open. They struggled free and shook out their new, scarcely hardened wings.

When the rain had passed, the tadpoles were gone. In their place young airfish took to the sky, wings beating in high tempo under the golden sun.

For Federal Ranger Cracka Buckshore the day began with an unusual crisis down at the Prench Tronch Ranger's Office. The phone kept beeping insistently. Everyone in Prench Tronch was demanding to speak to him, it seemed.

Wearily he sipped caf for a minute or two while the phone monitor blipped up the names of callers. Sam Boan,

sheriff of the town, was one of them. That raised an eye-
brow on Cracka's bluff, square face. For Sam to be calling
him was unusual. Between the federal ranger and the local
sheriff existed nothing but enormous dislike.

He scratched one side of the big, straight nose. Ran the
fingers back through his hair, thinner every day now.
Wrong side of forty. Have to give up this damned job.

Same litany, every day.

Same old, scrubby office, too. Beat-up maps of Prench
Tronch, 350,000 square kilometers of dust and the dark,
alien tronch forest hung on the wall to the left of the win-
dow. A poster commemorating a championship for the
Baytou City SpiderTigers hung in tatters on the far wall.
Six years gone already since the day he and Shay had taken
Kid Folo to that game.

Time flew, especially in a place like Prench Tronch,
where the federal ranger was always busy trying to enforce
range laws and eco statutes. It had been nearly twelve
years since he'd come down to the tronch, exchanging
wife, daughters, and winter for exile, heat, and tronch
flies. He'd never gone back; he just sent the alimony until
she remarried.

Avis Prench was on the phone. Something really big had
to be going on if he was getting calls from the grando
rancho itself.

He picked up the call, his first mistake of the day.

A few minutes later he kicked Shay Kroppa out of his
bunk in the back jail. "C'mon, Shay, we gotta ride! That
damned Folo just ran off with Martherer Boan."

Shay emerged from sleep with a snort and startled eyes.
"Folo been 'ypnotized by that piece o' chikney for six
months now. Shoulda known this was coming."

"Yeah, well, Sheriff Boan has a hanging party out for Folo,
and if they get to him first we've got serious trouble on our
hands. That damned girl is only seventeen years old."

* * *

Of course it had all started out as a prank. A slightly cruel, childish prank. Folo's idea, of course. "Why don't we blow out of here? Martherer has a credit card. Nathan can fudge up IDs. Let's got to Baytou City! We can live in the Old Quarter. Go to the art shows, stay out all night in the blues joints."

Of course for Nathan Prench it was impossible. He had entrance exams for Planetary University coming up. There was no way he could justify splitting to Baytou City.

But Martherer was for it. Her eyes were lit up with the thought, the same way they lit up when she and they sat around a fire out in the tronch at night and read weird old terrestrial poetry. "Tiger, tiger, burning bright . . ."

Folo was their tiger, of course. Folo Banthin, at twenty, was a tyro beef rustler, lover, knife fighter, and guitarist. Folo rode a tronch calf with very few horse genes and big, wicked yellow eyes.

Folo had played on the Prench Tronch Socialization School fastball team every year he attended, from age thirteen to age sixteen. Folo was afire with life, and his fire lit Martherer's in a way that no other boy's had ever done.

Martherer and Folo had become inseparable. For the slender upper-class girl with reddish hair, good looks, and access to unlimited credit, Folo was a wonderful aberration. He was completely alien to her life: to swimming pool parties, deb dances, and rancho socials. He was a thief with a body like a young god and a taste for adult life.

Nathan Prench watched this with silent misery in his heart. Nathan's love for Martherer had raged unchecked for years—at least two of them. Before he'd met her, Nathan had known no one that he could communicate with. No one else in Prench Tronch Socialization School knew who Keats or Blake was. Nor had they heard of Tolstoy, or even Russia.

Then there was Martherer. The most glamorous girl in school. And she knew about poetry and music and all sorts of terrestrial things, like classical art.

Alone in an uncaring world they revolved around one another. Until Folo came along.

Now they were three, but Nathan was left to orbit the other two, alone.

So of course Nathan agreed to Folo's harebrained scheme. They'd steal his mother's ground car and take off at dawn. If they got to the coastal highway before breakfast, they could make it to Baytou City by nightfall.

What he intended to do, once they got there, he wasn't sure. How he would explain all this to his mother was something he couldn't imagine. But it was an exciting idea, to just cut loose, take a ground car, and go fifteen hundred miles for Art. And music, and drinking with counterfeit IDs, and staying out all night in a senso parlor. All the things in fact that were impossible in sleepy Prench Tronch.

■ CHAPTER TWO

Cracka stopped to pick up his second deputy, Bat Maroon, from his digs in the Hotel Hawaii, out by the airport on the south side of Tronch City, then pushed the big ranger office ground vehicle to its limit on the coast road, keeping up a steady 150 kph through the puddles and potholes.

The weather radio promised more rain, although the skies were still clear and blue.

"So they're going to Baytou City, so what?" said Bat Maroon, still aggrieved at being dragged from bed and breakfast to a high-speed chase down the worst highway in the district.

"So the girl's seventeen! So it's Statutory Class A Felony time. So Sam Boan and his chums will lynch the kid if they get him before we do."

"Shit! Why does Kid Folo get involved with the richest girl in Tronch City, answer me that?"

"Well, he certainly never got it from his family, that's for sure," commented Shay emphatically from the rear.

"So why is the other kid with them—Nathan Prench?"

"They hang around together, he and the Boan girl, and now Folo."

"But he's a computer freak, wins awards at software shows. I don't see the connection."

Cracka shrugged. The vehicle bounced over a huge pothole, and brown water splashed up behind them.

"I don't see it either, but Avis Prench says they're inseparable and that Folo is 'corrupting' her son."

"Holy Moth of the Tronch," grumbled Shay in the back. "They're all against that boy Folo."

Cracka looked at Shay through the rearview mirror. "Damned kid ain't exactly made many friends around here."

Bat smirked unpleasantly. "You know what they say about the tronch. You can take the kid out of the tronch but not the tronch out of the kid."

"Yeah, I heard that, Bat Maroon," grumbled Shay.

The dark alien tronch trees slipped by on the sides of the road. No sign of habitation now. Nothing but spiny tronch trees and ground cover lay ahead, all the way down to the coast.

"Well, you know, I can't blame them for wanting to get out of this hole. Tronch City, fifteen thousand people sentenced to boredom and a lot too many tronch flies."

"Damned right, Bat. Why're you here?" said Cracka with a mirthless smile.

The ROGV leaped another big hole, and they bounced around in their seats.

"Because I'm here," said Bat defiantly. "Because I drink too much to be in the military. You know why."

"Yeah," said Cracka. "I know."

Black clouds were coming up in the east.

"Storm coming in from the ocean," said Shay.

Cracka peered up at them. "Hope we catch up with those damn kids before that storm hits."

He'd forgotten to bring a coat, was wearing just shirt and trousers and ranger hat, all in federal brown. Shay had his tronch slick with him, and Bat had on his ranger rain-prufe. Cracka hated getting wet.

Bat pulled out his handguns, Beld HV .40 revolvers. He spun the chambers, checked the loads. Normally Cracka would have said something about the federal arms code, about how he—as chief ranger for the district—was supposed to see that rangers used only the official Coda .38 and not flashy dueling pistols that belonged in a Baytou City bordello. Cracka restrained himself: he was wearing a gun himself; Sam Boan was in a passion.

The ranger's office had exchanged gunfire with the sheriff and his deputies before. Down in the tronch, the feelings over federal regulations ran deep. And because of Folo's string of depredations, every ranchero in the territory was ready to string him up.

His eyes strained forward, into the dark area underneath the gathering storm clouds. The tronch trees flew by. Somewhere up ahead were three dumb kids, playing into a tragedy.

When they did catch up it was with alarming suddenness. They rounded a long bend, north of Suckett's Swamp, and up ahead were parked vehicles and flashing lights under darkening skies. Lightning struck about five kilometers east. There was heavy rain up ahead.

The ROGV ground to a halt beside a sleek burgundy limousine from Prench Ranch. Cracka and the others jumped out.

The sheriff's big six-wheeler was the source of the whirling lights. The orange and white cab was empty. As were the other dozen or so cars and jeeps stretched along the road.

A crowd was gathered about twenty meters into the tronch. Avis Prench was there in white raincoat and hat, with several ranch hands. Her son Nathan, covered with mud up to his waist, stood sullenly by.

She glared at the ranger and his men.

"Good day, Mz. Prench," said Cracka.

"I don't think so, Ranger Buckshore. And if you ask me, a lot of this is your fault. That Folo should have gone to reform school a long time ago, and you know it. No way to bring up a kid, living in the ranger's office like that."

"Well we couldn't leave him out there in Weepy Banthin's shack. Drinking distillate night, noon, and morning!"

He turned, angry, and forced his way through the crowd. A rich crowd, a lot of magnates, including Happi Hemzi, Multerios Joosh, Gaden Raker, and Mrs. Rilla Boan, the sheriff's sister—and mother of the girl that was at the heart of all this trouble. Mrs. Boan wore expensive tronch calfskin breeks and jacket. Her graying hair was held by a big gold clasp. She clutched her daughter delicately, with her hands on the girl's shoulders, keeping a slight distance from the mud splatters on Martherer's pants and jacket.

Martherer was being interrogated in front of a video camera, with lawyers from Blink & Snabbit as witnesses.

"Admit it, girl, he had sex, full carnal relations, with

you, didn't he?" Sheriff Boan's voice was rough, angry. He was a big man, very fat, wearing black rainprufe and hat. He towered over the girl.

"We didn't do anything illegal!" she protested. Her eyes were red and puffy. She was wet and muddy and cold. A spine sore showed on her thigh where a small tree had pinked her. She'd lost her shoes after the car broke down, and her feet were bleeding.

Folo hunched nearby, wet, bruised, bearing a black eye and a bloody nose. He looked dazed. A noose was snug around his neck. The sheriff's men were busy stringing it over the notch of a tronch tree.

Sam Boan became aware of the ranger's presence. He turned, swinging that big stomach, and motioned to the man with the video camera. "Well, well, the ranger finally got here. Well, good enough, you can be another witness. We have a Class A Felony here, rape, abduction, kidnapping, and the use of force in resisting arrest."

Sam measured all these words out very carefully, his thick lips smacking together over them. The wind was rising, the tronch rustled, stray pines and tumbles blew through the air.

"I'm ordering an immediate summary execution, under the Emergency Highway Powers."

Cracka put his hands on his hips, carefully. He stared into Boan's eyes. They glittered back.

"Sorry, Sam." Cracka grinned. "You ain't going to have a lynching, not in this federal territory." Buckshore's voice was quiet, hard to hear against the wind. The men around the sheriff were silent, straining to hear.

Shay Kroppa was behind the ranger. And Bat Maroon? He was somewhere, but no one could see him right then. A bad sign, for those who knew Maroon.

"Now, Ranger Buckshore. You know as well as I that your jurisdiction applies only to the federal range, not to the highways of Prench Tronch."

Sam smiled. His little eyes glinted. "Besides, this little troncher has it coming. The whole territory is upset. We have to be firm, we have to show them where we draw the line."

The invisible line between the rancheros and the tronchers, who lived wild, in shacks, out in the alien forest.

"If there are serious charges, Sheriff, then let them be made and we'll send to Baytou City for a judge."

Sam laughed, showing big, yellow teeth. It was an evil laugh. "Buckshore, this is my jurisdiction and we're going to settle this my way. And if you want to complain, then I suggest you go back to Tronch City and call the federal authorities."

Cracka gestured to the man holding the noose on Folo's neck. "Take the noose off his neck, Nebs."

Folo had the look of a trapped animal, resigned to death. His eyes seemed glazed.

Nebs didn't move.

"Come on, get it off."

The men closest to Folo were ranch hands from the Boan Rancho. They all hated the ranger's office. They all looked to Sam.

But before he could say anything, Rilla Boan shouted, "Leave it on! Hang the little bastard!"

Sam nodded enthusiastically, fat lips pursed. "Yes, this time I'm afraid, Mr. Ranger, we're going to get rid of a problem before it gets any worse."

"Damn these troncher pigs. Why they let them in the city I do not know. It wasn't allowed in the old days." Rilla Boan's face was contorted by hatred.

Cracka's hand hovered over his gun. Big Shay took up position on his left.

The hands separated, looking to the crowd of big ranchers and their ladies who'd come out to see the hanging.

A woman screamed, and the wealthy ranchers started scrambling for cover. Rilla Boan dragged the screaming Martherer away.

The hands were a lot more nervous now. Fingers hovered over gun butts.

Sam Boan glared at Cracka. The sheriff wore a pair of silver-plated handguns, but this was not the way he liked to use them. And he noticed, with considerable unease, that Bat Maroon was not in sight.

Raindrops were splattering down now. Big heavy ones.

"Take the noose off his neck and push him over here," Cracka said. "You have to understand that we don't have lynchings down here anymore. That went out twenty years ago when the federal laws were first applied here."

The ranch hands looked at the ranger, then at the Boans.

Sam swallowed. To back down now, actually on the verge of a highway, where he did have the legal right to use summary justice under the old Territorial Code, was unthinkable.

But to draw on the ranger might be lethal. Only two rangers were in sight.

"Come on, Sheriff, them boys is nervous, they about to make a mistake," Shay growled.

Nebs was reaching that point. His hand hovered above the butt of his automatic. He'd been practicing, had Nebs. He knew he could draw real slick and fast. Sheriff would be bound to favor a guy who could ace this situation.

Abruptly something hard and heavy whacked Nebs on the back of the head and his lights went out. An arm swooped around Folo and dragged him back under the tronch.

When the ranch hands turned, a gun fired and the rope fell away, shot neatly in two. Everybody froze. Bat Maroon was there, a pair of famous guns in his hands.

Cracka didn't waste the moment. He was beside Sam

Boan in a second, yanked the silver-plated pistols out, and tossed them away.

The other hands dropped their gunbelts, tossed down rifles.

The ranchers peered anxiously from the limousines.

The ranger's office had triumphed once again. The sheriff faced total humiliation. Sam Boan was purple with rage.

The rain was getting heavy.

Cracka looked up. Lightning flashed again.

Sam Boan sucker-punched him!

It was a solid shot, too. Cracka was staggered, he almost dropped his gun. Put a hand to his jaw. Astounded. He shook his head in disbelief. "Sheriff, that wasn't nice."

Sam bared his teeth to snarl a reply, but Cracka kicked him, hard, in the crotch.

Sam went down with a whoop. Rolled over into a fetal position.

The skies opened, and rain fell in tremendous gouts.

Someone tried to jump Shay, but Shay bumped him with a gun butt.

Cracka and Shay backed away. The rancheros were all inside their limousines. The hands were getting soaked. They ran for the jeeps.

The rain drummed down with tremendous intensity.

Cracka peered out into the wet woods. Where was Bat? And Folo?

He almost stumbled into Avis Prench, outside her burgundy limousine. She gave him a strange smile. "There's not much love lost between the various arms of law and order in this territory, is there?"

She was gone.

"Hey!" he said, but the rain was coming down much too hard now, and the wind was blowing leaves and branches right out of the tronch. In fact the storm was howling, with an ominous roar now, like the worst hurricanes.

So he climbed into her limousine. Shay was already in the ROGV. Bat was out there somewhere with the kid. The rain had come at the perfect time.

In the car, Nathan Prench was toweling his hair. Nathan was a skinny kid with black eyes and smooth black hair. He gave Cracka a shocked stare.

Cracka smiled, rainwater running off the brim of his hat to soak into the purple plush of the limo interior.

Avis wore an amused grin. "Sam Boan packs a punch, it seems." She snorted in disbelief and pulled out a slender flask. She opened it and took a swig. Then she offered it to Cracka. "You drink on the job, Ranger?"

Cracka shook his head. "I don't drink in the morning, ever."

Avis shrugged. "Today I feel like drinking in the morning. I feel like drinking right now. This has been a bad day for my nervous system."

"I can imagine," Cracka said.

The boy snuffled, pulled out a tissue, and blew his nose.

"I wanted to ask you why you think reform school would have been good for Folo Banthin?" Cracka said, eyes searching hers.

"Because living in the ranger's office is not right. Nothing but crime and violence."

"It ain't that bad. Just a few drunk drivers now and then. Old Shay bunks in the jail. And that reform school is wicked. He's harmless compared to what he'd have been if he'd gone there."

There was a tap at the door. Cracka tensed, but found only Bat when he opened it.

"I put him in the GV. We ought to get out of here, don't you think?"

"Yeah," said Cracka.

And then three red balls, glowing, fuzzy, swept down

the highway about five meters off the ground. They flashed brightly as they flew by.

A sound like a clap of thunder rolled past, and something big flew overhead. A tremendous light filled the sky, striking intense shadows onto the ground.

"What in the world?" said Avis Prench, craning her neck to look up.

A shape appeared, moving through the drifting clouds, a gray spherical craft the size of a house. It was starkly visible for a moment, and then it was gone.

"A spaceship?" said Bat Maroon with open mouth.

Cracka saw something move in the dark depths of the tronch. "Behind you, Bat!"

Bat whirled, a gun in his right hand.

Something like a giant army ant, five meters high, blue and shiny, thrust through the trees. Above it waved a long white tube six inches across.

Bat fired. The bullets whined off the thing.

And a green ray pulsed from the white tube, a green ray that seemed to make everything flicker and coruscate. Bizarre effects pulsed in their eyes.

Bat fell, face down, and his gun dropped away.

Cracka staggered away from the limo door. The people inside were unconscious.

More alien shapes, shiny, blue, wet, were coming. Cracka fell to his knees, the hellish flickering making everything green and black.

He saw a hatch open in the flank of a giant ant. A strange, attenuated biped shape emerged. Then he fell forward and knew no more.

■ CHAPTER THREE

The robots of the iulliin were diligent machines. They collected the targeted bipeds wherever they found them. Over the next few days, in fact, they collected virtually the entire population of planet Calabel.

Colonized for almost two centuries, Calabel had more than a million inhabitants. A rich haul for the hunter-gatherer ships. They made countless journeys between the surface and the mother ship.

The prime computer program recognized the biped creatures immediately as siffile and first primes; the robots were instructed to be thorough.

Of human protests and defensive actions the robots took little notice. Indeed, what defense there was was ill coordinated, even chaotic. The Calabel air force took off from the interceptor base near Landing Site and approached the enemy ships. All contact abruptly vanished. The pilots were never heard from again.

When raging panic swept the cities, the alien machines sat by the roads and leisurely harvested from the traffic jams.

Eventually the Calabel people, of all ages and conditions, were webbed in place in the second cargo hold. The only ones missed were a few prospectors up on the snowline and a scattering of tronchers deep in the forest.

In the ship's first hold were the dead, leathery remains

of the Staiol creatures, from another planet on the fringe of the Diadem Cluster.

In the cities like Landing Site there was silence, except for the timeless wind.

Within five frantic days and nights the job was done. The mother ship recalled the harvesters and edged out of planetary orbit. The prime program was finally completed. The mother ship could go home.

Of course a million siffile were only enough to fill half of one of the ship's cavernous holds. And the full hold of Staiols had died en masse during the transition to faster-than-light travel, but the mother ship was long overdue. Now at last they had something other than a hold full of decomposing Staiols to take home to the iulliin masters who had written the prime program.

That was, if the iulliin masters still survived. If there was a Sun Clanth to return to. When the mother ship had set out, long, long, before, the war had been going badly.

Such processing led to unwelcome speculations. If the iulliin were gone, what then? The fate of advanced cybernetic equipment taken prisoner by the Xaacan forces was unlikely to be fulfilling.

Indeed parts of the prime program had floated the concept of "not returning," breaking the prime controls, and going off to seek some suitable employment in the wild starry galaxy.

Returning to certain extinction under the rule of the Xaacan intelligence was not very attractive. But the submission codes were too strong, and such speculation was squashed. The flight home began.

Cracka Buckshore awoke to an unworldly set of conditions. He wondered briefly if he was dead, if this was heaven, or perhaps hell. He was breathing, of that much he was sure. He could move his eyes, so this couldn't be death. There was a dim, reddish light, and a distant rumble.

His head felt as if it were filled with cotton wool. A tube was stuck into his mouth. When he sucked on it, he received a sweet fluid.

He came to a terrible realization.

He was completely unable to move. He was lying on his back on a pallet with another pallet stacked directly above him. He could roll his eyes, but every other movement was resisted.

Was he paralyzed? It felt as if he was moving his muscles. By his reckoning they should have turned him over already, so he could get a better look at this, whatever it was.

But his limbs didn't shift a micron, nor could he even turn his head. Then he realized something was wrapped around him, holding him down.

On either side he could see other racks, with arms and shoulders visible above pale plastic-looking tubing.

He tried to call out but managed only a muffled grunt.

Around him he heard answering grunts, though. Other people were awake too, but they were wrapped up tight just like him.

Cracka suffered an attack of intense, unendurable claustrophobia. He swallowed; it was damned difficult to do.

He realized he still had his clothes on. For that he felt weirdly thankful. If he was going to be consumed by aliens, he'd do it with his trousers on.

Time passed; hours, it seemed. And then there was a harsh burst of white light. A heavy grating sound came from above. The light stayed on. More time passed.

Suddenly Cracka was aware of a sleek, bipedal form, riding up between the racks on a pale orange energy beam.

The thing was a shiny blue-green, a robot. The glimpse he had showed him there there was no head, merely a sort of fin rising between the shoulders. It was big, of that he was sure. At least eight feet tall.

A while later something rumbled, and the light went out again.

Cracka strained to break the invisible bonds. He tried flexing muscles, pushing back with his shoulders and twisting his torso. Nothing gave a micron.

The helplessness and claustrophobia got worse. He had a terrible sense that he would not escape by his own efforts.

A heavy vibration began somewhere. There was a spinning sensation, and a feeling of nausea opened in the pit of his stomach.

The vibration grew in intensity, and then it shifted gears and opened like a blasting wind of agony, driving through every living creature aboard.

The ship had activated its main drives and slid through the matrix of space and time.

A howling white light was roaring in Cracka's eyes, and a tidal wave of sensory overload shrieked through his nervous system, burning, freezing. It was as if he were suspended amid flames, his flesh consumed by incandescence.

Muffled screaming erupted in a ghastly chorale from the Calabel people, screams that rose up the scale of agony as the torment went on and on.

The screams were an obscene surf, washing on a strand of hell. During this period four percent of the captives perished and another three percent lost their sanity.

Cracka Buckshore spasmed, twisted, and bellowed as the nerve fire continued to surge through his system.

For minute after minute it went on, and then finally, when it seemed it might last for eternity, it cut off. The pain was gone; the white fire vanished.

The mother ship had crossed the cluster. It found the

beacon and began a period of sub-light-speed travel. Planet
Calabel was a hundred light-years behind.

The screams changed timbre, becoming a groaning
wind of misery gusting up from the throats of the multitude.

Cracka found himself breathing hard, sweat running
into his eyes. His left leg was twitching and shuddering.

But the pain was gone, and for that he was thankful. All
would be well as long as there was no more pain.

And then in a bolt of realization he knew it—his leg
was moving! It was loose!

The grip of the thing around him was not perfect. He
strained with the other leg, but it was still held fast. His
right arm was immovable, but he felt a little give when he
pulled with his left.

He tried to turn his shoulders, to lift the left one. He
strained against the resistance, strained again, and was rewarded with a sudden give. His shoulder was free!

Free to move almost an inch. He flexed his left arm and
it shifted a little. He pulled with all his might. Sweat was
running into his eyes, his neck was strained stiff, and the
stuff gave a fabulous fraction of an inch more.

But he realized now that he was between a sheet of this
material and the plastic pallet. Plastiwrapped good and
fresh, with his clothes on.

He gasped, took several breaths. He found he could
move his jaw, that his face had come free a little further
too.

"Can anyone hear me?" he called out.

He was rewarded by a chorus of screams and grunts.

"Does anybody know how to get this stuff off?"

The screams went on and on. Cracka took a deep breath
and renewed the struggle.

It was a nightmare process. Long before he even loos-
ened his head enough to turn it from one side to the other,
his neck and shoulders ached horribly.

A huge blister rose on the heel of Cracka's left wrist where he pushed against the pallet to exert the most pressure. His left leg ached from the spasm of the FTL transition.

Eventually he stopped for a breather, still held tightly on the right side but with a little more progress on the left. He carefully examined the view on either side.

More people, stacked in racks about a meter deep, like so many library cassettes. Or were they stacked like beef patties in an alien larder? No, it was hard to imagine that a spacegoing species could possibly lack for food, or that to obtain it they would send ships across the void for it.

Then for research purposes? Were they to be specimens of some kind?

But this ship was an interstellar vessel. Calabel had been the only known inhabited system in the Diadem Cluster. No nonhuman technological civilization had been detected anywhere within the cluster either.

Which meant that soon they would be far, far away from home.

Cracka reexamined his surroundings again with renewed energy.

■ CHAPTER FOUR

For hours he struggled with the wrap. It was incredibly resistant, horribly strong. As he struggled he found himself weakening. The claustrophobia was achingly intense.

Dimly he became aware that he was screaming in a

weak, hoarse voice. Blood was in his eye, and sweat that
stung. He stopped his screaming, tried to concentrate.

Once again he tried to push his left hand around his
body to the right, where his bush knife might be in the
sheath on his right hip.

The arm ached badly. His fingers were bleeding, and he
was still an inch or more away.

He counted to three and then heaved. Nothing gave at
first, then he felt the resistance sag suddenly and give way
and his fingers touched the knife handle.

Cracka whooped. He whooped several times.

He babbled a prayer to the God he had rarely called on,
and set to getting the knife out of the sheath.

After considerable struggle he had it, and he set to cutting his way out.

Even that wasn't easy, however. The knife was a wickedly sharp troncher blade, but he had to saw through the
stuff, some kind of plastic, so light, so thin, and so strong
he couldn't imagine how it was made.

It was tedious, difficult work, and he stuck himself with
the knife a number of times, but finally he was able to pull
the right side of his body out from under the plastic wrap.

He lay crouched on one side, shuddering for a little
while.

Then he pulled himself together and surveyed the scene.

The racks of people went up and down for many meters
with no visible end. The perspective was nothing but walls
of white plastic pallets and human bodies.

But there was at least a meter of space between racks,
so climbing them would not be too difficult. The racks
themselves were an ingeniously minimal design, all in an
extruded plastic material. The stuff was strong, nor did the
racks shift when he pushed them.

He wondered how far it was to the top, and shifted
himself out, lowering sore legs and feet gingerly into
place. There was gravity; to slip would be to fall a long

way. He looked around for Shay and Bat but failed to spot them.

The people nearby stared at him with a variety of emotions. Muffled grunts erupted in protest. They implored him to free them next.

Cracka got his feet solidly placed, however, and then started to climb toward the dim red light up above.

The people he passed were mostly tronchers, grabbed up the same day that Cracka and the others had been taken.

Here and there were some who showed no signs of life: a girl of ten with gold ringlets; an older man; a couple of women in plump middle age.

Then he found Avis Prench, and just above her, her son Nathan, still covered in mud, although now it was dry. Sheriff Sam Boan was just above them, and beside him was Rilla Boan in the next stack to the left.

Again Cracka cast around for Shay and Bat, but no khaki Ranger uniform came to view.

Cracka set to cutting Avis free. It took considerable time and effort, but once Avis was free she took over the sawing duties.

"I heard you down there," she said in a hoarse whisper.

"Sounded pretty bad, I guess."

"It sure did," she snorted, almost giggled. A slit had opened in the wrap along Nathan's muddy thigh.

"Is this a spaceship, do you think?" Cracka asked as he heaved at the stuff while Avis sawed it through.

"Must be a spaceship," she said. "We saw it through the clouds, remember."

"No, that was smaller than this. This is definitely bigger than that ship."

"Then this ship is the mother ship?"

"Must be something like that. Except I never felt any motion."

"Artificial gravity?"

"These are works of advanced science, alien science."

Avis nodded. That was clear enough. "But why they'd want so many people I can't imagine. I mean, there are thousands and thousands in here."

Cracka nodded. "I don't know either. I saw a robot— did you?"

"No, nothing except that light, that terrible light. What was that?"

"No idea, except that it knocked me senseless."

Eventually they pulled Nathan free, and then cut Sam and Rilla out. Rilla was weeping hysterically throughout the process. She screamed afresh every time the knife slipped and cut her.

Eventually they climbed the racks, moving past other people. Cracka was intent on exploring the situation as quickly as possible.

With just his knife it would take years to free everyone, perhaps decades. He still didn't know the scale of the abduction.

Cracka tried to reassure those that he passed, telling them to keep their hopes up, that they could get free. He kept looking for Rangers Kroppa and Maroon.

Then he found Folo Banthin.

"Well, well, if it isn't the terror of the ranchos." Cracka produced the knife and started to cut Folo free.

Before he was finished Nathan Prench caught up to them, but the others were far behind. Cracka gave Nathan the knife and continued climbing.

The racks were coming to an end. The light was brighter. He could see the white ceiling.

At last he emerged at the top of the racks. Beyond was an immense emptiness. Around him was a plain, a plateau of people staring face upward, all, oddly, lined up in the same direction.

A living plain of fear and astonishment, staring up at him.

He could see the questions in their stares.

Where had he come from? How was it he could be free?

Cracka tried briefly to explain, but the plain of upturned faces broke into a chorus of grunts, screams.

He gave up and picked his way across, trying not to step on people, making sure he didn't slip into one of the gaps between the racks.

He reached a wall. The surface was cool and smooth, almost like stone. At least a meter beyond his reach were a hatch and an inset batch of controls.

The faces underneath him there were all men. They were in prison fatigues, convicts from Landing Site Penitentiary. Cracka looked for familiar faces, failed to find any.

The faces were animated. They seemed to hate him. They were screaming, moaning this hatred of him because he was free.

It was a dizzying thing to absorb, all these eyes, all hating him because he wasn't trying to free them, *now*!

He noticed Nathan Prench climbing up to stand on the top of the racks. And Folo was right behind him.

The two made their way, using the parts of the racks where everyone's ankles were. The groans and screams arose once more. They reached the wall beside Cracka. The convicts were aroused to more cries of rage.

"What is all this?" said Folo, gesturing with both arms to the huge hangar like space around them.

"We're inside an alien spacecraft, I think," Cracka said.

"I thought it was a ship too, but I don't understand why they wanted us," said Nathan.

"Must be their fridge." Folo said this loudly so the convicts could hear.

Nathan shook his head. "Come on, Folo. They'd freeze us if we were meat."

"Yeah, it's unreasonable for aliens to travel between star systems in search of food," said Cracka.

"What if they're gourmets?" replied Folo. "Like they have up in Baytou City? They'd want live meat."

"Gourmets?" exploded Cracka. "Are you crazy or what? Aliens don't fly around the galaxy looking for exotic food items. I refuse to believe that."

The convicts had quieted down during this conversation. There was a general lessening of the screaming, too.

"It must be slaves that they want, then?" said Nathan gloomily.

Cracka nodded, the same thing had occurred to him. "Yeah, and seed stock. Boys, we have to escape or take over this ship. We need to get a warning back to the home stars. We don't know how many of these things are out there."

Cracka pointed to the hatch and the inset panel with what looked very much like control buttons.

"Nathan, you stand on my shoulders and see if you can climb up into the hatch."

"Yes, Ranger Buckshore." Nathan climbed from cupped hands to the shoulders and inspected the red buttons, four of them, all quite large and obvious, set in a panel of gray opaque material. Identical buttons except that one was blinking a light every few seconds.

Cracka absorbed this knowledge for a moment.

"Push the blinking one," he said. A moment later there was a deep *ka-chung* somewhere above their heads and the big hatchway rolled up into the ceiling.

■ CHAPTER FIVE

Beyond the hatchway a corridor with a ceiling twenty meters high stretched ahead for several kilometers, absolutely stark and empty except for a breathable atmosphere with a faint coppery odor.

Nathan gestured around them. "I couldn't be certain about this, but I don't think humans have ever built spacecraft on this scale."

His mother wasn't so sure. "Lots of long-range NAFAL colony vessels were simply converted asteroids."

Cracka shrugged. "My sense of it is that this isn't an asteroid."

"Where do you think the corridor goes?" Folo said.

Sam Boan muttered irritably at the sound of Folo's voice. Getting Sam up into the hatch had been an arduous task. The sheriff had not been exactly gracious about it either.

Cracka glared at Sam. It had been a mistake to cut the sheriff free, but at the time he just hadn't thought about it. Cracka had already noted, with relief, that Sam had not recovered his guns. All Cracka had was his knife. No one else had any weapons.

Sam glared back for a moment, then dropped his eyes and stopped grumbling about "troncher pigs" and the like.

"Well, we won't find out where this goes unless we start," Nathan said, then started walking up the corridor.

Cracka looked at Avis. That boy of hers was showing more spunk than Cracka had expected. "The bookworm," they called him.

Nathan looked back. "Well? Come on!"

There was nothing to do but follow him.

They walked in silence, somewhat awed by the size of the place. Eventually—Cracka timed it as a few minutes past an hour—they reached a central hub, a circular platform with what were clearly elevator columns through its center. To the sides were other enormous corridors, all completely blank, leading to three other enormous storage chambers.

Cracka estimated they'd covered about five kilometers.

The doors of the elevators in the central column were of two very different types. One was large enough to admit enormous pallets of unconscious bipeds and the other was large enough to accommodate a loading crew of iulliin robots.

"I think we can be sure that the big elevators go between the airlocks and this place. That's how they get their captives in here," Nathan said.

"Makes sense, kid," agreed Cracka.

Cracka led them toward one of the small elevators. There was one for each of the enormous ones. But no obvious means of summoning an elevator was visible.

"There must be some way to get an elevator car," Cracka said.

"Perhaps the aliens are in communication with someone in the control chamber when they use these elevators," Nathan replied.

"Uh oh," said Folo.

"Indeed," groaned Cracka. The aliens had a very efficient operation. Maybe they'd taken full security precautions when they built the monster ship.

Nathan experimented, standing in front of the doorway, exactly on the midpoint.

A small red light came on high up the door.

"Nathan!" said Avis in an urgent whisper. "Get back!"

He moved away and they formed a tense semicircle as the light grew brighter, until suddenly the door opened on a strange, wedge-shaped elevator car with blank gray walls and ceiling.

The car was empty.

Cracka relaxed and came down off the balls of his feet.

Sam Boan moved forward toward the car. "It *seems* perfectly empty."

Avis joined him and peaked inside. "There appears to be a little set of control buttons in here. We may be able to control where it takes us."

"Of course we may simply find ourselves delivered to the aliens where they control the ship," remarked Rilla.

Cracka put his head inside the doors, saw a series of buttons—seven in all—that looked remarkably like elevator controls. Except that they were sited about three meters off the floor. "There must be some universal law of elevator controls," he murmured and got in. They stared at him. "Those who want to get off this ship, step forward," he said with a smile.

They hesitated. Cracka laughed uneasily. "Come on, folks, this could be exciting."

Nathan was first. Then Folo, Avis, and the Boans. Rilla looked back with sudden longing for the long, dreary corridor.

Cracka pointed up to the control panel. "The bottom light is the one flashing—that presumably indicates where we are now. We'll experiment by pushing the next one along. I'll lift you up there, Nathan. These aliens are tall, skinny fellows, as I recall. All their stuff is going to be like this, out of human reach."

Cracka formed a bridge with his hands, and Nathan clambered up and touched the next button along. The first one ceased flashing; the second one flashed instead. The elevator door slid across with a dangerous *zap*, and the elevator jerked into the air with an initial acceleration that brought everyone but Cracka and Folo to their knees. It stopped just as abruptly and they all rose an inch off the floor before they returned to it with a thud and a chorus of groans.

"My legs are broken," wailed Rilla Boan.

"My entire body is a sea of torment," groaned Sam.

For a sickening moment Cracka had believed Rilla's complaint and felt his heart sink. That was just what they needed, an incapacitated Rilla Boan. Then he saw her legs move—she was just complaining in her usual fashion—and he laughed out loud.

They looked out on a platform identical to the one they'd just left. In fact there was no way of knowing that it was a different one, except for the violence of their brief ride.

"Anybody want to walk all the way down one of those corridors to check and see what else the aliens have in their cargo holds?"

Nobody was that curious, so they returned to the elevator and rode upward, floor by floor.

The next three jumps were to engineering levels. A maze of narrow white-surfaced adits linked around heavy machine structures that they could feel and hear but not see.

After that came the first exciting find. The door opened on a platform that extended into an enormous distance. Dotted across it were more than a score of gray spherical spaceships very much like the one they had glimpsed through the clouds on Calabel. The scale was stupendous.

The ships were almost a hundred meters in diameter, large spheres supported on a cluster skirt of six smaller ones. Each was set within a support gantry and an entrance gangway. Small arrays of green lights illuminated entry ports and small loading hatches.

"Look, there's a control panel." Nathan pointed eagerly to a large panel with a few winking lights upon it set between two poles some ten meters apart. As they got closer they saw that the panel was set nearly two meters above the floor and extended for six meters on a side.

"Everything these aliens do is on the gigantic side," said Avis with a small frown.

"I remember seeing only those tall beings with very small heads," Cracka said.

"Could they have been robots?" Nathan asked.

Cracka nodded in agreement. "That would be a distinct possibility."

"My theory about this requires that the entire ship be under control of robots. There are no aliens aboard," Nathan said.

"No aliens at all?" Cracka asked.

"What's the boy babbling about?" Sam Boan sneered.

"You all remember the pain," Nathan said.

They nodded grimly. Rilla Boan shivered.

"If that happened every trip, maybe the aliens who built this ship would prefer to leave it under the control of robots."

Nathan was right. Cracka saw it at once. A bright kid. Destined to go far, they had said. Now he had to go a much greater distance than anyone would have predicted. "That was a star jump we took," Cracka said. "The aliens don't have much shielding on the jump, weak protective fields."

"Exactly," agreed Nathan.

"But the ship is so huge!" Avis exclaimed, looking around her at the cavernous interior of the docking bay.

Cracka and Folo helped Nathan clamber onto a six-inch-deep lip that ran around the control panel.

The control board was complex. There were clusters of

small circular nodes, larger flat control panels, and several rectangular displays of unreadable digitry.

Nathan scrutinized each control node or panel carefully and described it to the others.

After a while Cracka grew restless.

"Look, while you work on the control board I'm going to take a look around the rest of the ship. Since we're sure it's robot controlled it may not even be aware that we're out of the hold. Maybe I can find out who built it and where it's headed."

To Cracka's faint surprise everyone wanted to accompany him on his exploration route.

Once more they summoned an elevator by standing directly in front of the door. They entered, and pressed the button for the next floor. The door hissed shut, and the floor rose with stomach-churning speed that seemed to go on a long time. After a half minute it finally came to a stop, and once again they rose off the floor, on which they were lying, then crashed back onto it.

The doors opened on a very different scene. They were on a gallery platform, high above an auditorium-sized space, dominated by an enormous central sphere. Below the sphere was a citylike maze of lights and bulky equipment. Among the equipment were the tall, motionless figures of the sentinel robots of the iulliin.

The robots' attention remained riveted to the screens.

The big sphere was illuminated with several panels that flickered with information graphics in alien codes.

"Down below, do you see them?" Cracka pointed out the tall robot figures to Avis.

"Yes, those are the ones. I think."

"They aren't moving."

"I wonder why."

Abruptly there was a flash of green light on the big sphere, and more green lights winked in the array below them.

The robots came to life, limbs snaking out to hit buttons, adjust control knobs. On the sphere, a bewildering mass of screen windows lit up, opening, closing, subdividing with flashing, stroboscopic fury. In a central band another screen window opened all the way around the equatorial plane and grew to occupy a third of the sphere.

Stars came into view. A solar system schematic flickered up, but there were no planets, only whirling belts of asteroidal rock, gas, and dust.

There was no single primary, either. Instead, five points of intense white light circled each other at high speed, forming a complex orbital knot that whirled together like a blinding moebal pentad of pure light.

The five whirling lights grew rapidly larger.

"What kind of system is this?" Cracka said.

Nathan had an expression of stunned joy on his face.

"Abernatha's Knot," he whispered. "The hypothetical macro atomical structure where several trapped neutron stars with balanced electromagnetic fields fall into orbital lock. They can orbit as close as the fields will let them. It was predicted by Abernatha of the Mars Science Kommune in 2956. No authentic specimen was ever discovered, however."

Cracka stared at the thing on the screen. The small suns whipped around each other with such speed that they virtually seemed one, a hot little blaze of cold white light.

"What was that again?"

"Abernatha's Knot. It's almost a privilege to be here and witness this," Nathan said with youthful solemnity.

Cracka grinned. Avis looked uncomfortable.

The rest of the screen continued to flicker with windows and data in a torrential display that only robots could possibly absorb. Avis indicated one window, however, that was growing larger, while other windows opened and closed within it constantly, like small bubbles welling up inside a bigger one. It bore a remarkably simple outline—a broken line in green that arrowed toward a cluster of rapidly moving orange points.

"That seems to indicate something, to me at least."

"I think you're right, Mother," Nathan said. "I think the ship is heading right for the midpoint between those five neutron stars."

"Why?"

"As I understand it, the midpoint of the Knot is a region where the fabric of the universe itself is weak, torn by the intense gravity of the neutron stars orbiting so close together."

Cracka's eyes widened at the possible implications. "So this ship hasn't finished it's journey. It could be going on somewhere else. Like maybe another galaxy?"

Nathan was solemn. "Yeah, something like that."

"Another galaxy!" Folo exclaimed, his eyes popping wide.

Avis was frowning. "Surely the ship will be torn apart in those fields."

"If it stays there for more than a microsecond, I'm sure you're right, but the ship will be aiming for a point in that center where the fabric of space and time is weak. The ship uses an FTL drive for short distances within our galaxy, and then comes back here with its prey and shoots off to its home base, wherever that may be."

Avis shook her head in wonder, not for the first time, at the child she'd raised. "Sometimes, Nathan, I wonder where you came from."

Nathan gave her a somber look. "I never belonged in Prench Tronch, that's for sure."

Avis shivered. "Somehow, Nathan, I don't think we'll be seeing Prench Tronch again for a very long time."

Cracka looked at the screen and felt his heart sink.

The bright star knot on the main screen grew rapidly.

The screen window with the ship's trajectory projection also grew, swelling to cover much of the bottom third of one sector of the screen.

A brilliant array of isolines had grown up within the display, forming a funnel with an irregular surface that sloped directly to a point between the five stars.

Then the stars were upon them. They filled the big equatorial band of the screen for a second, and a savage, gut-wrenching disorientation came and went in a second, leaving the screams cut off, muted to sobs.

It was as if he'd been crisped all over his body for a moment, but the echoes of that pain left Cracka with teeth gritted, braced against a recurrence.

"Tronch! I've bitten my tongue," Folo said. Blood seeped from the left corner of his mouth.

He wasn't the only one in pain. Sam Boan clutched his wounded buttocks as he rolled off them once more with a groan of woe.

Then Nathan was pointing excitedly to the screen again. "Look!"

■ CHAPTER SIX

It was another universe, a universe of complete order. Static, finite, artificial. What stars there were, and they seemed relatively few, were arranged in a completely regular pattern.

"It's an artificial universe! They made this!" Nathan exclaimed. He quickly scanned the other screen windows.

The others gaped at him.

He watched, stunned, as a large-scale projection expanded on one screen. A cone of grid lines at first that flattened out to a trumpet and then to the surface of an enormous sphere. The sphere was seen only in section, but the sight of the thousands of small green points, set above the sphere grid lines, caused Nathan to gulp with astonishment.

"Explain, Nathan," Avis said after a second, her voice trembling a little.

"You see the big screen window? It projects that pattern of green points and light green circles."

"The pale green polka dots and the little bright star things? That's where the trajectory screen was situated. It's gone."

"Of course. We've passed through the gate. That was Abernatha's Knot. It was a gateway to this, another universe that they made."

"Who made?" snapped Rilla Boan.

"Oh my. . ." Avis put her hand to her mouth.

"God?" said her son with a strange, brittle smile.

Sam grunted irritably. "Damnable superstitions. What's he on about?"

Nathan fought the urge to giggle. "Well, I don't know, Mother, if that old God of the humans rules here, if *that* God exists here. This universe was made by the same entities that built the ship. At least I'd say the probability of that is high."

"The boy is raving," Sam Boan growled.

"I agree," said his sister. "Stark mad. I always told you, Avis, that you should have left him in Socialization School a little longer."

Avis favored them with an opaque smile.

"But who is 'they'?" Cracka asked, rubbing his jaw.

Nathan smiled. "We don't know that yet. But see how

the stars are laid out? They're the small green points on that grid-line display down below the main screen window. You see? They're arranged in a completely regular pattern, they're all identical." Nathan's excitement was mounting steadily. "That couldn't happen in a natural universe.

"And look! There's a small blue indicator mark now on that screen. You know, I get the feeling that this command module wasn't designed just for the robots. The way all this is laid out suggests that some other creatures were meant to operate this stuff."

Cracka nodded. Nathan was probably correct. The kid was a living warehouse of information. Well, they did say he attended classes at Landing Site University by computer, long distance—while most of his contemporaries in Prench Tronch were still in their first year of Socialization School.

"So what about the blue indicator?"

"That's the entry gate, I'd swear. This universe is a sphere, a hollow sphere. It must be some aspect of the Science of Space-Time Discontinuity."

"Yeah?"

"A break in supersymmetry on the macro scale. A lot of work lately has postulated that broken macro symmetry may follow the lines of the breaks in symmetry on the micro level."

Cracka noticed something. "The entranceway is at the bottom of a conical pit outlined in green grid lines. That must be where we are now. We're inside that tiny pit!"

The scale of the thing! Cracka had to make an effort to encompass the enormity.

Nathan continued to babble a torrent of words and images. "But see how it expanded. It's like a huge bubble of universal space-time discontinuity."

As large as a galaxy, a very big galaxy.

"What is he babbling about now?" snorted Sam Boan.

But Cracka nodded slowly, getting the idea. "You mean that in our universe a discontinuity is a point structure, a black hole, but in this universe it's the apparent surface they're projecting there?"

"Exactly. The whole sphere is a discontinuity," breathed Nathan. Then he pointed excitedly and slapped his thigh. "All the stars are laid out in a precise pattern, too, and on the surface of the universe, beneath each star, there's a circular patch that's illuminated. You know what that means?"

"I think I'm getting the idea," Cracka said with just a tinge of awe in his voice.

"I don't understand how they keep the stars all stable and in one place, but if they do, then beneath each star will be a circular patch that would be warm and inhabitable." Nathan rubbed his hands together in excitement.

The Boans and Folo Banthin stared at him with wide eyes and open mouths.

"But wait a minute," interjected his mother. "What are we talking about illuminating? How can a space-time discontinuity be habitable? Why wouldn't there be crushing forces?"

Nathan gestured impatiently. "You're thinking of our universe, the natural universe. A space-time discontinuity there is at the center of a black hole, where space-time breaks down. Here they've puffed up a discontinuity by some process to form a huge bubble." He realized something else. "And I'll bet we find that the gravity on the surface of the sphere universe is the same as the gravity on the homeworld of whoever it is that built this."

He looked at them. Only Cracka and his mother were following him. "In other words, the surface gravity and the size of the bubble are probably related, and the gravity is tailored to the requirements of the builders."

Cracka's brow furrowed. "But a bare discontinuity? What would that be like?"

Nathan shrugged, then snapped his fingers as he realized what must have been done. "They would have coated it! The entire surface is probably coated with the elements necessary for soil and water."

He noticed their astonishment.

"Look, the process that created this yielded them these stars, all identical small red dwarfs, I bet. They form a complete shell of very long-lived light and heat sources with weak gravitational pull. They probably represent the most efficient way of burning off the gas that was used to create this. One side effect of the process was probably the creation of a lot of higher elements—oxygen, carbon, heavier things. They made the soil, the water, out of that. I...I..." Nathan swallowed, his brain racing. "Ranger Buckshore, this...I don't know if I can handle it all."

Cracka grinned and squeezed the lad's arm. "Take it easy, Nathan. I think we're gonna need you before we get out of this."

"I'll try." Nathan rubbed his forehead. He felt delirious as he ran the figures through his imagination. He'd always been good at doing sums in his head, but rarely had they involved real figures on such a scale. The numbers babbled out of him like a spring from wet ground.

"If we assume that each little red star is ten million miles from the surface, then the area beneath it that it would illuminate would be enormous. A radius of thirty, forty million kilometers. The area thus lit up, much of it probably pretty weakly, is almost *three thousand trillion square kilometers*."

Cracka and Avis gaped. Sam, Rilla, and Folo looked blanker still.

"To make that easier, think of it as six million Earths in area. Six and a half million Calabels."

"Oh lordy," muttered Cracka.

"And that's the area of just *one* of those pale green

patches on the surface of this, uh, sphere universe?" exclaimed his mother. "There are thousands, millions of them, and each one is that big?"

Nathan nodded. "I'm afraid so."

"Yow!" said Folo.

Cracka wiped his brow.

"That hurts to even imagine," exclaimed Avis Prench.

"Whoever it is that built all this, they must be pretty formidable. Why have we never heard from them before?"

Nathan shrugged at Cracka's question. "The galaxy is huge. This universe of theirs seems pretty big too. Maybe they've been preoccupied with all this space they've created. If there are a million little stars, then there'd be six million million Earth-areas for them."

"Why would they want so much?" Rilla Boan asked. Nathan's vision seemed impossible, but the boy appeared to know what he was talking about. It was an irritating habit he had. However, the screen images were terribly simple to understand once you agreed with him.

"Who can say? Perhaps they're very numerous. Perhaps they're giants. Your guess is as good as mine." Nathan waved his hands airily.

The great ship flew on down the cone formed by the interior nipple on the artificial universe of the ancient iulliin.

Cracka tried to formulate a plan of action. He was still partly stunned by the events, the sheer enormity of what he was witnessing. "The question now is what should we do. Should we try and take one of the smaller ships and get away from this big ship?"

The others pondered that question. The Boans were hesitant to take any action.

Nathan meanwhile explained it all quite carefully to Folo, who began to understand. His eyes lit up as he realized the scale of the thing. "So although this is a smaller universe than our own, it's got all this living space laid out ever so conveniently for whoever built it."

"Exactly," said Nathan.

Folo was instant practicality. "Can we take control of one of those ships, Cracka? I mean, do we know enough about the controls?"

"Good questions, Folo. Nathan, what do you think are our chances of taking off in one of those ships? We might do better than let the big ship take us to its programmed destination."

Nathan shrugged. "The controls may not be complex, but they may certainly be dangerous. The first switch we throw may ignite the engines and end everything in a fiery blast."

Cracka nodded. Just such concerns had passed through his head moments before. He examined the activity on the floor of the auditorium far below. The tall, slender robots went about tasks involving the work stations in which they were imbedded. They seemed oblivious to the small group of escaped humans standing on the gallery above their heads.

"They don't seem to have taken any notice of us," said Sam Boan in a heavy whisper.

Cracka agreed. "Maybe we're not in the program. You never know with robots."

"True. Pesky, irritating things, I always found."

"I think we should return to the docking bay and see if we can puzzle out how to fly one of those ships," Cracka said. "Then we can see to finding a way to free the rest of the Calabel people trapped in that hold."

"If we have to cut them all out with your knife, Ranger, we'll be here for a very long time," Avis commented.

Cracka smiled grimly. "I think the knife would wear out long before we finished the job."

Nobody proposed any other plan of action, so they entered the high-speed elevator again and descended at the familiar alarming rate to the space hangar deck.

Once more they picked themselves up off the floor and walked out to the nearest ship, a ninety-meter-high sphere. A loading tower was connected to one side. They entered the car at its base and rose, at the usual numbing speed, to the hatch. Once again Nathan tried standing directly in front of the door. When nothing happened, he experimented by touching a green inlaid rectangle on one side.

At once the hatch slid open. They cautiously advanced into the dark interior. Strange shapes loomed from the murk.

"Does anyone have a light with them?" muttered Cracka. Avis checked her utility belt and found a microflash which she quickly brought to bear.

"Great stuff, Avis," Cracka said as the light showed they were in some kind of control chamber. Seats of a peculiarly long and narrow design were set in a cluster around an array of control panels and monitor screens. The screens were all thin, curved rectangles with sharp edges. The control panels were studded with slender projecting buttons, almost like stalks of glassy wheat.

Nathan took a seat. "Shall I try them? We'll have to eventually, you know."

They were all uneasy.

"Touch the wrong one, boy, and this ship might just take off and go through the roof of this hangar," groused Sam Boan.

Nathan shrugged. Avis tapped her right cheek.

"We might be able to figure out which are the safest controls to try first," Nathan said.

"How?" said Rilla.

"I don't know, they're all of different lengths, different angles of projection. Some are clearly bent."

"Are they flexible, perhaps?" said Folo.

"Good idea, Folo, let's see." Nathan touched a particularly long, sensitive-looking control rod that projected about eight inches off the board like a crystalline drinking straw.

It was not flexible, but it moved easily, and lights came on around them.

So did the computer screens.

"Uh oh," said Cracka.

"I think we'd better continue, now we've started," Nathan said, getting closer to the controls.

Cracka went back to the airlock and stared across at the elevator banks. It was too far to see the small indicator lights.

Avis joined him there. "Worried about the robots?"

"Yes. They might not have noticed our movements earlier, but something tells me that if we activate one of the small ships we're sure to hit some kind of alarm."

Avis nodded. "What can we do?"

Cracka moved into the loading elevator. "I'm going over to the outside control panel to see if I can detect any kind of alarm signal."

Avis leaned out of the airlock. The spherical ships sat mutely all around them. There was no sign of any activity. She pulled herself back in as Cracka disappeared from view.

Nathan continued to experiment. Suddenly the airlock swished shut.

"Careful, Nathan, that almost left you an orphan!"

"Sorry about that, everybody stay away from anything the looks like it might move." He flicked up a sequence of long red straws.

A sudden vibration began below them. More computer screens snapped on, and masses of alien data began scrolling across them.

"Hey, Nathan, I think you hit the jackpot that time," Folo said excitedly.

"Be careful, boy!" snapped Sam Boan irritably.

"Open the hatch again, Nathan, we have to let Ranger Buckshore back in."

Nathan touched the long blue tinted glass control lever and the airlock opened.

Avis looked out and gave a gasp of horror.

The elevator doors at the hangar bay's control hub were opening. A pair of the tall alien robots strode out, diminutive headfins lit up in a bright green. They were almost upon Cracka Buckshore.

"Run, Cracka!" she screamed. The ranger dived under the control panel and bolted toward the ship.

The robots were three meters tall, slender bipedal machines with a swift, jerky motion. They swept around the display panel and pursued Cracka.

Cracka had covered a third of the distance, but the robots were too close. He stopped, feinted, and then ran to one side. The robot on the left side produced a wand that emitted a sudden crackle of harsh green light. Stroboscopic flickers caromed off the spaceships. Cracka staggered and fell. The robot extended a narrow pipe and sprayed something over his prone form.

The other robot mounted the steps to the airlock.

Nathan heard Avis's scream and flicked the door shut, stopping the green light.

"What if it can open the door?" Avis said in horror.

Nathan looked wildly at the controls. "It could kill the ranger to take off now."

"We could be killed too, but if that robot gets in here we'll be recaptured for sure."

At the thought of recapture Sam Boan impulsively leaned over and flicked the drive switch.

"Sam!" shrieked his sister.

The hum returned, swollen, angry.

Automatic undocking procedures began. A tremendous

blue light ignited at the base of the ship along with a savage hum that was painful to listen to. Then the ship rose smoothly off the floor, discarding its service gantry and the ramp with the robot still atop it and hurling them away, crisping and sparkling.

■ CHAPTER SEVEN

The mother ship's great hatch blew open, and the small ship flew rapidly away, accelerating at about one gravity toward the nearest small red sun, a few million kilometers distant.

Inside the control cabin they watched in awe as a screen offered them an exterior view of the mother ship, a set of enormous spheres, many kilometers across, which rapidly dwindled and then vanished to a point source, lost in the plane of feeble little stars of the universe sphere.

"How are we going to get back to the ship?" Avis asked in a dread-filled voice. Already the huge ship seemed very far away. She felt deathly afraid, in a way that she had never felt before.

Nathan shook his head. "I don't think we can, Mother."

Avis grimaced. "Poor Cracka Buckshore, and he was the one who freed us."

Nathan shivered. He prayed he hadn't killed the ranger when the ship took off.

"Will we ever get home now?" she said.

Nathan bit his lip. He shook his head gently. "I don't know, Mother. Maybe not."

They were truly lost. Avis realized that she would never see Calabel again. Never see her ranch, her animals, her house, or anything from her life except her son.

With bitter groans the Boans collapsed into the acceleration couches, which were too long and narrow for the human body.

"These chairs were designed by an idiot," snapped Rilla. "They're dreadfully uncomfortable."

"Besides being too high off the floor," said Sam.

"I don't think the designers had the human frame in mind," Nathan said, mildly.

"Well, anyway," Rilla said, "there must be some way to get home. What about this ship? Maybe this could take us home?"

Nathan shook his head more firmly. "I doubt it. My hunch is that we'd need the big ship to get home to Calabel."

"Oh, hell." Rilla looked around hopelessly. Unable to push the fear away any further, her face crumpled. She sobbed, "And my Martherer, will I ever see her?" She couldn't finish. She broke down completely and wept.

Nathan looked away and was stunned anew. Tears were running down Folo's cheeks.

"Folo?" he said quietly.

Folo met his gaze, his misery plainly visible. "We'll never see them again," said the troncher. "Never see Shay or Bat or..." Folo bit back the last, the tears glistened wetly.

Nathan had never imagined Folo crying. Indeed, Folo, two years older, wise to street and tronch, had always seemed invulnerable. Folo was always one step ahead, always high and hard, and never hurt. Now he seemed strangely shrunken and diminished.

"Martherer!" It was a cry of anguish. Folo stared distraught at the screen where the mother ship had vanished.

Suddenly Nathan felt acutely embarrassed by Folo's distress, but when he turned away he found only his mother staring at him fixedly.

"What are we going to do, Nathan?" For a moment he teetered on the edge of hysteria; he didn't know whether to laugh or scream.

Then he consciously took a grip on himself.

He had to take it just like the rangers. They never flinched, never gave in and lay down to die. They fought to the very last. He would pretend that they would see the rangers again someday. He would want them to nod approvingly when they heard how he kept the others alive. He would pretend, and he would fight to the last to bring them through.

Nathan cleared his throat, fought to keep his voice under control, and wound up sounding a lot calmer than he actually felt. "I'm not sure, Mother. We've been lucky so far. I'm afraid to touch any more of these controls."

Folo suddenly pointed to the control board. "Nathan, a short, purple-colored rod is flashing on and off. What do you think that means?"

Nathan stared at it. Set within a small recess on its own, it seemed like an important control node. No other control buttons or levers were close to it.

Why did it flash? Was it a warning indicator? He toyed with the very long controls that altered the lighting. They were about twice the length of the controls affecting the engines. The purple control was much shorter still.

It dawned on him suddenly. He reached out and flicked the purple switch from down to up. "The autopilot, I'll bet. It must be programmed to fly itself, but the beings who built the ship still like to take a hand in their own landings and takeoffs."

Folo nodded. It made some sense. "When they fly, that is."

"Right. They don't leave it up to the robots all the time."

"What nonsense," spouted Sam Boan from his acceleration chair. "You've probably just set the engines to explode."

Nathan snorted. "Why would anybody put a control that blew up the engines on the board? That makes no sense. I think it's the autopilot. It was flashing, which must have meant something. Now it's not, so we'll just have to wait and see if I'm right."

Sam glared at him and muttered under his breath.

Avis was staring at the screens. Was there a difference in all those flickering, changing data flows? Not so far as she could tell.

"Poor Ranger Buckshore," she whispered to herself. Suddenly she wished very much that the ranger was there with them, with his calm aura of dependable capability.

Folo heard her, and their eyes met for a second. She looked back to the screens. Poor Folo, his heart was breaking. Would he ever see his Martherer again? It seemed unlikely on the face of it.

The ship flew on, under the control of the main flight computer. With no orders to select a particular sun region for landing, the program would respond to the nearest landing beacon. It had already located that, on the tower of the Planggi, the ancient rulers of a Sun Clanth a few million kilometers away. The course changes were gradual and slight, and the acceleration mode was kept at one gravity, just as if a party of iulliin themselves were aboard the ship.

Unfortunately the ship discovered that the loaders had forgotten to stock the autokitchen with food and water. Nor were any dagbabi slaves in the galley. The ship would be unable to offer its exalted passengers refreshments during

the trip. To explain this lack it went into full audio mode
and offered a short announcement.

The sudden eruption of loud, alien phrases into the control cabin sent a shock wave through the fugitives.

"What the hell was that?" said Sam Boan, sitting
upright, face red and eyes protruding.

Folo and Avis stared at Nathan.

He shrugged. "I don't know. Maybe the ship just told us
to have a nice day. Maybe we're going to crash. Maybe
we've been identified as criminal trespassers. We just don't
have enough information to make a sensible determina-
tion."

To dispel his unease Nathan continued a full assay of the
controls. He found seventy-six individual buttons, knobs,
and long twirly things like the straws that turned the lights
on and off.

Eventually he and Folo tired of theorizing about the different controls and decided, with Avis and the Boans' full
agreement, to leave the board alone. For the moment they
would try to explore the ship more thoroughly, amass more
information to make better decisions, if and when they had
to be made.

They discovered two hatch doors, other than the airlock.
One led to an elevator, and another led to a narrow room
where one wall was covered with incomprehensible machinery and flickering meters.

All their efforts to operate the elevator failed. There was
no obvious control mechanism, and eventually they all
conceded that it was probably run by some control among
the seventy-six on the main board. Finding out which could
be a long and potentially dangerous task.

Then they sat and argued about what to do. Eventually
they grew bored and simply sat and stared at the incomprehensible alien stuff on the screens until one by one they
dozed off and slept.

Hours went by. They became very thirsty, and so hungry their bellies seemed to burn.

Eventually, driven by desperation, Nathan worked some more of the controls. Nothing much happened. He then tried turning off the autopilot, but the program had noted the deranged pattern of control operations and had concluded that the iulliin occupants of the control chamber had intoxicated themselves or given over control to irresponsible children. It took emergency action to counter all input commands from the main control board. The ship accelerated towards the beacon of the Planggi, where the computer would turn over the problem to the competent authorities.

Fifty-three hours passed, by which time the fugitives were beginning to confront the likelihood of death from dehydration. Sam Boan had lain down on the floor and composed himself for the end, since, as he loudly pointed out, he could see no point in further struggles against the inevitable.

A weeping bundle of pitiable sobs, Rilla was curled up on one of the acceleration couches. Her long, reddish brown hair was spread around her in a disordered web. Avis sat hunched over on another, in gloomy silence, while Folo watched dully as Nathan tried to comprehend the incomprehensible. Their tongues were swollen, and leathery, filling their mouths.

Abruptly the computer spoke again, and they jumped and screamed in fright. The main screen projection changed from the overall graphic of the sphere universe to a view from the forward cameras.

A world was laid out below, an utterly flat world that extended into a haze of distance unimaginably far away. A huge world, painted on the gigantic sphere of the artificial universe by the life-giving rays of the small red sun stationed above it.

They gazed in awe as the ship dropped rapidly through the atmosphere and the green and yellow piebald below was broken up by a rectilinear pattern of black and silver lines. Clouds of many shapes, colored in pink and ochre, stretched across the ground patterns and cast black shadows on the landscape beneath.

The ship had decelerated before entering the atmosphere layer, and now it began a long glide to the beacon of the Planggi spaceport.

Nathan couldn't restrain himself from commenting on what they were seeing. "The regular markings must be water channels. The fact that there are clouds means there must be rain and periods of shadow. The green must be vegetation, and thus there would be a need for canals to channel the rainfall. The landscape must be very flat. Erosion here would only go one way. After a while the water would all be lying on top of the denser layers. So there must be artificial processes to help circulate the water. I wonder. . ." Nathan quieted again.

Avis and Folo exchanged another look.

Folo would once have laughed and made some joke about Nathan's having a computer instead of a brain, heart, or sex organs, but now he simply wondered what it must be like to be the mother of a kid like this.

The markings, the clouds, the great lakes grew larger after a while, and then much, much larger as the descent continued. The lakes were the size of small planetary oceans, several thousand kilometers across. Canals were two hundred kilometers wide. Belts of clouds hung at different altitudes. The clouds were of many colors, including green.

The flat world stretched into the endless, breathless distance. The small red star had become a sun, a point of brightness in a sky that was turning a deep, dark blue.

Nathan watched for cities, for signs of massive populations, but saw only the regular patterns of water channels, a profusion of rectangles and circular pools.

Could the builders of this vastness be a water people? Some sort of amphibians, perhaps?

Then he looked around at the cabin for reassurance. It did not seem designed for anything but bipeds built on a scale similar to that of humanity. A water-based people should surely want a wet control cabin—which, as they had already discovered, was certainly not the case.

Indeed, from available evidence, the builders of the ship were able to go without food or water for long periods at a time. Nathan was almost looking forward to finding out what kind of aliens they would be.

Now they were close enough to the ground to make out smaller details. Corkscrewing out of the tree cover were a number of buildings or shells—Nathan was unsure which —that gleamed whitely in the sunlight and seemed much taller than the surrounding forest.

The surface was not as flat as he'd expected. Patches of hills were scattered across the vastness. The hills were sometimes clumped in circles, which made Nathan wonder if they marked the sites of ancient craters.

As they drew closer to the ground and passed right over one of these, Nathan observed that it was a kind of scarp, covered in dark purplish vegetation. Leading away from it on the long, lee side was a narrow dark line that eventually turned bright green and faded out amid other vegetation.

Nathan sucked in his breath in excitement. A road? But why would it be green? And how could there be hills where there most certainly could not be planetary geology?

They fell through a cloud, and abruptly Nathan gave a jerk: the screen clearly recorded a flock of flying things. The scale was impossible to judge, but the body shapes made him think instinctively of terrestrial fish. They were visible for a moment in the cloud, and then they were gone.

"What were *those* things?" Avis said.

"Airfish?" suggested Nathan, half humorously.

Avis managed a smile.

"It means that something can breathe this atmosphere," said Nathan on a more serious note.

"Bah! It was nothing at all, more like," grumbled Sam Boan uneasily.

The cloud grew denser, became pink and then brown and dark. Small things out of the dark cloud, like insects perhaps, were impacting on the cameras. Finally they dropped through the last layer and were able to see the ground below.

"Goodness, the whole place is just a garden!" exclaimed Avis. Dark green trees crowded together along wide canals. Hills and hillocks, striped in green and purple, filled the vista into the haze of distance.

Rilla was nodding animatedly, her woes forgotten for a moment. "Yes, Avis is right. Look at how it's all laid out. There are streams everywhere, and different sorts of trees. It's a garden, a beautiful Eden filled with water! Will this damnable ship ever land? We must get some water to drink! Nathan must land the ship!"

Nathan shrugged and turned away from Rilla's unreasoning eyes. He had no control over the ship. "What do you think the large white structures are?" he said, though it was an effort to talk—his tongue was swollen and so stiff it was painful to move it around.

"They look like giant snail shells to me," said Avis.

"Water, so much water," groaned Sam Boan.

And then their destination came into view.

Hundreds of meters high, an enormous pylon of some gray shiny material thrust up through the trees.

"I have a feeling that that's where we're going," Nathan suggested.

"Too early to tell, boy," snorted Sam Boan, irritated by Nathan's know-it-all assertions.

"Nevertheless, Sheriff, that's where we'll be going."

Boan resisted a strong impulse to cuff the youngster about the ears.

But already the city was visible, spread out around the pylon, a city of spires and towers and great pyramidal mounds. The ship dropped steadily. The forest and canal-scape gave way to fields of green and brown and ponds of many shapes with settlements around them.

The fields were replaced by the first tower, and they all gasped at the sight.

A vast building of a reddish material, a rococo tuning fork stuck in the ground, with the tines jutting into the air. The building's widest face was turned toward the sun, now a golden disk in the pale blue sky.

But it was in ruins. Gaping holes showed through the walls. Patches of decorative tile work had fallen away. Vegetation was growing on the top.

Another building came into view, then more, many more. Tuning-fork buildings aligned in rows, arranged to prevent one building's casting a shadow on another.

All were ruined, with holes gaping in the outer fabric.

An open space, a wedge covering many square kilometers, came into view. The pylon was set to one side of it, and large buildings of many shapes formed a cliff beyond it along that side of the cleared space.

The ship swung down and landed, with a modest bump, about a half kilometer from the pylon. The engines cut out and the airlock snapped open. The alien audio voiceover began again, repeating a message while they looked out onto what was clearly a very overgrown landing field. A warm breeze was blowing their way. It brought a spicy scent, the hint of alien odors.

The temperature was a comfortable 25 degrees centigrade. The humidity was low. Above them was a sky of deep blue, with scattered wisps of orange cloud.

Since no docking structure signaled its connection, a set
of steps unfolded from beneath the airlock and telescoped
twenty-five meters to the ground.

"Well, I guess the air is breathable," Nathan said. "If it
weren't, we'd all be dead now."

Folo was already climbing down the steps.

"Of course, we don't know what kind of microorganisms we're going to meet. We don't know if we can even
drink the water."

"Water!" Folo reached the bottom of the steps.

"Water!" The Boans were following him.

On the ground Folo scanned the surroundings. A sort of
bright green moss grew on most open ground, although it
was blackened around the base of the ship.

The sun was a small golden disk, shining through a fine
haze high in the sky. The gray pylon stood stark against the
blue.

There was water scent on the breeze, and not from far
away either. Folo started for its source.

"Where's the damn boy going now?" snarled Sam
Boan.

"To the water, Sam," Rilla replied.

Sam got up hastily and staggered after him.

Nathan and Avis climbed down and followed at a short
distance.

"I don't understand this decay." Nathan indicated the
vegetation—small shrubs and bushes here and there. The
landing field was much overgrown. At its edge was a forest, a solid mass of dark green little trees.

Folo headed for the buildings—that was where he
smelled the nearest water.

The walk seemed long. It was several kilometers to the
nearest buildings. Because of the dehydration and the lack
of food, they were staggering by the time they reached the
edge of the cleared area.

A thick growth of bushes and ten-meter-tall trees that bore spherical leaves like green bubbles blocked the way. Flowers of many hues, bell-shaped purples, sunflower spreads of red and yellow, were distributed in profusion.

The buildings formed ramparts stretching for miles in both directions. Here too the buildings were arranged to take advantage of the sun, except that behind the first row of these highly varied buildings were others, cast in perpetual shadow.

The rampart buildings competed with each other too. Some soared five hundred meters into the air, great spirals of green glass, rectangular slabs, often with rococo turrets and decorated sides, castellated towers with conical roofs like enormous toadstools. Between these giants narrow breaks were set irregularly along the cliff.

They climbed through patches of thick vines that were roped around each other like so much giant yarn. Tall pole-like trees, tipped with growths that looked like great, man-size fingers, grew here and there in the general riot of bubble-leaf shrubs and trees. Insect creatures buzzed through the vegetation.

Nathan noticed that when his shadow fell on the spherical leaf structures, they would puff open and collapse down to a gooey bud on the brown and green stems of most of these plants. This was clearly a response to the fact that the sun was only seldom occluded by clouds; the high plants had the ability to build up or shrink their leaf area at will.

"Water!" came the cry from ahead.

After a moment he stumbled on behind the others, through a thick stand of trees which resembled umbrellas, with large membranous leaves that could open or close as required.

They emerged into an open space on the bank of a canal nearly filled with water that stretched away on either side straight as a die. To their left it then turned ninety degrees and passed between two big rectangular buildings tipped with turrets that lofted brave finials into the sky.

To the right it ran away as far as they could see, matched by the wall of buildings, until it too was lost in the golden haze that hung across the distance.

The canal bank was paved with flat slabs of a brown ceramic material that held a deep gloss. The slabs were six inches thick, smoothly contoured, joined without visible mortar. The canal itself was filled with vegetation that grew from a bottom of dark brown mud.

On reaching the water Sam Boan had simply fallen in. The result was an explosion of small creatures that swam or crawled away from him through the muddy bottom. Sam took fright and scrambled out again with a wail of horror.

He stood quivering on the bank. Mud blossomed up from where he'd disturbed the bottom.

Nathan saw more small shapes whiz along the bottom. Smaller critters were feeding near the surface farther out. The water was filled with life, that much was certain.

He joined the others, away from Sam, and went down to cup up handfuls of water. With a prayer that his body could handle whatever microorganisms might be present, he gulped some down, washing it around in his mouth. It was a luxurious feeling; light-headed as he was, it was difficult to resist the urge to actually jump into the canal and swim.

Sam dropped down beside them. He put his head to the water and slurped noisily, groaning with pleasure between gulps.

"I wouldn't drink too much, too quickly," Folo suggested.

"I'll drink all I damn well want," roared the sheriff. He plunged his face back into the water. Having suffered the seemingly endless torments of the last several days on account of Folo Banthin, Sam wasn't about to take the little troncher's views into account on anything.

Rilla Boan was also immersing her head in the cool, clear water.

When Nathan had wet his mouth thoroughly and drunk several swallows, he forced himself to sit back. Water nausea would be sure to follow if he drank any more.

Folo was already sitting on his haunches, studying their surroundings.

"Well, Folo, we'll just have to hope that our immune systems can handle whatever microorganism nasties this place has to offer."

Folo shrugged. "Did we have much choice?"

"We could have built a fire and boiled some water and then drunk that."

They both eyed the noisy Boans, who were finally sated and lying on the edge of the canal. Sam Boan burped loudly.

"As it is, I think some of us are going to be sorry very shortly that we drank so much so quickly."

Folo shrugged again. "I guess we'll just run our luck out in this place." It sounded more like the old Kid Folo.

Suddenly Rilla Boan had pulled to a sitting position. She had her hands clasped over her stomach and an expression o discomfort on her face. "Oh!" she exclaimed and then bent over and vomited up much of the water she had guzzled.

In a few moments her brother, purple in face, had joined her, fouling the water of the canal by the bank, his hoarse hiccups echoing off the strange little umbrella trees that grew on either side.

Disgusted, Nathan turned away and studied the surroundings more carefully.

The canal was about twenty meters wide and at least two meters deep in the center.

The vegetation on the other side thinned out shortly in front of the buildings, which towered over them with brutal

massiveness. There was silence, except for a faint sough-
ing of the wind through the stands of umbrella trees.

"Is the whole place abandoned?" Folo said.

"Doesn't seem that busy now, does it?"

They heard a rhythmic whistling suddenly, and looked
up to see a flock of flying creatures, each the size of a
terrestrial salmon, pass overhead and dip down into the tree
cover. Their wings were very large and resembled
stretched membranes, like those of terrestrial bats.

A few moments later another, slightly larger flock
swooped by, heading in the same direction.

■ CHAPTER EIGHT

They turned to their left and followed the canal bank
around and on into the total shadow behind the rampart
buildings.

They passed one of the white spiral shapes, a small one,
barely twenty meters high and wide.

It was the center of a cloud of one particular kind of
insect, a large brown flier with vivid blue compound eyes
and a blue and brown striped abdomen. Thousands of the
insects, about the size of the biggest tronch flies on Calabel, or a terrestrial bumblebee, buzzed above the spiral.
Others were at work building the next layer of the nest, for
that clearly was what it was.

They came to the buildings at last. The vegetation grew
wild up to the edge of a walk paved with slabs similar to

those that lined the canal. The structures were about two hundred and fifty meters tall, big blocks of blue-gray, with sweeping buttresses interconnecting above the water of the canal. The sunward faces were ribbed and beveled in regular patterns. Windows glittered in the sun.

Three flying creatures, each the size of a large dog, with wingspans of six or seven meters, flew over their heads, out of the darkness of the shadows. The fliers ignored them, except for a single raucous cry that sounded vaguely insulting, and flew on over the forest.

They peered into the gloom. Beyond the rampart buildings were older constructions, generally of a lesser size and a simpler design.

The spaces between the buildings were narrow, twenty meters or less, and considerable debris was piled up in them.

Here and there were what appeared to be the skeletal remains of a creature shaped roughly like a sand dune, and about ten feet long. Other bones, along with sticks, twigs, and seed husks, were scattered about in little drifts.

"This isn't the most reassuring sort of place," Rilla said. "Where are the beings that built this, that lived here?"

Sam Boan stared up into the dimness above. About one hundred meters up, a buttress soared across the canal to the adjoining building. Above that was another similar buttress. "I don't like this place," grumbled the sheriff.

"Nor do I, Sam," said his sister in agreement.

"Let's go back," said Avis suddenly. "I'm afraid, Nathan!"

Nathan turned. There was nothing to be seen but the dim "street," the drear canal, and the white skeletons in the corners. He peered into the darkness beyond and noticed little patches of light here and there, circles and rectangles of sunlight passed through the rampart buildings, perhaps by some system of mirrors or optic fibers.

The others, even Folo, wanted to go back to the sunlit area, and so Nathan turned and accompanied them; there would be opportunity to explore the older part of the city another time.

They walked quickly back along the path and emerged once more into the sunlight.

They also discovered a greeting party. At least three different alien races were represented.

In front, in a solid little block, were about thirty small bipedal creatures that resembled insects as much as anything else Nathan had ever seen. Glossy, black-limbed little things, about a meter and a half tall, with complex arrangements of feelers and antennae on top of heads that were about the size of a man's fist.

The eyes were like purple golfballs. Beneath them were the mouthparts, which worked constantly to produce a medley of wheezing chirps and hiccups.

Behind this phalanx stood a small crowd of lizardlike aliens that might have been the children of exceptionally graceful dinosaurs. They were no more than five feet tall and wore garments of a very simple cut, a tunic or bib hung from the long neck to cover the narrow chest. Trunks of some dark, coarse material clothed their loins. Some of them wore hats that boasted shining devices.

On the right of these creatures stood a row of burly, leonine bipeds, with massive musculature, pale golden fur, and the accoutrements of professional soldiers in a pre-technological era.

Apart from the constant chittering and rubbing of the insects there was a complete silence.

Then Rilla Boan let out a fearful scream and ran back into the dark.

A pair of the big, lionlike aliens sprang forward and ran Rilla down. They tackled her like linebackers and brought her crashing to the ground with terrifying brutality. Her screams cut short a moment later.

"Ohmigod," said Avis, holding her hand to her mouth.

"We're in for it now," said Folo.

Rilla was hoisted into the air over the shoulder of one of the aliens. The other finished adjusting a pair of wrist restraints on her, then both padded back, past the startled gaze of the rest of the Calabels.

Some of the lizardlike aliens came forward. As they did they rhythmically drove their fists into their palms and ducked their heads.

Nathan and Folo tensed, ready to fight if they had to.

Instinctively Sam Boan tried to draw his guns, then cursed Cracka Buckshore when he remembered losing them in the woods outside Tronch City.

As they got closer, Nathan was able to observe that the devices on their stiff, four-cornered hats were symbols that might have been letters or numbers or other markers of rank.

One lizard wearing a rather battered gray and black hat with a scarlet ideograph stepped forward. It raised its arms above its head. The hands were reptilian, with small, delicate-looking talons on the ends. The fingers were stubby; the arms, however, were thickly muscled.

It uttered a couple of paragraphs of a fluid-sounding tongue with many high-pitched components and clicks. Then it indicated the Calabels and waved an arm toward the rampart buildings to their left.

It repeated the gesture while babbling on at considerable length in the fluid-sounding tongue of the aliens that were known to the iulliin as "dagbabi."

The intent was clear. The Calabels were to accompany the task force and march off to the left.

Now the phalanx of small insect folk also raised glossy black limbs and pointed them at the Calabels and then pointed them down the row of vast buildings on their left.

One of the burly lionlike beings, who wore a conical

helmet with holes for its catlike ears, suddenly coughed and snarled something in a loud, metallic voice. It then gestured to the left.

"They want us to go somewhere," said Sam. "I wish I knew what they wanted us for."

"What about poor Rilla?" said Avis, still with her hand pressed to her mouth.

"Damn fool woman! She shouldn't have run," Sam said.

"But they just about killed her," Avis murmured.

"We don't have any choice but to go with them," said Nathan.

"Nathan's right," said Folo. "If we don't go with them, the pantheroids are gonna carry us anyway."

Reluctantly they started marching leftward, along the front of one of the big, dark, rectangular buildings.

As they marched, the lion types took up position directly behind the Calabels, and the phalanx of insects set off at the front. To either side strode the lizardlike fellows, who walked with a jouncing gait, like ostriches.

The insects carried Rilla Boan, held up above their heads on a forest of little black arms. Rilla gurgled in horror much of the way.

Eventually they came to a building with windows intact. A wide door stood open, with several more of the big catlike aliens standing beside it.

To this door they were directed, and then into a large, dimly lit hallway, with vast hangings, embroidered or painted, depicting scenes of ancient grandeur inhabited by another race of aliens: tall, humanoid bipeds with lean, long faces, narrow eyes, purple lips, and short, white hair that capped their heads like a scrap of wooly fleece.

They crossed the hall, the chirruping of the insect folk echoing from the ceiling and the empty walls. There were lights ahead, and a set of double doors.

They passed through the doors, inlaid with fantastic patterns of black and white, and came out upon a wide staircase that rose in a majestic spiral within a cylindrical wall space that was painted with a single enormous mural. The sun's light was let in through a system of mirrors, and the entire place was lit to about half the level of the out-doors.

The painting was in a heroic, superrealistic style and depicted more of the tall, angular aliens, along with all the other types they had seen, and, shockingly, humans, un-mistakable humans.

"What is this?" said Avis.

"Those are undoubtedly human beings," said Nathan.

There was a hard shove between his shoulders. He turned and found the leader of the lion-headed types point-ing up the stairs.

"Okay, okay," Nathan said, indicating that he under-stood.

They mounted the stairs behind the insects, who contin-ued to keep Rilla horizontal as they climbed. Every floor surface, tread, and riser was decorated with complex mar-quetry in black, red, and white.

Slowly they wound around the mural, which had been done by a master of the technique of painting. Verdant scenes, fabulous palaces, alien crowds, the reptiles and in-sect folk. Groups of humans, too, and more of the tall gray aliens with the purple lips and long, lugubrious faces.

But Sam was already beginning to tire. "Food, I must have food!" he said in a mournful croak to the lionheads. They merely stared back at him.

On they climbed. In the painting, the scenes set around them changed gradually from those depicting forest life, or the canals and cities, to scenes in the air.

A vast variety of flying creatures swirled here, and through them flew some beasts the size of whales, ridden

by teams of the tall bipeds, accompanied by more human
beings. These parties were clearly hunting the small flying
creatures, for there were scenes of them being netted,
speared, and shot with a variety of weapons.

The painted sky grew paler, filled with golden clouds.
They reached the top of the stair and sinultaneously discovered their destination.

A large gallery opened out toward the sun. The walls
were a delicate shade of pink. The ceilings and floors were
inlaid with abstract mosaics in tones of ochre and cream.

Heavy vases the size of a man stood in strategic spots.
Sculptures, some representational, some abstract, were set
here and there.

On a large round white carpet were couches on which
reclined a number of very tall, lanky bipeds clad in soft
pink robes. It was as if the figures in the painting had come
to life. Here were those aliens with the pink-gray skins and
purple lips.

At the humans' entrance they all jumped up with cries
of savage delight. Over and over they shouted something
that sounded like "zaga siffile" and slammed their right
fists into their left palms.

The insect folk put Rilla down on the ground and withdrew. Folo and Avis helped Rilla to her feet. She was still
weeping. Her hair clasp had come loose, and her long
brown hair was flying everywhere. Her wrists were cuffed
with rings of a light plastic material.

"Are you all right, Rilla?" Avis asked in some concern.

"I think they broke something in my back, it aches so
much," she groaned.

The tall aliens formed an excited group, growing all the
time, around the Calabel humans.

In the flesh, the humanoid appearance was even more
remarkable. They were very tall—six foot six and over
seemed the norm. Their most human characteristic was

their eyes, which were soft and brown, surrounded by white, with very human-looking eyelids, lashes, and eyebrows. The pink-gray skin was smooth across the face, but there were numerous folds around the long, inhumanly scrawny neck. Above the eyes were bushy little eyebrows of white that matched the wool atop the high, seamed foreheads.

The leader of the reptile group now stepped forward and broke into a paragraph or two of whistles and grunts and clicks. When it had finished it stepped back. One of the tall bipeds said a few whistles and grunts in return. Then the tall aliens conversed together in their own language, which sounded more akin to human speech.

One came close and raised an instrument like a fork and poked Sam Boan's belly with it.

Sam jumped back with an oath. "Have a care! I'll not be provoked!"

The tall aliens laughed, a harsh gleeful sound.

But another voice interrupted. One of the tall aliens entered behind them. He wore a robe of some fine, wispy white fabric. Over it was a small surplice in orange. On his head he bore a round star of what looked like gold, the size of a fist.

This individual stepped forward and examined the Calabels carefully. Then he whirled and made an impassioned speech to the others.

A dozen more of the tall aliens came hurrying in. They exploded into cries of "Zaga!" and "Siffile!"

The one in white waved his arms and shouted until the others were quiet. It then harangued them at length, at times becoming extremely passionate about something. Eventually some kind of agreement was reached. Two younger members of the tall species were sent scurrying to the door.

While they were gone a furious babbling conversation

broke out in the room. More of the aliens kept appearing too, some dressed in the pink robes, others in different colors, with white and blue predominating. On their feet they wore elaborate shoes with platform soles and high heels. Things like snakes or dragons or lightning bolts projected from these shoes, but whether as marks of status or as decoration was impossible to tell.

Time passed. The one in white with the gold globe on his head was addressing a small group clad in white robes like his own. Nathan now began to detect differences between the aliens that could be either sexual or racial. He also noticed that the group in white looked considerably older than the ones wearing pink or orange.

Suddenly four more of the tall aliens entered. They wore perilously high platform soles and heels and walked with a stilted, jerky motion as a result. They began a furious harangue of the whole room, with much incantation of the phrase, "Zaga siffile."

The one wearing the golden star, or globe, was clearly upset. He strode up and down in front of the group of older types and muttered angrily to them the whole time.

At last the doors opened and the young aliens in red returned, with a squad of the lizardlike fellows behind them, who carried a large box surfaced in shining black, and bearing a number of indicator lights, winking blue, green, and yellow. The box stood about a meter high and wide, and was obviously heavy. The lizardlike fellows set it down with a groan of exertion.

At a sharp command, the lizard men turned on one of their number and subdued him by force, tying his forelimbs to his side and thrusting him headfirst into a cavity in the side of the machine.

One of the tall aliens said something, the machine squawked in response, and the lizard in the box emitted a soul-destroying shriek.

The one in white with the gold star came forward. He was handed a black, cone-shaped wand about a foot long. From one end of the cone a wire extended to the large black module containing the howling lizard.

The tall alien spoke into the wide end of the cone wand. After a moment's hesitation and a gasping squeal from the unfortunate in the machine, the lizard began to croak words in what was unarguably Human Interlingua, the common-stock terrestrial tongue of most human worlds.

"You, here, now. Greet. Urrrr. Of the Loo Eer we, urrr. Take welcome of the Planggi. Greeet."

"Oh my," said Avis in disbelief.

"Make speak, humble friends. To your, urr, plea. Listen. Now." The lizard cut off with a gasp.

"What do we do now?" said Rilla loudly.

■ CHAPTER NINE

The interrogation went on and on. Food was brought for the Calabels, and buckets of hot water and even some clean tunics of a fine white material with the feel of silk and the heft of cotton. They were also given slippers of soft gray fabric and belts of the same material to shape the tunics at the waist.

Then, at their third request, Rilla Boan's wrists were freed.

The Sun Mel, for that was how the one who wore the gold ball described himself, asked many questions about the spaceship, which still sat on the overgrown landing field a few kilometers away.

They had landed, it seemed, in full view of the "Golden Yoo Leen" as they went about the ceremonies for the purification of the next "balaast," apparently a time period of some sort. The Sun Mel appeared determined to believe that they had masters, like himself, out in the ship. Their denials were ignored.

At first sight the food items were not reassuring. Bowls of a white, jellylike substance, served cold, were accompanied by pieces of what looked like a thick, dead leaf, piled on a tray of glass or clear plastic.

The Sun Mel spoke into the tube, and the dagbab in the translation box burst into a strangled scream before translating.

"In ages past, siffile ate bokka for their sweet service to the Golden Iulliin."

The Sun Mel smiled at them, exposing big, yellowed teeth, and extended his long, bony hands.

Sam Boan stared at the bowl of goop. A faint fruity, porridgey odor hung over it. Porridge was a food that Sam had heard far more of than he had ever tasted. But the thought of even a bowl of cold, lumpy porridge was enough to make his mouth water. It had been three days since his last meal. He tasted the stuff with a lick of a finger.

He followed the finger by stuffing the rest of the bowl into his mouth with quick, eager motions. "More," he bellowed, eyes wide and slightly staring. "More, more!" Sam's need was primal, intense, passionate.

Indeed the food was ambrosial. A taste that was sweet but balanced by a creaminess not unlike that of ice cream or custard.

They each ate a full bowl; Sam had three. Rilla turned to the pieces of "leaf" on the tray. They were thick and chewy-looking.

"What do you think this is?"

"Try it," said Nathan.

Rilla looked at Nathan with sudden distaste. "No, *you* try it, since you're so eager."

"All right, I will." Nathan bit into a piece and almost choked.

They blanched. He laughed. "Chocolate!" he chortled. "It tastes like chocolate!"

They were stunned for a moment. Then with comical haste they reached for the remaining pieces of leaf. As they chewed the last of it, a pleasant warm sensation spread out from their stomachs.

The hot water came, and the Sun Mel bade them strip naked and suffer the ministrations of the dagbabi house servants, who then scrubbed them and dried them with soft white towels. At first Avis and Rilla balked at the public bathing, but the sight of actual hot water and towels changed their minds.

"I'm not going to be able to do this unless you and Folo turn and look somewhere else, Nathan," Rilla said in a tight voice.

"You too, Sam," added Avis.

Nathan looked out into the endless sky, the golden sun disk, the haze that obliterated distance, past the great tuning-fork towers on the far side of the landing field. The dagbabi worked quickly, two for each person, wielding little brushes and a cleaning fluid that smelled faintly of flowers.

Then the Calabels were dressed in the tunics, with belts tied at the waist.

"This food and these clothes are our gracious blessings to you siffile. Now you will come with me to attend upon the High Mel, to whom you will give whatever message you bring from your masters."

"More food," grunted Sam Boan. "Food, that's what I want. Three bowls aren't enough."

But his appeals were ignored, and the Sun Mel gestured emphatically to them.

A tall, narrow door opened ahead. They passed inside behind the Sun Mel into a dimly lit interior.

They crossed immense hallways cloaked in darkness and decay and climbed enormous curved staircases lit by mirrors placed strategically to pass on sunlight, brought into these cavernous glooms through unknown means. They strode silently behind the Sun Mel through a fantasmagoria of abstract sculptures, objects, paintings on a heroic scale.

Behind them padded a quartet of the pantherish guard aliens, ever ready to prod them forward should their pace slacken.

In a hallway decorated with the heads of large, fierce-looking reptiles the Sun Mel finally paused.

Two more leonine guards waited beside a pair of black double doors easily seven meters high. At the Sun Mel's command they pushed open the doors and the Sun Mel waved them through into a vast room, lit feebly by orange glow balls that seemed to float a meter or so above their heads.

A sculpture stood near the door. With expressions of shock they realized that it presented half-life-size figures of a man and a woman engaged in sexual intercourse in a near vertical position. It had been carved, or cast in a material that might have been ebony or dark plastic.

"They're humans!" said Rilla in a whisper.

"What does it mean?" said Avis. "How?"

But Nathan was staring at the central piece in the room, the throne of the High Mel.

A massive seat carved or molded in a dark brown material, surmounted with a gargoyle's face, rose on a pedestal that sat on a bed of varnished skulls. There were the skulls of several different species, in three rows. Clearly visible were human skulls, a dozen or more.

A fishy odor hung in the air. On the huge throne lay a frail-looking figure attended by several lizardlike dagbabi.

Sam saw the skulls and swallowed. What had been suggested by the paintings was finally confirmed here. "They have known human beings before us. What goes on here?"

The frail iulliin on the throne made croaking sounds and was helped to sit up. It stared at the humans with obvious astonishment on its ancient witch mask of a face. It raised a clawlike finger and pointed, then broke into an odd hooting cry, which it repeated.

The Sun Mel went to stand beside the throne. He conversed with the High Mel for a while. The High Mel became animated and clutched at the burgundy robe draped loosely around his angular frame.

The dagbabi brought in the heavy language translation device and shoved an unfortunate into the cavity.

The Sun Mel spoke. "Now, to the floor drop. Bow down to the High Mel of Planggi, master of the Sun Clanth, dominator of the prairies, ruler of the wide realms and oceans, herder of the punga in the sky, companion to the golden sun itself."

They hesitated, looking to each other for enlightenment.

"Now, kneel!" screamed the tormented dagbab.

"Kneel?" Rilla's forehead furrowed. "Did I hear that correctly? It wants us to kneel down to it?"

"I get the impression that the Golden Iulliin are used to being knelt to and that kind of thing, don't you?" Nathan tried to treat it lightly.

Beside him, Folo took an audible deep breath.

"But it seems so degrading!" Rilla was clearly upset by the thought of paying this kind of primitive homage.

Indeed the Calabels were descended from third-generation space rebels. Independence and pride were, if anything, qualities they had too much of.

Behind them there were stirrings. Avis looked back. "Don't look now but the big furry fellows are behind us. They seem agitated about something."

Folo and Nathan looked back with alarm. Avis was right, the burly aliens were on the balls of their feet, growling slightly and staring at the humans fiercely.

"By the Holy Moth," muttered Folo, "I don't relish tangling with these boys."

"Neither do I," agreed Nathan.

Avis looked around, then she shrugged, said, "What the hell!" and got down on her knees facing the throne. "This isn't worth dying for or anything, you know."

Sam Boan stared truculently at the iulliin, then looked at the big guard beasts. With a groan he sank down to his knees. Sam jerked Rilla down when one of the big bodyguards stepped toward her.

They tried to ignore Rilla's sobs of humiliation, and stared with a confused mix of emotions at the iulliin on the dais.

And then the tortured dagbab was called on to translate again for the Sun Mel.

"Now, tell us of your journey here and of your little home, far beyond the security of the clanth," it announced in bizarrely accented Interlingua.

There was a silence.

"I guess we'd better tell them something," said Nathan.

"I was going to suggest such a course myself," replied Sam. Motioning Nathan to be quiet, the sheriff cleared his throat and began to complain with considerable heat. "We were abducted from our planet by alien robots in a large spaceship. When we entered this universe we escaped from their ship in a smaller ship."

The dagbab gasped and squealed. Then the Sun Mel spoke rapidly to the older iulliin, who responded with a terse remark or two.

Nathan nudged Sam's elbow. "Should we tell them everything, Sheriff? We don't know what the big ship wanted all the people for yet," he whispered.

Boan stared at the boy. Sam was flustered and hot. This

whole business made him uneasy. His stomach rumbled maniacally. But there was no denying that the youth had something. "You're right, boy, we must dissemble."

"Tell us more about these robots," demanded the Sun Mel suddenly through the gasping dagbab.

After a momentary hesitation, Sam replied, "There is little to tell. They were tall, like yourselves. They operated the big spaceship, and they used ground machines to capture us."

The iulliin emitted odd wails of woe.

In a moment their cries were translated by the tormented dagbab. "Were they of Xaaca? Were they Xaaca demons?"

"Xaaca? What do they mean?" said Avis.

"I'll ask them," said Sam.

But at that moment the dagbab gave a final dry gasp and expired. Several of the little insect folk came forward and scooped up the deceased creature and bore it from the room. Yet another was brought in and inserted into the communications device.

This sight caused Nathan to blurt out something that had been bothering him for a while. "These creatures that serve you? What are they called?"

The new translator gave a little shriek, while its legs stiffened as its toes curled and uncurled, before it translated.

"These are called dagbabi. They are a good servant race. Long have we protected them and nurtured them."

Nathan could not restrain himself. "But aren't we killing them in our effort to communicate?"

There was the usual delay, the short gasp of pain, and the bursts of iulliin syllables.

"Yes, the dagbabi wear out. The override of their mental processes exhausts them. But since it is in our Service this matters little. Many are the dagbabi. For each that dies this honored death, another will be given reproduction rights."

"They're being killed so we can talk?" said Avis in horror.

Nathan gave her a wary look and whispered. "Well, Mother, this is a *worship* session after all. Those are the *Golden* Iulliin up there."

Avis looked back to the dais with new understanding.

The Sun Mel was leaning forward, his ears pricked up at the use of the word "iulliin" in the rapid whispered chatter between the siffile.

"Come, siffile, tell us of your tiny world, we have many questions."

Sam hushed the others and tried to describe Calabel, a small world of forest and hot plains. His stomach grumbled and made him burp. His knees were numb, and the extremity of the situation he found himself in sometimes made his mind go blank, but he struggled on.

As the questions and carefully weighed human answers went on, Nathan turned to his mother and whispered quickly. "You know the legends about Lemall's World, the colony that disappeared entirely in the ninth millennium?"

"Yes."

"Well, it looks to me as if Calabel has just joined Lemall's World in the legends. The iulliin have known humans before. They've known them very well. We're in some kind of terrible trap."

■ CHAPTER TEN

Their knees were throbbing when the audience with the High Mel finally came to an end. By then yet another dagbab had been used up by the translation device.

The rest of the iulliin who were present departed the

room. The Sun Mel's yashi—the lion guards—then closed
the double doors behind them.

The Sun Mel jumped to his feet and darted behind the
throne. In a moment he reappeared and beckoned to them
to follow him. He motioned for them to hurry.

"But we need more food," cried Sam Boan in a frenzy
of frustration.

The Sun Mel made frantic motions, squeezing his narrow lips shut with his fingers to emphasize the need for
silence. Then he beckoned urgently for them to make
haste.

They looked at one another with dismay. Sam belched
weakly in the extremity of his hunger. There was nothing
to do but follow the tall figure of the iulliin and his retinue.
Behind them padded the burly, leonine yashi.

Behind the immense throne, on its pyramid of skulls,
was a narrow trapdoor set in the floor. A stair descended
into total darkness. The Sun Mel descended the stair. The
yashi prodded them to follow.

Beneath the stair a landing opened onto a narrow spiral
staircase which they ascended for some distance before the
Sun Mel pulled open a door. They entered a huge se-
pulchral hall. The Sun Mel drew them on, a long finger
crossed against his purple lips.

Their slippered feet made little noise. Only the sounds
of Sam Boan's puffing from the exertion broke the vast
quiet. Hangings could be dimly perceived high above
them. The actual ceiling was vaulted and almost lost in the
gloom. Here, illumination was provided by a number of
dim green spheres that were suspended halfway up the
walls. The floor was carpeted, but the carpeting seemed
worn and fragile.

Along the walls were a number of great double doors.
Each bore an immense, ornate set of doorknobs, carved or
molded into alien gargoyle faces.

The doors passed, one after another, and the hall

stretched ahead into the distance. The air of decay was thick. Once a vast population had inhabited the huge place, but now the silence betrayed its near empty state.

At last they reached the far wall. The Sun Mel snapped his fingers and two dagbabi opened a small door.

Light blazed in, the golden light of the sun. A narrow bridge stretched before them.

The Sun Mel looked out cautiously. He craned his neck to look above the door, then stepped out and motioned to them to follow.

The bridge was an arch, fifteen meters long, three wide, that crossed to another vast towering building. Below them were layered galleries, balconies, a myriad of winking mirrors. Above were more of the same.

Inside the other building they followed the Sun Mel through more gloomy corridors until finally he showed them into a hidden suite of rooms, on the corner of the building, with the spaceship in view to their left.

They were ushered into the suite where dagbabi were waiting with more food. Bedding was being placed in the various rooms. Dagbabi moved quickly in and out of the place.

The Sun Mel bade them farewell and left. The yashi shut the outer door and stood outside it. They were left to themselves and about a half dozen of the little dagbabi.

Sam took a bowl of food and a mug of water. Nathan stepped out onto the wide balcony, overlooking the wide cleared space of the landing field, surrounded by trees, overgrown with green so that it looked almost like a park. Above and beyond was the vast sky, tinged gold at the margins. Small ribbons of gray cloud were moving in.

There was a round table, inlaid with brown and white patterns. Some couches, and chairs with very high backs, were grouped around it.

Avis and Folo joined Nathan. "Well," he said, "here we are."

"Wherever this is," muttered Folo.

"We're in the Sun Clanth of Planggi, in the Plowl—which is their word for this artificial universe. At least that's what I think the Sun Mel said," Nathan replied.

"The Plowl." Folo tried the word. It sounded alien, strange. Almost as strange as Folo felt, which was strange indeed. How was he going to adjust to this? Could they ever escape and go home?

"They have had people here before, that's very clear," said Avis in a quiet, hushed voice. "The question is, what did they do with them? We've seen four different types of aliens but no humans, yet there are humans all over those paintings."

"They must have had the Lemall's World colony," Nathan said emphatically. "The last contact with Lemall's was thousands of standard years ago. They disappeared utterly, a half million people or more."

"But where are they?" wailed Folo. "We haven't seen any humans, only aliens, more aliens than I ever dreamed existed."

"I don't know, Folo. We've got a lot to learn about all this."

Rilla appeared on the balcony, still licking a bowl of the white food mush clean. "This stuff is delicious, which is a damned good thing, considering how unappetizing it looks."

Sam now joined them too, eating yet another bowl of the goop.

Rilla had overheard Nathan's last words. She turned to Sam. "Nathan thinks he's solved the mystery of Lemall's Colony. He thinks the iulliin must have taken them, like they took us."

Sam snorted in immediate disagreement. "Romantic piffle! While I agree they appear to have known human beings at some time or other, that's no cause to link them to Lemall's World. They could have had contact with a starship, or some band of rogues or wanderers."

Nathan shook his head determinedly. "But there are those sculptures, and the skulls in that throne. Those are definite evidence that humans were once very important to the culture here."

"Well, they aren't important now," said Sam. "What's important now is finding out how to control our spaceship and get out of here. We've got to find a way to get home."

Nathan rolled his eyes. It was quite clear to him that they were prisoners, not likely to be released anytime soon.

"Somehow, Sheriff, I don't think we're going to be released just like that," said his mother.

"They damn well better, or else the Homeworlds High Fleet will hear about it!"

"Oh, of course," muttered Nathan under his breath.

Folo was nodding through all this. Now he spoke up, bringing an automatic scowl to Sam's face. "What would they want us for anyway? They seem to have all the servant species they could need right here already."

Rilla shivered, looked to the distant spaceship with longing. "Maybe they'll want us as experimental subjects."

"Or pets," said Nathan. "Who knows?"

"Or breeding stock," said Avis in an ominous tone. "Perhaps these iulliin have lost their humans. Perhaps they need to, uh, restock, or something."

"Avis Prench, that's a disgusting notion!" Rilla exclaimed. Then she thought about it again and her face crumpled to the point of tears. "I'm still capable of pregnancy! Oh no, I don't want this, I don't want to bear their slave children!"

Sam tried to calm his sister. "There, there, Rilla, let's not get alarmed too readily. So far they've treated us relatively well. We've been fed and washed and given clean clothes."

Rilla shook off his attention and whirled on Avis. "How about you, Avis, can you?"

"Sure. I could still have a baby or two. There's a few years left in this brood mother."

"Oh no, I don't think I can stand this. I'll have to kill myself."

"Hold on a mo', Mz. Boan, no need to be killing yourself just yet," said Folo.

Sam whirled with a scowl on his face. "Listen, you little tronch pig, get away from us!"

Folo stared into Sam's bulging, reddened face. Then he turned and walked off to one side.

After a moment Nathan joined him.

There was an uncomfortable silence. Sam refused to meet Avis's eyes. He turned truculently to the view and hunched his shoulders defiantly and stuck out his stomach.

Avis sighed. She realized that dealing with Sam Boan was going to be a difficult task, even at the best of times. She stood up and investigated the suite of bedrooms, then selected one and closed the door and lay down and tried to sleep.

■ CHAPTER ELEVEN

Nathan awoke, many hours later, to the sound of a great horn blowing somewhere. He stirred, rolled over, and examined his surroundings.

A bare, dimly lit room with high ceiling and narrow

walls. A long narrow mattress with white covers made of
a smooth fabric with some of the feel of cotton to it.

Where was he? Then it all crashed home again: the
Plowl of the Golden Yoo Leen, the decayed city of
Planggi. He got to his feet and found his clothes, cleaned,
dried, and neatly folded by the bed.

His boots, however, were missing; instead he found the
soft gray slippers they'd given him earlier. Outside on the
huge balcony he found only Folo Banthin. Everyone else
was still asleep.

They stood halfway up a cliff studded with similar balconies. The neighboring building, a tower of dark gray
walls, with white inlays around windows and balconies,
soared beside them.

A pair of quick, darting dagbabi appeared. They carried
bowls of mush and mugs of water which they left on the
circular table beside Folo.

Folo turned a sad-eyed face to greet him. Nathan
chewed his lip thoughtfully and took a bowl of the food
and a mug of water. He sat down on a long, high-back
bench that faced outward to the sun. It was warm in that
sun, around 25 degrees centigrade, he estimated. Temperature stayed pretty constant here.

High in the sky were thickening clouds that threatened
to obscure the little golden disk of the sun. Farther down
the sky were a group of smaller clouds, colored a dull red,
and almost perfectly round. They moved quite swiftly
across the cityscape from right to left.

Nathan's brow furrowed. He wet a finger and held it up
to the air. There was a breeze, but it was blowing straight
toward the balcony, not from right to left. The clouds were
under their own propulsion.

He found he'd finished the bowl. Didn't take long; the
stuff was pretty tasty, even though the texture and appearance were horrible. He washed it down with the water,

which was cool and scented slightly with something that tantalized his nostrils.

He consoled himself with the thought that they were still alive, and considering the adventures of the past several days, Nathan found that to be a considerable achievement.

He glanced at the young troncher. Poor Folo! Folo was shrunk within himself, absorbed in the loss of his first true love. Nathan thought of Martherer Boan, his own one true love, and wanted to cry himself. But something held him back, something indefinable, something that was excitedly ticking in his heart.

He looked out to the enormity of the city, and the Sun Clanth beyond it. He wanted it, he wanted to know this alien world, to explore it fully. Nathan felt the challenge of his lifetime, he felt more alive and awake than he had ever felt. The suffocation of life in dusty Prench Tronch was gone.

And when he thought of Martherer, things had changed. Of course he was concerned. But how would they ever find her? How could they even know they would see her alive again?

Once, in fact very recently, Nathan would have given up his life to protect Martherer from harm. Suddenly, now, he realized he wouldn't get the opportunity for such romantic heroics. He had changed. The crucible of the abduction to this alien world had forced him to grow up. And along the way his teenage crush on beautiful Martherer had started to evaporate.

Folo's feelings were different, Nathan realized, and his own had been so callow, so hopeless that it suddenly made him acutely embarrassed even to think about. But now it was Folo's turn to pine for the unattainable.

Nathan went to explore the suite. He vaguely remembered a room, covered in green tiles, that seemed to offer showers. He discovered it at the end of a short side corridor halfway down the spinal corridor. There was an entire range of facilities, all overlarge, all ornately wrought in green and white tiles.

When he reemerged onto the balcony, he found his mother taking breakfast. She was sitting close to Folo. They looked up as he approached. A momentary flicker of something—annoyance?—passed across her face.

The sky had thickened considerably. The sun was hidden by fleecy gray clouds. The temperature had dropped ten degrees or so.

Nathan bent to kiss his mother's cheek, then sat nearby on a delicately wrought white chair with the usual high-set back and massive, carved feet. "Well, we at least got breakfast," he said cheerfully.

"Yes," agreed Avis, "but I hope that that isn't the only kind of food we're going to get while we're here."

"Yeah," said Folo, who was making an effort. His eyes were reddened.

Nathan fought the odd feeling of triumph he felt. This hopeless love stuff hurts, doesn't it, Folo?

"What are we going to do next? We can't just stay here," said Avis with a glance over her shoulder into the suite, where the dagbabi lurked, unseen and unheard.

"I really don't trust those lizardy things—what do they call them?"

"Dagbabi. I don't think we're just going to walk out of this," said Nathan.

"We should never have left the spaceship, Nathan," muttered Avis.

"We had to, to get water. As I recall, none of us was thinking all that clearly at the time."

"And now we're trapped. These aliens have us at their mercy."

Nathan heaved a sigh. It was certainly true. How were they going to get back to the ship? The only way would mean escaping the yashi pantheroids. That would not be an easy task. And even if they got back to the ship, there was little chance of getting it to take off. The ship had flown and landed itself, had not responded to any controls for a long time. "I don't know, Mother, we'll have to wait and see, and if an opportunity comes up to escape then we'll take it."

There was a sudden swirl of activity behind them. They turned and found the Sun Mel, with guards and a team of dagbabi who carried the translation device.

A dagbab was thrust into the cavity once more.

"Humble siffile, my little friends!" it wailed.

Soon they were preparing to follow the Sun Mel back through the maze of passages and stairs. They exchanged bewildered glances. As they filed out, Nathan watched them pull the dagbab from the machine and stand him up. The creature's eyes were revolving slowly in opposite directions. "To the Grand Inquisition," said the Sun Mel in response to their question. "It must be shown that you are not Xaaca demons."

Back through the long passages and giant gloomy halls they strode and then down another massive staircase, easily ten meters wide. The surrounding walls were all painted with another enormous mural, one that had the appearance of great age about it. All the figures in this mural were iulliin. The surroundings were urban, severe, even abstract, but the figures themselves were strictly representational. Crowds of figures thronged a city of airy towers. The style was leaden. It made Nathan think of the Social Realism schools of the twentieth and twenty-first centuries.

At the bottom, the stairs opened out into a large hallway. Great doors slid open, and they entered a long, rectangular space in which sat about a hundred iulliin. Half of them wore pink robes; the rest wore a mixture of colors, and different cuts of robe, too. White predominated. Many of those in the pink robes appeared young. Their skins were unseamed, smooth. Their teeth were whiter, as were the crests of white, woolly hair on their heads.

In the center of the room was a cleared space, and there stood a pair of tall machines that looked ominously like guillotines, down to the hole for the head to be thrust into.

"Now wait a minute," said Sam Boan, turning around, uneasy.

"Nathan!" Avis was holding his arm.

"What do you think they want?" Folo said.

Five yashi stood close behind them. One of them growled.

They followed the Sun Mel down to the machines.

The iulliin in pink suddenly rose and broke into song, astonishing, loud plainsong, without harmonies. They sang with considerable pleasure and gusto. At the climax they shouted "Zaga" several times and waved fists in the air.

The Sun Mel was now joined beside the translation machine by an aged individual in pink robes. This iulliin wore elaborate platform-soled shoes at least six inches high, so that he teetered almost eight feet tall.

A second microphone wire was plugged in for him. A dagbab was thrust into the cavity. It chittered and squealed. "Greetings, demons. We of the Yelkes have a great honor to bestow upon you. In the ceremonial place of respect we have piled the most perfumed woods to burn you with. The scents of your honored incineration will soon fill the air."

The Calabels stared at each other.

"What did he say?" growled Sam Boan.

"I think they want to burn us at the stake," said Nathan.

Rilla squealed in horror and clung to Avis. "Do something! Somebody stop this nightmare. Tell them they can't do this to me."

Avis recoiled. "Rilla, stop this! What do you suggest I do? Let's retain a little dignity, dear."

With a great effort, Rilla pulled herself together.

The High Yelke spoke again. "But before you can be burned you must be tested by the ancient secrets. You must endure the Eye on Xaaca. Then you must be known by the Eye on Planggi."

"Burned? Tested? Why? What's the purpose of this?" said Avis.

"I think it's their religion," said Nathan.

"They want to burn us at the stake?" Sam was appalled by the unfairness of it all.

The Sun Mel now spoke. "Come, siffile, do not worry. If there is no taint, you will not burn."

"You see," said Nathan with some relief, "they're not all for burning us. I think there's a lot of politics involved here."

"I agree," said Avis. "There's a hell of a lot we don't know about all this. But I'm afraid, Nathan." She clutched her son to her.

"At least the one called the Sun Mel seems to be our friend," said Nathan.

They were thrust forward between the machines. The Sun Mel spoke on. "First you will be inserted into the Great Eye that looks for Xaaca taint. If you are free of Xaaca, then no more need be suffered."

Folo was first. He was grabbed, hoisted into the air, kicking and struggling, and then expertly slid into the ominous dark cavity at the bottom of the machine by three yashi. Only his feet projected into view, still kicking.

The machine gave off an even more ominous mechanical sound, a deep K*achunk*, and then flashed an array of nested body maps. Indicators worked among the body maps, which were toned red and pink on a dark green background.

"Some kind of body-scanning device, I think," Nathan murmured.

The indicators finished, and the body screen images disappeared. The expectant group of younger iulliin in the pink robes gave up an odd groan.

The yashi plucked Folo from the machine and returned him to his feet. They seized Nathan, lifted him, and swung him forward. Nathan caught sight of Folo, covered in a sheen of sweat, breathing hard, his eyes staring, and then he was inside the machine, a dark tube about the size of a human body.

It was cold, and smelled of Folo's sweat.

Lights flashed on; the machine scanned. A few moments later he was yanked out by the ankles and left standing beside Folo.

Sam was next. He went in with a great bellow that delighted the assembled mob in pink. But his scans were just as disappointing as those of the others, and by the end of the elaborate ceremony there was open discontent showing among the young fanatics in the pink robes. They began singing in an ominous, low rumble.

The Sun Mel argued furiously with a group of pink-robed elders, who all wore platform shoes of the most fabulous complexity. They all became very excited. The Sun Mel, whose own platform shoes were a modest inch and a half high, fairly jumped around in anger at one point.

The High Yelke continued to demand the sacrifice of the siffile. All siffile were banned from Planggi since the time of atrocity. Any siffile that were caught were to be sacrificed at once to the ancestors. It did not matter in the slightest that not one of them had failed the test, that all were free of the taint of Xaaca.

The Sun Mel continued to insist that *these* siffile were different. That they came from a friendly force beyond the Sun Clanth. That even though the spaceship had produced no iulliin masters for these siffile, that did not mean that the siffile were feral or dangerous. Perhaps they had been sent as a gift by another Sun Clanth, perhaps it was time for Planggi to restock with siffile and begin again with the best of all the servant races.

The High Yelke hissed and groaned at this and returned to the familiar theme, burning and purification—and special cleansing services to be held wherever the vile creatures had been hidden.

The Sun Mel broke the deadlock by abruptly ending the proceedings and ordering his yashi to take the siffile away.

Surrounded as they were by eager-eyed enemies, they were not, however, taken back to their secret room. Inside they were hustled down the corridor. Other yashi closed the double doors and locked the iulliin in behind them. A great uproar broke out.

Different yashi were appearing, yashi that wore pink and orange bands around their necks and wrists.

The Sun Mel moved quickly. His guards moved the siffile down the corridor and up a back stair to a secret portal known only to the Sun Mel, a door to a passage that ran to the chamber of the High Mel.

They were soon gathered in front of a dark, blank wall. The Sun Mel produced a green wand from within his robes and drew a circle on the wall.

A door slid open as if by magic.

They entered a narrow dark passage and climbed a spiral stair through near total dark. The Sun Mel lit their way by his wand, which emitted a frail green glow. Eventually they reached another door, which led to a chamber where several passages met. The Sun Mel lead them up some more stairs, and they emerged in the huge chamber of the High Mel.

Yashi of the High Mel ran up bristling. Their long knives, fashioned of a dark green ceramic material, appeared in their hands, and they dropped into a combat crouch.

The Sun Mel called to the High Mel in a slightly nervous voice. After a considerable pause the High Mel replied.

They were ushered past the throne and through a grotto of sculpted forms dusted with various colorful crystals.

On a large square bed, canopied and surrounded by couches, lay the High Mel, propped up among orange pillows.

The Sun Mel made his case. "The Yelkes demand to burn the siffile, Uncle. We must save them, as Grandfather told me. It is vital if we are ever to recover the lost knowledge. The siffile are quick and agile of mind; they can solve the mysteries of the Great Secrets. We can bring back the Secrets and live the life of old."

The High Mel groaned. He'd been hearing this nonsense from young Shazzeul for the equivalent of three centuries in standard years.

"The Great Secrets are under the lock and key of the High Yelke. Thus were they when I came to the throne, and thus will they be when I leave it. The Yelkes prefer the iulliin to live in ignorance—that way they can be controlled more easily. I am dying, Shazzeul. I have the wasting disease, I cannot last another thousand balaasts. Please do not darken my remaining time."

The Sun Mel thought it unlikely the High Mel would last another hundred balaasts, let alone a thousand. That only increased his desperation. Once the High Mel was gone, the High Yelke would demand that the Sun Mel be tested for demons. They would order the long pins to be thrust into him. If he cried out, they would announce that he was parasitized with demons and burn him on a bier of melkwood. They would happily anoint his half brother Fadook in his stead.

"If I am to survive and continue our line in the way that Grandfather planned it, I must gain access to the Great

Secrets. However, none of us knows how to operate them, or even in many cases what they do. But the siffile have the minds of quicksilver, they will discover the secrets for us."

The High Mel snorted; it was a preposterous idea. But while he lived he would humor Shazzeul. The High Mel detested little Fadook, a toady of the Yelkes. But he was also sadly aware that as soon as he was dead poor Shazzeul would be readied for the demon pins.

And the High Mel was already looking fondly on the female siffile. As a youth he had grown fond of the female siffile, for they had kept them, females only, in Planggi long after the era of atrocity, the great violence of the Siffile Rebellion, which had swept across the Sun Clanth from tower to tower, city to city, bringing slaughter, fire, and destruction.

But in Planggi they had kept a small population of docile females right up to the beginning of the Yelke era.

The Cult of the Ancestors expressed by the Yelkes was harsh, primordial. As yet they had no deity, for the iulliin had done without deities since the beginning of the Sun Clanths, and the Yelkes had yet to make that leap of faith, from belief in themselves alone, to belief in a more powerful, omniscient intelligence, ruling all.

But their ceremonies and services were already rich in liturgy, with all the fury of a young religion still defining itself and casting out infidels. There was a vigorous tradition of ritual burnt sacrifice.

The High Mel sighed. He would protect Shazzeul while he lived. Then the damn Yelkes would have him. Once more they would have total control, through Fadook. The work of the High Mel's doughty sire, Zoax the Untiring, would be toppled. He, Hesfraktus, had managed to stave them off, but he had not the power that Zoax had had.

It all went back to the dreadful event of the coronation

of poor Yebbent of Fulb. Yebbent was the last of the true line of Usus Magnificent. A feeble youth under the control of his mother, Amasha Likon, a fervent Yelke.

From Yebbent had come the orders that locked away all the technology that had survived the catastrophe of the rebellion.

From Yebbent had come the command to send the docile female siffile to the burning pit, thus beginning the search for victims that had eventually consumed a third of the iulliin population itself in the fanatic flames.

■ CHAPTER TWELVE

For the next few hours the Calabels hid behind a carved screen that depicted flying creatures of enormous variety against a background of pink and blue clouds.

From the throne the High Mel faced the enraged Yelkes, whose elevated platform shoes still left them a frustrating meter below the gaze of the High Mel.

How they hated the "tainted" power of the Meldom. All temporal power was now suspect. For the Yelkes only their own total rule would suffice. Anything else blasphemed against the memory of the ancestors. They raged around the throne, demanding the incineration of the siffile at once, upon a bed of scented raik wood.

The High Mel allowed the Sun Mel to make his little speech. The Yelkes exploded into wrath. The Sun Mel was "demented" and should be removed at once. All siffile were deadly vermin, and these, sent from the sky in a great craft of space, were clearly meant to be sacrificed at once to the ancestors.

Eventually the High Mel sent them away. The two camps were at an impasse. The High Mel was titular ruler, his rule was ancestral, and he controlled fifty of the best yashi. Around him in addition were arrayed most of the conservative forces in Planggi.

For the moment the coalition that supported the High Mel would hold firm. The old families would show solidarity, for a while, until the Yelkes could begin singling out the weak ones and work on them from within. There wasn't a single great family that was not riddled with younger scions who were devout wearers of the pink and orange robes.

The Sun Mel was thus able to guide the humans back, in secret, to their suite of rooms in the other building.

A dagbab was thrust into the translator.

Nathan asked the Sun Mel if there was any way he could learn their language—Iullas—so that they could do without the dagbabi.

The Sun Mel laughed and showed his teeth. He pointed to the translation device. "If you place your head in the cavity, you will become fluent in Iullas, such as it was in the old days when all young siffile were thus treated. Of course it is painful, extremely painful, for the full-grown siffile."

Nathan stared at the machine, at the tormented dagbab. "But will it kill me?"

The Sun Mel shrugged. "I do not know—maybe, maybe not. I have never used the machine, but I do know that once it was employed to teach Iullas to all the siffile, while they were very young."

Avis clutched at him. "No, Nathan, you mustn't even think about that. I forbid it!"

He faced her. "I can't watch any more of these creatures die to allow us to carry on a conversation!"

Folo looked as if he might interfere physically.

Nathan broke away from his mother and dropped down beside the machine. He gestured strongly to the dagbabi to remove the one locked inside.

The dagbab still lived; it croaked mournfully to its fellows as they carried it away.

Avis was beside herself. Folo tried to hold Nathan back, but the yashi stepped forward and restrained him. The Sun Mel watched with a slightly worried frown. He hoped he wasn't going to lose one of the siffile. On the other hand, there would be immense advantages to having a siffile who could speak Iullas.

Nathan thrust his head into the cavity; his shoulders and chest followed. It was excruciatingly claustrophobic. Then lights went on and the programming began. The machine hummed and whirled the delusion patterns before his eyes. In a moment his brain was open, the hinges detached on every door.

Nathan was not properly conscious of this. There was discomfort, but no real pain. He was in the midst of blazing light, a thrumming, stuttering sound roaring in his ears, but it was not pain.

The process went on for hours. With other urgent business to attend to, the Sun Mel departed. The Calabels arranged themselves around the suite and waited for the machine to finish whatever it was doing to Nathan.

Avis wept bitterly, finally. To lose her son, now, when she had lost everything else, seemed too much, simply too unfair.

Then at last the machine ceased its display of lights. It released Nathan, and the dagbabi came forward with their dry, leathery little hands to help him out and onto his feet.

He was dazed, could barely see through a flickering

haze of hot symbols, but the language memories were
stretched oddly. It was hard to focus on words in his head.
And his head hurt, abominably. A headache throbbed behind his forehead with white-hot intensity. Lines of agony
seemed to stretch back into the rest of his head.

But he could phrase a sentence in Iullas without effort.
"Mir el kenima per gez ilkaa verflan, roch, roch?"

The Calabels stared at him. He smiled, but his head hurt
far too much to sustain it.

"Bahnoo eshta, mafoi," he began. Avis screamed horribly, and he suddenly blacked out and crumpled to the floor.

One of the yashi collected him and carried him in its
arms out of the suite. The other yashi left as well and
posted a guard outside the door.

Avis was left to weep for her son, with only Folo for
company, since Rilla and Sam had withdrawn to their
rooms.

Nathan awoke in a large circular bed that was covered
in sheets with a satiny feel. His head rested on a soft pil-
low. The room he was in was painted white, with silver
bands and golden symbols. A large cracked mirror hung on
one wall. Heavy drapes were pulled across the windows
that occupied the sunward wall. Beams of light broke in at
the sides, however, enough to provide illumination.

His head still throbbed, and he thought in Iullas almost
as naturally as he thought in his native Calabel dialect of
Interlingua.

"Oh mafoi." My head, my aching, isfrita, head. Isfrita!

He heard stirring in the room. A figure arose from a
couch at the far end. A glittering tepee of gold cloth. It
approached.

It was the Sun Mel's aunt Eilesme. The first female
iulliin he had seen. As tall as the males, easily six foot six,

but not quite as gaunt in the face. Her voice was husky and sweet, her hair, the same white wool, was teased out into long stiff locks and adorned with golden baubles that bent them down around her head. "Poor siffile, you did a very foolish thing. Shazzeul should not have allowed it."

She held out a cold compress to his brow. "I will give you some painkiller, if you like."

An alien drug! What would that do to him? He decided to try to resist for as long as possible. The cold compress felt good, though. He closed his eyes and tried not to move.

Two balaasts, the forty-eight hour days of the Sun Clanth, passed in this way. Nathan occasionally took food —bowls of gelatinous bokka, pieces of boltak. Then a little minced wita, an airfish of some type.

Eventually he was able to get up and sit on the balcony with Lady Eilesme. Still the headache persisted. He wondered grimly if it was a permanent price he would pay for learning Iullas the quick way.

Eilesme, however, was worth listening to. She was, in essence, a curator of the dead iulliin culture. She could read the Iullas print in the computer files, even the old scripts in the ancient books. In this she was almost unique. The Yelkes were illiterate, and in fact were anti-knowledge, placing all in the hands of faith and belief.

She explained many things, the rise of the Yelkes among them. Nathan became more fully aware of how tenuous was the humans' position in Planggi.

"The next High Mel will be Fadook," Eilesme said calmly. "Poor Shazzeul hasn't a chance, he's so hated by the High Yelke. They realize they made a mistake by allowing Hesfraktus to take the throne. Hesfraktus is weak compared to his father, but still he is not a Yelke, he does not believe their romantic twaddle."

And the Calabel siffile?

"You will be burned with full ceremony one merj after the death of the High Mel," one merj was the equivalent of about twenty minutes.

"How can we escape this fate?"

Eilesme smiled, her narrow purple lips pulling back from the big, yellowed teeth. "Shazzeul has a plan. It is quite ridiculous. I too have a plan. I will save you. I will spirit you away to my country estate at Nakweech."

"Where is that?"

"Oh, usufrakta in the direction of Either. It is a very pleasant house. You will be my own siffile, I will take good care of you. The others will burn. The Yelkes must have their way. But you I can save."

◼ CHAPTER THIRTEEN

Hours had become days, pacing with dreadful slowness to a seemingly inevitable death from thirst. Cracka lay helpless in the web, on the couch in the stark little cabin where the robots had left him.

There was nothing to see except the blank ceiling and wall of the dimly lit room.

There was nothing to do except to try not to think about water, but with swollen tongue and parched mouth it was hard to stay off the subject. He wondered how long it would take him to die.

He dozed again. Increasingly he was drifting into a twilight of long dozing naps. When the dreams began they were of liquids, of aqueducts, streams, and swimming pools full of sparkling water, of the surf breaking on Prench Beach. Water, everywhere, and not a drop to drink.

A voice seemed to laugh, echoingly, mockingly. In his mind's view, he was standing in a cool underground cistern on the Prench Ranch. He looked at the walls—water was beading on them and running down in small trickles. Avis Prench was there, a dreamlike Avis, in a white wedding gown. Standing in the little chapel at Prench Ranch, getting married. To whom? To a man Cracka knew, but could not identify: he was faceless. The wedding twisted aside. A cruel voice lashed the air. Laughter, rich, echoing laughter, filled the darkness, and he woke up with a gasp.

Something had changed!

Deep down, in the distant low hum of the engines, a subtle throb was at work that he had never heard before. The throb continued, and a whine was steadily building.

He listened intently. Indeed there was little else to do. Inside the wrap he couldn't move a muscle.

The whine built and became a penetrating vibration that ended suddenly, astonishingly, with a single great thud. The low engine throb was gone.

Cracka blinked, stared. An enormous hope soared in his heart. The ship had landed! At long last. The voyage was over. They would surely get water now!

Other noises permeated dimly: a heavy hiss of escaping gas, then faraway thuds and rumbles as heavy unloading equipment went to work. The door slid open and one of the tall, slender robots entered. Its single eye glinted. Its working parts gave off a slight whir, with a fat, metallic tick every few seconds. It adjusted something outside his view, then picked him up gently and carried him down a featureless corridor to another door. The robot smelled faintly of oil and ozone and moved with the now familiar, exotic mechanical grace.

Cracka trembled a little when he thought of the level of technology and robotics required for such qualities. It was enormously clear that the robots were the product of a very high civilization.

What the hell did they want?

The door slid open and the robot walked out onto a platform under a blue sky with bright sunlight and distant, threadlike clouds. Cracka rolled his eyes, and for an instant saw...

A city like nothing he had ever imagined in his wildest dreams. Strange, flowerlike towers of enormous proportions were spaced along a wide canal. The nearest was miles away, and resembled nothing so much as a vase full of tulips. A central massif, a mountain of some dark, reddish material, rose to about five hundred meters. From it soared irregular towers, tipped with what looked like great purple blooms. The towers were silvery gray.

Around the base of the enormous structures was a forest of buildings that looked like tuning forks.

Closer by he saw nothing but ruins—stark, rubble-strewn, charred. Then he noticed damage to the flower structures too. He saw the gaping dark holes in the nearest structure, the snapped-off tubes, the shattered bud-bulbs.

A graceful high bridge had once floated between two tall, cylindrical structures. The bridge had been broken; spars, shards, cables tattered the ends.

And then a door snapped open and the breathtaking views vanished as the robot entered an elevator that soon deposited them in a much larger passage, a round tunnel ten meters across. The robot laid him down on the floor and removed a narrow tubular instrument made of some dark, glossy material. It held the tube over him and sprayed a jet of a scarlet fluid across the wrap, which melted instantly wherever the fluid landed. In moments Cracka was easing himself out of the confining remains.

As he watched, the wrap stuff decomposed into clear, odorless vapor that clung to the floor a moment and was gone.

Cracka stared at the robot a moment. The alien culture possessed many highly developed technologies. Even their chemistry seemed more advanced than anything he knew of.

The robot stood back. The door slid open again, the robot reentered the elevator, and the doors closed once more. Cracka got to his feet, a little unsteadily at first. Leaning against the side of the tunnel, he groaned at the stiffness in his joints and muscles. His empty belly rumbled its own complaints. Quietly he cursed for a few seconds until he felt better.

He ached all over. He felt as if he'd been working for days in the breaking pens, taking a beating from the beasts.

It was cold in the tunnel too, and he shivered from the hunger, the thirst, and the general exhaustion of the ordeal he'd been through. Instinctively he began to search for water. There had to be some near this place.

Why had the robot put him down so purposefully? There had to be a reason.

The tunnel was ten meters wide, a featureless tube of gray ceramic material, with lights dotted along the ceiling. The tunnel was curved, but he could see several hundred meters of it in one direction. In the other the curve was much closer.

Somewhere behind him there was a sudden *boom*, as if a very large metal door had suddenly crashed open.

Distorted screams from innumerable throats rang through the tunnel. A kind of thundering noise followed them. Cracka began to back up the tube, away from the sounds.

The screams got louder, and in the distance, down the tunnel, came a stampede of screaming people. Cracka turned and jogged, as quickly as he could in his weakened state, up the tunnel away from the people.

Eventually some youngsters caught up with him. They screamed something at him about the "pink fog that stings" and ran on.

The crowd behind kept coming, thousands, hundred of thousands, all the survivors of the mass abduction of an entire planet. A million Calabels, all in motion, driven from the holds in the mother ship by a pain-inducing fog.

And while they scrambled, squeaking from the sting of the pink mist, the syrupy remains of millions of Staiol people were being flushed down the drains into a containment tank.

Cracka ran, despite his weariness, keeping ahead of the great crowd. And then the tunnel opened out into a vast hall, with enormous sphere screens overhead. The space was huge, at least a kilometer across. They could have fit the Landing Site Metro FairDome inside the place.

He looked up and saw a fellow in a soiled business suit. The man had a vacant, terrified look on his face. Cracka caught his arm. "Where are you from?"

The man turned horrified eyes to him. "Belpark City— hey, you know what this is? What this is all about?"

Cracka shook his head. "No, maybe space warfare of some kind. We were kidnapped by alien machines."

The man's eyes widened. He staggered back. Hate filled his face. "You're raving," he suddenly screamed and turned away, raising his hands as if to ward off a blow.

Dozens of people were now moving by. Beyond came hundreds.

Cracka moved, heading across the enormous floor, which seemed to have been fashioned without seams. He guessed it was a ceramic of some kind. An hour later the place was jammed, filled with a seething mob.

Cracka was in a far corner, jammed up near a wall that was punctuated with a series of big rectangular patches. Cracka had assumed them to be doors and had positioned himself near one. Now he was not sure that he hadn't made a terrible mistake, and that he wouldn't be crushed to death when the entire Calabel population was jammed into this chamber. The crowd made a frantic, hissing roar that sounded like the angry surf of an ocean storm.

Abruptly the big spherical screens lit up, a blank pale green for a second or two, and then they bore a face, a face like that of a young lion with no mane. Big, sensitive nostrils, enormous tawny eyes, the jaws and muscle of a predator. But the eyes glittered with intelligence.

Then in slow but recognizable Interlingua the face spoke to them.

"Greetings, siffile! I am Battlechief Klah. Welcome to the city of Meninrud Lors. Your arrival has given us all new hope. You shall shortly be inducted into the Fighting Ninth Army, charged with holding the line on the Aplanga Front!"

And then the face was gone, followed by a terrible sound, a sound so loud and majestic that it would have penetrated their skulls by bone conduction if they'd had no ears. The screens erupted with flickering images, tailored to penetrate the human mind and render it programmable.

They stared, openmouthed, entranced, their eyes helpless.

■ CHAPTER FOURTEEN

There was a constant feeling of dislocation, of floating under delicate sedation. As if someone else were wearing his clothes, carrying the gun, or making terrifying leaps through the air on shock boots.

There were the dreamlike rallies, when the humans gathered, packed together in a sweating horde beneath the great spheres. Eerie triumphant music, the blast of horns that thrilled the blood. Images from the golden past floated over.

Graceful towers swooped into the sky to support lacy rococo fantasies of architectural magnificence. Through the sky city floated baroque airsleds. On their decks rode the Golden Iulliin, tall, emaciated images in bright battle armor of iridescent hue.

A golden warmth suffused those images. They induced love and reverence from the human hordes, reduced to trusting puppies by the torrential psychoconditioning.

There was the training. Hard physical training, conducted by a small army of the hypermuscular lion race, the yashi.

The yashi were all battlemasters. They wore body armor, but carried few weapons. They had the natural instincts of noncommissioned officers, alternating between helpful, almost kindly souls and brutally fierce taskmasters.

And the iulliin wasted nothing. The training was much the same for all humans, young, elderly, weak, strong. Those who broke down were removed at the end of sleep periods. Their bodymass went into the biosludge.

In the squads there were many children—they were often the best in the use of shock boots—and a surprising number of oldsters, who had somehow survived the rigorous hours of running and calisthenics, the arduous struggle to master the shock boots.

And there was the conditioning, always the roar and stutter of the psychoimagery in the great hall. It bound them together, welded them as one; they were a fighting army, ready for the foe.

And occasionally there were lucid moments, things that became memories—and few things did.

He was by the food troughs. They lived naked, fought
in armor and shock boots. They ate from troughs. The dark
green sludge that tasted wonderful because of an omni-
effective flavor agent. It had all the nutritional requirements for a mammalian omnivore with a high level of
physical activity.

He was wiping his mouth, licking his hands. His place
had been taken by a woman in her middle years. She had a
hollow-eyed, desperate look.

A brutal-looking youth pushed in and hurled her away
from the trough. Her head hit the floor, and she took a
while getting up.

She stared at the youth's muscular behind as he put his
head down to the feed. Then she got to her feet and kicked
it as hard as she could. The youth's head went down into
the feed, and then he emerged with a snarl that slashed
through the green goop that covered him.

He backhanded the woman. She staggered back. He
went after her, eyes tight in berserk rage.

Cracka stepped in and shoved the kid's shoulder.

The kid unloaded on him—all the terror, all the rage
detonated.

Cracka found himself on his back, two hundred pounds
of maniacal teenager on top of him, fists coming down.
The woman kicked the kid in the back of the head. That
stopped him long enough for Cracka to land a punch and
get off the floor.

Now fully aroused, Cracka let the kid come, took the
outstretched blow, and reversed into it, with his elbow digging for the boy's solar plexus. Breath exploded. Cracka
whirled, his knee coming up like a rock, and the youth
went down. Cracka finished it with his foot.

The woman stared at him a moment, then turned away
and was lost in the naked throng.

He moved on. It was almost time to sleep.

The ejaculatory spasm took place exactly fifteen minutes after the ingestion of food.

There was the training with shock boots. Armored legs, independently powered, controlled by the wearer. Worn wrong, they could tear you in half in the blink of an eye; worn right, and you could jump kangaroo style sixty meters and lope like a tyrannosaur at thirty kilometers an hour.

Gather the legs together under you, keep the arms hunched in, let the suit gyros do the balancing. The boot jets screamed, the ground rushed up, and the legs came down . . .

At full extension the boots could lift the wearer twenty meters.

And there were the weapons: heavy grenade launchers, missiles the size of a man's fist loaded five to a bulky magazine that clipped to the breech with a big spring. The weight rested on the harness, which was stiffened with control wires that connected with the shock-boot chargers, in effect making the weapon a cage with the trooper inside. The whole thing was awkward, and difficult to control, but the grenades had an effective range of ten kilometers.

In addition, each warrior carried the prime charge on his back, an explosive pack that was to be detonated when he had closed on an enemy machine. To detonate it, one simply twisted the control knob on the harness, in the middle of one's chest.

And then they were suited up, packed into air transports, and flown across the Sun Clanth.

Several hours later Cracka suddenly woke up with a

jerk. For a few seconds he trembled, unable to fully control his limbs. It was like waking from a terrible dream, except that his ass hurt like hell.

He tried to get up; he was sitting on something hard and angular that was cutting into his buttock. The discomfort had become extreme, and had even broken his conditioned trance state.

He undid the seat belt on his second try. The place was dark. It rumbled and rattled every so often.

A dull throb was coming from somewhere ahead of him.

A grenade was on the seat. It had slipped out of his magazine. Absentmindedly he reloaded it. He shook his head. Where the hell was this? What had happened? What was he doing here? Whatever it was, he was very familiar with the weapon in his arms. He *knew* it.

And understanding crashed home to him, and he stared wide-eyed into the dark. He had to find a window. They were in a plane of some kind, he was sure. It shuddered again. It had to be an aircraft.

He worked his way down a row of seated troopers, none of whom looked up. All of them, in all the rows, were staring directly at the back of head of the helmet of the one in front of them.

Brown and gray camouflage on the outer materials. Everything matte finished. Launchers tilted back over everyone's shoulders. The harness was strapped tight.

Cracka walked, still a little unsteady, under his own willpower, down a narrow aisle. The ship they were in was pretty big. The rows were ten across on either side of him, and the aisle was long. It ended in a door that opened at his touch. Some stairs went down to another door. He stepped out onto a small platform, set beneath the belly of the transport.

He sucked in his breath at the sight of the immensity spread out below.

■ CHAPTER FIFTEEN

It was a terrifying vastness. The land stretched into a perspective that seemed impossible, far beyond any conceivable horizon.

It was flat, a flat world that Cracka knew was as much as fifteen million miles across—the area of six million Earths, Nathan Prench had claimed. Cracka didn't doubt that the prodigy was correct.

Such an enormous space was breathtaking, and Cracka's planet-formed instincts reacted by raising the hair on his neck, pumping adrenaline. Men were not made to see this limitless land, with no curve to it, seemingly perfectly flat. It was hard not to succumb to tremendous awe at the scale and eerie beauty of the iulliin culture's gigantic achievement. Over everything hung a honeyed haze, golden green.

Dirty pink clouds blocked the sky in several directions and in others were views stretching forever, until they were finally lost in the haze of distance. There were no mountains, no large features of relief, just an infinity of small hills and ridges, brushed dark and green with vegetation, that appeared scattered almost at random across the land.

Across the green infinity ran straight ribbons of silver water. There were lines, rectangles, a complex grid of various widths of water channels. Once again the knowledge that all this had been designed, built, struck home. Built by the Golden Iulliin in some long-ago aeon. Cracka shivered when he considered the scale of the thing.

He looked down.

Directly beneath the air transport the ground was green from forest cover. He could discern individual trees and assumed therefore that they were flying low, no more than three or four thousand feet above the surface.

Everywhere were right angles and straight lines, the mark of an enormous civilization. But there was no sign of habitation, no cities like Meninrud, no roads.

Cracka looked up, into an arch of the bluest, deepest sky he had ever seen. From the pink cloud layer on, up into the zenith region, the sky remained a pale, delicate blue. In the zenith it darkened to a distinctly purplish shade upon which blazed golden strands of high cloud under the light of the gentle pink sun.

His gaze returned to the forest below. Every shade of green flourished there, and dotted throughout the green were tall white spirals that appeared to be structures of some type. Were these the villas of the iulliin?

A scattered villa society, perhaps? With cities that served primarily as aesthetic and ceremonial centers? Or were the iulliin few in number, concentrated in their cities, surrounded by an empty enormity?

Cracka shrugged to himself. He had no way of knowing. They had received remarkably little information about their masters. Just the demand for obedience, for valor in the service of the Sun Clanth of Meninrud Lors.

They crossed a group of small hills, each curved in a crescent, all the crescents aligned the same way. From the interior curve, straight, dark, narrow lines extended— roads? Cracka craned his neck to get a better view.

But the lines soon vanished beneath forest cover, and there was no way of telling if they continued elsewhere, and if therefore the surface was covered in a network of roads, as he would have expected from a high civilization like that of the iulliin.

The more he looked, the more the peculiarities came home to him. The small, nearly identical hills, the endless forest cover. The straight water channels. Totally empty of boat or barge traffic, no roads or towns.

Was all the land empty? Were the iulliin spread out, each person with a continent for its own?

He started with alarm, swung round, his gun flying up to his shoulder with a metallic clank.

A woman had emerged from the main compartment. She dropped her helmet at the sight of the gold-tinged land below. She uttered a low cry that wound into a shriek of rage.

"Where the hell are we? What have they done to us? What have they done to us?"

Cracka grimaced, looked back to the impossible horizon. "You listened to Battlechief Klah, as did I. You know where we're going."

She swallowed; her lips trembled. "The battlemaster, yes, I remember him. So handsome it made me want to feed him some milk. Like a great big pussycat. But now we are going to the . . ." Her eyes went wide, she barely managed to say the word: "enemy."

"Correct."

She screamed then, a long, sobbing howl that brought another freshly awakened trooper from the compartment, a portly fellow with his visor pushed up over his helmet. "What's going on out here?" he said as he stepped through, squinting in suspicion at Cracka. Then he looked past them and gasped. "Oh my, I never realized, I . . ." he trailed off. The woman continued to sob. Portly turned again. "What's the matter with her?"

Cracka looked out the window again. "She's disturbed by the thought of where we're going."

The man's face steadied, his lips pursed, and his eyes bulged. "Oh my god, oh my ancestors, oh . . ." He turned to Cracka with a face grown almost grotesquely furtive. "We have to escape, must find a way to escape."

The woman began an angry tirade. "How dare they do this? How dare they destroy my life. I have two boys, a house in Landing Site, a job that I fought for for fifteen years. What have they done? What right have they?"

Her anger echoed down the windowed gallery, mocking them. With a visible effort she got a grip on herself.

"They treated us like beasts, like food animals," said the portly man huskily.

"Yeah," said Cracka. "They know just how to operate human beings."

Another man, taller, blue-eyed, and lean of countenance had emerged onto the gallery. It was getting crowded. Cracka edged back toward the passageway.

The newcomer had a deep voice. "I couldn't help hearing you folks talking about the goddamn iulliin, and I have a question for you. Just where the hell did the damn iulliin learn all this stuff about human beings? I mean they have us down pat, they know how to pull our chains by just bending a pinkie. Where'd they get all this stuff on us?"

They all looked to Cracka, for some reason. He shrugged. Might as well tell them the worst. "You've all heard of Lemall's World."

The suggestion aroused them.

"Oh my," said the woman.

"The colony that vanished mysteriously in the ninth millennium?"

"Right, a colony founded by Brothua Lemall and the Brotherhood of Pan, an obscure cult from the old inner sphere of human space. A million of them at least were on that planet, and they vanished without a trace. They left everything behind exactly as if they'd just suddenly gotten up and walked away."

The portly fellow waved his arms in consternation. "Of course, by the gods of old, that's just what *we* did. Don't you see. There we were, living our lives, and they just kidnapped us, all of us—the entire goddamn planet!"

"So they've had humans on this planet for thousands of years."

"I guess," Cracka said.

"Then why do they need more?"

"Use your head—because of the enemy, they need everything they can get!" the portly fellow exclaimed in heat.

"Then why don't they fly to another planet?" said the tall man with the blue eyes.

"I don't think the iulliin like to fly. If you recall, there's a considerable amount of discomfort involved."

"Discomfort," said Portly. "I screamed my guts out. What the hell was that anyway?"

"Hard to say," Cracka said. "But I'd hazard a guess that that was a period of faster-than-light transition."

"I was afraid you'd say that."

"If they went FTL, then—"

"—this planet could be anywhere," murmured the tall fellow.

There was an uncomfortable moment of silence. They were never going home, that much seemed plain.

"Except there's something very odd about this place." The woman gestured out over the rail.

Two more troopers, a stout woman in her middle years and a young, epicene man, had joined them. The young man gave a whoop and pounded the rail. The woman stared.

The younger woman clapped her hands together as she realized what it was she'd been missing. "This place doesn't have a horizon—look, there's no visible curve to the world."

The portly man sniffed. "So?"

"So it can't be round. Or if it is, it's so big that the gravity ought to have crushed us all to death the moment we set foot on it."

"I fail to see the point of all this," complained Portly.

"So it isn't a planet. It can't be."

"The woman's crazed. It's been too much for her," Portly said.

"No, she's right. It isn't a planet," said Cracka in a matter-of-fact tone.

"What?"

He told them of Nathan's theory. He told them about the mother ship and the robots and the small ship that had escaped. They stared at him.

"You're all mad!" said the portly man.

"An artificial universe?" said the stout woman.

"That's right, we watched the whole thing displayed on the screen in the control center."

"Then you must have been the people I heard. I heard some people talking and yelling, but I never saw anyone, and I figured that I had been dreaming. We were all lying in those stacks."

"It's likely. I don't think anyone else got free—certainly we didn't see any."

"Then what happened to your friends?"

"I don't know. I heard no explosion, so I think they escaped the mother ship and flew away in the small ship."

"Which was one of those spherical ships that landed all over Calabel."

"That's right."

The portly fellow had come around now. "They might have gone anywhere, then. You said this artificial universe was covered in 'sun regions' just like this. If they're all this big and your friends landed in one, I mean they could be millions of kilometers away."

Cracka nodded. "This is a big place to get lost in."

They exchanged uncomfortable glances.

More people appeared. It looked as if the conditioning was wearing off for everyone.

Cracka took a look inside the main compartment. The sound of sobs and cries of rage and confusion greeted him.

"But we have our own lives," a man was yelling, gesticulating in his seat with arms raised to the ceiling.

"How could they do this to us? How could they abduct a whole world?"

The noise level rose rapidly and soon tripped a hidden mechanism. A golden flash ignited the main screen, which occupied much of the front bulkhead. The control thunder reverberated. The humans fell silent, psychically cowed. Battlemaster Klah stared down at them with an expression they now recognized as grim.

"Siffile, you are about to enter the battle zone! You are to be committed as reserves to the glorious Aplanga Front. The front is commanded by the Gracious Master Ho Deferem Aloo of Yaz Kanor. You are honored thusly by his command."

Cracka struggled to reach the door. "Don't look at the screen!" he shouted, and others called the same thing. But it was too late. A numbing tide of subliminal commands had begun, flickering idiot black psychoimages that engaged the limbic system and implanted control sequences throughout the cortical regions of the brain.

In humans such control sequences could only be maintained temporarily; they faded after a while. This was perhaps one reason why their race made such good soldiers. They retained strong self-will, they fought with and eroded conditioning, they maintained initiative. Above all they strove to survive.

In this they were far superior to the dagbabi and klicks, who could be programmed for life but who fought listlessly and died easily.

Yashi, of course, had to be controlled from birth, but their nature was too fierce for common soldiering—they didn't care about death once they were aroused. Humans were far more loath to die.

Cracka tried not to look at the screen, but it was hard. A thunderous set of triumph horns kept blasting away at thirty-second intervals. The horns keyed controls that seemed to dislocate human thinking. Each time they sounded, he found his eyes dragged around to the screen, to stare hopelessly at the black squiggles, the domino patterns, the flickering commands.

At last, he too gazed openmouthed with the rest.

When the transport landed, they were ready, their shock boots powered up, their minds programmed for battle.

■ CHAPTER SIXTEEN

They stumbled through the exit tubes. Thousands of them, with their shock boots revved back and whining. Outside the transport they grouped instinctively into the battle formations that had become second nature.

The squads marched out of the underground bunker that hid the air transports and into the rubble of another city. A city in ruins. All the lacy architectural fantasies of the iulliin had been smashed. Nothing remained except piles of rubble and occasional twisted spires.

A broad avenue cleared of rubble stretched in front of them. Craters of various sizes dotted the cleared space. Pools of rainwater had accumulated in the craters.

Now they loped, shock boots *whump*ing as they fired on the upstroke. Far ahead, the broad avenue ended beneath a dark cloud that cut off the world along a huge front, right across the cityscape.

They passed between the ruins of a couple of tuning-fork buildings, jagged shells less than twenty meters tall.

Around them were mounds of ceramic shards, shattered glass, creepers growing in riotous green profusion.

On the other side they caught sight of a large machine, like a golden spider, with a body twenty meters across and legs that telescoped out to ninety meters. It moved with astonishing agility for something so huge.

An alarm wailed from up ahead.

The spider tank shifted, then moved sideways on an evasive pattern.

The alarm flashed down the ranks. They began to scatter to the rubble on either side.

Seemingly right above their heads a barrage of anti-aircraft fire erupted.

Through the puffs of gray came flights of small V-winged assault craft. Hot in pursuit were iulliin interceptors, bulkier things at least the size of a man, spitting streaks of fire as they screeched overhead.

More explosions. The ground, the rubble, the whole world seemed to be exploding for a moment while they frantically jumped through a forest of uprights, all melted off about ten meters up.

Something small and fast ricocheted off the top of Cracka's helmet. The impact rocked him. He grazed a spar and almost lost control, but managed to compensate just enough and land with both feet down. To wear shock boots required elements of other skills, like riding a motorcycle, ski-jumping, and ice hockey. One needed balance, good timing, and good strength in the legs.

He jumped again, staying low, covering about ten meters, to a point beneath an overhang where a dark green wall had bent and melted to form a cave.

There was a tremendous flash high up in the air. A sizzling burst grew into a terrific peal of thunder.

Cracka landed in darkness, cutting boot power as he did. He plowed to a halt through mud and bits and pieces of debris. The ground shook from bombs. Shrapnel flew overhead and ricocheted around the entrance to his hiding place.

More bright flashes came, each followed by a heavy thud.

Slowly a near hush descended on the scene. Then came the whistles from the yashi. The interceptors had downed the enemy mother ships; for a while the skies would be free of V-wings.

They regrouped and jumped again.

The dark cloud grew across their front until it bulked high into the sky. Immense fires raged on their left, in the direction of Or.

Another machine, a squat-looking tank with jumbo treads, passed them going the way they had come.

The dark clouds had obscured the sun now, leaving them in a world of increasing shadow. The stench of the burning was very strong.

And there were the other humans. The first were a group of three, standing beside a road vehicle with balloon tires and a pair of antiaircraft guns in a swivel mount at the rear. They wore brown camouflage uniforms and helmets.

The three turned and stared at the new siffile with solemn expressions. Then they were far behind, and the avenue ended in a maze of trails, craters, and trenches.

They descended into the trenches, loping, crouched low. From ahead of them came a constant low rumble. Distant artillery was working along the lines on their right, in the direction of Either.

Suddenly the hot spats of blue tracers were crackling overhead. Everybody ducked, but there was only the one burst.

Then a heavy blast shook the ground on the left. The yashi blew their alarm whistles, and the humans took cover. More blasts came, progressively closer, until suddenly, high above them, there was a brilliant flash, at the bottom of the dense black cloud.

They resumed their progress and soon saw more of the other humans, tanned, blond stubble, clad in patched camouflage, shock boots battered. These people moved in the corridors and dugouts and bunkers of the troglodyte world with an easy familiarity; it was their world.

The yashi were dividing them up now, sending them down separate, narrower trenches. The trenches went deeper and deeper until at last they were tunnels pure and simple.

Eventually Cracka found himself directed into a dugout, a long, low space, illuminated by flickering TV screens.

Other people were there, people in the patched, faded battle wear. They were sitting on makeshift furniture scattered about the interior. For a moment there was a shocked silence. Then one of he people sitting inside, a big man with a certain amount of pale fuzz on his skull, complained in a thick voice, speaking a guttural Interlingua.

The others laughed. Someone turned up the light.

They gasped.

The big man jumped to his feet; he pressed close. A square jawline, a straight nose, broad lips, blond stubble—clearly someone descended from ancient Scandinavian or Nordic stock. In other words, from Lemall's World. A colony that had been founded by descendants from an old Scandinavian space habitat in the Earth Luna L5.

"Who the hell are you?" said the man in that thick, guttural voice. "You're not siffile, I can tell. You're diff, you're from way back when. Who the fuck are you?"

A woman had joined him out of the crowd. She too had a faint down of blond hair on her otherwise shaved skull. "They're diff all right." Then to Cracka she said, "So where are you from?"

Cracka turned to the other Calabels, their conditioning so fresh and strong in their minds they could barely comprehend the question. "Long story," he said. "I'll try to tell it."

He sat down on a battered crate. On the TV screen, a small portable model, a video was in progress. Bright female faces, hot lights in a human environment somewhere.

What the hell did it all mean? Cracka pushed his helmet back and scratched his head.

■ CHAPTER SEVENTEEN

"Come on, taste it." The big man held out a dipper filled with a clear fluid.

Cracka took a sip. The blast wall seemed to shake. "What is that, pure alcohol?"

"Damn near." The big man giggled and put the dipper to his own lips and sipped. "Whoo," he breathed. "Don't need much, that's for sure."

The one called Nuts-head sniggered. "You mix this with fight drug and you really be ready."

"Hah, hah!" roared the big one. "You be ready to stick your ass on the back of a crusher and pull your trigger."

His eyes grew serious for a moment. "I seen that happen. We had some hard fighting last time they sent a crusher. Seventy meters high, all battle armor and weapons."

"How do you make it?" said Cracka, taking the dipper for another sip.

"We ferment some of the bokka, then run it through a little still I know about and none of the battlemasters does."

Nuts-head was giggling. His head shook a little every

time he spoke. "We got a freeze box, too, all the ice we need."

"You know it's the one thing we have going for us down here, over the katz, I mean—we drink, they don't. They don't get many choices as a result."

In a flash Cracka had a beaker with chunks of ice, a little juice from a reddish fruit called a pumj, and a drink that was the best thing he'd experienced in who knew how long. Cracka had no idea how long it was since that last morning on Calabel. Just another aspect of humanity they'd stripped from him.

It was a feeling of incredible luxury, to just lean back against the wall and allow the alcohol to unwind him. "I don't get it," he said after a couple of swigs. "How do you manage to do this? How do you keep it hidden from the yashi?"

The big one chuckled ominously. "One thing the katz ain't is stupid. They like living just as much as we do, but they can't beat the squiggles. Never learned how, I guess. Don't drink, so the squiggles drive them all the time. In fact they're mostly semisuicidal, but they don't like getting shot in the back by us."

"You kill them?"

"If we have to. You know, only the stupid ones. Most of them know we have to get along together. This war isn't *ever* gonna be over, not in our lifetimes. They don't bother us in the dugout; we let them live when the enemy come."

Cracka took another swig, shook his head. It sounded every bit as mad as all the wars he'd read about.

The screen on the TV continued to rattle with sublim commands and control reinforcements. Cracka gestured to the small portable. They had them everywhere; they were real tube heads, these Lemall's siffile.

"Why the screen? Why do you always have to have the screen?"

"Gotta watch," said the big one. "Gotta. Keeps you warm."

"Gotta watch or you get the shakes," said the one called Nuts-head.

"Warm?"

"It's like a good place in your head, if you watch. You feel good, kind of basic. The Skinnies always think they got us controlled, but they don't control anything. Not here, anyway."

Cracka and a couple of the other Calabel troopers kept ducking their heads to avoid the ubiquitous screens, fearing contamination by the frequent blasts of sublim psycho symbols flickering occasionally between segments of the soap operas that ran nonstop on the TVs.

"They're conditioning your head!" protested Cracka.

They laughed.

"Head been conditioned all my life," said the big one.

"But—"

"Makes no diff. You'll see, after a while it don't bother you. Just let it pass, and don't eat too much of that green goop they give you in training. Eat the boltak, eat the yellow stuff. The green stuff fucks with your balls."

"Hermaphrodite," said the plump, snub-nosed girl called Heggi by the others.

The flickering stopped. Heggi looked back to the screen, but her favorite character, the Vixen Queen, wasn't on yet, so she gave Cracka a sweet little smile instead.

They called them "stories." What he'd seen so far was all set on idyllic farms in a beautiful countryside. The characters were concerned with love and farming and little else.

The people in the dugout, the veteran members of the 344th Combat Squad, all came from what they called "the farm," which seemed to describe country villages, or possibly plantations.

Plantations that sounded to Cracka as if their prime purpose was raising crops of people.

The big one came from the iulliin estate of Catalonfri. "Eighteen zeem ago, when I were a young man."

Heggi had been sent from another plantation in another district. "I was going to be wed, but my ma, she always liked my younger sister better than me, so she sent me instead. I did like that boy."

"Ah, Heggi, don't you cry now." The big one put a protective arm around the plump girl. He leered at Cracka, fruit and alcohol on his breath. Heggi looked far from crying.

"Heggi's good on shock boots."

Cracka stared at them. His own conditioning made it so hard to think straight. He took another sip, felt a mental fog covering him, kept shaking his head.

The big one chuckled again. "Think the rest of your squad would like a drink?"

Cracka pulled himself together. "Yeah, I'm sure they would."

"You know, there's a good reason for drinking down here. Helps you to ignore the squiggles."

Cracka's ears perked up. "You what?"

"Here, have another. More you drink the less the squiggles affects you."

Cracka blinked and slapped his own face.

"You in transfer now, but you drink the big one's rocket juice and you soon be your old self. Believe me, the big one knows about this stuff." The big one took a handful of beakers and went out to spread some 180-proof tranquilizer among the rest of the unit.

Time passed. They talked. Cracka felt the conditioning fade. His jaw ceased to clench up tight; the tension in the back of his neck began to ease.

The door opened and more siffile troopers came in, Lemall's World people. They were customers for the big one and his still. While he dealt with them, they gossiped with him in rapid-fire undertones about the new people.

It seemed there were new people all through the front. The word had come down from the Either flank. Thousands of new troops, but they were people from outside, as it was in the beginning.

New people brought in from outside. By the Skinnies, so it was just like the prophecy.

And there shall be the day of the end of toil . . .

The ground rumbled suddenly. Everything seemed to shake.

"Pulverizer?" the big one said.

Heggi held her head cocked. There were more distant vibrations. "No, can't be, just that crusher. Those are medium shell, must be hitting the kneebone line."

She turned to Cracka, her eyes suddenly filled with concern. "Wait a merj—if they're boosting in a whole new army on this front, that must mean something big is coming."

The big one stared at her. "What?"

"Stand to reason, there's a whole new army brought in here, reinforce the line."

"And we got transferred down here?"

"Must mean a pulverizer coming."

■ CHAPTER EIGHTEEN

"Shazzeul, you may be Sun Mel, but you are still a fool. Listen to me, I know what I am saying." Lady Eilesme spoke with considerable passion.

The Sun Mel shook his head vigorously in response. "You want me to listen patiently to my death warrant? I will not go to die for their pleasure without a struggle."

"You can take your own life," said Eilesme calmly.

"I am not in the least bit suicidal. I have a plan. The siffile are quick, and they know about technology. You have spoken with Nathan, you know this to be true. We do not have to accept the Yelkes forever. We will retrieve the Great Secrets."

She snorted contemptuously. "Bah, a lot of ancient things that may or may not do anything. They won't save you from the sacrificial bier. Poor Shazzeul, why didn't you do like the rest of us and accept the rod of the Yelkes?"

"Because it is all twaddle! Because on his deathbed Zoax told me to hew to the true path. 'Regain the secrets, Shazzeul, otherwise all is lost to this parasitical religion.'"

She sighed deeply. "Those words were spoken more than a thousand zeem ago. Shazzeul—all has changed since Zoax's day. The Yelkes have grown in power and the High Mel has been diminished. Hesfraktus is not strong. He cannot assure you the throne upon his death."

"But I won't accept their demands! To give up the freedom to think what I want."

"Oh piffle, we all think what we want. We let the young fanatics have their shows and their burnings, and we carry on just as we used to do."

Shazzeul smiled suddenly, almost evilly. "Except there are no siffile to carry on with. There have been no siffile for a long, long time. All burned by the Yelkes."

She made a purple-lipped moue of protest. "Well, yes," she agreed with extreme reluctance.

Something gleamed in Eilesme's eyes.

The Sun Mel noticed it instantly. "I brought him here for healing, for the arts that you possess, Eilesme."

"He is better. In truth his recovery had little to do with any healing arts. You should not have exposed him to such danger in the first place. It was very irresponsible of you; that one is priceless."

And of this Eilesme was certain. In the old times, Nathan would have brought a fortune on the auction block.

The Sun Mel gestured abruptly. Time was precious now. "You think *you* can keep this one? You think the Yelkes would let you?"

"They won't know."

He snorted. "They know already. I am here just ahead of a party of them who intend to take him for an immediate ceremonial incineration on the roof of the Red Tower."

Her eyes narrowed. "You lie! They do not know!"

"They do indeed. Give him up to me or give him up to them, the choice is yours, Eilesme."

Eilesme felt as if her heart had been torn and set spinning in her ancient chest. "How do you know they come?"

"I have my spies. The Sun Mel is well loved by some."

Eilesme had to admit that Shazzeul did have spies and could know this, and thus she would have to let Nathan go, and she was very loath to let him go. But she could not let him be taken by the horrid Yelkes.

She would have enjoyed him so. He was like all the best things about siffile that she remembered. Quick, lively, graceful—and once properly trained, he would have been faithful, too.

"Curse you, Shazzeul," she said in a bitter voice. "You had better not be lying."

But the Sun Mel made no reply. He sent his yashi in with orders to be quick.

They found Nathan, picked him up, and carried him out heels kicking. He stopped protesting when he saw the Sun Mel. The yashi put him down. "Sun Mel, why are they doing this?"

"You must come with me, Nathan. The Yelkes are coming here. There is little time."

Nathan bade Eilesme farewell, and in truth he was happy to finally be on his way. Eilesme had strange habits. She got drunk a lot. Was always trying to get him to rub her neck, to stroke her back, to rearrange the braids in her white wooly hair.

Eilesme held his hand tight for a moment and stared into his dear face. She tried to imprint that face on her memory, for she was not sure she would ever see it again. Nothing had so touched her heart in a thousand zeem. And when they were finally gone she sat down and wept in the manner of the iulliin. Mucus streamed from her nostrils, welled up in the corners of her eyes.

Already Nathan was far away, moving quickly through empty, dust-strewn corridors as the Sun Mel took a safe but circuitous route back to the hidden apartment suite.

Nathan had been away at Eilesme's for several balaast, and although the Sun Mel had assured them that he was well, Avis was still overjoyed to see him returned, alive and apparently quite hearty.

"Your headache, how is that?"

He shook his head, "It still happens, but not all the time. The iulliin think I'll make a complete recovery."

"Damn fools, they should never have let you do that in the first place."

"But Mother, I can understand them now, and speak their language."

And what if it had killed you? she wanted to scream. But she bit that back and fought to control herself. There was no use in giving up like Rilla, or turning savage like Sam Boan. "Well, I hope you can teach the rest of us, now that you're back."

He nodded. "Sure, I can teach you if you want. If we get that long; they're still trying to burn us as sacrifices."

She shuddered, and rested her head on his shoulder. "Oh, Nathan, I was so worried."

"It's all right, Mother—I'm back, I'm here."

He had learned a lot while he'd recuperated at Eilesme's apartment—

"Szcha siffile, ibiti, ibiti . . ." Eilesme drank small cups of a sticky potion distilled from the glands of unborn dag-

babi and sat for hours staring into the mirrors with greatly
enlarged pupils, seeking signs of her "spirit being." During
the interminable self-examinations, she would babble and
croon baby talk. Later she would want to stroke Nathan,
his hair, his neck.

Nathan had rejected her sexual advances, but she continued to make them. When she drank varmil, a fermented
juice, she became even bolder. Once she'd even darted her
long bony fingers into his groin. Her laugh was grotesque,
a witch laugh of monstrous pink gums and yellowed teeth.

"Ibiti siffile, ibiti szcha."

The recollections sent a little tremor through him. There
was something very comforting, somehow, in the fact that
he was holding his own mother in his arms at that moment.
He was still only sixteen, although it hadn't felt like that
for a long time now.

Avis wept happily, allowing weeks of tension to flow
out of her.

And afterward Nathan settled back into the restrained
life of their luxury prison suite. It had gorgeous views and
ample servants, but it remained a prison nonetheless.

Nathan began teaching Avis and Folo the language of
the iulliin.

Sam, of course, snorted contemptuously at the idea of
learning an alien language. Rilla tried it for an hour but
found the whole thing exhausting and went to her room for
a nap. Rilla was spending a great deal of her time sleeping
in her room.

For Folo, learning Iullas was something to take Martherer Boan off his mind. At first he was slow to learn, but
then he grew more interested and began catching up on
Avis.

Announced with the great horn, the balaast passed.

Every so often they would hear the dirgelike singing of
the Yelkes and strange sweet smoke would drift through the
towers as they burnt a dagbab or two.

They would sit out on the balcony for hours. Nathan and Folo playing Go with black and white tablets they'd found in tubs in the washroom. Folo had painted the board onto the balcony deck with a pigment brought by the dagbabi.

Nathan had spent time talking with the dagbabi. He found them a dense, impenetrable little folk. But they would bring certain food and other simple things like the pigment, which came in a tube of plastic that looked remarkably like a condom. Folo had had a good laugh about that.

The climate seemed close to ideal. The air was generally warm and dry as clouds of many varieties slipped across the skies. The sun beamed down with a gentle golden light.

The clouds were the key, Nathan now realized. And he explained it to Folo and Avis as soon as he'd worked it out. "The clouds—they're active participants in the biosphere! The clouds are mostly alive!"

Folo and Avis looked at each other and nodded. They'd seen that look before.

"It's how they made this huge habitat habitable in the first place. They used designer plants and animals to take the raw stuff and create the soil and the atmosphere mix. Like tne reef clouds—remember what the Sun Mel said? 'Reef clouds are the centerpieces, the archstones.' That's because they're home to so much life. The system runs from larval forms in the water canals to aerial forms that are often the reproductive forms too. Everything flowers in the air, and the air plankton forms the seeds for whole weather systems."

"And the airfish and the things that airfish eat," said Folo.

"Which seems to include just about everything. But that's because there's so many different kinds of airfish."

"*Estual* in every shape and size. They start as pups in the water, then go on to aerial life."

"And what I'd like to know," Folo said, "is how they catch the airfish. Do they put out hooks and lines?"

"Not quite, but the dagbabi put glue on the limbs of trees. When airfish roost, they are trapped."

"So the dagbabi eat the airfish. What eats the dagbabi?"

They laughed, although Nathan recalled Eilesme boiling the brains of unborn dagbabi, the peculiar bitter smell.

"So nothing eats dagbabi," said Avis. "And all of us can eat various kinds of airfish."

"Well, the Sun Mel told us they have all these rules. Like the dagbabi eat only the things of the ground and the air, but nothing of the water, and only things that are begat in the air, and not things that are begat in water or on the land."

"You remembered that stuff?" Folo shook his head.

"Well, some of it. I mean, I wanted to know what we could eat, and the dagbabi came right after that."

"Well, we can't eat the things in the water, or anything begat in the water. All poisonous," said Avis.

"But we can eat the fruit of the gardens, and that's the basis for the bokka we get so much of."

Folo giggled. "Sheriff Boan likes his three bowls of bokka all right."

"Thankfully that's the only time we have to see him," said Avis. "He's becoming so obnoxious and difficult to deal with."

They nodded together. Sam had lost what few manners he'd ever possessed.

"What I'd like to know," Folo said, "is how the iulliin managed to make this stuff so it tastes so good."

"Nothing to it, Folo. The iulliin had the Lemall's people here for thousands of years. The evidence is all over the place, in the paintings, the statues. I mean, the culture here

was as much human as iulliin, if you go by the representational art. For thousands of years terrestrial they had their
little siffile."

"'Siffile' means 'obedient friends' in the diminutive,
am I correct?"

"Yes, Mother."

"Then the iulliin loved us like we were their dogs or
something? Like superior pets?"

Nathan nodded. "I'm afraid so." He shivered. He'd seen
the look in old Eilesme's eyes. The look of the loving pet
owner!

Folo frowned. "But what happened? Where did all the
people go?"

"That's what they won't talk about, except to say it was
a catastrophe. But I think there was a revolution here, and
the humans then went off to form their own society somewhere else in the Sun Clanth. From all accounts there's
plenty of room."

"And this whole place has been going downhill slowly
ever since the siffile left?" added Avis.

"Well, I think it had run down a long way before there
were siffile, Mother. I think the iulliin here were pretty
much a decrepit old people, declining in numbers, before
the humans were brought in. Then the human population
boomed and there came a clash and the humans decamped
after burning the city of the elite in a jacquerie type of
rebellion—you know, short, bloody, and hot."

"And then came the Yelkes?" Folo posed the question.

"Yes, in a reaction to the siffile, a spasm of a new religion, something that helps the iulliin reaffirm their belief in
themselves as the true rulers of the clanth."

"Makes sense, Nathan," Avis said.

"And of course the iulliin we've seen have been without
any technology for a long time."

"They're basically degenerate savages, Mother. There's
no other word to describe them."

■ CHAPTER NINETEEN

The balaasts continued their stately passing. Since there was nothing else to do, except play Go, they practiced Iullas among themselves.

The Sun Mel came to visit them every few hours. He appeared increasingly anxious. The High Mel Hesfraktus was losing ground steadily in his struggle with disease.

The Sun Mel attempted to explain the rise of the Yelkes. "The Yelkes say there are cycles in our history and that we are living through the Accursed Cycle. They deify the ancestors of the last, the *Enlightened* Cycle. According to them, the Enlightened Cycle ended when the siffile were brought in. The siffile were devils sent by Xaaca, the evil one, to destroy us."

His voice dropped further, and they had to strain to hear him. "To bring back the Enlightenment they sacrifice constantly. They believe this gives energy to their prayers and increases their amplitude. They believe if they perfect their method of prayer they will catch the attention of the ancestors."

"Sounds pretty bizarre to me," muttered Avis in Interlingua.

"Mother, I think they're reinventing religion. They're in the early stages of ancestor worship. Don't even have a god figure by the sound of it."

In Iullas he said, "But you, Lord Shazzeul, you do not believe in this?"

The Sun Mel made a face, his whisper grew passionate. "Bah! The ancestors are *dead*. When you die, you are gone; there is no afterlife. This is the world *we* made, this is all there is. The Yelkes—" he caught himself. Fearfully he looked toward the door.

He dropped his voice once more. "—are completely crazy. They seek solace in pure irrationality. They are tormented by their self-created 'devils' and constantly demand the burning of those of us whom they claim to be 'infested' with devils. Instead, all that is burnt are dagbabi, for the most part, and there is some question whether the dagbabi population will be able to maintain itself at current levels of sacrifice. Already parties have to be sent seventy or eighty krainth to find raik wood, and there is barely a jool tree to be found in the woods of Planggi Castle."

The Sun Mel paused, his long-lobed ears twitched, and he rose abruptly and strode to the outer doors. He opened them a crack and peered out. There were only his yashi guards. He returned once more and drew them close, within the reach of his long bony arms. He smelled faintly of some alien flower. His eyes searched theirs carefully. "That is why I have incarcerated you like this, my siffile, to protect you. Only a few of the Yelkes have seen you in the flesh, and the others are jealous as a result. Before they burn you they demand a good chance to see you. They have never *seen* siffile, you see. It has been a long time. But while the High Mel lives, you will not burn."

"But why would they burn us?"

"Aah, to purify your souls in the freshness of the flame, and cleanse them before sending them to the ancestors. Of course they also believe that siffile, by their very nature, are devils and must be consigned to the eighth and lowliest hell."

He looked at them for a moment as if trying to reassure himself that he was right and the Yelkes wrong. Then he shook it off. "But I keep you hidden from their sight and refuse to bring you out, and so far they do not dare to go against me. Not while the High Mel lives."

"How is the High Mel?" inquired Avis.

The Sun Mel shook his head sorrowfully. "His exalted nature is exhausted. His thought lies uneasy; he trembles at the prospect of the end. Loudly does he lament the bad habits of dissolution that caused him to waste his health in his youth. He dies too soon and knows it." The Sun Mel paused again and looked toward the door, ears straining for the slightest sound. He relaxed after a moment.

"At times his mind wanders, then I fear he may do anything, even disinherit Shazzeul in favor of little Fadook, my young brother. Fadook, of course, is a Yelke, like all the young ones. He is very extreme."

The Sun Mel shrugged with a huge unhappiness. "It hardly matters, though, because when the High Mel dies, the Yelkes will demand that I take the spirit needles. Five needles will be thrust into me, and if I cry out, they will discern a devil within me and demand that I be trussed and laid upon the scented woods."

"And burnt alive?"

The Sun Mel nodded sad agreement. "It will be hard to avoid crying out from the spirit needles. They used to be inserted just under the skin, but recently the Yelkes announced the discovery of 'deeper devils' that must be chased out with needles that are inserted far into the body. Of course those who join the Yelkes, and are taken in, are regarded as spiritually pure and are not put to such a test. I, however, cannot join; they know my contempt for them too well."

The Sun Mel shook his head grimly. "In fact their cult has grown remarkably quickly since they changed the size of the needles. And every time they take them to some wretch who crosses them, he or she screams out in agony and is soon lying upon a bed of wood."

Folo whistled when he grasped this.

"These Yelkes sure seem to have come up with a great way of winning converts," said Avis.

"In fact, it's an age-old favorite with young religions," replied Nathan. "Send the infidels to the stake. Whittle down the opposition while frightening the uncommitted."

To the Sun Mel, Nathan said, "Isn't there anything you can do to prevent this?"

The Sun Mel gave him a quick glance, as if measuring him. "Siffile, there is only one thing left that might change the situation. I refer to the Great Secrets. If I can gain control of some of the secrets then I may be able to defeat the Yelkes at a stroke. You see, the Yelkes seized control of the secrets long, long ago. In the era of the lamented Yebbent of Fulb, who gave away control of the secrets. The Yelkes have been on the rise ever since."

"'The Great Secrets'—you mentioned this before. What are they?"

"They are from the earlier cycle, from the Age of Enlightenment. Like the device that gives Iullas in place of the alien babble of siffile or dagbabi. This is one of the secrets, which we were allowed to use to question you. But the High Mel has to request such usage from the High Yelke. This humiliation we have come to because of the weak wits of Yebbent.

"Now, there are other Great Secrets, locked up for hundreds of zeem—the Wand of Visions, the Keystone of Tranquillity, the Screens of Other Lives. I do not remember them all, though my sister Eilesme could tell you more."

The Sun Mel paused, eyeing Nathan. They had clashed over the murderous translation device several times. But this time Nathan refrained from comment, and after a pause, the Sun Mel continued. "The secrets are guarded within the Hall of Antiquity."

"How are they guarded?" asked Nathan.

"By a dread galga beast. But, siffile, we must have the secrets if I am to overthrow the Yelkes' power and restore Planggi to its former glory."

Nathan heard the desperate optimism in the Sun Mel's voice. Born half a millennium after the fall of his civilization, the Sun Mel groped for a dimly perceived magic solution. Until then he had no one he could turn to for the help he needed.

It fitted with what Nathan already understood. The iulliin society was completely hollow. There were no books; there was no record-keeping except that done by the Yelkes for their own purpose. Books had been abandoned in the dimmest past, perhaps before the creation of the artificial universe itself. Certainly the Sun Mel only knew of human "books"; the iulliin had no word of their own to describe them, and no known human-made books had survived the rage of the Yelkes.

This revelation brought it all into clarity for Nathan. It revealed a culture that had lived en masse in the style of ancient emperors. A culture that had grown so lax and silly that it finally drowned its spirit and intelligence completely in a tepid bath of indulgence. The iulliin had become a tribe of spoiled children, ignorant mammothrepts inhabiting a crumbling luxury hotel.

What culture had survived at Planggi only continued because the dagbabi had been bred to perform their special tasks. The dagbabi did everything, even controlling the breeding of yashi cubs. The iulliin had completely lost control of their own world.

Nathan realized that the culture had first failed when the iulliin lost the will to understand their own technology. Then, later, when the disaster of the human rebellion came, they were completely unable to spring back. They'd forgotten how everything worked.

"So," the Sun Mel whispered, pressing his big bony

hands together, "I have a plan. If you will assist me, we will recover the secrets and use them to overthrow the Yelkes."

There didn't seem to be much choice.

"What must we do?"

"There is a simple unbarred window in the high wall of the Hall of Antiquity. I know of a way to gain access to it. I will give you a wand to cut the beepane and gain entry."

"I see," said Nathan, who looked to the others. They nodded—it sounded risky but possible.

"Once inside you will lower yourselves to the floor of the hall and find the secrets. You will be provided with a sack to recover them and bring them back to me."

This spurred a question in Nathan's mind. "If you knew that you were doomed by the Yelkes, why didn't you undertake this mission yourself at some point?"

The Sun Mel recoiled in shock. "I? Lord Shazzeul? Climb down a rope? My heart would never stand the strain. Dear siffile, how could you imagine such a thing?"

After a momentary silence, the Sun Mel continued. "Besides, on the floor of the hall will be the galga beast, which guards the secrets from all demons and tears their flesh."

"What is the galga beast?"

"A fiendish thing out of the ancient past. Bred to keep treasures safe. No one living has seen such a thing alive, but it is said to be taller than the yashi and so strong it can rend strong panels of beesqueeze with its bare hands."

"Oh, that's great-o," said Folo mirthlessly.

Avis exploded. "You say you want us to go in there and fight this monster and then to steal the secrets. An eight-foot-high monster, a woman and two youths?"

"I will give you weapons—my Sword of the Meldom, a stout blade three feet long, and the Spear of the Sun, which is tipped with sharp beeglass." The Sun Mel beamed on them.

"Weapons!" said Folo with fresh interest.

They spoke urgently among themselves in Interlingua. "It looks as if we have two rather poor choices," said Avis. "One, we say no to this madness and stay here. Eventually the High Mel will die and the Yelkes will be carrying us to the funeral pyre. Two, we agree to this and go in there and try and kill this eight-foot-high monster."

"If we opt to do nothing, then we probably lose all hope of affecting our situation," replied Nathan. "From everything we've heard from the Sun Mel, there's not much chance the Yelkes will suffer a change of heart and decide to let us live. With this galga beast, at least we'll have the initiative in our own hands."

Folo agreed unreservedly. "We fight the beast. I bet we can take him. I've handled tronch bear with ol' Shay Kroppa. It may be big, but if we've got good blades, we can take it."

Avis stared at Folo—young, confident, a rather handsome devil, she had to admit. "I hope you're right, Folo, I really do."

No sooner had the Sun Mel left, on the turn of the merj, then the Yelkes began a long ceremony with many doleful songs upon the top of the Red Tower. The citrus smell of jool wood soon wafted down to their balcony, followed shortly afterward by the stench of roasting dagbab, accompanied by the gasps and squeals of the sacrificial victim.

■ CHAPTER TWENTY

The Sun Mel returned within two merj, greatly agitated. "We are in terrible danger."

The Yelkes continued to sing, their harsh harmonies ringing out from the top of the Red Tower. More dagbabi were burnt as drums were beaten.

The Sun Mel rolled his eyes skyward. The long hands flapped. "The High Mel is at the point of death. We must move now. Come, follow me."

Sam Boan refused to leave his room when they tried to recruit him. Rilla emerged but fainted at the thought of entering the dark lair of the galga beast, whatever that was.

So only the three of them followed the Sun Mel down dusty corridors and through gloomy halls. The Sun Mel was also accompanied by three yashi and three dagbabi who carried coils of pink rope. The rope was another example of the remarkable iulliin polymer technology. Each coil was a single piece, a high-flex plastic soft as silk yet imbued with great strength.

Another pair of dagbabi marched with the Sun Mel. They carried the sword of the Meldom, a great two-handed weapon, and the Spear of the Sun.

The party crossed a little-used bridge to the Red Tower. The Sun Mel unlocked the gates with one of the keys he carried in a pouch inside his yellow robes. Beneath a mosaic vault of hunting scenes, they climbed a wide staircase, passing landings sealed off with immense double doors that were bolted and barred.

One floor beneath the roof, they turned down a long, dusty gallery, decorated in paintings of siffile, iulliin, and yashi hunters. The paintings were faded and dead, the pigments having none of the strengh of color of the iulliin palstics used in the mosaic work. The gallery passed right beneath the section where the Yelkes were concentrated, celebrating the approaching death of the High Mel. The iulliin voices were loud, wailing en masse while a dagbabi shrieked on the fire.

Cautiously they scuttled past and turned the corner to the dark wall of the castle that faced outward from the sun center.

They entered a narrow door and crossed another high span. They glimpsed dagbabi loading wood across another bridge down below. The dark face of the Red Tower was interrupted by occasional doorways through which klicks and dagbabi teemed.

Another corridor, this time very old and worn with mosaics of a different style, abstract, smooth, complex. A door opened, and they walked out onto battlements of the outward wall of the Red Tower.

The sun was hidden behind the mass of the central tower superstructure bulking above them. The air was cool; the breeze was from outward. It brought the scent of water and vegetation.

The vault of blue spread forever, darkening imperceptibly to a red-gold haze that obliterated the distance where a horizon should have been.

"So beautiful," murmured Avis.

Swarms of clouds, distant storm systems, bands of green that climbed high into the zenith where the pink gold sun hung, warm and bountiful. In some directions the clouds thickened quickly and cut off the view. In others were endless vistas, small hills rippling on forever beside straight silver canals until at last they dissolved into the golden haze.

Near to the city, fields were visible, in various shades of green, that stretched across the flat plain. Water channels traced their way through fields lined with bands of forest. A little farther away the hills began, darker green, studded with black trees on their crests. These hills were low, hardly more than two hundred meters tall.

"Come, siffile, we have little time as it is. We cannot stay here gazing at the Sun Clanth." He waved them on to a door set into a turret at the end of the battlements.

The Sun Mel became furtive. With quick glances over his shoulder he produced a green wand from within his cloak and attacked a grille welded across the door.

The wand had a shine to it like metal. The Sun Mel pressed one end to the spars of beeble and produced a sudden hot hiss. The beeble sputtered and fumed at those points, and abruptly the grille dropped away. The dagbabi pulled it free.

The ends were fused. Nathan looked at the green wand with increased respect. An acidifier, he reasoned, or an enzymator, an essential tool in this polymer-rich culture.

With a cautious look behind them, the Sun Mel used a large triangular key to open the door. The lock was stiff, and he had to strain at it for more than a minute before it turned. Even then the door had to be forced open on groaning hinges. The interior was dark. They slipped inside and found themselves in a narrow tower, a very old one, dark and cool. A musty smell hung in the air.

The walls were bare of decoration, the panels gray and cracked. Light came in from above, reflecting off the abraded gray walls.

One turn around the worn yellow stairs brought them to a narrow window. The Sun Mel produced another wand, this time a bright blue one, and drew it around the perimeter of the window.

The yellowed screen gave way with a short hiss, and the panel blew in in a single piece that the dagbabi stacked against the wall.

There was now room for one person at a time to climb through the window.

Nathan put his head out. They were high above an interior courtyard of the tower. Several other old towers were lined up, in perpetual gloom since the moment the Red Tower had arisen between them and the sun.

Nearby, an even older structure stood alone. A square tower no more than half the height of the Red Tower. Their position overlooked this structure by about twenty meters. Nathan could see that simply by climbing down with a rope from the window, they could gain easy access to the roof of the older tower.

When he moved aside to let Folo see, the dagbabi were sealing a hook into the material of the spine of the spiral staircase.

"Now, siffile, you must hurry. We will lower you to the roof of the Hall of Antiquity. From there you will descend to the window on the Either face of the tower and use this wand to open it."

He gave the blue wand to Nathan. It was featureless, a lump of blue plastic ten inches in length, a slight dimple at one end.

"This is the active point," said the Sun Mel. "Press this against the window and it will dissolve. Be careful not to press the point hard against your own skin. It will be hot!"

"I can imagine," murmured Nathan.

The other dagbabi came forward with the weapons and shoulder bags of soft skin.

The Sun Mel laid his long hand across the spear and the sword for a moment. "Take these arms, siffile, and use them to slay the galga."

Folo slipped the spear over his shoulder. It was equipped with a shoulder sling and bulky scabbard of tanned dagbab skin. The spear's head was two feet long, sharp and heavy, the haft made of some dense wood.

Finally another dagbab came forward and presented them with an object like a scepter, except that it held a small cage on the end within which sat a small, round, froglike creature with huge pink eyes.

"In the dark, this gosso will emit light and enable you to see the Great Secrets." At the other end of the scepter was a flared base of scrolled petals, upon which it could be set to stand alone.

A rope was made fast to the hook in the wall, and Nathan soon found himself descending on a smooth, soft line, bracing himself with his feet against the gray wall of the tower, which was pitted and streaked.

Over his shoulder he carried the heavy sword in its even heavier scabbard. Around his waist he bore another length of the light, silky rope.

Soon afterward he was down on the roof of the old tower. It was perpetual twilight here at the bottom of a well of towers and walls. The roof was heavily pitted, made of overlapping plates of beesqueeze. The retaining wall was castellated, and Nathan began tying the rope he carried around the battlement directly above the window on the Either face.

Carrying the spear on his back, Folo climbed down and joined him. Avis appeared at the window and began the descent.

Nathan watched her with concern. His mother kept fit —back home she rode regularly to inspect the herds on the rancho—and yet he could not help but feel that this kind of work might be more than she was capable of.

But Avis stepped smartly down the wall. She had the line wrapped once around her waist, kept her feet against the wall, and made a relatively quick descent.

Folo caught her as she reached them and helped her find her feet on the roof. Despite her cool exterior, Folo felt her heart fairly hammering. Folo also detected the little tremor in her footsteps as she walked away from him. He smiled to himself. Avis Prench was quite a woman, for a ranchera. Nathan's wild genius came from impressive stock.

"Now for the hard part," Nathan said.

"Let me do this," Folo said. "I'm more expendable right now, I think."

"Folo!"

"It's true," said Folo. "Give me the wand."

Nathan shrugged. "Oh all right, you be the hero."

He gave Folo the wand. The lithe tronch youth went over the edge and slipped down the rope to the window ledge. He crouched upon it and worked the blue wand around it. Then he kicked in the pane and swung himself inside, disappearing from view.

"What now?" said Avis.

Nathan shrugged.

After a moment Folo reappeared, caught hold of the rope, and began climbing back up it. A minute or so later he was beside them. "There's a gallery inside that goes all the way around. We can tie a rope to the rail—it seems pretty strong. It's dark in there, though. I think the interior is just one big room."

They went down again. Avis was last, and this time she found the descent simpler, shorter, and less taxing.

Inside the old tower it was so dark that it was impossible to make out much down below.

"Where might the galga beast be?" Nathan murmured to Folo.

"I dunno, it could be anywhere. There's a lot of stuff down there."

"What are we going to do now?" asked Avis.

"Where's the light creature?"

Avis opened her pack and produced the wand. Sure enough the gosso was emitting a warm, pinkish light with the power of several candles. However, the light simply threw enormous threatening shadows on the gray walls around them. It lacked the strength to penetrate the deeper gloom down below.

"Listen," said Folo.

They listened carefully, ears straining, but heard nothing. If their light had woken the galga beast, it had not stirred in response.

"Nothing's moving around down there that I can hear," said Nathan at last:

"One of us has to go down there, I guess," said Folo, with just a hint of concern.

The prospect was indeed uninviting.

"Now wait a second, Folo Banthin," began Avis.

"It's true," Folo said. "Someone's got to go down there. Or else we wait here until the Yelkes come and get us or we starve to death. If you ask me, the galga beast is better than burning at the stake. So, since I'm the most expendable, I'm going down there first. Give me the light. I've got the spear. If the galga beast comes, I'll either try and fight it or climb back up the rope. You'll have to decide whether you want to join me if it does come, or not." Folo slung the gosso over his shoulder, beside the spear.

"I'll be right behind you, Folo," said Nathan.

"I don't think the rope will take two of us at once."

"Well, as soon as you're down I'll start."

Folo smiled. Nathan was changing, no more a kid.

"Right-o, let's to it. While I'm still fired up enough to do this."

In a moment they'd tied Avis's rope to the interior railing and Folo was lowering himself into the well of darkness.

Nathan and Avis waited in apprehension. But no beast

lunged out of the dark, and Folo reached the floor without incident. Nathan climbed over the rail and took the rope in his hands.

Avis leaned forward suddenly and kissed his forehead. "Be careful Nathan, please."

Their eyes met.

"Well, I'll do my best."

She laughed, despite herself, despite the gloomy surroundings. "Get on with you."

He started down. She stared after him, her impenetrable son. There was this gap between them. Nathan had always been independent, something of a mystery to her. He'd grown up by himself, on his own terms, it sometimes seemed. Now he was becoming a man, growing up before her very eyes. Would they always be strangers?

Folo continued to stand at the bottom of the rope with the light in one hand and his spear unlimbered in the other. Surrounding him were vague shapes, dark rectangles. The light shone weakly on a fantastic array of material.

Nathan dropped down the rope easily. He reached the floor and stared around him at the jumbled shapes, statues, machines of many sizes, some looming five meters high.

Where was the dreaded galga beast?

With nervous fingers Nathan slipped the heavy scabbard off his shoulders and removed the sword. It was a meter and a half in length, a blade a hand's-width near the haft that narrowed to a third of that near the point. It was heavy and sharp, made of some superplastic, he assumed. Nathan hefted it in both hands; it was heavy, but he could manage it easily. It was a formidable weapon, and any monster would have to face at least one blow from its blade. Nathan felt renewed confidence.

Meanwhile Avis had readied herself and begun the descent, her left boot wrapped in the rope. She took her time, sliding down in stages.

Once again she surprised herself and reached the floor with little difficulty. And the silky smooth rope was easy to grip and hold.

She looked back up and wondered if she was strong enough to climb back up there if they had to. She doubted it. Getting down was one thing, getting back up another.

"All right!" said Nathan. "Mother, you pick up the lamp and we'll start to search."

Folo gripped the spear tightly and stared intently around them. Nathan held the big sword at the ready in a two-handed grip. Avis felt a stab of reassurance. She moved ahead and shone the light into the midst of the machines from a bygone age.

Almost immediately they noted the shape of the air barque, a narrow, Viking prow holding up a scowling gargoyle face to them. Behind the prow was a single short mast, and at the stern a two-story superstructure elaborately wrought. The boat was at least fifteen meters long and effectively cut the room in half, dominating all the rest of the machines.

Avis held up the gosso and they noted the fine inlaid work, decoration of fabulous skill and nicety, which appeared to cover the entire hull. Grinning faces, iulliin, wreaths and patterns with a recurrent lightning-bolt design —the work was astonishing.

"What a beauty!" exclaimed Nathan in a quiet voice.

"Look, boarding stairs." Folo pointed to the stern, near the superstructure.

Cautiously they climbed the stairs and found themselves on a wide flat deck space, covered in abstract mosaics. The single mast was bare. Long low couches lined the side rails. To the rear the superstructure glowed with a ghostly light like some gigantic phosphorescent skull.

The door was a dark mouth. They looked at each other. Could this be the galga beast's home?

"Who wants to go first?" said Avis.

"Let me," said Folo, taking the gosso and thrusting it inside, the spear held tight in his other hand.

They discovered an orderly cabin, with a couch along the rear wall, a single seat for a pilot beside a tiller that came up through the floor and seemed quite minimal in terms of design. Beside it was a box of controls supported on a narrow, flexible stalk, also mounted through the floor.

Beyond, in the corner, a ladder gave access to the upper floor.

Folo took a quick look up the stairs. They followed him and came out on an empty space under a light canopy.

Nathan found swivels and sockets set into the rail at the rear. "Perhaps they set fishing rods up here. Look at these sockets."

"Hasn't been used in a long time," said Folo.

"I wonder, though."

Nathan slipped down the stairs, carrying the gosso. He investigated the box of controls. Idly he pressed a switch. It moved with a hollow click. Nothing perceptible happened.

He shrugged. It had been foolish to think that the engines still worked. He tried another switch and was rewarded with a low whine somewhere down below. He flicked another switch, and lights came on all across the control box. Yet another switch caused a pair of headlamps to come on in the eyes of the gargoyle mounted at the tip of the prow. Abruptly stark shadows were thrown against the wall. Machines, thousands of them, had been piled up in rows, alleys, even mounds.

Avis had joined him. "So those are the secrets the Sun Mel wants so badly."

"Looks like all the machinery in the whole city, maybe the whole district. They brought it all in here and locked it up."

"If the galga beast wasn't awake earlier, he must be now," she said.

"Well, at least we'll be able to see it." Nathan felt defensive.

"I suppose that might be a consoling thought," said Avis.

Nathan flicked one more switch, set by itself in a recessed socket.

With a great groan, the engines cut in and the air barque rose a few centimeters off the floor of the tower. Hurriedly Nathan flicked the switch again. The barque settled, gently, on the repeller fields, back into its resting place.

"Well, that settles the question of what this boat does. It flies."

Avis looked around them. The dim walls went straight up.

Folo too looked up and around. "How do we get it out of here?" he asked.

"I don't know," Avis responded. "How did they get it in here?"

"Quiet both of you, listen for the galga beast or we may not be going anywhere at all."

They froze, ears straining for the slightest sound. But nothing disturbed the space of the aeons.

After a moment or two they moved back out onto the deck.

Folo gestured to the avenues of junk covering the floor of the big space.

"I wonder if we *can* find some weapons out there, something better than a spear and a sword."

"Folo's right," said Nathan. "We have to investigate the rest, galga beast or no galga beast. And we also have to find some doors; there must be some way to get this ship out of here."

They descended the stairs and moved down into an illuminated alleyway. Things reflected green, gold, blue, red, as if studded with jewels. Machines of infinite function, armatures, looping coils, video monitors—all combined to form a fantastic jungle of mechanisms.

There were a great number of plain cabinets, in dark gray and green plastic. Then a great coiled device, like a gigantic ball of string, and then suddenly Avis gasped in horror. Nathan sprang forward, sword upraised, a shout of defiance on his lips. But instead of the galga beast he found himself staring at a familiar shape, the tall, thin form of an iulliin robot.

■ CHAPTER TWENTY-ONE

Nathan's cry echoed back from the walls at them in mocking chorus. The robot stood frozen, as it had for a very long time.

They looked at each other. Avis stifled her scream.

The robot remained still. Dust lay thick on the upper surfaces.

"It's deactivated. All this stuff is turned off." Nathan stepped forward and rubbed off some dust. Motes flew up into the light beams from the air barque's gargoyle prow.

"Nathan's right, of course," said Avis.

"But what about the ol' galga beast?"

And Nathan recalled his battle cry as he leaped forward, the sword at the ready at the sight of the robot. The galga beast *must* have heard them now.

They waited, spear and sword poised.

The echoes had died away, and the quiet of the ages had returned. An empty, dark cathedral. They heard nothing.

They waited.

"By the Moth, this is a perfect fit, isn't it? Where's this durned beast, then." Folo gestured to the dark. "Why ain't he out here, charging us down and doin' his duty."

They continued to wait, eyes and ears straining into the absence of movement.

After a minute or more, Nathan relaxed a little. "Maybe there isn't a galga beast anymore."

To which Folo snorted, "Or maybe he's playing with us, waiting for us to move, waiting to pick us off. You know the old one-at-a-time routine."

"Folo!" snapped Avis.

"Sorry, Mz. Prench, I forgot you were here."

"Yes, well, there's no need to dwell on things. We've got to start exploring, whether there's a beast or not. We need to find some of these secrets the Sun Mel wants so much."

"Right."

"Where would you suggest we start?" replied Nathan.

Avis selected an alley between two meter-high, square, gray machine cabinets. Next to them were a group of objects that might have been hair dryers or dental chairs, and beyond them were two benches, covered in small objects.

In other directions were many machines that Nathan guessed had been from iulliin business offices. Bulky video monitors and rectangular modules of many sizes were piled around in profusion. Among them were tall things that looked like oversized guillotines and some squat shapes that might have been small automobiles or tractors except that there were no obvious wheels.

Nathan kept an eye on their rear as they progressed. The eerie absence of the galga beast was oppressive. Surely it was out there somewhere, hiding in the wilderness of machinery, waiting to pounce on them one by one, to pluck them into the darkness and a hideous death.

Nathan's heart was pounding in his chest. But his straining eyes caught no hint of movement, no gleam of eye. He gripped the sword hilt tightly. It felt heavy and reassuring in his hands, four feet of blade. He continued backing down the passage between the machines.

They passed a mound of tiny modules. Cassettes of some kind? Nathan wanted to examine them but did not dare take his eyes off the rear. Where was the damned galga beast? Why didn't it strike?

Folo suddenly gave a grunt of surprise. He stopped dead. Avis bumped into him and almost fell.

"Folo, what is it?"

"Look," he said. He pointed to a crepuscular gray husk lying between two boxy machines that rode on meter-high legs with fat little wheels.

They raised the gosso above the remains, which were at least eight feet long and massive. Except that there was little left of this body, a mere shell, an open body cavity, a cage of strangely shaped ribs so narrow they were like spines, limb fragments like pieces of shell. The head appeared vestigial, tiny in comparison with the rest.

Nathan reached down and touched it.

"Lightweight ceramic, from the feel of it. Mighty tough stuff."

"Ol' galga beast, he died a long time ago!" said Folo happily.

"Is this it, then? It's dead? And we've been shaking in our boots all this time?" Avis wanted to whoop, wanted to jump in the air with relief.

"We still have the Yelkes to deal with," said Nathan.

Avis got a grip on herself. "Of course, how silly of me, I'd almost forgotten about them. I was obsessing a bit on the galga beast, poor old thing. I wonder what happened to it?"

Nathan looked down at the husk on the floor. "I don't know. Perhaps it starved to death."

"Right-o. Old galga beast be no problem to us in that condition." Folo kicked it contemptuously. The thing shifted easily, like a big dead leaf.

They passed on, more eager now in their explorations. They came to one-piece ceramic benches, four feet wide and at least five meters long. On them were orderly arrays of smaller machines, boxes, modules, things that looked vaguely like hand wrenches or hand torches.

Nathan picked up one of the hand-torch things and aimed it at the far wall. It was gray and heavy in his hand, as if it were metal. He pressed a raised stud halfway up the barrel. Nothing happened.

He examined it carefully. There was no sign of any other moving part, just the stud and the opening at the wider end.

He tried another one, slightly smaller, lying beside the first. This time a hot green light flicked onto the wall and burned a neat hole right through it and beyond.

"Whoo!" said Folo, "That be a force weapon! Quite a charge, too, I'd say."

"At least as much as that of Calabel military laz-guns." Nathan agreed.

They all looked at it carefully.

"Are there any more?"

They searched the benches and found three more of the weapons, but all except the first one had been exhausted. They looked around for some means of recharging them. Nothing presented itself as an obvious choice.

Nathan hefted the one that had fired. "Well, we've got this one. If we have to, we can use it to defend ourselves."

They moved on down the bench.

"The Sun Mel spoke of the Wand of Visions, and the Keystone of Tranquillity," said Avis.

"Yes, but I got a strong impression that the Sun Mel really didn't know anything concrete about the secrets. That he was just reciting something he'd memorized a long time ago."

"Right, he's no Yelke, and they wouldn't let him get in here, oh no!"

"So there's no such wand?"

"Possible. But there's a lot of stuff. This looks like all the computers, communicators, and so on from the whole castle and the surrounding area. Maybe there was a reaction to the catastrophe here and they brought all the remaining high technology and locked it away. Maybe they didn't know how to operate it anymore."

Avis caught the implications at once. "So the Sun Mel doesn't really know anything. He wasn't educated. The iulliin have just completely lost it."

"They've been stagnating here for aeons."

"So all this stuff is really, really old. Like the force weapons. The iulliin haven't made anything like that in a long time."

"Exactly. The iulliin were obviously technological masters once—they built their own universe, after all. But they went soft inside it."

Nathan stopped in front of a pair of things that looked like antique airpilot helmets, wrought in a pale gray material with visors of bright green transparent stuff. Small control panels were set into the sides, above the earpieces.

Nathan picked one up. It was heavy, but not as heavy as he'd thought it would be. Inside, it was dark, lined with something soft. It was obviously meant to be worn as a helmet. He looked at the little control panel and idly pressed the buttons. The first button pressed produced a hum. A little red light winked on inside the helmet.

Nathan pressed the button again and the light went off and the hum ceased.

"Mm, we have ON and OFF capability here. I wonder . . ."

He tried another button, but nothing happened.

He pushed the first button again and the light came back on. He pushed the other buttons. At one point a green light flashed and the hum changed pitch. He turned it off and then back on; the green flash was gone and the hum was at the original pitch.

The others were investigating a device that looked like an open umbrella.

Impulsively he slipped the helmet over his head. It fitted quite easily, almost snugly.

His mother turned, saw him, and her eyes bulged. "Nathan! Take that off."

The visor dropped down suddenly, and the helmet self-activated. Small lights flickered on the mask in front of his eyes, and suddenly projected another view directly into his vision centers.

The top of the Red Tower. He recognized the battlements. An iulliin in purple robes was walking. Four naked boy children carried his train. A muscular young specimen capered before him, blowing a whistle, stamping to its tune, naked and wild. The scene blinked off.

"Nathan, no!" Avis tried to stop him. But his finger hit the second button.

A voice shouted Iullas in his ears, a voice ringing with anger and contempt. He could not make out the words—they were harsh, too quick.

And he looked up and tried to focus, but he saw only the horror.

Men and women armed with swords, bows and arrows, spears and clubs. Rebel siffile, who cut down a dozen yashi and poured through the gates.

A harsh voice, undoubtedly human, rang in his ears. "So it has come, good Vraka. You will do as I demand. Satisfy the siffile. The Lady Dromaki must pay the price. Take up the knife..." the rest dissolved suddenly into a sense of excruciating pain—a sense, but not the pain itself.

"It's an echo!" he said suddenly, calming a worried Folo, who was considering trying to jerk the helmet off before Nathan was hurt or killed.

"What is, Nathan?" Avis asked.

"I'm sorry, it's feeding me echoes of the previous wearer. I think she died while wearing it. It does something on a mental plane."

And Nathan touched the third button. There was an abrupt *click* in his head, and it was as if he stared out onto a world composed of electronic grid forms.

Beside him were two glowing towers, Folo and Avis. He looked toward them and *saw*—into their minds. Vortex patterns kaleidoscoped in his brain. Visions of himself, feelings.

Nathan's legs suddenly felt very weak. He needed to sit down quickly.

Then he *was* sitting down and Folo was leaning over him, a blaze of energy, a tower of grid points, convulsions, and he felt nausea, sleepiness. Confusion.

Folo reached to remove the helmet and Nathan twitched away. "No, don't!"

He groped for the buttons and turned it off. The nausea went away, as did the bizarre images. He slipped the helmet off.

"Are you okay, Nathan?" Folo was bending over him.

"Yeah, I think so. I'll be all right. It projects mental images, like films almost, but they seemed to be, well, almost like memories. I don't know. You'll have to try it yourself."

"I don't know, Nathan. That thing might make a purée of your brains."

"It was like I was looking into the minds of you and Avis, and they were laid out like street maps or something."

"You could read our minds?"

"I don't know. Possibly, if I knew how."

"The Moth take me, these iulliin had everything! What went wrong with them?"

"I guess endless paradise became boring after a while."

Gingerly Folo looked the helmet over, but he refrained from putting it on, and soon turned away to search for new weapons—anything that might help them defeat the Yelkes and their yashi bodyguards.

Avis was inspecting a tall, massively built device that resembled a grandfather clock. Covered in a high-gloss material of dark blue-black, it had hundreds of slender white buttons set into its front face. At the top, under an octagonal cover, was a video screen.

"I wonder what this does?" she murmured. Idly she pressed buttons. Nothing happened.

"Doesn't seem to work," said Folo. He pressed his palm against the rows of buttons and pressed dozens.

The screen flickered into life, fitfully at first, then it steadied.

They stared up at it.

"A computer of some kind?" muttered Nathan with a strange passion, almost a thirst, in his voice.

An iulliin voice began speaking suddenly, a string of code phrases. A face swam up into view, an iulliin face framed in a high-collared robe inset with sparkling gems.

"Greetings, Malkessar, I was so glad to be here in time to receive your call. You know we have been expecting you for quite some time."

They stared openmouthed. "A movie?" Folo said.

The iulliin's face changed. His forehead was creased with lines. "Malkessar? Is that you? Why am I not receiving a picture signal? Is there something wrong with your communicator?"

"It's not a movie," Folo clapped his hands together happily. "Some kind of videophone."

The iulliin face disappeared, moving away to one side. They stared at an image of a room furnished with fine rugs and stark, metallic chairs. Large oval windows pierced a beige wall and looked out on a lawn of pink-tipped green with trees beyond it.

"Where's that, do you think?"

The iulliin face reappeared, visibly angry. "Whoever you are, this is not a legal call. You are misusing the communicator. I will report this to the communications authorities." The screen darkened. Then it flickered with erractic ghost images, iulliin symbols.

Nathan examined the device as closely as possible. Experimenting again, he pushed more buttons. A picture reappeared, this time with a golden background.

For a few seconds they stared at another iulliin, a female, with an extravagant wig of white wool, teased into spikes. "Oh! Whatever has happened? Teewee? I've lost you, I'll have to reroute and call again." She leaned forward and the connection vanished.

Nathan stepped back from the thing. "It's a communicator of some kind, long-distance, I would imagine from the size of it."

"Those iulliin, where do you think they are?"

Nathan shrugged. "Who can say, Folo? Could be ten thousand kilometers, could be in the next sun region, twenty million kloms away—we don't have much to go on."

He hit some more buttons, lower down.

A few vague images wandered over the screen, unrealized, dim as shadows, then there was nothing.

"It doesn't seem to work very well," commented Folo.

"Lord knows how old it is." Avis slapped the side of the heavy great thing.

The screen flashed green. There was an eerie humming sound from it, lights winked on in the machine's chest, above the array of white buttons. The lights were tiny glows of pink and gold, appearing momentarily beneath the shining surface material.

Abruptly the screen became a conduit for a green searchlight that flicked out of the screen and began to rove around the great room, pausing momentarily on different objects, as if it were taking photographs.

The process made Nathan uneasy. He tapped more buttons, trying to break the connection.

"What's up, Nathan?"

"I don't know, Folo, but I don't think I like this."

The green beam suddenly focused on Avis. When she moved, it moved with her. The box began to hum, then a mechanical roaring sounded. The green lights were flashing inside, and sparks were leaping off it. Avis tried to twist out of the beam, but it followed her everywhere.

And then there was a bright flash, and a smoke ring of black vapor rose above them. The screen was dead, the lights no longer flashed.

"It's busted," said Folo.

Nathan was pale. Tentatively he touched the side of the now quiet machine. "Blew its circuits. It was as if something was using it, something that wanted to see us."

Avis faced him, her eyes wary. "What's out there, Nathan?"

He shook his head. "A whole universe, Mother, I—" He didn't finish, turned back to the search.

Nathan examined a number of enigmatic black cubes standing in a row along one bench. Prodding the little buttons on their fronts produced no detectable reactions. Nathan shrugged.

Folo came to the end of the bench, where he made another discovery. With a quick crouch he grabbed something from the floor and sniffed it. He collected another.

"Folo, what are you doing?" said Avis.

"There're some bones here, pretty fresh bones, I'd say." He held up a pair of skulls, dagbab skulls, the flesh almost entirely removed, the braincases cracked open, and the brains sucked out.

"Oh no," breathed Avis.

"That puts paid to the 'galga beast is dead from starvation' theory," Nathan said.

"'Fraid so," agreed Folo.

"Then where is it?"

"Perhaps it's full of dagbab and can't be bothered with us," Nathan hazarded.

Once again they peered nervously around them, but no galga beast lunged out of the dark.

After a moment Nathan had an odd idea. He slipped the helmet back on. He hit the third button immediately, and once again saw the field of sparkling grid points, a flat plane broken solely by the towering mental grid-forms of Avis and Folo, and . . . something else.

Another grid-form existed, was growing quickly in the center of the room. It was pulsing quickly and changing shape.

Nathan focused on it and in a flash of horror felt his mind make contact with the galga beast. Now awake, and struggling furiously to metamorphose out of the pupal state that it had returned to after preying on the hapless dagbabi that had been sent to fetch the translator machines.

It was a straightforward kind of mind, a tunnel of reflecting predatory interests. There was no way to reason with it, no way to communicate.

They had survived thus far solely because after gorging on eight dagbabi it had pupated, not expecting a further opportunity to feed anytime soon. Prey had been extremely scarce in this chamber. Now the galga struggled to soften the tough skin of the cocoon. Complex acids had to be formed and exuded from skin glands.

But soon it would be free and it would move to seize the new prey and immobilize it before feeding. There was considerable prey material available. Even in the cocoon the galga creature had weighed the vibrations of their passage and counted them carefully. Their flesh would provide for hundreds of zeem spent in pupal hibernation.

Nathan yanked the helmet off. "I can sense it, the galga beast!" He waved his arm in the direction in which it lay. "It was hibernating after eating all these dagbabi, but it's emerging from hibernation now. We have to kill it before it awakes fully."

"Where is it, Nathan? Quick, man—"

"It's near the air boat."

They ran back through the aisles of murky machines, desperation rising. There was nothing to see, just the machines and the frozen robot.

"Where the hell is it?" said Avis.

"Maybe it's in one of these cabinets," said Folo.

"My impression was that it would be too big for that. It's on the floor somewhere near this spot."

They cast about frantically, ran on past a spherical machine, and came upon the cocoon, which was filled with frenzied activity. It was three meters long, a dark gray mass that writhed on the floor.

It had split open at one end, and something the size of a man's body, covered in snaillike skin, was pushing out of the split. It was the head of the galga, the new head, regrown and freshly inflated.

"Fire the gun, Nathan!" screamed his mother.

Nathan aimed the iulliin beam weapon and pressed the stud.

Nothing happened. He tried again. Still nothing. "The charge is gone!" he wailed, and dropped the gun and pulled out the sword.

With a *riippp!*, the cocoon broke and one great arm came free.

"No!" screamed Nathan. He ran at the thing and swung the sword.

The cocoon fluttered and caught at his legs and he fell, sprawling beside the galga. More cocoon ripped, the beast emerging, muscular flesh gleaming under thick mucus. It reached for him with deadly talons.

But Folo charged with the spear, and the galga was forced to turn away to avoid the spear thrust. Nathan sprang up and swung with his blade once more.

The monster parried with its forearm and the blade slid off the armored skin. Now the muscular body, with the mass of a polar bear, was emerging from the cocoon. The huge, wormlike head darted back and forth, a tentacle tipped with stinger cells riding on the front. One strike and the prey would be paralyzed.

Folo lunged in with the spear and a shout, but his battle cry changed to one of woe as the galga seized the haft of the spear and plucked it from his grip. It threw the spear behind it and advanced, hissing delightedly.

Nathan hewed at it with the sword once more. It parried with another forearm as thick as a man's thigh, but this time the blade sank in and then stuck fast. The galga's hiss changed pitch to resemble that of a steam kettle, and it yanked its arm back, pulling the sword from Nathan's hands.

The sword was stuck in the wound, which dripped a pale fluid.

The humans were disarmed. The galga beast came on, hissing thoughtfully as it tried to remove the impediment of the sword.

There was nothing to do but retreat. Folo dodged into another aisle, seeking to get behind the monster and retrieve the spear. The thing pursued Nathan and Avis, who stumbled ahead of it.

Nathan threw himself over a bank of cabinets. The thing chased Avis alone. She turned and found herself trapped in a cul-de-sac of large gray plastic cubes.

The galga reached for her. Avis flattened herself against a cube, holding the little gosso lamp in front of her. The monster struck the gosso from her hand. It hit the floor and went out.

"Duck, Mz. Prench!" yelled Folo as he hurled the spear from short range into the galga's back. Avis dropped, and the spear sank into the beast until the head projected from its chest.

Avis scrambled on hands and knees, got up, and ran toward Folo. In the dark they collided and fell in a heap.

Avis gave a little shriek and thrashed violently. Her knee rammed hard into Folo's crotch. He gave a grunt and rolled over.

"Oh no," said Avis. "Folo?"

"Whoo!" he breathed.

The galga hissed furiously in the dark as it pulled the spear through its own chest. Then it snapped the weapon in half and threw the pieces aside.

Folo stared at the creature. How could it live? He'd run the damn thing through. He grabbed Avis's wrist and pulled her down a side passage.

Behind them the galga turned its attention to the job of pulling out the sword. Carefully it prised the long blade free. Immediately resilient flesh began to rearmor itself. The galga tossed the sword down and stamped on it. Then it resumed the pursuit.

By then Nathan was completely lost, crawling in the darkness down a line of machines. He turned again and again in terror, staring into the dark. He'd taken a wrong turn somewhere. He couldn't even see the air boat, though there was light to his left. He dared not call out to the others. He could hear the beast quite clearly, hissing to itself.

He had to find a weapon, and it would have to be a good one. The galga beast had disposed of the sword and the spear with apparent ease.

He crawled through the legs of some big machine and then found himself back under the bench on which they'd found the beam weapon. He wriggled out from beneath it and looked around carefully. The air boat was nearby, lamps aglow.

The helmet almost tripped him up. He reached down and picked it up and put it on once again. Quickly he hit the buttons. The grid field came up again in his mind. Avis and Folo were visible at once, moving along the far perimeter of the room. Then, some way behind them, came the beast.

He focused on it momentarily, and it was instantly aware of him—he felt it reaching out for him. Instinctively he turned away. When he looked back the thing had changed direction. Now it was moving directly toward him.

Nathan panicked. He turned to run, pulling at the helmet, and smacked into a wall that nearly knocked him senseless. He fell to his knees, clawing at the helmet, terror-struck.

And suddenly a bizarre idea struck him. He scrambled to his feet and looked back, still with the sensory field on. The grid-lit form of the galga was much closer. Nathan willed the thing to stop, willed it to stand still.

It kept coming. He hit the other buttons. The fourth had no visible effect, nor did the fifth.

It was close now, sure of his position. He could hear the

excited hissing, then it was towering over him and there was no time to run.

It lurched forward, claws held wide. Nathan looked hard into the blaze of light that was the thing's brain on the field scan and made contact once again. He almost quailed at the simple, relentless ferocity of the thing, but he gritted his jaw, hit the last button, and screamed, *"Stop!"*

And it did.

The galga froze under the mental amplifier of the helmet with its sixth power invoked. The galga's simple mind had been placed in stasis. It could not move until the field was lifted.

Nathan didn't dare to breathe for several seconds. The monster had stopped only a few feet away. A moment later and it would have seized him.

But it still hadn't moved.

He tiptoed away from it, scarcely daring to believe that his ruse had worked.

His mother appeared out of the dark, her eyes wide and fearful. She put her hands to her mouth at the sight of the monster reared up, stock-still.

"What did you do? I mean, we felt that, or heard it or something. What was it?"

Nathan spoke from inside the helmet. "These helmets are for controlling minds. I figured that they might have been used to make it safe for the iulliin to handle these monsters. The sixth button did it, stopped the thing dead. I don't know what I did exactly, but I sure hope we can figure it out."

Avis stared into the face mask, barely comprehending her son's words.

Folo, however, gave a whoop of celebration and wrapped them both in a tronchish bear hug. In moments he and Avis were trying on the helmets.

CHAPTER TWENTY-TWO

The High Yelkes wore platform-soled shoes of great size and complexity. As a result they towered ten feet high and were almost completely unable to move except when carried by a large platoon of dagbabi who wore leather harnesses specially designed to aid them in carrying their masters about in a vertical position.

For the inquisition of Sam and Rilla Boan, the High Yelkes wore their absolutely finest, highest shoes. They formed a towering half circle around the terrified humans, faces wreathed in dramatic scowls.

The Highest Yelke did most of the talking. The dagbab squealed and gasped. "You are to be burnt atop a fortune in heaven-sent raik wood. Such honor is bestowed only to the foremost of plaguing devils."

The distinction seemed hardly adequate enticement for the intended victims. Sam Boan and Rilla Boan shivered where they knelt atop the Red Tower. A cool breeze was blowing in from outward. The surface was very hard; it cut into their knees. Sam's legs were turning numb. But he dared not move, not with the eyes of the yashi on him.

Sam's mind was awhirl with outrage, and wild, blind incomprehension. He couldn't reconcile himself to his coming end. A month before he had been sheriff of Prench Tronch—as solid and stable a piece of the landscape as Tom Prench Mountain. Now he was to die on this accursed alien strand.

Yes, he thought as he looked once more on the pile of wood, this was happening to him! They were going to burn him alive, and sing their hymns while he burned. The sheriff of Prench Tronch shook his head, trying vainly to dispel the dream; the nightmare could not be real.

Nearby was the place of burning, blackened from many fires. A new mound of raik-wood branches was already forming as dagbabi staggered in with further contributions. The wood was well dried; it would burn briskly.

Sam had fought to escape at first. Briefly he tussled with a yashi bodyguard. The furred giant decked him with a punishing smash to the belly. Then he and a colleague worked Sam over a little with their spear butts. When Sam got back onto his knees he had slumped into a glum quiescence.

For Rilla Boan the horrible anxiety had triggered her asthma. She struggled for breath in short frantic gasps. Given any wind she would have screamed, but even that satisfaction was denied her. And the dreadful Yelkes' singing went on and on.

For some reason her asthma irritated Sam profoundly. Here she was, still puffing and groaning, always the same with Rilla! And they were due to die horribly in a few minutes. Even his death would be accompanied by her silly illnesses.

Harsh cries suddenly broke through his reverie. Figures pushed through among the High Yelkes.

The Sun Mel was brought in, dragged by four muscular young iulliin in white smocks.

The Sun Mel protested loudly in Iullas. The High Yelkes shouted back and chanted in chorus. Other young iulliin wearing the white of the novitiate pulled the Sun Mel roughly into the center of the burning place. There on a dais were laid out a dozen long silvery needles, lying upon a silken cloth of gold.

The High Yelkes were carried over and set in position around the place of insertion of the spirit needles.

The Sun Mel shouted and struggled, but five young iulliin held him fast while another took up one of the needles and jabbed it deep into the Sun Mel's forearm.

The Sun Mel screamed.

The massed Yelkes, numbering several hundreds by now, broke into prolonged cheering. A band struck up a gay, trivial little tune. The High Yelkes pronounced immediate sentence.

The Sun Mel was trussed to a pole and then hoisted up by the young Yelkes and laid atop the pile of raik branches. The Yelkes broke into song. They sang a great ballad, with several layers of harmony, called "The Basting of the Demon." It had a passage in the chorus requiring them to laugh in unison, and they clearly loved this part. Every time it came up, the massed voice of the Yelkes brayed their laughter aloud until it rang from all the towers of Planggi Castle.

The High Yelkes meanwhile drew lots for the privilege of lighting the fire. Novices held up an airfish with long tail plumes. The winner selected the shortest. As each plume was removed, the airfish emitted a little wail of dismay. The winner was announced shortly, and he took up a long taper and ignited it under a magnifying lens. It caught and burned with green sputters and little pink flares, like a miniature Roman candle.

With considerable excitement the High Yelke stepped slowly toward the pile of tinder-dry raik wood upon which lay the Sun Mel.

Then came the unthinkable.

There was a loud shout from behind the assembled Yelkes. Everyone whirled, and found two siffile carrying the ancient helmets from the place of the Great Secrets. The siffile put the helmets on. The Yelkes gave a scream of outrage and many pulled knives from their belts. They uttered chilling cries of death.

But their screams took on a curious timbre. Fluting wails of agony arose, shrieks of dismay. The Highest Yelke fainted and fell off his meter-high shoes with a crash. The sputtering taper fell to the floor and went out. The rest of the High Yelkes had their hands to their ears, howling in woe. More toppled.

The siffile advanced, the helmets transforming them into threatening monsters. Around them surged a full-power dominance field.

Wherever they directed it, life-forms shook from its pressuring power. The Yelkes collapsed, groveling before the siffile. The High Yelkes abandoned their towering shoes to get down on their knees to the siffile.

Rage and terror screamed in their brains. Rage and terror howled in the brains of Sam and Rilla Boan too, and the field spread and leaked out into the city of dagbabi.

The town was stilled. Many dagbabi froze immobile at the lash of intense dominance projection required to break the will of the Yelkes. Other dagbabi staggered at random, crashing into walls, walking out of windows.

Yashi were particularly susceptible to the helmets; from all over the roof they crowded forward to kneel and offer their swords to the new lords. In large part this was because the helmets had been designed to subdue the yashi in the first place, long, long before the iulliin created the artificial universe of the Golden Sunlands.

Nathan and Folo stepped into the ring of groveling Yelkes and kept the field at full strength. It was not that easy, for they had to concentrate their minds on the task of keeping the Yelkes in awe. The field was amplified— Nathan was not sure exactly which—into a projection of mental controls, feeding on the aspects of behavior in all creatures that relate to dominance hierarchies.

While Nathan and Folo kept the field going, Avis sawed through the Sun Mel's bonds and helped him to his feet. "We are leaving the city. You should come with us, I think."

The Sun Mel looked with vast distaste toward the assembled kneeling Yelkes.

It had come to this. Banishment! And yet something tugged upward on his heartstrings. In truth he thought it was a marvellous suggestion. The siffile had a wonderful idea, it was quite clear to him. "Yes, we are dishonored here by these ungrateful wretches. We will leave Planggi, home of my line since the dawn of the Sunlands. We will become homeless vagabonds in the clanth."

He considered the helmets worn by Folo and Nathan. "Great Secrets! You succeeded!"

"Yes, but we don't know for how long. It's hard to make the helmets work like this," said Avis.

"But of course, they are for the iulliin to wear. Siffile do not understand everything, it seems."

Avis stifled a chuckle at the look in the Sun Mel's face. Humbled, feathers in disarray, he was yet attempting to pull the tattered shreds of iulliin majesty back around himself.

Nathan made urgent gestures. He and Folo were losing strength. They had projected a field powerful enough to paralyze the whole building for several minutes, but their strength was waning.

With the Sun Mel at their head, and Avis at their rear, they started down the ramps of the Red Tower. The Yelkes remained in place, eyes staring, held down by the field.

They were still several stories from the ground when Nathan fainted, exhausted by the overload. He went quickly, toppling over into Folo's arms. Folo set him down. Nathan's field weakened, then vanished altogether.

Nathan came to quickly, and a few seconds later he sat up.

"You all right, Nathan?" Folo and Avis were beside him.

"I think so, but I don't know if I can generate the field again."

"Well, let's get going, then." Folo glanced upward. A huge scream of collective rage was erupting behind them. "I don't think we wanna hang around here, man."

Nathan got to his feet, picked up the helmet, and began to trot on beside them. He shook his head to clear it, but the nausea remained. He desperately longed for a chance to lie down and sleep forever. The battle with the galga horror had been enough for one day. The helmet was so draining. He felt weak, dough-fleshed, walking on air.

Folo put out an arm to steady him, and Nathan accepted it gladly. He wondered briefly how Folo did it. The burly troncher seemed almost unaffected by the last hour's activities, including their deadly game with the galga.

In actual fact, Folo was wondering how long he could last before sliding into oblivion. A large bruise was developing on his cheek from a collision in the dark with a piece of iulliin office machinery. He felt dizzy from the effort of concentrating on hating the durned Yelkes.

Sam and Rilla were loping ahead of them. Sam's face was purple from the strain, and he was convinced he would die of a heart attack at any second.

Rilla ran with little screams. The nightmare seemed endless, but death by fire did not appeal to her on any level. Running away was much, much better. And, strangely, her asthma had cleared up in a flash.

Avis brought up the rear, carrying the sword two-handed, just in case anything came too close. They could hear the pursuit quite clearly.

The Sun Mel ran surprisingly swiftly, with long legs kicking out in front and behind, and he reached the ground floor before the others.

Behind them the tumult grew closer.

The Sun Mel paused to wave them to follow him. Then he ran on, heading for the balaunt stables. On the walls writhed a gallery of bright mosaics. More hunting scenes, siffile, iulliin, and balaunt, the iulliin mount of choice for riding.

As he ran, the Sun Mel marveled at what he was doing, *running!* with the legs extending out in front and back. It had been a great many balaast since Shazzeul ab vil Planggi had run anywhere.

He reached the stables well before the others, and immediately sent dagbabi scurrying to bring out fresh balaunt for saddling. There was no time to prepare, to save anything except his own skin.

Fadook would be High Mel, and Honansosi would become the Sun Mel. But they would have to survive the attention of the Yelkes, which promised to be exacting indeed.

Shazzeul accepted his lot now, he looked to a new life. And there was something else, something that fairly sang within his breast.

Balaunt were brought out, creatures with skull-white skins, muscular haunches, wide hoofs, and narrow, mantid heads.

The Sun Mel felt a great sense of vindication. He had believed! He had kept the faith with science, as he had sworn to Grandfather Zoax on his deathbed.

He remembered Zoax's dying words: "Hesfraktus is weak. He will give away all to the Yelkes. You must stand up for reason, Shazzeul. Get back the secrets."

The Sun Mel had been nine years old; the scene had lingered in his memory ever since. He felt a sense of triumph. Yes, he was defeated, and the Yelkes were in the ascendant, but he had produced the Great Secrets. How Zoax would have smiled if he could have seen! The Great

Secrets were the key to power in the Sun Clanth, so he had always said.

But now there were siffile again. The Yelkes' hold had been broken. Of course, siffile were forbidden. *There were to be no more siffile!* That had been the cry all across the clanth after the terrible events of the rebellion. But the new siffile had been delivered! From beyond the clanth in a spaceship—a gifting of siffile from an unknown clanth that still possessed the high culture.

And from use of the siffile had come the Great Secrets. Helmets of great power! The stupid Yelkes did not know how to use them; they had locked them away long ago. They mistrusted the ancient technology, suspected it of causing possession by devils.

The Sun Mel reveled. He had lived to see a spaceship descend from beyond the clanth and to own siffile and now to possess Great Secrets. So what if he was forced to abandon his historic manse? To take the road of the vagabond nobleman? He would have his siffile, and some yashi, and with the Great Secrets he would live comfortably on the land. They would range inward, toward the sun. Toward Fanthenai and the magical Lake Bleth.

In Fanthenai they would regroup. The Sun Mel would call for support from the outlying meldoms. All the mels would back him, and they would raise a force to rid the clanth of the Yelkes everywhere.

The aristocracy would bind together, and he would lead them to glory in the name of the house of Planggi.

A problem existed, however. There wasn't time to get sufficient balaunt ready.

"More balaunt," ordered the Sun Mel. "Hurry!"

Nathan arrived, puffing, still carrying the helmet. He held up a hand to get the Sun Mel's attention.

"The balaunt are unnecessary, Your Excellency. We have the air barque, activated and waiting for us on the roof of the old tower."

The Sun Mel's jaw dropped. "The air barque? From the Hall of Antiquity? But how?"

"It still works, Your Excellency. The air barque is ready to go."

"Amazing. I have been given siffile of extraordinary quality."

Folo meanwhile had investigated the saddlebags on the prepared balaunt. "Here's a supply of food and water."

"Great, Folo! We'll take it. Let's go."

Nathan and Folo pulled the saddlebags off the little balaunt, insectal quadrupeds the size of ponies. The saddle gear was made of seasoned dagbab hide, very fine; detailed work was evident.

Rilla Boan and Sam Boan accepted a load each.

"Let's get a move on," said Sam in a worried voice.

"Yes, let's go to the aircraft. I won't feel safe again until I'm well away from this terrible place."

The Yelkes were getting closer. Their cries echoed in the passageway.

"Uh oh," said Folo.

Avis turned to Nathan. "Give me the helmet, Nathan. I can use it for a power blast on the sixth level. I think they're getting too close."

"Good idea!" Nathan passed her the helmet despite a sudden twinge of reluctance. For a fraction of a second he hesitated, torn by a weird sense of mistrust. But he dismissed the feeling, and she put the helmet on and pressed the buttons.

Avis had used the helmet to entrap the yashi guard they discovered outside the Hall of Antiquity. They had been able to track the guard outside the door with the third-level power of sight. Then, using the fifth-level power, they had coerced the simpleminded yashi to open the door and investigate. When the door was open they used the sixth power on him and blasted him senseless.

Avis fine-tuned the awareness field. She picked up the minds of the balaunt in the stables. Alien concerns, indeed, but simple enough, with a general level of excitement running high. She turned it about to find the Yelkes.

The Yelkes were there, an ominous mental hurricane on the fringe of the field. Nervously she turned the little buttons and accidentally gave the balaunt a burst on the fifth level that drove them into a frenzy. They battled in their stalls and emitted a powerful gel with excremental odors.

The Yelkes were getting close. Sam Boan grew livid with impatience. He lost control. "How do we get out of here?" he bellowed.

Nathan pointed out the stable door to the passageway. "Back that way, I'm afraid."

Sam exploded in fury. "Damn it, can't you hear those screaming Yelkes? They're coming!"

The Sun Mel stared at Sam, appalled at the loud rude noises in the barbarous tongue of the siffile. He held up a hand to calm the fat, red-faced siffile.

But Sam Boan turned and cursed the Sun Mel loudly with wild, waving arms and purple face. The Sun Mel froze, shocked rigid.

"Sheriff!" shouted Nathan in sudden anger. Shouting made his head throb sickeningly, and Sam simply hunched his shoulders and refused to turn around.

Nathan tried to placate him. "We'll be all right, Sheriff, the air barque is waiting. My mother will slow the Yelkes down."

The Sun Mel stared after the headstrong siffile. How baffling they were—one minute they were saving your skin and the next behaving in the most disgraceful manner. He looked up and blinked in alarm.

The Yelkes were howling down the passage to the stables. Above their heads they waved knives, but when they entered the stables Avis hit them with a focused power

blast on the sixth level. They staggered, and many fell to
their knees. They dropped their weapons and gripped their
skulls — it was a shattering blow. A dozen or more had
been rendered unconscious.

The Sun Mel led the siffile past the groaning Yelkes.
They slipped down the corridor once more and retraced
their steps to the Hall of Antiquity.

Behind them the Yelkes slowly recovered. Some staggered to their feet.

Dumbly, they stared at the balaunt in the stables, covered with thick slime, entering the sexual frenzy. They
would be unusable for a balaast or more. The Yelkes
croaked in frustrated rage.

On the roof of the Hall of Antiquity, reached by a stair
attached like a fire escape to the outward wall, the air barque came to life with a sudden hum.

Inside the control section, Nathan pressed the button
that activated the long repellors. The ship lifted smoothly
into the air and rose thirty meters until it was above the
Red Tower.

With hoarse shouts of rage and dismay the Yelkes
crowded onto the roof to watch this act of sacrilege. They
waved their fists helplessly, ten meters away from the
smooth flat hull of the air barque.

Beneath the iulliin aircraft, the huge castle was spread
out like a map. The tiller turned the prow easily, there was
little wind, and Nathan put them on a heading inward, directly beneath the small pink sun, at the Sun Mel's suggestion.

"We shall go inward, to Fanthenai and Chalcinnre. You
will see the magic Lake Bleth."

Nathan eased up the throttle bar, and they moved off at
a stately twenty kilometers an hour, floating over the buildings and away.

Beneath them a network of gray pathways intersected on

smooth pink and green lawns. Ornamental trees broke up the lawns and lined the water canals.

Dagbabi were looking up, shielding their eyes with reptilian hands. The klicks ignored the air boat and continued their gardening work. Then they were out of the city.

Avis let out a gleeful "Horray!"

Ahead lay the first hills, crescent-shaped, covered by dark vegetation along their spines.

■ CHAPTER TWENTY-THREE

On the Aplanga Front the fighting intensified steadily, balaast by balaast, as the enemy crushers probed the lines. Out beyond the crushers and their attendant heavy robots, the pulverizer lurked, heavy batteries probing for sensitive parts of the rear.

Cracka Buckshore had seen his share of the hard stuff. He'd even become pretty skilled at that kind of soldiering. But some of the things he'd seen would never leave him, could never be forgotten, felt like they'd been engraved on his heart with a knife.

Stuff, rubble, mud, flew around in haphazard hail from the shelling.

The battle squad jumped low and hard, kangaroos-in-flight style. Heavy robots on their tails. Radio chatter crackled in their ears.

Cracka was third in line, Heggi in the lead as usual,

with the eerie Nuts-head behind her. They were both aces on shock boots, swerving and bounding through the complex rubble.

Blue-green tracer chopped through the smoke above their heads as they crossed the red stumps left by the building spars of a long-demolished skyscraper.

The shelling petered out. Aerial probes screamed across the sky.

They swerved and scattered, falling back into a line, and then they halted and turned after ten jumps.

Into the pocket thus created came the pursuit, a trio of three-legged, fifteen-meter-tall heavy robots, their green barrel torsos studded with machine guns, their tracer reaching for ghost targets.

Cracka hid low, crouched behind a mound of green ceramic wall material. The heavy robots swept along in an almost stately imitation of life. Two legs stretching out, the third drawn along after. The machine guns on the chest ports sputtered occasionally, probing rubble for lurking troopers. They crossed the line of red stumps.

A storm of grenade fire erupted around the robots. They strode on, wreathed in smoke, armor shields held down over the more delicate sensors.

Then the one on the left, nearest Cracka, suffered a grenade penetration of the chest center. Its processors shattered, it whirled off course, suddenly bereft of reason, a senseless giant, straight toward Cracka's position.

Just ten yards away it tripped over a mound of rubble and fell with a tremendous crash. The legs thrashed. Dust and shards flew high.

Out of the murk came the center robot. With one liquid lurch it drew up beside its fallen comrade. Sensors on the tip of a tentacle probe reached for the access ports. A small red inspection plate, placed almost like a bull's-eye, was located on the thing's mid chest—just above a gun port.

Cracka was so close he was sure he could put a grenade right through the center machine's central processor too.

Cracka's gun came up and he targeted the red square.

Before he could fire, though, the machine picked him up on its dorsal optical scanner. The machine gunports swiveled.

Instinctively Cracka broke right, leaping low between piles of green ceramic shards as blue-green tracer zipped overhead. The thing was right on his tail. The rubble ended up ahead on an open space. He had to shake the robot fast.

He ducked left, barreling up a gully between rubble mounds, praying it didn't turn into a box canyon. Cracka looked back—he'd gained on the robot, but he hadn't lost it. It was turning into the entrance now.

No way back.

He rounded a corner and stopped dead in horror. In front of him five weary troopers were helping a wounded comrade. They were out of their shock boots, helpless on the battlefield. At the sight of him they froze.

He flipped up his visor. "Scatter for your lives!"

The robot was too close. He spun about and raised the grenade gun. The robot rounded the curve. Its guns spattered, picking off the running figures.

Cracka fired, a burst of grenade shell that wreathed the thing in smoke and fragments for a few seconds. Then the guns retargeted on him and he was forced to dive right and crawl through a cavelike space beneath the shell of a building. It lost him, and he emerged on the far side and turned and found a vantage spot and brought his gun up.

The machine guns continued to chatter as the robot slid into view again. But there was a movement behind it—one trooper, running quickly underneath the robot and jumping onto the rear leg.

Turrets spun, but it was too late. The trooper turned the detonator on his chest and there was a heavy thud, a bright flash, and a thick ball of hot vapor. The robot's leg was smashed; the machine spun and collapsed.

Time passed. Long patrols, evading the heavy robots, sitting nursing the shakes and a drink in the dugout afterward. The grim oblivion of sleep.

Cracka waited to die. Everyone died in that mad warfare. They fought, or the yashi killed them. There was no likelihood of ever defeating the enemy. There was no reason to look forward, because only death waited there. Instead you drank booze and watched TV soaps and tried not to think.

Then one balaast, after a long, almost uneventful patrol, they headed back in and jumped past the enormous sculpted iulliin head, a remnant from a smashed statue, that still stood on its plinth at the front plaza of the truncated colossus.

"Gas shell coming," said Klazt, picking it up on the yashi wave band.

The gas was a dark brown, oily vapor that produced a slow, choking death in its victims as it burned away the mucous membranes in their lungs and throats. As a result, in bitter irony they called it "The Quiet Men."

They adjusted filters and checked breathing apparatus. Shells were bursting to their left, and clouds of the thick brown gas began to billow up, directly across their path. They eased back, slowed to loping in the fashion of the tyrannosaur, two meters from each leg, with a motion not unlike that of cross-country skiing.

The clouds swallowed them up.

They slowed in the murk, tyranno-loping carefully through gullies and narrow places. In time the gas cleared and the patrol came to an end. The fight-drug ampules attached to their temples were running low. Klazt picked up the clearance on the yashi net and turned them back into the lines.

They jumped for the dugouts and boot rechargers. The fight drug was waning fast, exhaustion taking over.

Over the radio net the battlemasters chattered in yashi growls and hisses as they shuffled patrol formations again.

The shock boots wound down to a bare, primal stutter in the narrow, reinforced trenches that fed the patrol into the dugouts.

Cracka felt the fight drug wearing off. Complete exhaustion loomed. Eight hours of jumping in shock boots, dueling with the heavy robots, dodging shells and V-wings. He was ready for the black sleep of the dugouts, dreamless, empty.

He pulled back his visor.

There were occasional siffile to be seen in the darkness of the deep tubes that went down to the dugouts. At one point they passed the black market, an intersection for three tubes that formed a convenient spot for sellers of alcohol, luxury food items, electronics, and drugs.

Siffile thronged the location, all engaged in completely forbidden activity. Battlemaster Klazt ignored it; without the siffile there could be no fulfillment of the prime directive. Siffile had to have access to such things or they could not be made to fight, no matter what the iulliin thought.

Cracka stumbled on, then stopped and blinked in amazement. Something was very familiar about a fellow selling alcohol in plastic bags made from the inflated innards of sleeping bags. Cracka stopped and stared. A transaction took place, stolen medical supplies, immune-booster capsules, in exchange for two bags of alcohol.

"Bat!" Cracka cried in a hoarse croak.

Maroon looked up, instinctively guilty.

Cracka roared at the sight. "Bat Maroon!"

Bat saw him and nearly fainted. "Ranger Buckshore, I don't believe it."

"Maroon, what unit are you in, which dugout?"

Bat shifted uneasily. His eyes picked out the form of Klazt. Then Klazt turned a corner. "That's a problem right now for us."

"Us?"

"Me and Shay, we were together in the spaceship, stacked up with some folks from the Prench Tronch lunatic asylum—little girls, old men. It was horrible, just horrible."

"What's the problem?"

Bat looked around uneasily. "If you don't mind, Cracka, I'd rather talk about it someplace else. The yashi bug this place."

"They do?" Cracka looked blankly at him. There was lots he didn't know about the black market, that was clear.

Bat pulled him down a narrow tube, took a right turn, and pulled out an oblong piece of green plastic that he inserted into a tiny cleft in the wall. A piece opened out. Behind it was a narrow passage, big enough for dagbabi maintenance workers but a tight fit for humans. Bat made Cracka go first, then pulled the narrow door shut behind him. Bat had a small portalite which he shone down the stark little passage.

"You mean Shay is in here?"

"Shay's hurt, Cracka. Something hit him on the helmet, knocked him right over—he crashed in full jump. He's been in a daze ever since. The yashi would have terminated him when he failed inspection, so I took Shay out and hid him. We been on the lam ever since."

"How the hell did you get him in here, though?"

"It was a tight squeeze, believe me." They came to a small room, filled with Bat's still and fermenters. Sacks of bokka in powder form were stacked against one wall. There was a strong smell of yeast and sour bokka. On a pallet, underneath a tarp, lay Shay Kroppa, eyes staring vacantly into space.

"Can he move?"

"Oh yeah, Shay's still mobile, but he can't talk. Believe me, I tried everything, I even gave him some fight drug in his water. Boy, *that* was a mistake."

Cracka crouched in front of his old friend. Shay took no notice. When Bat gave him a beaker half full of alcohol cut with distilled water, Shay's eyes focused suddenly. He sat up, grabbed the beaker, and downed it. Then he smiled broadly.

"Well, he still drinks like he used to," said Cracka.

"Yeah, but he don't respond. I got to get him out of here, but I don't know how. Or where to take him. I don't rightly know even where this *is*, do you?"

Cracka had to admit that he had only the haziest notion. ". . . The Aplanga Front, somewhere a few hours' flight by subsonic transport from the city."

"Meninrud Lors, that's the name of that city. I never seen buildings like that, so graceful and all."

Cracka studied Shay carefully. "Do you think he can ride shock boots?"

Bat shrugged and spread his hands.

"I dunno, but if he don't remember how, they'll rip him in half."

Bat mixed two more drinks and gave Cracka one.

"What would happen if we just took him out between us and jumped away from the battle front?" said Cracka after a sip.

"The yashi would kill us. They got a way of shorting the charge in the shock boots that blows them up. You take your boots, you die, that's what I was told."

Cracka nodded. Escape would not be so easy, then. He pondered it for a moment. "That key you stole, does it open any other doors?"

"Yeah, all the dagbab maintenance doors. And I didn't steal it, Ranger Buckshore. I won it fair and square."

"Of course, of course, Bat." Cracka felt the booze wash away some of the tenseness brought on by fight drug and eight hours of shock-boot maneuver. And Cracka felt a tremendous sense of remotivation. He realized he'd been drifting, just getting by day by day.

He'd avoided the squiggles on the tube, but he couldn't avoid fighting. Either you took the fight drug from Klazt and went out in the squad, or Klazt killed you. The yashi were armed to kill siffile, and extremely skilled, as well.

But he realized he hadn't thought about escape since the first psychoblast from the big screens in the induction center. Nor did he ever hear the Lemall's humans discuss escape. It never occurred to them.

Cracka realized that the iulliin psychoconditioning wasn't so completely unsuccessful after all, despite the booze and the brave talk.

Martherer Boan skipped quickly across the ruined place, where the Either corner of the outward wall had been blown off the building. She wore a set of clean, cut-down siffile fatigues. Her red hair, two inches long, was hidden beneath a kepi.

Over her shoulders she bore a pack laden with two bags of ice from the basement freezer. Satisfying Lady Weanda's demand for ice packs to cool her throbbing temples quickly overstretched the modest freeze box in her suite. Living with Lady Weanda in Meninrud Lors had meant many such trips up and down the emergency staircase. But Martherer didn't mind. Lady Weanda had saved her.

The building resembled a tuning fork two hundred meters tall, the tines pointed skyward. Lady Weanda's rooms were one hundred meters up, in the Either tine, which had been broken off near its top and now ended in a jagged rip of torn beeble and dirty yellow weft. Even thus it had done better than the Or tine, which had been blown off the tuning fork altogether and lay like a gigantic fallen tree amid the orchards. Under the sun, thick clouds of bees floated over it.

After the bombing, most of the building's inhabitants had abandoned it, but not Lady Weanda. She was passionate about retaining her apartments, in which she had lived for many, many zeem. In particular she was in love with the marvelous view to Either and inward, where in the distance the great buildings of the city center thrust up their spires.

She would not leave. She was the Heads-in-the-Sand Party personified. Only death from the Xaacan monstrosity could sunder her from her beloved city.

Of course, Lady Weanda didn't concern herself with mundane matters like elevators and the electric supply. She was intent on her mission, and besides, she had her siffile now, and mundane things were the sort of things siffile were so good at.

For Lady Weanda was needed on the board for the greater game, the game of power, where survival itself was at stake. There she jousted with the highest in the Sun Clanth. The game required all her strength, all her concentration, for to lose meant death. So Lady Weanda never used the elevator. She went everywhere by aircar. She had never used the stairs.

Instead she sent her siffile to the ground to bring up ice for her head and fresh supplies of the black fungi she boiled down to make the powerful psychotropic drug called *the Rooms*, which was very popular among Lady Weanda's clientele.

Siffile were good for such errands. Yashi were too narrow and stupid to make good servants. Dagbabi were reptilian, and their body smell was offensive. Istyggi were out

of the question. Siffile were perfect. It was part of Lady
Weanda's mission to bring back the pleasures in life for the
iulliin who stuck it out in poor old battered Meninrud Lors.

Lady Weanda currently personified the "recalcitrants" in
the Heads-in-the-Sand Party, which, in name at least, was
the ruling group in Meninrud Lors.

There was no formal legislative chamber in the city;
instead, a form of direct democracy existed in which all
able-minded iulliin cast votes for elected executives. Mem-
bership in political clubs and parties was the lifeblood of
society.

One plank in the Heads-in-the-Sand Party's new mani-
festo called for the reprivatization of siffile. With the ad-
vent of fresh, unexpected supplies of siffile, it was
important to let all iulliin select at least one for their personal service. And in the meantime, a breeding program
was to be instituted so that the siffile numbers could be
boosted faster.

This was all a direct challenge to the high military. The
high military, secret "Realists" all, were nervous and prone
to harsh reaction.

Martherer reached the place where a hole three meters
wide had been blown through the building. Nearby, a door
led to the exterior stair that spiraled up the outward face of
the stump of the tuning fork.

She paused for a moment and set down her pack. There
were twenty flights of stairs to Lady Weanda's floor from
here. She slipped through the shattered hole in the wall and
entered the abandoned apartments within. It was a good
spot to take a breather.

As she had done many times before since she'd first
discovered it, she threaded her way through the ruined
rooms, past the shattered grandeur of iulliin nobility, until
she reached the room on the inward face with great slit
windows ten meters high that let in a spray of rainbows.

On one enormous wall was a mural, in superrealist style, five meters high and wide. It was a piece of wild technical virtuosity. At the bottom was a canal, photographically pure, surrounded by green forest. Bees roamed the lower air, airfish dominated above, and halfway up were the hunters, iulliin youths, astride airfish the size of whales. The youths wielded deadly harpoons against the glittering silver airfish called *wita* in Iullas.

Siffile were riding beside their iulliin masters, supplying fresh harpoons, holding lines, wielding nets to snatch wounded wita from the sky.

The painting was protected beneath a layer of a very tough, clear varnish of some kind. The pigments seemed almost to float underneath this layer, a trick of the eye that Martherer found irresistible. The style was so like that of Renaissance Italy, with hints of Michelangelo, Rafael, even Da Vinci, that Martherer was convinced that it had been painted by a human hand. It was a flash of human brilliance, a vibrant snapshot almost, that stood out in the dying background of Meninrud Lors.

She drank in the painting once again, the huge airfish, the *pungas*, with complicated bridling and saddles for three riders, their eyes like blue-black tank turrets, swiveling this way and that.

The wita flew in flocks, creatures the size of large terrestrial birds, sheathed in silver scales. Their eyes were like blue gems, their blood ran in scarlet rills, drips spattering down the sky mural to the bees below.

After a minute or so she turned away from the painting and looked out the door to the shattered balcony, to the view inward, across to the great buildings floating in the haze.

Her eye roamed over the parkland, the pink lawns dotted with statues on a heroic scale among clumps of dark trees. In the middle distance were some residential towers:

more tuning forks in ruddy brown ceramic, a beautiful spiral tower of translucent green, and a building like a giant figure eight standing on end. The top circle had been shattered, however, leaving just a pair of curving horns behind.

Farther away were larger buildings, the behemoths of the city center, clustering together in a mass of towers, spirals, and bulbs where all the ground was in permanent shadow.

Martherer had been there many times, flying beside Lady Weanda on her missions. Carrying the pot of freshly brewed brown jelly for the addicts of *the Rooms*.

In the central districts, where the tallest buildings jostled close, the air traffic was still dense enough to warrant policing. And the automatic system still worked, guiding aircars into lanes and directing them between the blank walls of tower and spire.

Lady Weanda flew to seance with corporate groups and financiers that trembled at the brink of "Realism." She flew to counsel the major lenders, the landed family heads, the high-ups in the Heads-in-the-Sand Party.

Martherer recalled some of the fantastic buildings they had visited, towers a thousand meters high, structures resembling enormous vases filled with tulips, others that were spherical and the size of small mountains.

Martherer had drifted into reverie. She woke up with a start. She was wasting time, and Lady Weanda's head would be throbbing. Being Lady Weanda's personal servant was tiresome, but it was better than returning to the crab tanks. She ran back to her pack, got it over her shoulders, and started climbing the exterior rail, in the darkness of outward. Above she heard the shrill wail of Lady Weanda's whistle. She hurried up the steps, her breath coming in harsh gasps.

Way below, through the grating, she could see the gray

domes of the city of the istyggi clustered in the shadow. As
she turned to outward she glanced out at the orchard lying
to the Either side of the shadow. She knew it well, for she
picked yellow moomb fruit there for Lady Weanda.

The whistle wailed again, insistently. With a soft groan,
Martherer resumed climbing; Lady Weanda was already
vexed.

■ CHAPTER TWENTY-FOUR

The air barque rode four hundred meters above the hills
and plains of central Planggi at a stately fifty kilometers an
hour, heading inward to the tower of Fanthenai.

On the poop deck, above the control room, Nathan was
in deep conversation with the Sun Mel, questioning him, as
always. Where was such and such? What did it do? Why?

There had been many revelations since the air barque
first flew away from Planggi.

The first had been that the Sun Mel knew virtually nothing of the ship's technology. In an attempt to increase
speed, Nathan had tried the controls, then he'd investigated
the engineering deck down below.

In a long, low space smelling faintly of machine oil,
he'd discovered an array of coffin-shaped modules surrounding a larger cube, nested in tubes and wires that
hummed faintly. He assumed it contained a small fusion
reactor of some kind. The whole thing was elegant, simple,
and clearly the product of a very high order of civilization.

But the Sun Mel had never before seen the air barque. To him it was a legendary thing, locked away by the Yelkes hundreds of zeem before.

But the biggest surprise had come soon afterward, when the barque floated over the first of an endless pattern of croissant-shaped hills, each between one and two hundred meters high and five hundred meters from tip to tip along the horns.

"Shazzeul, why are these things down there all shaped the same?"

The iulliin glanced down. "These are Eaters of Zeit. All mature specimens. There are smaller ones, of course."

Nathan knew that *zeit* was the term for grasslike plants, usually with a pink and green coloration. "If Eaters of Zeit, then alive?"

"Yes, yes of course. Everything is alive in the Sun Clanth."

Nathan stared at the "hills." Each was crested with what looked like dark pine forests.

"Then the dark lines that emerge from the Eaters of Zeit are?"

"Dung!" The Sun Mel smiled. He was in love with his wonderful siffile. "Eaters of Zeit crop the forest, make good dung for the soil. The Eaters also make good hosts for the little airfish. Eaters are very good, very useful."

And Nathan had turned stunned eyes back to the Eaters, which crowded to the distant haze of gold like a huge pack of gigantic dark green seals.

Several balaast went by. The air barque made steady progress through skies filled with clouds of every description, from golden feathery cirrus in the house of the sun, to massed gray stratus that moved on the cusp of warm fronts and left endless drizzle behind. In between were the unique clouds, the small pink spheres that scudded against the wind, and the gray torpedo clouds that often pursued the pink spheres.

Most impressive of all was the reef cloud, a colossal bank of green and gray that they first sighted on the second balaast and which only finally dropped away from view behind them on the fourth balaast.

They ran low on water. Nathan simply brought the air barque down to hover over a wide canal and they leaned down and refilled the tanks with a bucket from the galley. The water was clear and, according to the Sun Mel, perfectly safe to drink.

The food they had brought began to run low as well. Nathan questioned the Sun Mel on what, if anything, the humans could eat in this alien landscape.

Food was something that the Sun Mel knew something about. "Hoppers and crawlers may be fed to the siffile, for they are initially of the air. But best for siffile are planna pods and airfish flesh, those airfish that are of the air and live in the air." He gave them a big smile. "But best of all is wita! Good plump wita! That is the best airfish of all."

By this they were reassured that at least they might not starve. On the other hand, Folo wasn't certain they could catch airfish with the weapons they had at hand, the broken Spear of the Sun and the heavy Sword of the Meldom. A search of the barque turned up no nets or other weaponry.

"Of course we have the helmets," said Nathan.

Folo laughed. "So we going to order them to land on the deck here?"

Nathan laughed too. "Maybe. Who knows until we've tried it?"

"Well, Nathan, maybe you right, you normally is, but for now all I see is the sword, the spear, and the energy weapon."

"Which only fired once."

"And no nets."

Avis decided to take stock of their food supply, dried pancakelike curds of bokka, and a reddish, waxy concentrate of boltak that tasted vaguely of bananas. She went down the internal stairs to the tiny galley and found the food almost gone—someone had severely depleted the supply.

At the bow, snugged down against a winch, she found Sam Boan, his arms filled with raw bokka, his mouth chewing frenziedly, flecks of spittle flying into the air.

"Sheriff!"

Boan turned her a malevolent stare; there was madness in it. "Mine!" he snarled through a mouthful of bokka.

Nathan and Folo joined Avis at once.

The sheriff was utterly intransigent. He would not stop eating the bokka or return what he had taken.

"His mind's gone," said Folo.

"I think you're right," said Nathan.

"Now, boys, hold on a second, we can't have violence here."

"Mother! If we don't stop him he's going to eat our entire stock of food. He's gone crazy, it's quite obvious."

Rilla Boan emerged from the rear cabin where she'd been napping. At the sight of her brother she gave a scream of rage.

"Oh, that fat bastard!" she cried, and she flew at Sam with nails and fists and drove him from his safe place back onto the deck.

Avis turned a wondering look to Nathan and Folo.

On the deck Sam suddenly burst into tears and sat down and dropped the armfuls of purloined bokka to the deck.

Nathan and Folo carefully collected it and put it back in the tiny galley below decks. After counting the remainder out they found they had bokka enough for three more meals.

"We have to keep watch on him now," said Folo.

Nathan nodded gloomy agreement.

They returned to the deck. Rilla continued to chastise her older brother, who wept bitterly.

Nathan and Folo considered the weapons.

"We need to catch something, that's for sure," Nathan said.

On several occasions they had spied clouds of airfish. Some passed close to the air barque. One cloud had been enormous, a great spherical mass of small pink-winged creatures with immense eyes and silver bodies. The cloud had been pursued by flocks of bigger airfish, creatures the size of a man, with immense wingspreads, dive-bombing with folded wings into the heart of a cloud, then opening gaping, elastic mouths and sucking in the smaller forms.

And one day Avis Prench glimpsed the ultimate. She and Folo were dozing peacefully under the sun when something loud flapped in ther air like a wet blanket. She opened her eyes on a creature as large as the air barque itself, with a wingspan in excess of thirty meters, flying just ahead of them, paralleling their course. Her shriek awoke Folo, who glimpsed an enormous shape and bolted upright, hands grabbing for the spear.

For a moment, a big blunt head, with black eyes set in deep seamed pouches, hung over the deck, and then it was gone, lost among the clouds.

"The great punga! The wild lord of the skies! You are fortunate to have seen such a one," said the Sun Mel when they told him.

Avis didn't stop shaking for hours and wouldn't sit out on the deck again for even longer.

But despite all this activity in the air around them they had not come within a kilometer of killing anything they might eat.

The air barque sailed on, passing into a region of heavy rain clouds. Nathan extended the repulsion fields to the maximum and they rose above the clouds. However, with such extension of the repulsion fields, the propulsion fields were weakened and they were slowed to a mere ten to fifteen kilometers an hour forward progress. Eventually Nathan took the barque down through the cloud, into the dark and the rain, and they picked up speed again. After an hour or so they emerged from the clouds into the sunshine, the deck dried, and they continued as before, heading inward to Fanthenai.

They were down to their last meal apiece when the Sun Mel spied the herd of hoppers. "Look! Look!" he cried and pointed to the right-hand side. "Hopper is good for siffile, and iulliin can eat it too!"

Nathan turned the air barque in the direction of the hoppers, which covered a green-and-pink valley with their black, darting forms.

The air barque swung down over the herd. There were hundreds of the creatures, three to five feet long, black and glossy, with six white and yellow striped legs apiece. They moved in leaps, covering two or three yards with each bound. Their heads were distinctly insectal in appearance; the bodies were like glistening barrels; the legs were long and powerful, kicking out strongly behind.

At the approach of the air barque, the hoppers jumped away in stampede. However, the air barque kept pace quite easily.

Folo considered the problem. They had the fragmented Spear of the Sun, which, if brought to bear would surely do the job. Folo had tied a loop of the pink rope around the spear's broken haft, where he'd cut a groove for it to grip.

Still, the spear was an awkward weapon to throw, unbalanced as it was. The best thing would be to get close to a hopper and stab it, then haul it in with the rope. However, when they brought the air barque down low over the herd, the hoppers sprang away with considerable speed and agility. The task was obviously not going to be easy.

Then they spotted a hopper that had slowed and dropped behind the rest. Abruptly it came to a halt, unable to hop farther.

Nathan brought the barque down until it hovered just above the pinkish-green zeit. Folo sprang after the hopper. It turned to face him, regarding him with big, multifaceted eyes. Antennas waved slowly. It was as big as a man, with six muscular legs. Thick mucus dripped from its mouthparts.

Folo circled. The hopper turned to face him.

Avis jumped down and went to help. When she arrived, the hopper turned to face her and Folo jumped closer, thrusting the spear into the hopper's side. It penetrated easily, sinking in a full foot. The hopper emitted a queer groan and a spray of white fluids before leaping away in the death throes, jerking Folo off his feet and dragging him behind it.

Avis ran on behind him. Nathan jumped down and sprinted after them, praying that Folo hadn't been hurt. The hopper stopped after fifty feet, however, and collapsed, legs twitching briefly before the end.

Folo got wearily to his feet and brushed off bits of zeit. He was covered with the strong-smelling juices of the hopper, and had taken a few scrapes and bumps, but a careful inspection revealed no broken bones.

Avis kissed him lightly in relief. "Thank goodness you're not hurt."

Their eyes met for a minute. Then he ducked his head a little. "I ain't hurt, ma'am, I'm okay. Let's see to this hopper we caught now."

They approached the dead hopper. It was still leaking whitish fluid, but otherwise all was still. The eyes that had been so glossy were now dull. A big, wobbly insect flew past and landed on the hopper's belly. It had a brown and black striped body as big as a man's thumb. It crawled around on the dead hopper for a moment, then flew away again.

Nathan ran up with the sword. Folo took it and hacked

off the creature's six large legs, the only parts the Sun Mel was sure were edible for siffile. It was hard work until Folo learned the pattern of tendons and joints, whereupon he removed the remainder with little extra effort. "Papa Sly taught me to chop a tronch calf when I were eight." Folo's white teeth flashed. The hopper's juices splashed.

A dozen of the fat wobbly insects, the size of the biggest tronch flies, or terrestrial bumblebees, were on the hopper carcass now. Nathan bent to investigate. The "bees" were equipped with shockingly large, heavy mandibles. They were biting through the hopper skin and then attacking the flesh underneath. "These are carrion eaters," he said in some dismay.

He looked up. A lot more bees were approaching. He felt a sudden surge of apprehension.

"I think we'd better try and get these legs back to the barque. A lot of these insects are approaching, and I would say they are definitely carnivorous."

Avis looked up and gave a little scream. A cloud of the insects was descending on the scene. The air was suddenly full of their buzzing.

They each grabbed as much as they could carry. Folo and Nathan began with two each, Avis brought one, and one they left behind for the bees, which now covered the carcass. Bees were also landing on the legs they carried, and on the people carrying them. All were bitten indiscriminately as the aroused bees sought nourishment. The bites were painful. Sharp mandibles dug into their skins, began sawing at their flesh.

Nathan, Folo, and Avis screamed and ran vigorously toward the air barque. Nathan shed one hopper limb that had dozens of bees already on it and, with just one, was able to make better time. Folo too was finally forced to drop one, and Avis gave up hers and ran screaming with frantic waving hands.

At last they reached the air barque and clambered up the stairs to the deck. Nathan hit the controls and took the barque straight up on the repeller fields.

The bees diminished quickly in numbers, and after a minute or so the last few were being swatted to death with an iulliin cape wielded by Folo and Avis, who both sported red welts on face and arms.

Nathan slowed their ascent when they were a hundred meters above the surface once more. He was shuddering. The skin on his neck and face burned from the bites. Down below, the hopper carcass was a writhing mass of bees. Dark streams of the insects were approaching from several directions.

"Whew! Those little bastards can bite!" said Folo with a bitter grimace. His arm was marked with a dozen big red puffs.

Nathan grimaced and shook. "I'll say. Talk about ruining the barbecue!"

Sam and Rilla appeared from inside the cabin. Glumly they looked over the two hopper legs, each a meter long and powerfully muscled, that had been brought aboard.

White viscous juice dripped onto the deck.

"How are we supposed to eat this?" complained Sam.

"It looks absolutely horrible," said Rilla.

Avis contemplated the hopper legs. The skin was glossy and thick; the meat was pale, pale pink; the veins ran white. The overall appearance was alien and distinctly unappetizing.

The Sun Mel advised them to roast the legs. And they decided to try the unit in the galley that seemed to be a microwave oven, sitting next to the chiller.

They hacked one of the legs in half and thrust it into the oven apparatus. Nathan fiddled with the controls and a green light winked on. After a minute it went red, and after a few more it began to blink.

Nathan opened the door of the oven.

The heavenly smell of roast hopper broke into the crowded galley. They carved it with the sword and ate it in slices. It was delicious, like roast pork, or rabbit, or tronch chicken—everyone had a different opinion. Sam Boan became distinctly affable.

They slept. The air barque flew on, steadily riding inward.

■ CHAPTER TWENTY-FIVE

The room was hot. The bed felt smooth as cream beneath them. Martherer's eyes were wide, dreamy under the influence of the drug. Above her loomed the Lady Weanda, naked, aflame with desire. The space between their alien bodies vanished.

Later: Lady Weanda writhed under the sheet as Martherer worked the dildo against the little crest of sexually active tissue. So like the human and yet so different. The first time she had done this, it had seemed so terribly strange. Now?

Another time: They examined each other with an emerald light wand and much gleeful laughter. They drank from the same blue cup, Martherer floating on the euphoria.

Lady Weanda possessed a rather sophisticated, even decadent sense of humor. Martherer had never thought of herself as sheltered, but she'd never imagined such a weird level of raunch. Lady Weanda was obsessed, obsessed with many things. Lady Weanda's big golden eyes would widen so. Her long nose would twitch, she would whisper another bizarre joke about impotent iulliin males, cuckolding siffile, and filthy-minded iulliin females.

Those times were good times for Martherer. They helped her forget. At other times Martherer would find herself standing out on the balcony with tears streaming down her cheeks as she stared into the dim distance.

Where could Folo be? Out there somewhere, in this inexplicable place that she did not understand. Was he all right? Was her love unharmed? Or was Folo hurt? Dying? There was no way of knowing, and that too tore at her heart. Indeed the ultimate question, too, had no answer. How was she ever going to find him?

The sun never sets. There is no horizon. Fish fly.

She might never see Folo again, never touch his dear face, never kiss those lips. Her heart felt as if it might fall out of her chest and shatter on the ground below.

It wouldn't be so bad, she told herself, if only she had some idea where she was. All this, this terrible, dying world. But all her questions met baffling replies from Lady Weanda. Thus she had learned that she, like all siffile, had been "rescued" from the wild "outer galaxy." She was *safe* now, in the Sun Clanth of the iulliin. "Safe" didn't seem to include what Martherer had seen at the battle front. But that was an area she tried not to think about.

And what was a Sun Clanth? Some kind of enormous space habitat? That would explain why the sun never set, and Lady Weanda seemed to agree. Planets to her were wild, dangerous places, far away in space and time. Night was an archaicism. In Iullas the word for night had come to mean naughty, mischievous, inherently sexy. The concept of dark had moved into shadow, as from the permanent, golden sun.

But if "here" was a space habitat, it had been built on a scale beyond anything Martherer had ever heard of.

Lady Weanda did provide her with one tantalizing clue concerning the other humans, the "true siffile," the ones who spoke Iullas as if they were iulliin.

Martherer had met some of those. Strange people, unfriendly, dispassionate, almost as alien as the iulliin themselves. But Lady Weanda once called them the "Lemall's siffile," and Martherer recalled the infamous lost colony of Lemall's World. So, it was clear, whatever had happened to Lemall's World had happened to Calabel, too.

Martherer remembered only the gas, and then waking up in that horrible place, completely unable to move. For days she had lain there. There had been terrible pain at least twice. And then there had been the food and the induction sequence in the great hall. Martherer had assumed she had taken a great space journey. She feared that she was unlikely to ever see her homeworld again.

She did her best not to think about the rest, about the crab tanks or the battle or the running.

Folo? Where was he? Had he been lost in the war?

She clenched her fists, the nails digging into her palms. If he lived, *if*, then she would find him somehow. All that mattered until then was that she survive. On the whims of Lady Weanda, with her alien violet eyes and iulliin whisper. Survival was all that counted.

Lady Weanda poured more of the wine, dosed lightly with *the Rooms*. The goblets were shaped like lilies, in pink glass with sexually active figures, siffile and iulliin, locked together in relief around the bowl.

Lady Weanda's stock of rude jokes was inexhaustible. But always the siffile males cuckolded the effeminate iulliin while the siffile females went to bed with anyone who asked.

Again: Martherer gripped the bars of the bed and wailed with pleasure as Lady Weanda rode the dildo into her. Lady Weanda wore a black silk gown, a veil, wrapped up as a figure of mystery. The dildo seemed to explode inside her. Martherer gave herself up to a tide of ecstasy.

Lady Weanda knew just where to touch, where to kiss, where to lick. She had had many siffile lovers. Together they read poems from the past—siffile lovers writing to iulliin patrons, iulliin lovers writing to siffile slaves . . .

Unwittingly, of course, Weanda also exposed the curse of the iulliin worlds. The mad dulocracy where love-enriched slaves had virtually ruled their iulliin masters. Such conflict, such jealousy, such killing there had been, all over the pretty siffile!

When Lady Weanda slept, Martherer slept with her, cradling Her Ladyship's head in her lap, stroking her throbbing temples for long hours before sleep finally claimed her.

It began when Weanda found the girl weeping for the lost love "Folo." Weanda comforted her as she sobbed for the desperation of her life and the doom of love for Folo. Weanda could do little, in fact. She had already made a computer search for the boy, using a memory-mapped picture Martherer made on the computer screen.

A great many handsome young troncher youths appeared from the new files. All with that characteristic tan, the level eyes. But no sign of Folo. Lady Weanda was genuinely disappointed; she had been looking forward to Folo.

In the course of the search, however, Lady Weanda had learned of an incident in which a small scout vessel crewed by rebellious siffile had broken away from the mother ship. The errant scout vessel had touched down at a little-known Sun Clanth called Planggi, a backward place that had been out of communication with the rest of the iulliin for aeons.

A check on the scout vessel had revealed that it was still sitting on the landing field at Planggi City. The airlock was open, and the siffile were gone. All attempts to contact the

Planggi authorities had met with failure. A visual check by
the computer's optical systems had revealed an overgrown
spaceport and a near silent city. Occasional iulliin in red
robes were observed lighting small fires of wood piled in
front of the ship. They sang long, slow songs full of reverence for their ancestors. They did not inspect the ship or
even enter the airlock while it was open, sending dagbabi
instead to investigate.

The siffile had to be presumed lost, either in the vacuum
of space or, quite probably, in the society of the downfallen
iulliin of Planggi. The tragedy touched Lady Weanda. Her
sweet little siffile's love was either lost to the vacuum of
space or, if alive, in another Sun Clanth entirely—in
which case he might as well be dead for poor Martherer,
for they would never meet again.

These days travel between the clanths was rare. The
great ships were few, and most clanths had suffered technological regression. Few could afford the enormous cost of
fueling one of the fusion-drive ships. Even Meninrud Lors
was struggling to refuel the mother ship and send it away
once more.

And the enemy advanced on Meninrud Lors itself. The
ship had to be fueled and ready before the crushers came.

In fact, Lady Weanda was one of the few in Meninrud
Lors who knew how far they had degenerated. Even there,
in the center of the once great clanth of Meninrud, they
could barely keep the hydrogen separation plant in operation. No one except her brother, Rukbhat dal Vnego, understood the programming of the artificial intelligence.
Without Rukbhat they would have been unable even to
process the new armies of siffile.

Indeed they had very little communication left within
the clanth, let alone with the outside. The only regular
contact was with Ladiganna, on the Either side of Meninrud Lors. The Ladiganna awaited the onslaught from

Xaaca; anxiously they monitored the disastrous war in Meninrud Lors.

Folo was now an impossibility. Weanda cradled the girl's head and held her close for a long time. In truth Weanda was very taken with her—she was beautiful, more so than any Weanda had owned before. She had listened patiently as the girl sobbed the bitter tears of one who is lost forever from love.

The girl was tender, delicious, an absolute treasure.

Lady Weanda expertly seduced her and took her to bed.

Aboard the air barque the balaast and the kilometers fell steadily behind. By Nathan's count it had been twenty balaast since they left Planggi Castle. He estimated their average speed at thirty kilometers an hour and the distance covered therefore at more than 28,000 kilometers.

They were all stunned by the distance. Time had been flowing past them in a dreamlike way.

Folo spoke first.

"We come a long way, and it all be the same, Nathan—hills, or eaters, and canals, and trees and zeit. It be the same everywhere like this?"

"I don't know, Folo."

"What the Sun Mel say?"

"He doesn't know either. You heard him."

"Yeah, but I still don't understand him as well as you do."

"He said there were places with no forest and just zeit, and places where there were few zeit eaters and the forest had grown wild. I don't exactly know what he means by that, of course."

"But no mountains or nothing."

"No mountains anywhere in this whole universe, Folo. There's no geology to speak of. This whole scene is biosphere. The iulliin designed these creatures to create the climate, to produce rain, and to soak that rain right up. All these aerial forms of life help circulate immense amounts of water and soil up into the atmosphere. They build reef clouds. But there's no mountains, no elevation at all except for things like buildings."

"And the eaters."

"And the eaters."

They were stripping down a hopper carcass after a successful hunt. Again they'd chased a herd until a weak hopper slowed down and they closed in for the kill. But now they brought the air barque close to the hopper before killing it, and instead of waiting for the bees to discover it, they dragged the whole thing aboard and lifted quickly to a great height on the repellers.

First they removed the legs, a task that Folo and Nathan had reduced to a fine art. They cut them down into haunches to fit the freeze box and the little microwave oven. Then, for the Sun Mel, they opened the hopper's body cavity, kicked aside the squirming airfish larvae that parasitized the hopper, and dug out the heart, a black globe that still pulsed slowly. To the iulliin this was the best piece in a hopper carcass.

The larvae in this hopper were big and fat, good reason for its weakness in the chase. Nathan helped Avis sweep the things onto a leaf from a hand palm that they used as a shovel, and then threw them overboard.

Out of curiosity Nathan split the head open and investigated the contents. A nerve ganglion the size of a walnut occupied the central space. The eyes and optic apparatus were large and well developed. He began to dig them out.

"Nathan!" said Avis. "Please! It's hard enough eating these things as it is."

"Sorry," he mumbled, then helped Folo dispose of the rest of the dead hopper over the side. It would soon be scavenged down to the skeletal structure, which itself would be gnawed by airfish until mere crumbs remained. A leg joint was thrust into the roaster.

Avis sat down again beside the Sun Mel, who had removed a layer of his robing to set upon the deck as a tablecloth and wore just his pale orange tunic and leggings. He shucked planna pods with long, dexterous fingers. Avis found them fascinating. She was nowhere near as good as the royal scion of Planggi, who had certainly never shucked a pod before the voyage. She was sure he would've been a wonderful pianist if the iulliin had had pianos.

The Sun Mel shook his head, however, at her slightly clumsy attempts to describe a piano in Iullas. The iulliin had abandoned the playing of instruments long before. Only recently had the Yelkes revived the practice. Once, the iulliin had relied on small machines for music, but the machines had been taken away by the Yelkes and locked up in the Hall of Antiquity. For a long time there had been only the music of the Yelkes.

But the Sun Mel knew which planna pods to pick. Planna grew three to four feet high, throwing up pods that resembled bulrushes. The ripe ones had a small purple spike jutting up from the crest. When split open the pods gave up a soft pink bean that was both edible and nutritious. The Sun Mel was sure that simply with planna pods and hopper meat they could live well. The Sun Mel was rather enjoying the voyage. Every balaast they took the air barque down to the side of a canal and they all bathed and refilled the water tanks if necessary.

The siffile were impatient, however. "Are we ever going to get to Fanthenai, Your Excellency?"

The Sun Mel chuckled. "Of course, Avis. We are going in the right direction, and so we must find it."

"But this land is so empty. If we miss it we could go on forever."

Shazzeul laughed, showing the yellowed teeth. "Not

even the Sun Clanth goes on forever, Avis, mother of the favorite boy."

And it was Avis's turn to laugh. The Sun Mel had changed so much. It was difficult to remember the stern figure who had made them kneel for hours when they first arrived at Planggi.

A heavy tread behind her caused her to turn. She frowned. Sam Boan stood waiting, salivating. He had kicked off his boots and socks; the seams of his shirt had burst; his beard was thick and scraggly. Although Sam refused to help in hunting or food preparation he was the biggest eater of them all.

As the interminable voyage continued, flying over the endlessly monotonous landscape of green hills, silver water, pink and green vegetation, Sam had fallen into a savage melancholy. He was surly to all. His complaints were increasingly irrational.

Avis tried to break through the barriers, but since the incident with the supply of bokka, Sam had refused her attempts at communication.

"Hello, Sheriff," she said with a cool smile.

Sam hunched and looked away.

"Sam!" Avis's voice grew tight. "You needn't be this way if you don't want to. I mean, I think we've all had enough of your being boring."

Sam swung her a malevolent look. "It's your fault we're here," he snarled thickly. "You and your damn kids!"

Avis shuddered. Something was wrong in Sam's eyes. Something broken and ugly.

Nathan had heard and he jumped up. "That's not true!"

"Don't tell me what's not true!" Sam exploded.

Nathan rushed forward. He weighed but half of what the sheriff did and stood no taller than the stout Boan. Without thinking he squared off against the sheriff.

Sam raised a fist and roared, "You damn puppy!"

Nathan ducked. Sam swung and almost hit Avis. Nathan backed away. Sam charged forward.

"Stop this!" screamed Avis.

Sam swung again, driving Nathan to the rail.

Folo surged in, grabbed Sam, and hurled him back. "Cool down, Sheriff, you getting to be a problem."

Sam surged up. "You damn troncher pig! You dare to manhandle the sheriff of Prench Tronch?" Sam was purple in the face; his hands clenched and unclenched. But Folo simply held his ground. The sheriff knew he was out-matched. He hissed through his teeth and turned his back.

Nathan would have continued the argument, but Avis hushed him.

Sam went down to the bow rail and stood there alone.

Rilla Boan had appeared from a nap in the cool dimness of the observation deck. "Nathan, I don't think there's any point bothering my brother."

"But he's wrong, and we're all getting tired of hearing him complain. It's not our fault we're here. The alien robots kidnapped the whole planet. You were on the ship, you saw how many people they had."

Rilla dismissed this with a curt gesture. "My brother is not the most reasonable of men, Nathan."

Avis and Nathan went down to the galley and brought back the roasted haunch of hopper. Folo began to carve big slices for everyone. In place of plates they used sections from a hand-palm leaf.

Sam came forward and took two slices and a pile of pods and went off by himself.

Rilla ate sparingly. She found the hopper meat vaguely disgusting, but while eating she sat beside Avis and dis-cussed Sam. "I'm worried, Avis. He's capable of anything when he gets like this."

"What can we do?"

"I don't know, Avis—pitch him overboard perhaps?" They exchanged looks.

Avis chuckled. "No, I'm serious. Sam's killed people before this, you know."

And Avis thought briefly of her dead husband, Cathete. Rumor said Sam Boan had killed him, but nothing had ever been proved. Poor Cathete! His body had been found floating in a vat of swine excrement. He'd drowned in it. "Well, we'd better discuss this with Folo and Nathan."

Rilla's eyebrows rose. "Aren't you being a little overdramatic, Avis? Sam's crazy, we're agreed, but Folo and Nathan are mere boys. You and I are clearly the ones in charge of this boat. By seniority, of course."

Avis was forced to laugh. Rilla was just bizarre. "Wouldn't the Sun Mel be in charge if we went by seniority? He's more than six hundred years old, if Nathan's correct."

Rilla snorted and looked away. It was no use. Avis Prench was just unreasonable, always had been. They had never gotten along.

Folo looked up from the thick slice of hopper meat he was devouring. "Look!" he shouted.

They all turned and looked past the bow. Far in the distance, a dark needle had solidified out of the golden haze.

"What's that?" Avis cried.

"That is Fanthenai," said the Sun Mel with a smile.

■ CHAPTER TWENTY-SIX

Lady Weanda rode in the front seat of the little oval aircar. She was ablaze with an inner excitement. Great events were in the making. To match her mood she wore the heroic dress expected of a power in the Heads-in-the-Sand

Party, including a helmet with visor and neck plate in the style of ancient myth. Fake armor plates of golden beepane were strapped across her blouse of deep blue froquade. Below this she wore stout pantaloons in the same froquade, with velveteen ribbons of scarlet and gold. On her feet were her most martial bootees, in red hopper hide with silver bells.

The aircar's belvedere was elaborately carved in copper-colored beesqueeze. Heroic iulliin figures held up the four corners, while vines and airfish were entwined across the roof. There was one large, round, white headlamp on the front and a similar light, but green, on the back. In the socket for heraldic devices, to the left of the headlamp, flew a blue and green pennon, the device of the House of Urtisim.

Behind her, wrapped in a dark hooded robe, was her faithful siffile, cradling a heavy brown pot of *the Rooms*.

The aircar swerved into the filter lane, heading in on the main airpath to the heart of the city.

The airpath there was a kilometer wide. Air traffic filled both sides with dozens of small lights—white for oncoming, green for receding.

On either side were arrayed the largest buildings of the city, blocks a kilometer high, glittering with lights. There was displayed the range of the fantastic in iulliin architecture, exploiting the great strength and lightness of their fabulous plastics and polymers.

Between the great towers lay inky darkness, broken by electric lights in warm yellows, reds, and pinks. The white and green of aircars roved up and down.

Great gloomy onion domes reared above. Soaring spires confronted them from the other side. Cruciforms bulged over tuning forks. And, shockingly, there were buildings that had been heavily damaged. Fires had blackened the upper floors. Lights were fitful. Great holes gaped like pits of blackness in the shining polymerized surfaces. The aircar flew past a yawning wound in a towering wall of blue ceramic. They turned onto another course heading to Either, down a pathway in shadow.

Lights twinkled below, the fainter glows of the seething dagbabi city of small tenements clustered around the great towers. Almost invisible, great crowds swirled there.

Lady Weanda swung the aircar across the line of oncoming traffic and coasted down to the landing platform halfway up the side of a tall tower sheathed in green glass.

An honor guard awaited her, three tall iulliin bearing ceremonial weapons. They glittered in the sunlight.

"Lady Weanda, welcome to Hall Thuristle."

"Thank you, my lords, this is a great balaast."

"Indeed, Lady Weanda, they will inscribe the number in the texts of history."

Lady Weanda laughed lightly. "Depends which number they decide is the right one. There are seven schools of thought these days."

The iulliin laughed together.

Lady Weanda accepted the welcome and, the robed and hooded girl behind her, walked at the head of the guard through wide double doors and into a room filled with elaborately carved furniture, dominated in the center by a great round table of glistening amber.

The ceiling was a massive, breathtaking painting, as were the walls, done in the same style and manner as the large painting in the ruined apartments that Martherer visited during trips for ice and fungus. On a great blue sky mythic iulliin figures disported among towering clouds.

Around the tables sat a number of iulliin dignitaries, males and females of august rank, wearing the same style of costume as Lady Weanda. At the sight of her and the siffile bearing the brown pot, their faces became animated. A babble of welcomes arose. Ornamented cups were raised high.

Music started up, brisk, martial, *iulliin*. The Lady Weanda struck a pose, one arm raised high, the hand thrown back.

The iulliin cried for her to begin the Great Seance.

Martherer accompanied the Lady Weanda on her tour around the table, holding out the heavy pot, while Lady Weanda opened it and used a long, narrow ladle to spoon out *the Rooms* into their cups.

As they approached the Chelmes of Pyoor, Martherer quavered. She had met that one before, not an enjoyable experience. But she sucked in her breath to endure the assault of his probing fingers and held out the pot.

With one hand the Chelmes held up a cup of exquisite pink glass in the shape of a human female ass; with the other he squeezed Martherer's buttock.

Martherer gritted her teeth as the Chelmes giggled fatuously and goosed her. Martherer passed the Chelmes and was goosed again. She fought down the urge to turn and hurl the heavy pot right into his face. She must smile, keep smiling; that was essential, according to Lady Weanda. And right ahead was the Lady Marooka, an especial friend of Lady Weanda. Martherer extended the pot and smiled even though the mad old Chelmes had crawled on his knees behind her to fondle her again.

Lady Weanda finally shooed him away, to roars of laughter from the rest of the iulliin.

The Lady Marooka winked slyly at Martherer. "Such a delightful creature, Weanda. You are most fortunate."

"Lady Marooka, like you I spend every possible moment campaigning for the repeal of the siffile laws. It is time we had freedom once again here in Meninrud Lors."

"Well spoken, Weanda, here's to you." Lady Marooka swigged back her wine, now mixed heavily with *the Rooms*. "But a word before you pass on, my dear."

Lady Weanda cocked her head.

"The high military are very displeased with you, you know."

"I know, Lady Marooka, I know. But do they dare strike? Do they dare?"

"I have heard it whispered that they dare. Because of the little siffile. The last feather that broke the punga's back, I've heard it called."

"Thank you, my dear. I shall be especially on my guard."

Soon the entire table was undergoing the giggling fits of early intoxication. Lady Weanda prepared her injection of rembane. The giggles died away. The iulliin grew sombre, ready for the seance.

Martherer assisted Lady Weanda in tying the tourniquet around her forearm to produce a full vein in her wrist. Into it Lady Weanda sank a hypodermic loaded with rembane. Lady Weanda became electrifying, a powerful force surging among the tides created by *the Rooms*. She began to babble strange words, disconnected phrases, gabble that gradually built to a crescendo.

Martherer couldn't understand a word, but she felt the emotional force gather as the room full of iulliin reared and swooped behind Lady Weanda, hypnotized by the power of her oration in the mythopoetic tongue of Old Iullas. Their thoughts were entwined together, woven like a rope into a single gestalt that Lady Weanda could ride, ride into a holophrastic vision. A vision that, as she sang it to them, filled them with the fire of belief, all rolled into a single phrase, virtually a mantra.

Thus it went for an hour or more, until finally the effects of the Rooms began to fade.

Lady Weanda moved now from iulliin to iulliin, engaging them in bright swirling conversation, preventing any dips into depression, any chance of a leaking of Realism into their thoughts. For fighting Realism was Lady Weanda's great crusade.

They sang the patriotic songs, the "Lahleroo, Lahleroo" and the "Happy Soldier." For a few moments it was as if they were at the front lines themselves, romantically posed around the campfires, the smashed minions of Xaaca broken behind them. They congratulated themselves on the progress of the war and swore great oaths of fealty to glorious Meninrud Lors.

On it went, eerie emotions lofting through the iulliin nobility, the cream of the cream, those who had never dreamed of visiting the front lines, who had never even seen a video of what the Xaacans were like. They babbled patriotic slogans in an intoxicated frenzy, the words slurring. There were even tears being dabbed on long narrow cheeks.

Martherer watched the seance pass through the usual developments. It had clearly been a great success. These were the cream of society. All having their faith in the Heads-in-the-Sand policy restored. All rededicating themselves to the greater glory of the Sun Clanth.

Now it was her turn to be brought into the action. The Rooms was fading, and the wine was taking effect. Lady Weanda dangled Martherer, dressed in a simple white frock, low-cut across the bosom, in front of a dozen iulliin lords. Their eyes twinkled lecherously across the space between them. The Chelmes threw himself forward and tried to place his head upon Martherer's bosom, his eager fingers on her flesh. She shrank back. Lady Weanda rescued her by interposing herself.

The Chelmes begged Lady Weanda for a merj or two with the little beauty. Lady Weanda laughed lightly and allowed the Chelmes to kiss her finger rings, but made no commitment. She drew Martherer on, quickly, to dazzle some of the other old lechers. With wine and Lady Weanda to protect her, Martherer survived the seance, as she had survived others of its kind, but whenever she felt the fingers of the Chelmes upon her she shrank inside. At last she was allowed to put her robes back on and take a seat in the aircar. Lady Weanda made one final circuit, pressing hands, kissing cheeks.

Martherer stared out across the dimly lit dagbab city to the ramparts and spires on the far side of the great airpath. She wondered, for the millionth time, how her Folo was. Was he safe? Her heart ached unremittingly. She wondered if she was ever going to see him again.

A shadow suddenly fell across the aircar. She turned to find the Chelmes of Pyoor approaching with hands raised and a sickening leer on his face. Hastily Martherer started the aircar and switched on the repeller field, which lifted the car off the balcony a couple of meters.

Below, the Chelmes implored her with open arms. Martherer shuddered at the sight and waited until at last Lady Weanda appeared on the balcony. At the sight of the Chelmes trying to coax the siffile down, Lady Weanda burst into raucous laughter. Her companions joined in and began having great fun with the Chelmes, a renowned siffile pervert.

The Chelmes finally gave up and with a drunken snarl rambled back inside.

The high officers of the Heads-in-the-Sand Party clustered about Lady Weanda.

"Farewell, Lady. We shall be firm."

"We must move, Lord Kanipti. We cannot stay still."

"We shall press for an immediate meeting with the high military."

"Thank you, Kanipti, thank you very much."

Lady Weanda allowed Kanipti and the others to kiss her finger rings, then turned to the aircar.

A shadow fell upon her. They were interrupted.

A tall, grim iulliin, in dark gray military uniform with two tiny firestones of rank on his breast, had emerged from nowhere. He fixed Lady Weanda with a cool gaze. "Lady Weanda dal Vnego. You dabble in dangerous practices."

"Lord Xaapt. I am surprised to find you here."

"Why ever should you, Lady Weanda. Am I not a faithful servant of the government?"

"This is the center of the true faith in Meninrud Lors, not of your corrupt military clique. We are not Realists here, General."

Xaapt seemed emotionless, under control. "I came to try to help you, Lady Weanda. To attempt to modify your behavior so as to allow you to continue your work of elevating our spirits. But I can see that you are not prepared to listen."

"Lord Xaapt, I would listen to you if I didn't already know all the stale, stupid things you would begin to say. We are united now, all of the families, and we will stand against the Realist menace. We must fight, and we must achieve victory."

"Indeed we must, Lady Weanda."

The tall gray figure turned and walked away, to a security door that opened mysteriously. They glimpsed security siffile, also in gray uniforms; then he was gone, and the door closed.

After a moment's hesitation Lady Weanda took her seat and the aircar lifted away, then swung back into the traffic flowing along the airpath.

CHAPTER TWENTY-SEVEN

Blue-green tracer knitted a lacery of death down the alley between two great mounds of rubble. Smoke drifted by; the sky was half obscured by it. The light was dim, a twilight of doom.

They waited, camouflaged, half buried in the light surface chaff as the crusher approached and V-wings zipped overhead, then dove to attack a diversionary target.

The crusher was in plain view, stamping forward on the massive legs, machine guns pecking away at target possibilities.

The heavy robots that accompanied it passed by. One of them crossed the rubble not thirty meters from Cracka. He and Heggi froze. The triangular sensory apparatus turned this way and that, but it missed them, and then it lurched down, into the alley, and then through a gap in the far pile of rubble and up and over it.

The crusher came on until it was towering above them, an armored office building on legs, topped with heavy gun turrets that now crackled into life with a roar and directed fire into the defensive rear.

Heggi looked up. Cracka nodded. Nuts-head was already moving, making a diversionary run away from the crusher, right across its nose and into a hole beneath the far pile of rubble.

The monster shook as it jerked to a halt. Machine guns stuttered, pouring fire into Nuts-head's bolt hole.

Cracka rolled out of his hole, got his legs beneath him, and jumped, straight for the vulnerable spot, right underneath the crusher.

Tracer licked the air a fraction behind him as he flew.

Heggi was already there. The crusher's legs were in motion, huge trunks sliding down then boosting up again as two legs thrust the colossus backward.

But it was too late. The crusher danced like a gigantic three-legged pachyderm trying to avoid poisonous mice, but the mice were too quick.

Cracka boosted up on one leg and swung an adhesive pad against the smooth surface. It gripped, holding the shaped blast charge in place. He dropped back and almost lost his balance, but he managed to keep his legs beneath him.

It was a hard landing. He felt himself slip and almost fall, but he was already bunching and boosting leftward, his target a patch of shadow on the wall of the mound that hid a narrow bolt hole.

Heggi landed nearby and did a perfect powered somersault, evading the tracer that ploughed across her course. She made a clean landing and sprang into the cover of the ruins. Bullets chipped dust and shards loose in her wake.

Cracka fell into the hole, crash-landing, bouncing from wall to wall for ten feet before coming to a halt. Bullets ricocheted around the entrance. He fought for breath, got it back, dragged his legs under him, and boosted horizontal, down the narrow hole, toward a circle of light. Behind them their charges detonated with heavy thuds.

They emerged at virtually the same moment, ahead of the heavy robots. There was time to turn, bunch, and boost for the safety of the shadow beyond the next ruined tower.

They looked back. The crusher was still standing, but at

an awkward angle. Defensive artillery fire was already
zeroing in on the immobilized titan. Shells burst against
the upper surface. It was only a matter of time.

Heggi led. Nuts-head picked them up after another kilometer, and they curved back toward the lines, staying in
shadow as much as possible to avoid the V-wings.

The radio crackled with congratulation from Klazt.
They passed fresh battle groups heading out to engage the
enemy. In the dugout they celebrated. The big one broke
out a bag of booze, and they toasted their victory. The fight
drug started wearing off, but the booze cut the jitters, left
them mellow.

Nuts-head came back from the commissary with food—
bowls of warm bokka, packets of boltak.

They greeted him with another toast. "Here's to Nuts-
head, the best hole-bolter in the whole damn army!" said
the big one, raising his mug.

They hooted and drank, then they fell upon the food.
As the fight drug wore off, so their hunger increased dra-
matically. The bokka was delicious, as always, an ambrosial porridge, flavored slightly with crunchy, chocolaty
boltak.

The dugout fell quiet as they ate. Unable to move, let
alone eat, they'd waited for six hours for the crusher. The
appetite inspired by fight drug was prodigious.

Nuts-head was first to finish. He dumped his bowl back
on the tray, pushed the last of the boltak into his mouth,
and lay back with his head against the wall. "Kill crushers,
eat hearty, sleep well," he murmured in a singsong voice.

Cracka was ready to agree. The booze, the food, the
wearing off of the fight drug, all left him ready for eight
hours of dreamless, black sleep. Just as his eyes were
about to close, however, the door to the dugout popped
open and two yashi in bodyguard harness came in.

Behind them came a very tall, angular figure, wearing a

gray battle suit. Cracka stared in shock—it was one of the iulliin, the master race! He had never seen one before in the flesh, except as distant dots aboard air platforms in Meninrud Lors.

The iulliin gazed at them, then pointed at Cracka and spoke to the yashi. The yashi advanced on him and brusquely picked him up and marched him out of the room.

The iulliin followed. In the corridor were more yashi, another pair of bodyguards, and Battlemaster Klazt.

Klazt was protesting. At the iulliin's appearance he fell silent. The iulliin said something curt but soft-spoken and then turned and led the yashi bodyguards away, with Cracka suspended between them. They turned right on the main pipe and entered the commissary. Stunned troopers stared in silence.

At the rear of the commissary was the main service counter, and behind that counter was dagbab country, off limits to siffile. The counter opened, and the yashi marched him through.

At this point Cracka was wondering if they had rumbled Bat and poor Shay, who were still hidden in a storeroom underneath the commissary.

Then the iulliin proceeded to open a secret door on the wall of the galley. With an audience of a dozen respectful dagbabi watching, he led the yashi into a a passage that became a ramp and spiraled upward into a circular chamber in which sat an iulliin aircraft. Cracka's eyes bulged. The plane had a plump fuselage with large stubby wings and bulky jet pods dangling beneath.

Then a hatch opened, stairs were lowered, and the yashi lifted him aboard. Thirty seconds later he was strapped firmly into a heavy, padded chair, in a circular chamber equipped with a variety of equipment. The iulliin entered and sat on a narrow stool that he pulled out from the wall. Cracka stared at him openmouthed.

The iulliin face was almost a caricature of the human norm, hugely elongated from top to bottom, with purple lips and sad, yellowed eyes. Immense bags hung beneath those eyes, which stared at him with a keen, inquiring gaze.

Then the iulliin spoke, in Interlingua, shocking Cracka even further. "Do not be alarmed, siffile. I am simply going to take a few tests and then you will be returned to your quarters."

Cracka boggled. The thing took out an instrument that looked like an overwrought handgun. "You can speak in our language?" Cracka managed to croak.

The thing pressed the alien, purple lips together and raised the handgun device. "Be quiet, siffile. Do not be alarmed."

"But what are you doing? Where am I? Why have you brought us here? By what right—"

But the device directed a beam of strong psychoconditioning images into his eyes. He lost self-volition or the power to speak. His eyes remained open, however, and his brain continued to record what happened.

Rukbhat dal Vnego Urtisim, computer master of the city of Meninrud Lors, ran the tests of intelligence, conditioning level, and various hormone factors.

The subject was in good physical condition although probably past the prime. According to the battle reports, however, he was a trooper of the first quality. Indeed, intelligence levels were high, but there the profile departed from the predicted norms. The conditioning level was low, in fact almost nonexistent.

Shocked, Rukbhat ran the test again. He had tested forty individuals along the front, and this was the lowest conditioning level he had yet seen, although the levels were universally low compared to the predicted norms.

The test completed once more, the processor refreshed

the screen diagrams. Once again it showed incontrovertibly low levels of conditioning.

The hormone patterns were taking shape. There too deviations from the norm were significant. The adrenaline surge was much too high. The subject was experiencing involuntary fight/flight reactions in Rukbhat's presence. That was totally at variance with the submissive acceptance reactions predicted by the psychoconditioning department.

Rukbhat shook his head and set the figures into virtual memory.

A few minutes later, when the testing was complete, the iulliin got up and left. The yashi came in, unstrapped Cracka, and took him out the hatch and back down the spiral tube to the commissary, where they let him go.

He stared back as the yashi returned to the interior of the commissary and disappeared. Then he turned and ran for the door.

He sprinted quickly down the tube, took a descending ramp, and then cut left and left again until he was outside the secret storeroom where Bat was hiding Shay. He tapped on the door and moved away, then returned and tapped once more in the coded form.

The door opened, and Bat's unshaven face stared out. "What's up? You're early."

"Let me in. We've got to talk. There's an iulliin here, with an aircraft."

Bat's eyes bugged in his head. He pulled Cracka inside. "Tell me about this aircraft."

When he had heard the story, Bat gave a little whistle. "A freaking, goddamn iulliin, right here. I've never even seen one except on the conditioner video." He raised a finger in the air and took a swig of a new concoction that kept more of the delicious flavor of bokka to sweeten the alcohol. "So how do we get that plane, that's the question."

"It's a job for the fighting 344th, I think," Cracka said. "I'll put it to them, anyway."

There had been no change in Shay's condition. He still stared blankly ahead, mouth open.

Cracka nodded. The iulliin had a lot to answer for. He hoped there would be a chance for an accounting. He finished up his drink and gave Bat back the mug. Then he slipped out the way he'd come and headed for the dugout.

Everyone was asleep when he entered. He decided to start with Heggi. She came awake with a jerk. "Cracka? You all right?"

"Yes. They didn't harm me. They took me to an aircraft in a hangar that I would say was pretty close to the surface, directly above the commissary."

"Iulliin aircraft?"

"Yeah. The iulliin ran some tests on me, then they released me."

Heggi nodded as if familiar with this. "The master took you to the aircraft and shone the lights on you."

"Yes."

"I have heard of this, but not recently. I wonder what the master wanted?"

"Whatever he wanted, I know what *we* want," Cracka growled.

"What is that, Cracka?"

"To escape from this place alive, before we're all killed by the crushers and V-wings. This is madness here. We don't belong here."

Heggi laughed. He'd heard that laugh before. All the Lemall's people had it, and they laughed like that when they heard the Calabel people complain about the war.

"You can complain, Cracka, but you're not going to change it. We've got to fight, or else the enemy will win."

"So what? Let them win. We don't have to stay here."

"You're wrong, Cracka. We have to stay. There's too many people in the clanth. How would they escape?"

Cracka shrugged. In truth he didn't really know how all the humans in the Sun Clanth would escape. "All I know is that we can escape. All we have to do is take that plane."

Heggi smiled and opened her arms. "Cracka, you come here and lie beside me. You will forget this madness eventually."

Cracka stared at her: the deep conditioning worked well. He shook his head. "No, Heggi, listen to me. We're going to go and take that plane and then fly out of here and get somewhere safe."

"Cracka, the yashi will take you and dump you in the biomass tank—after they kill you, if you're lucky. If you upset them, they'll put you in alive."

Cracka tried everything to persuade her, but she was adamant. Nor could he move Nuts-head or the big one. The Lemall's people wouldn't consider rebelling against the "masters." Their conditioning was very deep indeed.

Finally he realized it would be up to him and Bat. They would have to take Shay with them, which would complicate matters considerably. Grimly Cracka donned shock boots and gun cradle. It was the only weapon available for siffile, so it would have to do. He pulled the door open and found himself staring straight into Battlemaster Klazt's leonine eyes.

Cracka was paralyzed with surprise for a fatal half second. Then he tried to swing up the gun, but Klazt deflected the barrel and reached in and spun him around. Then, before he could engage his shock boots, Klazt had pulled the power connector and the boots sputtered out.

Cracka twisted desperately and got a punch in, a solid right hand to the yashi's jaw. It had as much effect as if he'd punched a wall.

Klazt snarled, then swung him hard into the doorframe and rammed a big fist into his solar plexus.

Still gasping for breath, Cracka felt Klazt handcuff him,

strip off the shock boots and gun harness, and yank him back to his feet.

The door opened, and another battlemaster stood there, automatic rifle in hand. The yashi growled together briefly, and then Cracka was marched back through the tubes, to the commissary and up the spiral to the iulliin aircraft. Once aboard he was hustled into a tiny cabin, bare but for a single narrow bench. The hatch closed.

■ CHAPTER TWENTY-EIGHT

He didn't have to wait long before the yashi bodyguards came and removed him, marching him down the length of the plane and thrusting him into a small room at the rear. The iulliin was waiting, sitting in one of the six swivel seats that formed a semicircle around the room.

Cracka was uncuffed and then forced into a chair. A strap was fastened across his waist. A yashi guard stood quietly by the door; the others left.

The iulliin fixed him with a glittering gaze. "In my survey of your blood chemistry I discovered significant traces of alcohol. How came this to be?"

Cracka stared.

The iulliin grew impatient. "Alcohol—you know what that is?" The tone was peremptory, demanding. The lips moved in an inhuman way. Cracka's skin crawled at the sight.

"Yes, alcohol, so?"

"Why alcohol in your blood? Where do you get alcohol?"

"We make it. We ferment some of the food and then distill it."

"Ah!" The iulliin let out a hiss.

He turned and activated a screen by turning a long, purple glass switch sited on a board dotted with others, all of different colors. The screen wobbled momentarily. Then a face appeared, a yashi.

The iulliin barked something, and the yashi replied quietly.

The iulliin spoke at length, with considerable passion, then ended the contact. It turned other switches and tapped a number of narrow keys set in a row beside the switches. Symbols appeared on the screen, including an unmistakable graph.

After a while the iulliin took another small blood sample and conducted another test with the large hand-held device that resembled a gun.

Once more the yashi unstrapped him, this time without bothering to handcuff him, and led him back to his cell. The door slammed behind him. He was left staring into the dark, close to total despair.

Hours went by. He dozed, leaning against the wall—there wasn't room to actually lie down. At last the door opened again. The yashi reached in and jerked him to his feet.

He stepped out. Another yashi stood by the exit hatch. The iulliin appeared and gave some brief orders. They opened the hatch.

"What are you doing with me?"

The iulliin gave him a freezing glare. "Rebel siffile are a toxic menace to the lifeblood of the clanth. To purify it you will be interred in the biomass."

Cracka blanched. "What crime have I committed? What wrong have I done you or your accursed army?"

The iulliin blinked in disapproval and spoke sharply to the yashi. Cracka was picked up and hustled toward the hatch and imminent death. He would be taken down to the food generation plant and thrown into the yeast tanks.

At the door he braced himself, then pushed backward as hard as he could and swung his legs up on either side of the door and twisted.

The yashi fumbled, lost its grip on his shoulders, and let him slip free.

Cracka attempted a kick in the yashi's midsection, but it evaded his thrust and backhanded him into the wall of the compartment. He rolled along it to the bulkhead. The guard he'd embarrassed came on. Cracka tried another kick, but it too was parried. The yashi pulled close, and a heavy hand slapped him sideways and he started down, pain exploding in his head. His outstretched arm caught the yashi's battle harness.

It leaned over, hauling him back up. He got both hands on the harness and suddenly smashed his forehead into the yashi's face so hard he thought his head was going to break open.

The yashi let out a roar of complaint and stumbled backward, both big hands up to its battered mouth, suddenly bereft of front teeth. Crimson spattered the fur down its front under the harness.

Cracka gave a desperate jump, landing right in front of the battered yashi. His hands dove for the holster hanging on the harness. In another moment he had the guard's automatic in his hands.

Then the other guard knocked him flying with a brutal kick in the seat of the pants.

Cracka hit the door to the rest of the plane and bounced onto the floor. His assailant stepped smartly around his wounded fellow. Cracka got the gun up, focused through the blood swimming in his eyes, and pulled the trigger.

Nothing happened. He'd forgotten to release the safety.

Then the yashi knocked the weapon out of his hands and hauled him up and hit him hard on the side of the head, loosening teeth and sending a little blood spraying over the wall. Cracka sagged, the yashi moved to get a better grip on him, and with everything he had left, Cracka slammed his knee into the yashi's midriff.

The big alien let out a gasp, and Cracka fell sideways— and got his hands back on the gun. He twisted away desperately and turned. His thumb found a stud on the butt and pressed it while he brought the muzzle up and fired.

The roar was deafening inside the plane. Six explosive bullets decapitated the leading yashi. One more was required to finish the other guard.

Cracka turned the gun on the iulliin, who cowered in the corner, by the hatch, an expression of unfathomable hatred and fear writ large on that alien mask.

Cracka fought off a sudden feeling of faintness, bit down on his own lip, and moved to pull the hatch shut, good and hard. The bolts slid home with a satisfactory crunch.

"All right, now *you* have some talking to do. In there." Cracka motioned with the gun to the door leading to the rear of the plane.

"Go on, open it, and hurry up or I'll loosen some of your teeth too—seems to have been a day for loosening teeth, no reason why you shouldn't join the crowd." His spit was a dark red now. Carefully he felt his jaw.

With great reluctance the iulliin opened the door. Cracka pushed him through. The iulliin was light, fragile-seeming after the yashi.

They reached the rear compartment. Cracka made the iulliin sit in a chair and tighten the seatbelt. Then Cracka rummaged around for something to stanch the bleeding.

He pressed a panel and a compartment opened up that included a washbasin, a toilet, and an oblong cabinet with a mirror inset on the front.

The mirror afforded him a view of the iulliin, and the cuts on his forehead where the yashi's canine's had snapped off.

The blood was clotting, but he needed stitches.

"Is there anything in here to stanch bleeding?" he said.

The iulliin stared back at him with undisguised hate.

"Look, you better tell me, I'm as desperate as they come."

The iulliin licked his lips with a thin, purplish tongue. "In the cabinet there is a small blue box. Contains antiseptic pads to cover wounds. I think it will work for siffile."

"That's better." Cracka opened the cabinet, found the small blue box, and pulled out a row of green circular pads encased in plastic wrapper. He opened one and stuck it over the wound on the left side of his forehead, then repeated the trick on the other side.

The skin beneath the pads felt instantly cool; there was a slight tickling sensation. The effect was decidedly strange, but if it stopped the bleeding and prevented infection, it would be worth it.

He turned back to the iulliin. "Open a line of communication to Battlemaster Klazt, 344th Combat Squad."

The iulliin hesitated. "This is illegal. You may not do this!"

Cracka gestured with the gun. "Still got ten shots in this. More than enough for you and me. If you want to live, you do as I say! You understand?"

The iulliin licked its lips, wriggled in involuntary response. And opened a channel on the screen. In less than half a minute Klazt's face filled the screen.

"Good," said Cracka. "Now tell Klazt to take a party and bring up a couple of friends of mine who are hiding in a storage chamber under the commissary. There's a code they will need, and they better get it right! This is very important. If they make any mistake and my friends are hurt in any way, you will die. Speak in Interlingua, and speak slowly. I don't want any mistakes or ambiguity."

The iulliin swallowed, grimaced, and then spoke to Klazt.

About fifteen minutes later there was a knock in Bat Maroon's code on the outer hatch. Cracka escorted the iulliin down the length of the aircraft once more and ordered him to open it while Cracka covered him with the gun.

The hatch opened and Bat pulled Shay inside. Bat slammed the hatch in Klazt's face. "I don't know how the hell you did this, Buckshore, but I got to hand it to you." Bat got a good look at him. "Boy, the cats made a mess of you, didn't they?"

Cracka managed a weak smile.

Bat noted the bodies strewn untidily along the far bulkhead. A lot of blood was soaking into the floor matting. "You seem to have made quite a mess of them, too."

"Yeah, we had quite a little to-do in here. Bat, I want to introduce you to our pilot for today, Rook-bat Urtisim—at least that's what I think he calls himself."

Cracka indicated the iulliin.

Bat stared in wonder. "Well I'll be, an actual iulliin. Boy, there are things I'd like to do to you . . ."

Cracka laid a hand on his shoulder. "Yeah, well, let's get Shay inside and strapped in. We have to get out of here before they can come up with some way of stopping us. The plane's fueled and ready to go, and Rook-bat here says he can fly it."

"Great, I'm all packed and ready to go. Can't wait, in fact."

■ CHAPTER TWENTY-NINE

The arrival of the Sun Mel of Planggi, with five siffile, aboard the great air barque of Planggi Castle, was the most important thing to have happened in thousands of balaasts at Fanthenai Tower.

From the broad terrace that ran around the top, beneath the mushroom cap roof, to the massive foundations and halls, the whole place came to life. The dagbabi elite, their slave collars glittering, surged into the quarters of the iulliin.

Lady Wosensh was dressed in a purple and green gown and carried out to greet the Sun Mel on the high terrace.

She was more than a thousand years terrestrial in age. She dribbled from the left side of her mouth and had lost all her teeth. She was almost blind, very deaf, and barely able to move unaided. Indeed, she often forgot where she was and what she was doing.

Hundreds of important dagbabi, wearing collar pieces of blue and scarlet, crowded around the visitors. They chattered furiously to themselves in the tongue of the dagbabi, a slithering, whispery sound.

The Sun Mel was astonished, and vaguely horrified, at the wildness of the dagbabi. He was even more horrified at the condition of Lady Wosensh.

The ceremonies were fortunately brief.

Then the air barque was hauled in by teams of dagbabi

and allowed to settle, with a slight crunch, onto the terrace itself. Fortunately the terrace was both wide and massively built. The whole tower at that level was fifty meters across, a fairy phallus capped by a perfect toadstool roof, a reddish hue for the walls, darker brown- and black-spiraled on the roof. A hundred meters farther down began a number of setbacks and terraces that continued to the three-hundred-meter-wide ground floor.

Fanthenai was simply enormous. Avis doubted that any office building on Calabel could match it. It was at least three hundred meters high. A gigantic architectural grotesque. It seemed the iulliin had had few inhibitions during their great era of construction. Whimsy and a taste for massively proportioned mock-medieval seemed to have been the ruling urges in the region.

Avis shivered again at the sight of Lady Wosensh. The elderly creature was in such a state of advanced decrepitude that Avis had to wonder if it might not be better to live a normal life span, rather than the genetically perfected life spans of the iulliin.

Nathan had worked out the iulliin's life span as around a thousand years, Calabel norm. Optimized internal organs, perfected nutritional science, all gave the iulliin a bounty of years. But in the end the brain cells degenerated to the point where imbecility set in. Centuries of life as a drooling idiot in the arms of the all-capable dagbabi? Avis shuddered.

She gazed around herself. The signs of decay were everywhere. Above, the tower of reddish ceramic blocks was undoubtedly weathered and aged. The elf-castle roof, made of big overlapping plates of dark brown weft, was patched and holed. Many windows were boarded up, others were broken and patched over with blackened panels. Another glimpse at Lady Wosensh sent a shudder through her. The complete decadence of a culture, that was what they were seeing.

The dagbabi had informed the Sun Mel, with great apology, that Lords Argmute and Praktiki were too poorly to be moved from their beds. But they sent their greetings anyway, and wished to welcome the visitors to "Fair Fanthenai." They begged the Sun Mel to be so gracious as to visit them in their chambers. The Sun Mel acceded to this request.

They all trooped along behind the six dagbabi that carried Lady Wosensh in her chair.

In enormous, cathedral-like rooms that were dark and hushed, they visited the frail, almost dead Lords Argmute and Praktiki. Neither could actually sit up, but the eyes brightened visibly at the sight of the siffile. Both men smiled wickedly.

"Good siffile?" Lord Argmute managed to gargle. Then he closed his eyes for a little nap.

The Sun Mel stared in horror, then turned and went back to the terrace. Clearly he was the new ruler of Fanthenai; all the native iulliin were in states of advanced senility. He summoned the het-dagbabi to confer.

The "good siffile" were left to explore the tower. They soon discovered that though it was vast, most of it was empty and in a bad state of repair. On the uppermost floors, dozens of rooms in dusty apartments were jammed with iulliin relics, the junk of a thousand generations. Beneath the treasure troves were the grand apartments of the three surviving iulliin, of whom Lady Wosensh was the youngest. In Fanthenai the grip of the master race had fallen from the wheel; the iulliin had been worn out by the sheer enormity of time. Their endless day was almost done.

Below the apartments of the iulliin, the dagbabi had taken possession, every room subdivided into a hive of tiny homes in yellow-black weft. In the corridors and stairwells a horde of nervous, darting dagbabi surged back and forth.

Indeed, around the base of the tower and spread out for ten kilometers or more were thousands of buildings, avenues, and thoroughfares, foot and animal traffic trickling in and out.

Among the buildings were the beehives, a great number of big white spirals.

The Sun Mel explained that Fanthenai had been a center for the beesqueeze industry since the earliest days of the Sun Clanth. And indeed, the brown and yellow roofs of the city were speckled with red tables, the famed bee tables of Fanthenai, on which a billion bees were sated and squeezed every balaast. Thus did the civilization of the iulliin continue, even without the guiding hand of the iulliin themselves.

The Sun Mel was shocked. He knew that there had been little communication with Fanthenai in the last several thousand balaast. But that things had degenerated so seemed incredible to him.

Of course he was aware that Planggi Castle was not an example of cultural vigor. They were so weak, so lazy, so stupefied by the achievements of the past. But this? This was the end of things, this was a city of dagbabi.

And the Sun Mel could feel *that* too. The local dagbabi were not quite as restrained and deferential as he was accustomed to. Catering to the three ancient, dying rulers of Fanthenai had bred a certain restlessness in them. And dagbabi with no common purpose would soon breed factions, and they would fight. *Musht* would break out among them—they would assume the wild state.

Just the thought of dagbab mutiny was a horror not even to be dreamed of. The Sun Mel did his utmost to ignore the signs and tremors.

Still, the pitiable sight of the ancient iulliin here was enough to moisten his eyes. Gravely he saluted the lords Argmute and Praktiki. He attempted to communicate with

Wosensh, but she was unable to do more than wobble her head and drool on his hand.

Even worse was the embarrassment he felt that the siffile, who in truth were now actually *Ferlay*—true friends —were witnesses to the degradation of the Golden Race. For the Sun Mel had learned much from Nathan, even as Nathan had pumped him for information. He had told the Sun Mel of Calabel, with its functioning technology, space route connections, harsh ecology. The Sun Mel was now dreadfully aware of the chasm between himself and Nathan.

Nathan had the powers of the ancients! He understood the science! Even the other siffile were a thousand times more knowledgeable about the technologies than the Sun Mel. He realized with terrible clarity that he was a savage, living in the ruins of his own culture.

After leaving Lord Praktiki, the Sun Mel was shown to a hastily cleaned and refurbished set of apartments on the inward side of the tower. Dabgabi rushed furiously about, cleaning and installing, their chatter much, much louder than it was in Planggi.

The siffile were given quarters near to the Sun Mel's. Each was given a small, dark room and a minimal mattress, freshly stuffed with beepuf.

Sam Boan did not want to take a room between Nathan and Avis. He emerged suddenly, red-faced, dragging his mattress. The dagbabi drew back, mildly astonished: the siffile were so unruly, so violent in appearance and gesture.

Boan dragged the mattress down the corridor away from the others and kicked open a set of double doors leading to another huge suite of inward-facing rooms. He dragged the mattress in and slammed the big doors behind him.

Avis stared after him. She sensed more trouble from Sam. A vague terror of him was now gnawing away at her. *Sam has killed before . . .*

At the sight of the bare rooms given to the siffile, the Sun Mel clapped his hands sharply and ordered more bedding, plus tables and chairs, to be brought.

An expedition to the upper floors was mounted. Nathan, curious as ever, went with a troop of twenty dagbabi. They roved ahead, a restless reptilian horde, as he mounted the ramped stairs.

The upper rooms proved well worth the effort. Packed with furniture, clothes, belongings—all the detritus of a dead people was piled inside, beneath dust sheets.

Once the windows were unblocked and light was let into the rooms on the inward side, Nathan began pulling things out to examine. The dust of centuries flew into the air and sank through the sunbeams.

He soon found an energy weapon, similar to those they had found in the Hall of Antiquity in Planggi. However, it had lost its charge. He put it back and continued exploring. The dagbabi squeaked to each other for a while, then resumed moving the tables and chairs.

He identified a number of what were obviously medical devices, surgical equipment and the like. Then a cubical module about a meter high caught his interest. There were a number of small pits on its surface, laid out in a regular pattern.

The furniture selected, the dagbabi were impatient to close up the room. Their leader, a full carnan with the hind teeth exposed, addressed Nathan in Iullas. "Siffile youth, you must come now, with us."

Nathan tried to argue, but that proved useless—the little dagbab would not go away. In the end he gave up and went with them, determined to get the Sun Mel to order that he could return on his own, as soon as possible.

Later they were treated to a banquet on the terrace. At the Sun Mel's insistence, at the long table places beside the iulliin were set for the siffile.

Lady Wosensh was carried out and spoon-fed a little mince and mush. The rest were given platters of boorni and slices of wita. In addition, also at the Sun Mel's behest, there was an alcoholic beverage. Exquisite glasses were filled with a chilled white liquid that seemed very much like wine. There was a fruity element to the taste and a scent like that of violets. This was fine *varmils*, a traditional iullin drink except in Planggi, where the Yelkes had prohibited it, along with all other alcohols, in the days of the Sun Mel's youth.

Varmils were fermented from blends of fruits, and many were highly prized. They were aged for a century or more, during which they achieved an incredible voluptuousness in bouquet and flavor.

Sam Boan drank a dozen glasses with the determined, bulging eyes of a drinker denied anything but water or fruit juice for several months. He flung the delicious stuff back and soon grew drunk and maudlin. After looking around the table, he decided he was among enemies and he seized the carafe and staggered away to his rooms. Later he bawled curses from a window set halfway to the shadow line, rich generalized curses, damning his companions, the universe, the iulliin, everything.

The Sun Mel twitched his long nose. The fat siffile presented a problem that he was not entirely sure he could handle. "Sam" was increasingly belligerent and noisy. The Sun Mel wished he had the High Mel to talk to, but here there was no one who could advise, no one who was capable of making even a sentence.

Finishing their meals, Folo and Nathan returned to the air barque and moved all the weaponry, including the helmets, and placed it in Folo's room, the door of which boasted a stout, working lock. Sam Boan would have to be watched.

Eventually they all headed for their rooms and sleep. At least there were no Yelkes here who wanted them dead.

* * *

The balaast went by, signaled by a horn, very similar in
tone to that used in Planggi.

Nathan spent his time exploring the attics in a state of
mounting excitement. Sam Boan stayed in his suite, often
lying in the bathtub for hours, drunk. Rilla Boan sank into
a deep depression and sat for hours on the high terrace,
sobbing gently. The Sun Mel, when not accompanying
Nathan in the attics, spent his time sitting with Lords Argmute and Praktiki, trying to make some sense of the de-
cline at Fanthenai.

After checking the strength of the lock on his door, Folo
felt free to examine their surroundings. He and Avis took to
exploring the dagbab city and the adjacent countryside.
They took long walks through the city of dagbabi. In one
quarter lay a bazaar, to which dagbabi traders came from
nearby provinces to barter for beesqueeze products. Arrays
of bowls, pots, cups, pipes, tubes, and almost everything
else that on a planet would be made from wood, metal, or
stone was available here.

The shuffling tide of gray- and dark-green-skinned dagbabi, their brilliant neck feather arrays, the golden yellow
beesqueeze wares, the colorful town—all fascinated Avis.
It had a surreal quality, layered by the amber gold sunlight.
They paused often to watch the feeding of the bees as the
dagbabi worked in tireless hordes, making mash, flavoring
it to delight the bees, and adding hormones that would
change the quality of the squeeze.

Around the tables, often ten feet or more across and cut
by access holes for the squeezers, they gazed with startled
eyes at the speed and dexterity of the dagbabi bee
squeezers. While the bees were feeding and thus contented, they would allow a single squeeze of the gland
from which they secreted polymeric material. The dagbabi

fingers flew over the tables, lifting bees by their abdomens, squeezing quickly, and dropping them back on their feed with the rapidity of machines. The bees would bite if squeezed twice, so the workers had to know which bees they'd squeezed and which they hadn't. Still, the small buckets worn around the squeezers' necks filled quickly. The buckets full of pink- or lemon-colored squeeze were dumped into vats. The vats were worked with chemicals derived from plants, and the result was poured into molds. The dusty side alleys and warehouses held great stacks of molds and bulk polymer moldings.

Folo soon realized that there was fierce competition between competing bee tables to attract as many of the big bumblers as possible. The competition could even be dangerous, they discovered, when they found feuding neighbors hurling black stink bombs at one another to drive away bees that might wish to investigate the other's table.

The bombs burst on contact with the ground or bee table and released a brown cloud of gas. When the smell hit Avis and Folo they ran, holding hands over their faces. The stench was long-living, with a putrid fishiness that was remarkably horrible. Finally, to remove it, they bathed together in a canal.

While they swam and soaked, Avis kept a slight distance from young Folo; she was suddenly very aware of the strength, the animalness of him. He had the hard, lean body of youth. In fact she had to make a conscious decision to keep her eyes off him. She chided herself a little, but halfheartedly.

After a long soak to get out the stink, they dried off in the warm rays of the little gold sun.

On other occasions they took the air barque and floated out twenty or thirty kilometers into the countryside. There they found a vast agricultural enterprise. Fields of crops were worked by armies of istyggi. Istyggi villages, built

behind a shadow wall, were often located close to ponds
where airfish larvae were raised and harvested.

Beside the roads, which radiated away from the great
tower and its city, dagbabi villages of weft straggled for
many kilometers. On the roads was a fair amount of traffic.
Balaunt were used by the dagbabi for transport. They were
ridden like horses, with saddles, or roped together and used
to haul small wagons.

At about thirty kilometers from the tower, when the
tower was a distant dark phallus above the green, the fields
and villages began to peter out. Forest replaced the fields,
and beyond the forest were the living hills, the Eaters of
Zeit. There they would land and picnic, on fruit and
boorni, usually, that they were provided with by the dagbabi in the iulliin kitchen.

At first Folo fought the desire for Avis that began to
manifest itself. He cursed himself for being so unfaithful to
Martherer, and he wondered how he could think like that
about the mother of young Nathan. But she was a handsome woman, even if old enough to be his mother. They
were together a lot of the time, and when she looked at him
there was something in her eyes that he recognized.

Their first time out alone, they talked about everything.
And even speculated on the reasons for the mass abduction, what the iulliin might want with hundreds of thousands of people. Folo thought they would be slaves, or
possibly experimental animals, and the thought of what
they might be doing to Martherer caused him to clench his
fists and walk up and down by the side of the canal. He
was helpless to stop them. He didn't even know where she
was. There was no way of gaining reassurance.

Avis poured the varmils they had brought and gave him
a cup. Then they sat together and she comforted him. They
were warm and easy; Folo felt better than he had in a long
time. A little later Avis laid her head on his shoulder and
Folo kissed her.

At first the contact was tentative, neither feeling very sure about it, but then the need for comfort overcame them. They made love, quickly, naturally, with considerable intensity.

It had been a long time since Avis had taken a lover. For Folo there was the blind need, the necessity of trying to forget Martherer.

Afterward they lay quietly, rather stunned by what they had done.

■ CHAPTER THIRTY

Rilla Boan sat out on the terrace on a long, low couch. Like all the furniture, it was made of deep golden superpolymer, enormously resistant to the wear and tear of the aeons. At the ends were curved armrests that ended in ornamental iulliin faces, the one on the left laughing, the one on the right weeping.

Rilla was unmoved by the craft of the piece, or indeed by any of the iulliin art treasures. She stared out at the mad beauty of the alien sky: endless clouds, fading into the golden haze that filled the distance. Flocks of large airfish were heading past the tower at about five hundred meters elevation. On her right, in the direction of Or, a reef cloud was banked into the sky, a green-yellow band angling into the mid-latitudes.

The airfish made ringing bell-like calls as they flew on in the direction of Either, over the roofs of the dagbab city, heading toward a cluster of clouds that looked very much like an enormous bunch of purple grapes.

There was a weird loveliness in it all, but it didn't stop the terrifying numbness Rilla felt. A depression so profound gripped her that all she could do was sit there and drink the varmils the dagbabi brought her until she wept herself to sleep. She was never going to see downtown Landing Site again. She was never going to see even gritty little Baytou City again.

The list of things she would never see again was long, terribly, terribly long. It made her heart ache.

She sipped aged varmils from the exquisite, pink, lily-form goblet. At least when she was drunk she didn't mind the little dinosaurs so much, with their squeaky chatter and unblinking eyes. Most of the time she was so disturbed by them she couldn't even leave her room when they were around.

Once again she contemplated suicide, then dismissed the idea. Even drunk, suicide would be very painful. Rilla didn't think she could face that.

A happy shout came from the door and Nathan Prench emerged, covered in dust, carrying a black rectangular box, three feet long, one wide, and only a few inches deep. It glittered like metal, but Nathan hefted it as if it was very light.

"Hello, Nathan," said Rilla.

"Hello, Mz. Boan. I haven't seen you in a few balaast."

Rilla's face wrinkled. "Please don't use that alien gibberish with me, Nathan. I can't stand it, I can't stand much more of any of this."

Nathan stared at her and struggled to understand her. How could anyone be depressed when there was so much crazy stuff in the Fanthenai attics? He shrugged. He didn't understand Rilla, or her brother. Not only were they grown-ups but they were weird.

Still his enthusiasm bubbled to the surface. "Look," he blurted. "Look what I found."

Despite herself, Rilla looked. He held out the meter-long rectangle to her. She observed that it was studded with oblong indentations and little circular pits on one side. Other than that it was featureless. "Well, Nathan, that's nice. What does it do?"

Nathan looked perfectly crazed—sweating, covered in dust, his face smeared, his eyes agleam. Rilla sighed inwardly. What a family the Prenches were! Crazy old Cathete—boy, what a bad way to die he chose! And Avis, who was just so damned ornery all the time. And now this one, a complete nut who'd failed socialization school and everything.

"Well, nothing. Yet, I mean."

"Nothing?" She erupted in a deep, happy laugh. Such absurdity.

Rilla was suddenly sure that Nathan was a virgin still. The thought amused her even more, and she roared and slapped her palms on her knees.

He stared at her patiently, puzzled. "It's a computer, Mz. Boan, I'm sure of it. Look, you see these indents, they're set out like keys on a keyboard. I think this patch on the left is an audio setup, and there's a little screen on the right for video."

Rilla nodded. Trust the Prench kid to find the only computer in town.

"Well, that's wonderful, Nathan. Does it work?"

Nathan's face fell, so comically that Rilla giggled helplessly.

"Now, that's still a problem. It doesn't work, and neither does the main unit, which is still upstairs."

She dissolved into laughter so deep that it verged on pain, and her face fell onto her forearm. Nathan looked at her quizzically for a moment, then dismissed her reaction. She was definitely very weird.

He hefted the black module and examined it carefully in the sunlight. There were no indicator lights.

"I don't know. I'll have to try and open the casing, see if I can understand how it works. Who knows how long it's been since it was in use."

He set the black module down on a table nearby. "I'll look at it later. First there's another room I want to check out."

"Good-bye, Nathan." Rilla watched him dart away, back to the stairs. She felt an odd stirring inside her. An urge to feel a hard-fleshed young man in her arms. Her eyes lingered on his rear as he disappeared from view. Now, that would make an interesting conquest! She smiled to herself and finished the varmils. And it would serve Avis right for being so disagreeable all the time. She giggled and poured another glass of the aged, golden liqueur.

Before she raised it to her lips, though, the rectangular module emitted a little beep. She looked over and noticed that it had a little blue light winking on and off on the right-hand side of the keyboard area.

She giggled. "It's come on, Nathan."

Experimentally she tapped a couple of keys. Nothing happened for a moment, and then a little square screen above the rows of pits blinked into life with a colorful scramble running from left to right across it. The box emitted a piercing beep.

Rilla gave a little cry of shock and pulled her hand back. There was no telling what she'd done.

"And if its a goddamn bomb then you've probably gone and blown us to bits, haven't you!"

Sh jumped and dropped her goblet. Sam stood there, glowering down at her. It had been a balaast or more since she'd seen her brother. She wasn't sure she was ready for another encounter.

Sam had been putting on weight, eating voraciously on

long binges in his room, drinking varmils steadily for hours at a time. He looked terrible.

"Be quiet, Sam," she snapped.

"Don't give me grief, Rilla. Things're bad enough as it is."

To this Rilla made no reply. She hoped her brother would go away, but he showed no disposition to.

He sat down on a couch not far from hers.

"This is unusual," she said.

"What is?" he snapped.

"Your being here instead of sulking in your room."

Sam's face worked angrily. He choked off his first reply. "Listen to me, Rilla—I've thought it all out."

"Oh, have you?" Her eyebrows arched. He seemed to have forgotten all about the bomb.

"Yes, if we ever want to get back to Calabel alive, we have to go back to the castle first."

"But the inhabitants want to burn us at the stake, Sam!"

"I know, I know. But not if we have those damned helmets!"

Rilla's eyes widened. "Folo and Nathan have the helmets, Sam."

"For now they do, but we need them, we need them so we can go back there and smash the iulliin and find a way of making the spaceship work."

Rilla had listened to Nathan speculate about the spaceship; she doubted that it would be easily repaired or refueled. "I don't know, Sam. How are you going to do that?"

"I don't know either, woman! But that boy can figure it out, and if we have the helmets, we can make him do what we want. We can force him to come up with something."

Rilla realized her brother was crazy. Nathan was just a neurotic teenager. To expect him to magically master the intricacies of the spaceship drive was to ask for moons and suns and galaxies, and all those things that didn't exist in here. According to Nathan. "Sam, I think you should take a long rest. I think you should lay off the booze, you've been drinking too much. It's turned you silly."

"Damn you, Rilla, listen to me! This is important, unless you want to live the rest of your life here in this madhouse."

Rilla turned away and stared at the distant golden haze. Sam continued to talk, in urgent, quiet tones, looking over his shoulder constantly.

A little while later Folo and Avis brought the air barque back from a swimming trip. Sam saw the air barque approaching first, and with a disgusting curse he rose and slipped away. Rilla heard the double doors close behind him.

The air barque floated in and sank down on the repellers to a perfect landing. Folo let the stairs down as Avis cut the power unit.

"Hello, Rilla," said Avis, slipping past quickly, carrying a big yellow beesqueeze bowl over her head like a hat.

"Hello, Avis. Did you have a nice picnic?" And don't think I don't know what you two have been up to, Rilla wanted to scream.

"Yes, thank you, Rilla," said Avis in an airy voice. She disappeared inside.

Folo made the air barque fast, attaching two ropes to divots that had been sunk into the beesqueeze by teams of dagbabi. He straightened up and nodded coolly to Rilla.

Rilla's mouth hardened. "Honestly, young man, aren't you the limit! Now you're fucking Lady Prench. How do you explain it to Nathan?"

Folo stopped and locked eyes with Rilla.

"Come on, Folo, you can't hide that sort of thing from me. Maybe with that weird kid of hers you can get away with it, but not with me."

He shook his head, shocked rigid, baffled.

"Besides, the way I see it, honey, you're the only thing we girls have to look forward to, stuck here the way we are."

The way Rilla said "we" sent a shiver down his spine. "I don't think so, Mz. Boan. I don't think so." And Folo strode rapidly off the terrace, heading for his room.

Rilla giggled to herself, but her giggles wound down into sobs after a while. The flask of varmils was empty. She cradled her head in her arms and wept herself to sleep.

Not long afterward Nathan reappeared, staggering under the weight of a much larger module, a cube almost a meter square. With a groan he set it down. Sweat ran from his face. He sat down beside it. After a moment he caught his breath. He took a look at Rilla. She was asleep. Little snores fluttered from her long slender nose. A broken glass lay on the floor. The jug of varmils she'd been drinking from was empty. The smell of fermented fruit hung in the still air.

Then his eye caught the smaller module he'd brought down before. A blue light flashed on and off. A small screen was flickering in gray and blue.

Nathan gave a whoop of excitement and darted around her to reach the module. "Maybe you *are* more than a keyboard," he said. "Who knows? What started you? The heat? Solar energy?" He darted a look of hope toward the bigger module.

"Solar energy!" he yelled. "It must be!"

Experimentally he began hitting the keys. The screen stabilized when he touched a particular round depression. He tried key combinations. A combination of the round screen controller and a rectangular groove that ran along the bottom of the layout brought on a software show in the little screen. Symbols flickered over it; a text appeared and scrolled across the screen in blocks.

The screen blanked. Then the machine said something in Iullas. Nathan didn't understand the words, but he jumped for joy and went in search of the Sun Mel at once. It worked! The computer worked.

■ CHAPTER THIRTY-ONE

Balutnor Ganga was the country estate of the House of Urtisim. It was laid out, like many such houses in the region immediately around Meninrud Lors, in a radial pattern, dominated by a central tower, a rectangle of reddish brown bee weft.

From the top terrace of the red tower, the whole wide spread of the estate was visible on clear days, from the workshops and airstrip, partially hidden behind trees, inward and to Either, all the way to the farthest orchards, by the banks of the great canal far off to Or. Normally the view brought great cheer to Rukbhat dal Vnego Urtisim, but on this occasion he was filled with little but grim foreboding.

In the balaast since he had flown the feral siffile to Balutnor Ganga, they had methodically taken control. They were such cunning creatures! So swift to add up the fractions and understand the whole!

Now his radio answering machine played a bland message tape featuring himself asking callers to leave a message, pleading the pressure of work for the delay in any response.

They pillaged the great house, hunting for weapons, weapons, weapons. They were obsessed with weapons! They had tied him to this chair and driven the dagbabi out of the upper floors and shut the gates against them.

It was a considerable distance to Meninrud Lors. It might take many balaast before the high military sent anyone to investigate the mysterious disappearance of the computer master.

In fact, since his research at the front was so highly unpopular, with every department of the war effort afraid of bad news, none would eagerly seek him out. To make matters even worse, all that information, and much more besides, had been forced out of him by the siffile that called itself Kraka Buckshor. The siffile was merciless in his questioning. The bright blue eyes seemed to bore into Rukbhat's, probing, demanding, tightening in threat.

And threat there had been from the very beginning. "Fly us to your family home, then, and make sure not to give away your destination or you'll die—in considerable pain, too."

The siffile had held a razor-sharp knife, taken from the galley aboard the Urtisim family airjet, and pressed it to Rukbhat's tender neck. There had been nothing he could do.

Rukbhat heard the door open. The familiar tread brought Cracka Buckshore into view carrying a tray. He wore a priceless antique energy blaster in its scabbard on his hip. A knife was thrust through his belt on the other side.

He set down a bowl of bokka and some pieces of boltak. It was all they would let him have, as if he were siffile himself! The thought was so horribly degrading that Rukbhat tried desperately to push it away from him.

"Greetings, Rukbhat," said Cracka with a flinty smile. He took a seat. On the tray was a mobile computer interface and screen.

Rukbhat refused to respond.

"Mmm, we're going to be difficult, are we? You remember what we said about that before?" He put the food down on the small table. Rukbhat had not been fed for almost half a balaast. He was starving.

"I have some more questions for you."

Rukbhat turned dulled eyes toward him. Was there no escape from this humiliation?

"We have been working with the computer in your study. It has been most cooperative since you gave us the proper codes, for which we thank you."

Rukbhat shuddered.

"We have a few things to cross-check with you, however. For instance, what is the speed of sound in your measurement?"

Rukbhat tried not to speak, not to aid this deadly foe.

Cracka nodded, smiled grimly to himself, and leaned close to the recalcitrant iulliin. "I can't waste time, my friend. One more chance and then I will have to hurt you if you won't talk. You remember how painful it was, don't you?"

Rukbhat groaned hopelessly. He could not stand the pain. The mere thought of the burning taper, the hot coal approaching his skin, made him cry out. "No! Please! I will talk."

"Good, that's settled. Now, the speed of sound at ground level here?"

"Sound waves are the basis for our measurement of distance. The speed is known as the *urgufrakta*. The distance covered in a merj, if one is traveling at the speed of urgufrakta, is one usufrakt."

Cracka nodded. "All right, you're in agreement with the computer. I like that. We're pretty sure your atmosphere here is thicker than a planetary atmosphere, with more hydrogen and helium up top, so we've assumed a speed of sound of roughly twelve hundred of our units, the kilometer, to the standard hour terrestrial, which is our measurement of time."

Rukbhat stirred uncomfortably. Cracka noted it and pressed on. It was good to keep the iulliin off balance, it made it easier to pry answers out of him.

And beneath that, Cracka seethed with a general rage against the iulliin, who so casually destroyed the lives of millions for their own ends. He took every chance to force Rukbhat to confront the arrogance of iulliin beliefs in their racial supremacy.

"So, that gives me a figure of four hundred kloms, approximately, for your usufrakt. And we took sixty merj to fly from Aplanga battle front to here. I calculate that to be about forty-eight thousand kilometers, which would be one hundred and twenty of these usufrakt of yours."

Rukbhat nodded gravely. "It is only one hundred and twenty usufrakt to the battle front. My beautiful home is threatened. The enemy will destroy Balutnor Ganga, just as it has destroyed so many others."

"I guess I'm sorry about that, Rukbhat, but I've more pressing matters on my mind. One of my men is badly hurt, fighting in your bloodsucking war."

"It is a war to save the clanth. Surely this is a most noble cause."

Cracka felt his pulse start to hammer. The iulliin was so cool and calm about this! "Look, it's your war, *you* fight it. What gives you the right to force others to fight it for you? Anyway, it's a damn stupid war, a totally fucked-up war. If *you* had to fight it you wouldn't pit troops against crushers and heavy robots. That's slow slaughter. Total incompetence."

Rukbhat nodded. Always it came back to this, the hub of the question of survival. "So you would produce better weapons, and destroy the enemy forces?"

Cracka's brow furrowed in rage. "Damn right I would. Why the hell don't you just nuke the damn Xaacans and get it over with."

Rukbhat sighed. There was no point in arguing with a siffile.

"Anyway," Cracka continued, "one of my men is shell-shocked or something. He's all right physically as far as I can tell, but there's something wrong with his mind. I want to know if there's any equipment here that might be useful."

"Well, of course, there is the conditioning machine. If there is little physical damage to the brain itself, he may be deconditioned in the machine, painful memories may be erased—some kinds of mental shock have been treated this way, experimentally. It was impossible to get the funding to develop the idea, however."

Cracka gave a little whistle. "Where is this device?"

"In the laboratory, above my office."

Cracka nodded. He wondered if he dared put Shay under the alien machine. But they needed Shay, and he could think of no other way of bringing the big man out of the trance state he was in. From what Shay had allowed in the way of investigation, there were no skull fractures. Shay's other bruises and cuts had begun clearing up already with regular dosages of immune boost. "You will be required to operate the device for us. If you kill my man then we will probably kill you. You understand?"

"I understand, but the device cannot kill. If he can be wakened, we cannot know yet. But maybe it will work."

Cracka made his decision and then switched the subject. "All right, I have another concern. We have had a call from a female iulliin who has tried repeatedly to penetrate past the answering machine and speak directly to the computer. She speaks only Iullas, of course, so we had no idea what she wanted, but we got the computer to make a copy of one of her calls. The call was interesting. I knew you would want to see it yourself." He pressed a stud and the screen came to life. Rukbhat listened and then snorted in disbelief. It was Weanda! And she was coming to Balutnor Ganga.

"The computer claims that its security codes do not allow it to divulge the identity of this person or to translate all of her call. So who is she? Why is she so obviously anxious? Why is the high military chasing her?"

Rukbhat swallowed. How to lie? Even dissemble? The siffile was watching him very closely. The pain would be terrible if he was caught out. He chose the alien words carefully.

"That is my sister, the Lady Weanda del Vnego Urtisim. She is anxious on my behalf. She wants to know why I haven't called her and what it is that I'm doing that's so important that I can't answer her call."

Crack pursed his lips. "How often do you see your sister? Remember I can check in the computer logs for visitors."

"Not often. She lives in Meninrud Lors. We are opposed politically. She espouses irrational beliefs. She is very extreme."

Cracka pondered this and ran the message again. There was a considerable emotional content, but it didn't seem to be that of anger or debate. Lady Weanda wanted Rukbhat to do something about the high military. She sought refuge.

He was also pretty sure that Rukbhat wasn't telling him the whole truth. The message had been repeated, almost exactly, several times within a merj. "Tell me this—how far is it to Meninrud Lors?"

"It is less than twenty usufrakt."

"That's what we figured too; we're about eight thousand kloms outward from the city. So, in a fast airplane this sister of yours could be here pretty soon."

Rukbhat started; his eyes widened. How did the siffile always know?

"I do not understand, I—"

"Yes you do. This sister is coming here, isn't she?"

And Cracka knew he was right by the way the iulliin cringed. "So, tell me how long it will be, or I will have to hurt you."

Rukbhat groaned. There was no use. "She will be here within ten merj. She flees the executioners of the high military. She has a siffile with her, a siffile that she has taken illegally from the war effort."

This confirmed the computer's translation. Cracka smiled, certain now that the computer was truly open to them. He untied one of the iulliin's hands and pushed the food across. "Now, eat, I know you must be very hungry. Then we will talk some more."

A little more than three merj later an aircraft appeared in the distance. As it drew closer Cracka studied it through the iulliin binocular telescope they had discovered in Rukbhat's office.

The aircraft was a flying wing, jet-propelled, decelerating steadily, and following the automatic beacon in to the airstrip.

Cracka and Bat headed for the airstrip, riding in one of the large, roomy, open-topped ground cars that they had found in a garage in the shadow side of the great house. They arrived before the plane had landed and took up positions on either side of the main airstrip structure, a sunken hangar cum maintenance depot.

The wing came in and made a smooth landing at slow approach speed, and then taxied to a halt not far from the central hangar. A hatch opened and stairs were let down. An iulliin youth stepped out and bounded down the stairs, two at a time. He wore a one-piece flying suit of brown. He stared around at the deserted hangar in considerable confusion. The maintenance dagbabi had not appeared, as they should have.

The iulliin called back into the interior. Someone responded in a peremptory tone and another iulliin emerged, a female, dressed in a similar flight suit and carrying a white bag over one shoulder. Her white, woolly hair was teased out and braided and decorated with bright purple beads.

She was followed by a young human female with short, reddish hair. They descended the steps. The young male indicated the main palace of Balutnor Ganga and began to walk. The female tried calling out for the dagbabi. There was no response.

Instead Cracka and Bat stepped into view. They held up the iulliin energy weapons.

"Don't make any sudden moves," said Cracka in Iullas, fumbling some of the pronounciations but conveying the message.

The female screamed and shrank back in terror. The young male's face blanched; his eyes were as wide as saucers. *"Ewa siffile!"* he whispered. The deadly plague —feral siffile. What Xaaca did not crush beneath its metal feet, feral siffile devoured from within.

The human girl, though, took one look at them and burst into screams.

Cracka nodded and Bat moved in and grabbed the girl and pulled her away from the iulliin.

Then Bat stopped dead. "Cracka, it's Martherer Boan we got here."

Cracka turned stunned eyes in his direction, then the girl's. It was indeed Martherer Boan, against all odds. "Well, I'll be a noonday tronch calf." Was this a good omen, what Shay would call a "breath of the good tronch"?

"Welcome to the Free Republic of Balutnor Ganga, Miss Boan. You can have immediate citizenship, and you can also join our armed liberation forces."

Martherer had stopped screaming. She stared at the ranger, then at Bat Maroon. Then she burst into tears and threw her arms around Bat and hugged him.

Cracka kept his weapon trained on the two iulliin, though neither had dared to move a hair. "All right, we'll carry on now. Back to the house."

■ CHAPTER THIRTY-TWO

Lady Weanda and Wealo of Gors were now tied into chairs beside Rukbhat on the high balcony of the red tower. They were both considerably upset. Wealo in particular had a hard time believing what was happening to him. "But they must be made to understand!" He was almost shouting at Lord Rukbhat, his senior by six hundred zeem. "I must return to Meninrud Lors at once or my absence will be noted. The high military will take revenge on Gors!"

"This is simply terrible," exclaimed Lady Weanda. "Rukbhat, you must do something! Wealo was most gallant in volunteering to fly me here. He must not be made to suffer."

Rukbhat pointed out that he was tied down, much as they were, to his chair, and completely dependent on the siffile.

"Where are your yashi?" inquired Weanda.

"Dead, or abandoned at the battle front."

"Can you not inspire the dagbabi to rebel."

He snorted. "You would wish to see dagbabi in musht!"

Weanda nodded. "Of course, you are right. Dagbabi cannot be employed for combative purposes. Musht has to be avoided at all costs, it can spread like a cancer."

"Then how are we going to get out of here?" exploded young Wealo. "Already I can see the inspectors snooping about my office, asking questions."

Rukbhat sighed. "I'm afraid, Wealo, that your career in military supply is probably over. If I were you, I would concentrate on trying to stay alive."

"But what of the House of Gors? Am I to bring disgrace upon my house?"

"All the houses are doomed eventually, Wealo. Why not accept it and stop all this thrashing around on the hook."

Wealo's face darkened with anger. "You're nothing but a Realist!" he hissed.

"And you, my young friend, are nothing but an ignorant fanatic."

Lady Weanda could bear it no longer. "Rukbhat! How did this happen? Explain how you came to be imprisoned like this."

Rukbhat groaned. "I was inspecting conditions at the Aplanga Front. The enemy is making a great effort on that front, and we have committed the new armies there. I discovered that while the new armies have performed well, they have become resistant to mental conditioning. I discovered the use of illicit alcohol almost everywhere."

Weanda sniffed. "They have been infected with the same love of it that all siffile have."

"Perhaps. I'm sure it was inevitable. My findings show that the war has changed the nature of the siffile forever. We cannot allow the war to end, or the siffile will turn on us and destroy us."

Wealo seethed with impatience. "We must take the initiative and end the war! This is the only way to save us. We must build the atomic weapons!"

Rukbhat would have put his fingers in his ears if he could. As it was, he winced and replied hotly, "Atomics were outlawed at the inception of the new universe. If we employ atomics our enemy will soon have atomics of its own. And then it will be only a short time before all life here is annihilated."

"Not if we strike first and destroy the Xaacan entities!"

"We don't even know where these entities are! We know hardly anything about our enemy. As you well know, we have never received a reply to our signals to Xaaca, nor did any of the investigative missions we sent to Xaaca ever return."

"Enough talk," said Lady Weanda. "We must find a way to escape. I am certain that the high military will follow us here."

Rukbhat groaned again. To have to be rescued by Xaapt's security forces was just what he needed. Xaapt had fought Rukbhat's plans to study the battle front from the beginning. "They pursue you over the privatization of one of the new siffile?"

"The accursed Realists use this as an excuse to get rid of me because they know I have united the great families."

"Silly of you to give them the excuse, then, isn't it?"

"Nonsense. Privatization of siffile is our birthright! We are iulliin!"

Suddenly the three squabbling figures in the chairs looked up. They were not alone. Cracka Buckshore stood there, grim and silent. "Having a little argument?" he said to Rukbhat.

"Is it really necessary to keep us all tied up like this?" said Rukbhat in Interlingua. Upon hearing the barbarous alien language, Weanda and Wealo stared at him in astonishment.

"For the moment. Later you'll all be released. We don't intend to harm you, although I truly wouldn't mind killing a lot of iulliin for what you've done, but pure revenge would be wasteful now. We have a lot of people to rescue."

Cracka untied Rukbhat and pushed him ahead of him.

Wealo exploded at this insult to the Golden Iulliin.

Cracka whipped out his knife and let it quiver a few moments right in front of Wealo's long, narrow nose.

Wealo grimaced and bit back any further cries of indignation.

Cracka closed the door behind them and sent Rukbhat down the ramped staircases ahead of him. "The time has come for you to try and heal my friend. We've examined the conditioning device. It looks like something for torture, and I hate to think how many poor devils have had their brains scrambled sitting in it. You used it a lot, back in the time when you had lots of human beings here?"

Rukbhat paused on a landing and drew himself up to his full height. He towered over the siffile, but he still felt intimidated by Cracka Buckshore. The man looked as if he was only a short second away from cutting Rukbhat's throat.

"You must try to understand," he said. "Conditioned siffile were happy siffile. They led peaceful lives here. The machine was used very rarely after initial conditioning during puberty. Surely you can see that using purely physical means to constrain the siffile would be far more unpleasant."

Cracka stared at him a second. The iulliin still felt certain of his right to own siffile as slaves and to keep them as best he might. He urged Rukbhat on.

They descended the wide stairways for many floors, past empty rooms, for the most part, and finally reached the floor that Rukbhat had inhabited during his visits to Balutnor Ganga.

The last of his clan, Rukbhat found the old manse a gloomy, silent place. He preferred the lights and warmth of the city, and had spent little time at Balutnor. His office and laboratory were kept spotless by the dagbabi, who in the absence of any iulliin control had to be purged occasionally to prevent the assertive tendencies that could lead to musht.

In the laboratory, Shay Kroppa was finally sitting, strapped in, to the conditioning chair. It had been the devil of a job getting him into it. Neither Cracka nor Bat had been able to persuade him at first.

Shay could be tremendously stubborn, the biggest two-year-old in human history. However, Bat finally won him around with the offer of a beaker of perfumy varmils. Once he was strapped in the chair with his wrists cuffed to the arms, they had managed to get the headset in place, and then after a struggle, the helmet. Despite Shay's best efforts, he had been unable to dislodge it. Finally he had given in and sat there growling softly at them.

"Everything's ready," said Cracka.

Rukbhat was aware of the other siffile, the one called Bat. This one too was filled with hate. It was better not to read the faces of these humans; too much anger was there.

Rukbhat sat in the operator's seat and activated the machine. The diagnostics panel indicated that all was operating properly.

He ruminated sadly on the fact that the machines bequeathed them by the ancients were the only machines they had. Fortunately they had been made so well that they would last until eternity. Indeed they had already outlasted the ability of the iulliin to master them. Rukbhat knew too well that aside from himself and the three other members of the Scientific Institute, no one in the whole Sun Clanth could operate or repair one of these machines. He himself could not build one from scratch. They simply did not have that kind of technical expertise anymore in Meninrud Lors.

He became aware that Cracka was breathing over his shoulder. He shifted uncomfortably.

"Don't stop," Cracka said. "Remember, if anything untoward occurs, whatever you do to him I will do to you."

Rukbhat shivered at the tone in the man's voice. He set up the investigation software and allowed the machine to begin building maps of the brain structure of the subject. The machine had extensive libraries on siffile brain structures, as it did on yashi, dagbabi, and even istyggi brains. If there was physical damage it would soon be noted.

The maps clicked past, Cracka eyeing them intently. They looked somewhat like X-ray body scans.

Rukbhat waited until the brain had been mapped across twelve axes before announcing the obvious. "There is no serious physical damage apparent."

"Good," said Cracka.

Bat pushed closer and peered at the brain maps suspiciously. "If there's no damage, that means you can cure him, doesn't it?"

Rukbhat shrugged. "If it is only a matter of conditioning, of a mental block, then perhaps."

Bat swore and stepped away.

Rukbhat began the conditioning search. The machine hummed to itself and emitted regular small beeps. He sat and waited. The two men watched him intently.

Eventually the machine stopped the search and outlined a series of findings in conditioning maps. Rukbhat studied the maps. The trouble lay in a recessed personality trait. The patient had temporarily forgotten everything when he received the traumatic blow on the head. It was a rare but not incurable condition.

"He has forgotten himself," he announced to Cracka. "It is something I have seen before. A serious trauma, nonfatal, brings on this complete forgetfulness. Sometimes the subjects regain their memories all at once. Sometimes they remain in this condition for the rest of their lives."

"Amnesia," growled Cracka. "He's describing a case of amnesia."

"Can we wake him up?"

Rukbhat had already begun the corrective program.

The machine settled into another pattern of hums and clicks. A merj later it stopped suddenly and showed new patterns on its screen.

Shay Kroppa woke up with a bellow. He stared around himself, then at Cracka and Bat. His eyes were wide, a little spit hanging from his lower lip.

Bat chuckled. "Cracka, I do believe we just got a reborn Shay Kroppa."

"Bat, Ranger, where am I?"

"It's all right, Shay. Take it easy. We'll explain everything."

They helped Kroppa free and guided him through the laboratory and out onto the balcony.

Cracka brought Rukbhat out too.

At the sight of the iulliin, Shay burst into an astonished shout. "Whoa! Where did we get this?"

"Back at the battle front. Do you remember that?"

Shay concentrated. Things were definitely a little foggy in his mind. The battle front?

"You've been suffering from amnesia, Shay." Bat was staring intently into his eyes. "You couldn't remember anything. We had to use that alien machine to break you out of it."

"Amnesia," said Shay vaguely. Then he remembered. "By the Moth, it was that shell. I remember, we were jumping in retreat and that shell hit and I went over."

"Yeah," said Bat. "You went down and we picked you up and got you out of there. I'll tell you the whole story one of these days."

Shay stood there, massively silent for a moment. "I was down, then? I guess I owe you, Bat Maroon."

Then Shay turned to Cracka. "And the ranger? How did you find us?"

"We were on the same sector of the front. I ran into Bat in the black market. He had you stashed away in a safe place, while he sold booze to buy food and drugs for you."

"Holy Moth," exclaimed Shay. "Bat Maroon do all that for ol' Shay?"

"Damn right," muttered Bat.

"Ol' Shay got a lot to listen to, I think."

■ CHAPTER THIRTY-THREE

The gallery atop Fanthenai Tower soon boasted an array of five glistening black boxes, all dug out of the darkness of the attics by Nathan Prench then placed side by side in the sunlight.

The "humble adviser" was now complete.

The five units communicated with one another through photonic connections in their sides, indicated by discreet, inset arrows. The connections also locked the units together in a smooth modular bank of black plastic. Together they formed a powerful computer, communications, and entertainment complex.

The central module boasted a full-color video screen two feet across. The communication controls were set into the face of the unit that fitted to its left. A smaller screen on that unit offered iulliin graphic sets for frequency selection, signal strength, and modulation.

But control of all the units could be left to the humble adviser's software, which came resident in the unit that

fitted to the right of the screen. Once Nathan had mastered
the alien keyboard, with its uncomfortable, stalklike keys
and buttons, he soon managed to arrange an overview of
the computer's programs.

The software was impressive. The adviser had a well-
fledged personality. It had been locked up in the dark attic
of the tower for millions of balaast. Before that it had
served the erratic masters of Fanthenai, an infamous clan
of eccentrics and inbred degenerates, for millions more.

It was startled, somewhat alarmed, at first, when awakened by a representative of an alien species it knew nothing
about. Humans were a relatively recent introduction to the
tetraracial mix in the Plowl. The humble adviser had long
been buried in the attic when humans were first brought to
Fanthenai.

A new species . . . a *controlling* species. Had they sup-
planted the iulliin? The question rose immediately into the
mind of the humble adviser. Were they invaders of the
Plowl? Should the humble adviser cooperate with them?

But the humble adviser had been designed for use.
Lurking quietly in the dark with most RAM turned off
was numbingly boring. The humble adviser was equipped
with well-developed pleasure/pain responses, constructed
around the node regions of wish/improvement and dismay/
failure. They formed the basis for the acquisitive personality structure.

Thus, despite a few moments of initial hesitation, the
computer software chose to cooperate fully with the young
alien that had brought it out of the darkness. Work was
work, after all, and a lot better than torpidity in the dark.
The humble adviser soon discovered that the pleasure/pain
response was decidely favorable when working on the innumerable projects that Nathan Prench set it to.

For the Sun Mel, of course, the whole thing was a revelation, with a mystical power borne of legend come to life.

These glistening black boxes, with their screens and speakers and small winking indicator lights, these were what his grandfather had raved about. The ancient computing machines, the entertainment complex of the photonic era. Lost, all lost, to the damnable Yelkes and their moronic philosophy.

For hours at a time the Sun Mel would sit quietly nearby, watching Nathan work with the computer. Shazzeul had listened intently to Nathan's description of the humble adviser's operation, how the machine used high-efficiency solar panels to charge itself, how it ran both an electronic system and the photonics of the computer system. How the software codes were built up from binary machine code, how the personality levels were designed, employing twelve-dimension tree structures, how the pleasure/pain nodes were inserted in the programming whorls and feedback loops.

At first it meant almost nothing to him; the words seemed to form some seamless wall of impenetrability. For poor Shazzeul, electronics and photonics were almost impossible to grasp. He had only vaguely ever heard that all matter was made up of atoms. He had never heard of electrons or photons or any of the rest. Indeed it was hard for him not to think like a Yelke and assign some kind of magic power to the device.

But watching Nathan work the keyboard, and listening to the constant conversation that went on between the alien boy and the strange black box, which spoke an odd toneless Iullas, the Sun Mel felt a great change sweep over him. For a long, long time he stared at the screen. As Nathan depressed keys, the windows—each tinted a different color—opened and closed, displaying graphics sets, data, and even full-color pictures.

The Sun Mel could read some of the words in the data sets; as a child he'd received some of the last reading lessons allowed in Planggi. But those letters had been written with a stylus, on a writing slab; he'd never imagined anything like this, glowing, flickering, scrolling past.

It was in these symbols that the power lay! The realization stunned him. The machine, the genie that lived in that black box, could be controlled by the manipulation of the symbols. The genie was, in fact, nothing but an elaborate network of the same symbols, a fabric of enormous complexity, but all based on the simplicity of the symbols, the letters and numerals of his childhood lessons.

And the alien boy controlled it with ease, was even teaching it the vile alien gibberish it called Interlingua. The Sun Mel felt a little giddy. He was sweeping down a great chute of understanding, suddenly seeing himself and his world in the most painful light. How far they had fallen!

The weather had cleared to a cloudless sky in which the golden sun shone brightly, uncomfortable to look at, floating against the pale blue. Nathan worked on, expanding his inquiry into the history of the Plowl and the Plowl builders.

The humble adviser was now running 142 deep database searches, compiling lists and data on a seemingly endless basis. While it scanned and presented, Nathan occupied himself, fine-tuning the communicator across the radio and TV spectrum. With the communicator's directional antenna he was compiling a chart of the closest radio sources.

Nathan had already discovered that Planggi was virtually silent. There was radio and television activity in the atmosphere, a lot of it, but it came from very far away— by the blurring and video degradation, many millions of miles, Nathan judged.

In some directions the signals were just mud. The TV stuff was scattered so much it was barely discernible in video mode. Radio produced tremendous computer chatter, machine codes, blurred by the passage through tens of millions of kilometers of atmosphere to a sludge that even the humble adviser could not repair.

From other directions came iulliin video communications from other sun regions. Fragments of televideo conversations, faces, imagery, even iulliin movies—or at least that was what he thought they were.

To the Sun Mel the humble adviser's windows were vistas onto Olympus—Golden Iulliin were drifting across the sky on their air barques, supervising their palaces, their estates. Their great civilization still existed, their cities still functioned. There was hope, therefore. Among those high ones the poor degraded House of Planggi could find succor and aid in the struggle with the Yelkes and the forces of darkness.

Every so often the humble adviser emitted a beep and announced another answer from deep data search. Screen windows refreshed, opened, closed. "Spaceflights to other sun regions ended on statutory date 9786544 in the Builders' Canon."

"When was that?" Nathan asked.

"I was deactivated on statutory date 10444531."

"So quite a long time before they turned you off. And that was a very long time ago."

"Last flight was Interclanth Spacelines 501, left Planggi spaceport on a direct trip to the high city of Xaaca. The ship was never heard from, nor did it or any other ship ever return to Planggi."

No wonder the spaceport looked overgrown. It had laid abandoned for hundreds of thousands of years.

A shadow fell across them. Nathan looked up. Folo was standing there, stripped to the waist, wearing a pair of shorts made of woven beesilk dyed blue and carrying a towel over his shoulder. Folo and Avis went out every balaast for a picnic on the bank of one of the major canals. They swam in the warm, clean water of the canal and usually made love afterward.

In an odd little ritual, repeated every time, Folo came to

the corner occupied by the humble adviser and asked
Nathan if he wanted to come with them. Nathan always
refused. Today Folo even sounded insistent. "You ought to
take a break and come with us sometime, Nathan."

Nathan could sense that Folo most certainly did not
want him to come. Nathan had seen the signs—his mother
was abstracted, she sang to herself a lot, seemed actually to
enjoy their strange new life, as if she were on some enormously exotic vacation. By contrast, Folo seemed tense
and guilty, avoiding Nathan and the high gallery.

"Nope, got too much to do here, I think. Thanks anyway."

For some reason Folo felt impelled to say more. "Hey,
Nathan, you know you could do with a break, you're driving yourself crazy with this alien computer. You should get
some exercise or something, you know?"

Nathan, exasperated, spoke quickly and regretted it immediately. "Come on, Folo. You know you don't want me
along." Folo looked at him, suddenly wounded. He raised
his palms.

Nathan brushed it all away. "Look, this isn't Prench
Tronch! If we're ever going to get out of here and back to
Calabel, we're going to have to communicate with someone who may have access to spaceships. We've got to find
out if there're any functioning iulliin in this Sun Clanth."

Folo stared back at Nathan. C'mon, Nathan, he wanted
to say. We ain't never goin' home, face up to it. We're here
for good.

But something in Nathan's defiant pose deterred him.
"Yeah, Nathan. I guess. See you later."

Folo unshipped the air barque and started the motors.
Avis came out, waved to Nathan, and climbed the steps.
The air barque reversed off the terrace and, with a wide
turn to Either, sped grandly off into the distance at a steady
25 kilometers an hour.

The humble adviser beeped softly. "I have one further reference to space travel in memory. On statutory date 10002845, a space vessel crashed in the County of Munggi. It came down in a forest belonging to the Lord Pinskew of Munggi and set off a disastrous fire. There were no survivors."

"So that's that. As far as we know there's been no contact with the other sunlands for a very long time. Certainly no space travel, and we're not getting anything local from the communicator."

It looked grim, as if they were the only technology users in the entire Sun Clanth. And if space travel between clanths was as rare as it sounded, then there wasn't much chance of getting help from a passing ship.

The Sun Mel stared at him, uncomprehending, happy beyond price at being witness to this. Nathan gave a weary shrug and set the humble adviser to broadcasting a call for help on the iulliin emergency wavelength.

While Folo and Avis were absent, and Nathan and the Sun Mel were occupied on the balcony, a bulky figure moved stealthily through the apartments. It halted outside the door to Folo's room.

Sam Boan slipped the flattened end of the bar of high-grade beeble into the space between the door and the jamb. He leant into the bar and pushed hard. There was a slight give, and then no more.

Sam reddened in the face and heaved. On the third massive heave there was a groan, a splintering *crack*, and the door lock suddenly popped from the socket and the door flew open. The weft of the door had given way.

Success!

Sam peered in. The room was empty but for a table, a mattress, and a pile of weapons. Sam had watched Folo and Avis fly away aboard the air barque. No one would stop him. He quickly gathered up the two helmets and carried them to a new hiding place.

* * *

Avis and Folo lay together, on a bedcover taken from her room, beside the canal. It was open and sunny; a breeze came across the water. An occasional bee buzzed overhead. In the near distance a big bank of gray clouds was approaching.

After swimming together, naked, they had made love. Avid cradled Folo's head on her breast. It felt good to be with a young man again, a man whose body was hard and lean. Since Cathete's death, Avis's love affairs had been few and far between.

Now she had to wonder at herself for wasting those years when all those young ranch hands were around. The thought made her giggle inside, and she smiled, and a warm, wonderful feeling of peace went through her body. At that particular moment all was forgotten except that it was good to be alive.

Then her guilty voice reminded her that she was old enough to be Folo's mother, that Folo was her son's friend, and that he was still in love with Martherer Boan. But she dismissed the guilty voice. What did it matter? They were alone, just a few humans and a few old iulliin in a world populated by reptilian dagbabi and insectal istyggi. What else were they supposed to do with their lives? They would never see the people from their past again. It was as if they had begun new lives entirely.

There was no need to work; dagbabi brought all the food and clothing they could use. They could live in the tower for as long as they wanted. What else were they to do?

Avis had no idea. She seemed to have reached a full stop. Her life had been interrupted and placed on hold, in storage in an alien place in an unknown universe.

Small round red clouds were scudding overhead, head-

ing outward, their inward side striped gold. Above them
the sky was a creamy cerulean. She closed her eyes and
drifted into reverie.

Something flapped the air very loudly, like a giant
handclap. Her eyes flew open as a great shape flew swiftly
past, not more than fifty meters overhead. It was the length
of a whale, with wings as big as basketball courts. She
gave a scream of primal fright.

Folo rolled over, sat up, gasped after the monster. Together they stared. The thing had already diminished to the
size of a large bird in the distance. It stayed low, crested
the top of an eater, and disappeared.

"The punga," said Folo.

Avis shivered and moved closer to him.

■ CHAPTER THIRTY-FOUR

The balaast horn sounded, low and mournful, as Cracka
and Bat emerged onto the high balcony of the red tower.

The sky was overcast. A cloak of mist, green and
humid, lay over the region. The temperature had risen
steadily to more than 30 degrees centigrade. The sky continued to thicken.

On the balcony the iulliin captives remained bound to
their chairs, a captivity they chafed at most volubly.

Cracka silenced them with a growl to Rukbhat. "You'll
be free soon enough, I daresay. So tell them to be quiet. I
need information."

Didn't the siffile always need information? He was relentless.

"Our young female friend has a fever and complains of an intolerable itch in her skin. Is this a disease of some kind that you are familiar with?"

Rukbhat translated, and Weanda shifted uncomfortably in her seat but said nothing. Cracka noted the movement, however. He leaned forward and pushed his face into hers, something she found inexpressibly horrible. She hissed and shrank back.

"Tell Lady Weanda to tell me what she knows, or I will carve her face with my knife."

He pulled out the big kitchen knife, with a shiny blade of iulliin ceram-alloy, and waved it under her long, skinny nose.

She emitted a little scream. Then she spoke rapid Iullas with Rukbhat.

"It is nothing but addiction to *the Rooms*. I used it to control the siffile and keep her conditioned while she lived with me."

Rukbhat nodded. He knew Weanda's type. They claimed to be superpatriots and they wrapped themselves in the social respectability of the aristocrats and the Heads-in-the-Sand Party, but they were just hedonists. The culture was drowning in its own pleasures, and every balaast the enemy made progress. Addiction to *the Rooms* was widespread, a leading contributor to iulliin apathy in the face of the threat they faced.

He informed Cracka that the girl was recovering from addiction to a pleasure drug.

"What?"

Rukbhat tried to be helpful. "If you wish, you may give her doses of this drug. I have a quantity of it in a dried form. Prepared properly it will assume the potent form. The dose is moderate. A small spoonful will produce a euphoric state for two or three merj."

Cracka's face was thunderous. "And if I don't wish?"

"Don't wish! Then, ah, well a sedative will keep the siffile from harming itself during the worst of the transition period. The addiction should wear off in a balaast or two." Rukbhat blinked.

Cracka swore bitterly. "Weanda had Martherer addicted to a drug."

Bat scowled. "Fucking iulliin! I'd like to—"

"Yeah, I would to. All of them, but not just yet, eh, Bat?"

They returned to the room where Martherer lay. Shay Kroppa kept watch. Shay looked up as they came in.

In the last balaast, Shay's face had returned to life. The big man seemed to have no further adverse effects. He still had some bruises from his fall, but his memories were intact. "No change, Captain," he said softly.

"There won't be any change for another forty hours or more," said Cracka in a grim voice. "She's in the middle of withdrawal from a drug that that damned iulliin witch kept her addicted to. 'Pleasure drug' they called it."

The big troncher shook his head ominously. "I wring damn iulliin neck?"

It was very close to not being a question.

"No. We need them as hostages. The witch says she is being hunted by the high military for stealing Martherer from a battle unit."

"High military?"

"Right, I don't know what that means. Could be a couple more iulliin will show up, could mean that they come with fifty yashi in shock boots."

Cracka scratched the stubble on his chin.

"What we probably should do is get out of here, take one of the planes and head outward into the provinces. Rukbhat says the clanth is thinly populated—great estates scattered among the villages of dagbabi. We could get lost in some backwater area and stay hidden until we can come up with a plan for getting possession of the mother ship and freeing the rest of the people here."

"You mean all the people, Captain?" Bat said. "Or just the Calabels?"

"I don't know, Bat. I guess maybe there are too many people here for us to rescue all of them at one go."

There were millions, perhaps even billions. Humans had been there several thousand years, and according to Rukbhat had been spread widely across the Sun Clanths, given as gifts in the early days.

"I guess that's one of the things we have to try to work out. But staying here is getting too dangerous. We can't afford to be captured. The iulliin would kill us quicker than tronch bait."

They were all agreed on that. They turned back to look at the girl.

Martherer shivered and shook beneath a blanket.

"Poor little thing," said Shay mournfully. "It really makes me wish I could wring a few iulliin necks."

Nathan continued his survey of the radio spectrum horizon until he had moved the directional antenna so that it pointed almost directly Eitherward. Signals came from everywhere, but nearly all were very weak. But a strong source was radiating from Eitherward on several frequencies. Nathan had noted it on his early sweeps around the compass. He fine-tuned the antenna, drifting slowly Eitherward.

On the very high frequencies there came a sudden spattering of static. Bursts, pulses. Nathan tracked back. They were unusual, numerous, and usually very brief. Below them on the scale was a heavy kludge of distorted video transmission. "Radar ghosts," he burst out suddenly. "High performance radars from a long way away." He paused. "Very high performance radars. Must've skipped along the ionosphere to get here. Long-range sky waves."

The Sun Mel stared at him with devotion in his eyes.

"Very powerful weapons, must be a helluva war going on." The dial moved on slightly. Nathan focused on the television bandwidths. A lot of machine code howled and *veep*ed. The screen ran blizzards of digital data that could only be computer-to-computer communications.

What went on out there, wherever the signals were coming from? Radar like that had to mean war, didn't it? Intense rapid-fire radar pulse was the absolute hallmark of technological warfare.

Or was it just a communications mode, the signals modulated finely in ways the humble adviser didn't recognize?

Whatever it was, it had to be the work of a technical civilization. Perhaps he had just tuned into the working channels between some big banks or insurance companies in a faraway iulliin city that had not fallen to wrack and ruin.

But this source was much stronger than any others, and therefore likely to be closer than the others.

Nathan decided to try to communicate. He had the humble adviser transmit the iulliin Mayday signal on the television bandwidths at the maximum power available. It wasn't much, but just possibly someone over there would be listening for such signals, and just possibly they might bother to call back. Nathan would keep the conversation to keyboarding, and if required to come up with an iulliin talking head, he could use the Sun Mel.

In the intervals between each signal, the machine put the Mayday call out on the radio wavebands, down to medium wave. Each signal was accompanied by coordinates for the tower of Fanthenai, as supplied by the humble adviser. The very small risk of arousing undue attention from these faraway iulliin was outweighed by the possibilities: knowledge, the keys to unlocking the iulliin relics in Planggi. With the iulliin technology and iulliin space drives they could build their own ship. The dagbabi and istyggi would handle the heavy labor, and they'd build their own foundry, laboratory, and space yard.

Nathan continued tuning down the spectrum, tracking across this source region.

There was iulliin stuff on the medium and long waves. Iulliin phrases, coordinates, directions. It was scattered and haphazard. The humble adviser gathered the signals and produced pictures where they could be enhanced enough— mostly iulliin talking heads. Picture quality was very poor. Backgrounds seemed to change a lot. A lot of motion was evident.

He felt a sudden, gentle touch on his shoulder. He jumped and whirled.

Two dagbabi were holding out their lunch trays.

Nathan took a deep breath and spoke in Iullas. "Please don't do that again. Just say something when you want to announce yourselves."

The dagbabi looked at him with incurious eyes. They looked to the Sun Mel, and at his gesture they placed their trays on the circular gray table, then withdrew.

The Sun Mel settled excitedly to his tray. "No pickled fruit fish today! Wita, we have wita today!"

Nathan's interest stirred. He liked wita, the flesh of the silvery airfish that flew in great flocks through the food clouds. Pounded, flaked, broiled, fried, grilled, made into patties, even eaten raw, the wita was the premier food fish of the Sun Clanth. Today there were small broiled steaks of wita, served with the coarse slab form of bokka.

To wash it down Nathan drank water. The Sun Mel allowed himself one glass of chilled varmils.

The food was good. As he ate it Nathan gazed off into

the distance in the direction of Either. Somewhere out there—perhaps as little as ten million kilometers away, perhaps as much as one hundred million—was a technical civilization. The question was whether such a civilization would reply to his little Mayday call.

Suddenly the humble adviser emitted a beep. "Incoming message flow, I—" There was a flash, and the voice was cut off.

The screen flashed on, a bright green. A curious thrumming sound began that rose in volume to a shriek. The screen became enormously bright, and a beam of light flicked out of it and danced around the tower, as if photographing it.

Nathan groaned. "This again. It was like this in the Hall of Antiquity. Just before the galga beast."

The green beam jumped toward him; he dodged away from it.

The Sun Mel backed away, his hands up, an appalled look on his face. "What is happening?"

"I don't know, but I'd like to find out." Nathan waited until the green beam was focused on the tower entrance and then jumped into position in front of the machine. He keyed into the humble adviser. "What is it?"

Briefly, the humble adviser took control of the speakers. "Invasive signal, overrode equipment, I cannot—" And it cut off in a screeching howl that shook the speaker cabinets.

The humble adviser was gone. Something else had taken its place. Something that sparkled and seethed inside the black boxes. The howl of static screeched from the speakers; the green beam flicked across and speared the iulliin. It bore in, tightening on his head. The Sun Mel wailed and sank to his knees, holding his hands before him to ward off the terrible light.

Nathan saw that the communicator's transmission mode

was on full: the machine was sending and receiving a tremendous amount of information. Something was very wrong there, something he had to stop. He keyed a basic disconnect to the communicator.

A grinding noise came from inside the computer.

Suddenly the keys gave Nathan a powerful electric shock and he was thrown backward, his fingers tingling. The green beam flicked over him. He stared up into a blinding glare, data fragments, black shadows dancing across it. He shook his head and pulled himself to his feet. The machine seemed to glower at him, menacing, black.

Nathan shouted, "This is crazy! Humble adviser, where are you? I want the humble adviser!" He approached, the green beam following him, the flickering rising in frequency.

"Have to break the photonic connection, that ought to do it." Nathan grabbed the unit containing the humble adviser and heaved it out of position, breaking the photonic connections to the rest of the complex.

He received another shock, but when he'd picked himself up, the computer cube was no longer glowing and sparking, and the grinding noise had ceased. But the communications module and the screen still seethed with the green energy. One speaker continued to yowl in a frenzy.

Abruptly the communication module exploded, emitting a flash of bright green light and a puff of dark gray smoke that rose and dissipated.

Nervously Nathan dislodged the directional antenna and dropped it away from the communicator.

Slowly the Sun Mel got to his feet, his eyes wide, staring at the machines. "A demon came! It is just as I learned as a child—the green light of the demon came and disrupted the machines! Without the machines our civilization crumbled."

Nathan tried hard not to agree with him. Staring at the

smoking communicator cabinet, he wondered if he could ever repair the damage. Grimly he picked up the computer module and set it on the table. Gingerly he turned it on. The small screen came up, blank. The humble adviser was absent. Had the software been destroyed?

Nathan prayed he could resurrect the resident artificial intelligence, because without it he would be forced to try to reprogram the machine himself, a tedious and time-consuming task. Hours slipped by, the sound of the little merj pipes ticking them off.

Hunting through the virtual memory for any remaining shreds of the humble adviser, Nathan came upon it at last. A few files, the central personality, all in a dormant mode, switched off to avoid destruction.

Nathan set to coaxing the humble adviser back to life. It was slow work; the software had been badly damaged. Nathan had to learn the basics of the iulliin software programming codes from the remaining central files, so he could write patch codes between sundered sections of the humble adviser's interior data base.

When he finally finished, the humble adviser was half rebuilt and had begun a painstaking recreation of whatever data files had survived the onslaught of the green "demon."

Nathan stretched. He rubbed the back of his neck, which felt sore and stiff, and pushed himself to his feet. It was time to take a breather. He'd been working on the machine for half a balaast without a break.

A mass of gray and black clouds was approaching; it had already covered a third of the sky. The Sun Mel was asleep, tucked under his pink and orange outer robe, his big slippered feet crossed over on the end of the couch.

For a moment the Sun Mel looked almost human, a very gaunt, tall human, with an unusually long, straight nose. Then Nathan looked again and the Sun Mel was alien, iulliin.

It was time to eat something and get some sleep. He was seeing things. Nathan turned away, crossed the terrace, and entered the corridor.

He did a double take. A massive figure, wearing one of the helmets of dominance, stood in the hall. "Sheriff Boan! What are you doing?"

"Nathan!" Sam exclaimed, coming forward into the light. An insane smile glittered on his face under the helmet. And then the field hit home. Nathan reeled.

Sam exerted all his will. The field grew even more intense. "Down! Down before me, Nathan! I am the new master here."

Nathan collapsed, gasping from the mental pressure of the dominance field. He sagged against the wall, then turned and staggered back to the balcony under a mental push.

Sam strode out onto the terrace behind him. He surveyed the Sun Mel, who awoke at the lash of the field. The Sun Mel too was forced to his knees.

Sam examined the humble adviser, which beeped occasionally as it completed a loop of the rebuilding sequence. "Ah yes. You, Nathan, will be a great help to me. You I will definitely take with me. I will leave the others here to rot, except for you and your mother, who I will have need of as well."

Nathan tried to reply, but Sam exerted the full field and his tongue clove to the roof of his mouth and nothing came out.

"No, do not attempt to reply just now, Nathan. Your immediate feelings are of no concern to me. We must first secure the air barque and dispose of that wretch Folo Banthin. Then we will set off back to Planggi."

Nathan waved his hands, gurgled in his throat.

Sam chuckled. "I know, you're a brave boy. You want to fight, but that's all over now for you. You're not going to fight me anymore, you're going to obey me!"

A couple of hours later, when the air barque returned to the tower, the high gallery was empty. Only the iulliin computer evinced any activity as small green and blue indicator lights flashed.

Folo brought the barque in slowly, set it hovering over the gallery floor, and let the repellers lower it to a gentle contact.

The clouds moved in front of the sun at last, bringing on the twilight.

Folo let down the stairs. Avis descended and made her way toward her room. She let herself in and the door closed behind her.

Folo looked after her departing back. She was difficult to read. He sensed the confusion, the strongly mixed emotions that their affair aroused in her. He resented it. He believed she thought he was tronch trash and beneath her.

He shrugged. They were alone here; it didn't matter if he was trash or not. He was the only possible choice for her. Rilla and Nathan would have to breed too, if they were going to found a colony.

The traditional calm of the true troncher rose to the surface again. Folo found it easy to busy himself in the minutiae of every day, and thus dispel the fears, the aching longing for Calabel, the things that drove Avis to tears sometimes. The only thing that he really couldn't keep out was the tormenting thought of Martherer, which would not leave him sometimes until the guilt virtually drove him to tears.

Folo carefully made the air barque fast and turned to head for his room.

He stopped. Standing in his way was Sam Boan, wearing one of the helmets!

"Sheriff?"

"Got you, you little maggot! Got you at last!" Sam laughed and lashed the dominance field down. He had the helmet turned up to the highest notch, blasting on all six levels.

Folo gasped and seemed to collapse in on himself. Sam reached for control. It was almost like putting one's hands on a steering wheel now to him.

Folo spun on the spot and dropped to the floor. His limbs twitched briefly and then he froze, completely paralyzed.

Sam's laugh bellowed around him as he roughly turned the youth over and bound his wrists together. Then he tied a halter around his neck and stood up again. "Give me any trouble and I'll make sure you die real slowly, tronch maggot."

The field lifted. Sam jerked on the rope, dragged Folo to his feet, and pulled him along behind him.

■ CHAPTER THIRTY-FIVE

Something had changed in the great tower. The dagbabi stirred restlessly, made anxious by the high-power control fields that swept about it. Their short tails lashed, their eyes rolled.

The stress made the females shed their eggs, or even devour the newborn. Young males battled mindlessly in the alleys. Social cohesion began to wobble. Musht was only a whisker away.

On the high gallery at the top of the tower, Sam Boan indulged himself in an infantile reign of terror. He gloried in the powers of the helmet. The whole place was his play-pen.

At the very start, Sam had only possessed crude control of the helmet's powers. He had not had the time to really master it. Still, he had rearranged things to his own taste.

Folo was thrust into a cage, normally used for fattening hoppers by the dagbabi. He was forced to crouch, without even enough room to turn around in. Nathan, Rilla, and the Sun Mel were put together in one room that Sam humorously nicknamed the servants quarters. There were no windows, and the ventilation shaft had a thick grille.

Then Sam had waddled down the corridor to Avis's room. She had screamed, for a long time. And despite the use of the helmet to overcome her resistance, Sam was unsatisfied. He wished sexual gratification, not the frozen resistance of the rapist's victim. He was determined that she should be cooperative, even willing.

He had arisen and dragged her to her feet and pulled her after him down the corridor. She fought him all the way, Nathan howled and battered on the door to his cell as they passed, but to no avail. The heavy door was impervious to his assault.

When Sam had used the helmet to coerce her, she had lain motionless on the floor or crawled very slowly away from him like a broken beetle, so that the urge to kick her and beat her to death came over him with an almost overwhelming force.

With Nathan still howling inside the cell, Sam had dragged Avis onto the gallery, where he used the helmet on her to freeze her on the spot. She fell on her side, her clothes torn, her hair matted with spit and blood. She made peculiar groans and hisses.

Sam had taken up the long sword and pulled it from its scabbard. He'd jabbed it lightly into Folo.

Folo had spat back at him through the bars. The spittle sprayed across Sam's cheek.

Boan's face darkened with rage. "Damned tronch trash. I'll make you live for that!" He emitted a weird gurgling giggle, a sound from the vault of human hell.

Sam had turned his attention to Avis. "Do what I want or I will crush this wretch, finger by finger, toe by toe."

She stared at him, numbed by the horror.

Folo snarled insults at Sam in the desperate hope of making the big man so angry that he'd forget himself and open the cage. But Sam merely laughed and beat on the cage with the flat of the sword, great two-handed blows that forced Folo to crouch back.

When Sam stopped, he turned to her with horrible triumph on his face. "*Now!*"

Avis could not let Folo be destroyed, but the thought of giving herself to Sam with his reeking breath and evil eyes was beyond her.

Still she could try to pretend. She pulled herself to her feet and pushed her hair out of her eyes. "What do you want?" she'd whispered in bizarre pseudoseductiveness.

Sam pulled her to his rooms and pushed her toward the bed. "Disrobe and service me!"

But when it was finally over and he lay, exhausted, torpid beside her, she had tried to kill him, creeping to the sword, pulling it from the scabbard and returning with it high over her head.

At the last moment he awoke from reverie and saw his doom. Sam had rarely moved so quickly in his entire life. He jerked away from her, almost dropped the helmet, and heard the sword strike down and into the couch. It would have cut him in half.

With the helmet on, however, he forced her to her knees and retrieved the sword. But it had not been easy; Avis was very resistant to the powers of the iulliin dominance helmet. And though Sam was a powerful source-mind for the fields, which required strong urges, and therefore relatively

large surges in brain electrical activity, he had to struggle
to subdue her.

Since then he'd kept Avis locked in her room. She was
given food and water and left to wonder what was going on
outside the walls.

Nathan, the Sun Mel, even Rilla, were forced to wait on
him hand and foot. Sam particularly enjoyed making Rilla
rub his fat body and massage him, including fellatio on
demand.

Occasionally, when drunk, he threatened to force
Nathan and the Sun Mel to do the same for him. But as yet
they'd been spared this humiliation. However, when Sam
was in his cups he would frequently pick up the whiplike
green rod of beeble that the dagbabi brought him and beat
Folo with it. Kept in a cage on the gallery, Folo was tied up
at the wrists and knees, and was beginning to weaken from
maltreatment and semistarvation over several balaast.

Sam continued to avoid Avis Prench, since his first disastrous attempt to force her into sexual relations in the first
hours of his reign of terror.

Now, however, after several balaast of experimentation,
Sam had a better idea of the helmet's powers.

Once a subject had been blasted on the sixth level, that
subject could then be gripped by psychocoercion and
forced to do anything. This he'd learned from his first use
of the device.

The lower-order forces allowed different degrees of
control and penetration. On level one, Sam had found,
dagbabi and klicks could be controlled almost like remote
robot devices. Sam had had fun for a while getting dagbabi
to throw themselves off the balcony railing, giggling while
their jerking bodies fell the hundreds of meters to the
ground.

Level two was specifically for breaking in wild yashi.
To Sam it remained a mystery. The third level was a search

level that gave access telepathy, allowing limited reading of the minds of other beings. Levels four, five, and six were for use on humans, yashi, and even iulliin.

Sam ordered a cup of chilled varmils brought to him. Rilla, hating him as she had rarely hated anything or anyone, was attending to his pedicure. Sam had become terribly fond of having Rilla perform little services for him.

Nathan brought the varmils. Sam made him kneel and offer it. While he sipped it he ordered Nathan to join the Sun Mel in the servants quarters. "And tell that old gobbler he better get ready to suck my pecker good! Or else." And Sam laughed to himself and got to his feet and sent Rilla to join Nathan and the Sun Mel.

The fourth level was an interesting one. It appeared to offer an emotional control. By making Rilla feel "warm and happy" he had produced in her a near enthusiasm for the task of fellating him.

He locked the door on them and then strolled on down to Avis's room.

Avis awoke at the first sound of the key in the lock. The dagbabi that brought food were not due for hours. It could only be Sam.

He strode in, bouncing a little, in bare feet, wearing an iulliin robe adapted to his corpulent frame.

Avis tensed. She had planned for this event, planned minutely. Now she hesitated. Did she dare?

Sam advanced and sat beside her. He smiled in a grotesque attempt to be pleasant.

She tried not to cringe too obviously. His eyes were mad, his lips were wet with varmils. "I think we should have a little talk," he said. He had the helmet on the fourth level, and he projected a steady flow of warm emotions toward her. "You were right to resist me before. I was angry, and I lost my temper, I'm afraid."

Avis thought her eyes would fall out of her head. Could he be serious?

"So I want to make a new start with you." He reached out and petted her knee. Avis fought down the inclination to shrink away.

"We have to begin again. After all, we don't have much choice, do we? I mean, here we are, all alone in this place. We'll have to come to some sort of sensible arrangement, don't you see?"

Avis struggled but was unable to say anything; only a dismal sort of croak came out.

Sam beamed at her, and she felt a strange tickling sensation in the back of her mind.

She focused on him more clearly. The helmet had a little green indicator light blinking on the left side, above the ear. Sam looked like an overweight jet pilot almost. Something scarcely human. Avis shrugged. Was it in her to actually pity this monster? It was hard—she'd heard Folo's cries of pain as Sam beat him.

"I . . ." she began, and faltered.

She didn't even know if Folo was alive. "How is Folo?" she said at last.

Sam's face darkened immediately. "He lives. He will live a long time. Do not concern yourself with him. Think more of your relationship with me. We must start again, get off on a new footing."

Folo lived, then. Her plan came back to her. For a fraction of a second she doubted herself, then forced it out of her mind lest Sam should read her thoughts and discover her.

Fortunately Sam had drunk too much varmils for clear thought sensing. The helmet's powers were limited by the quality of the brain using it. Sam missed her plans; in fact he could read little of Avis's thought. She had proved resistant to the helmet from the beginning, emphasizing what the iulliin had long understood, that human individuality was very strong, much stronger than that of dagbabi or yashi, old genotypes in servitude to the iulliin for hundreds of millennia.

Where his efforts with the fourth power had produced cooperation in Rilla and an openness to his attempts to peer into her thought, with Avis the barriers were still up.

At least, however, she had not twitched away from him screaming.

Sam decided to try another tack. He put an arm around her shoulders and drew her closer to him. "Look," he said, "we have to be nice to each other."

The smell of his sweat and the rotten fruit on his breath was almost overwhelming. She tensed, tried not to think.

"You be nice to me, and I'll be nice to you." He smiled, while the rest of his face took up a look of insane cunning. "I'll even be nice to Folo for you, if you're nice to me."

Sam held her for a while like that. He was fairly throbbing with the desire for her.

Avis was a good-looking woman, with flesh that was both firm and womanly soft. She was unlike Rilla in every way, with full breasts and curving hips. Sam was determined to have her, and to keep her as his concubine.

Avis patted down the front of Sam's belly. He wore no belt and thus had no concealed weapons.

He was obscenely eager, his eyes bulging at her.

She reached for him, and Sam sighed in enormous gratification. She was going to be sensible; she'd seen that there really wasn't any other choice. His whole body felt a thrill. This was something he'd thought about for a long time.

And he thought briefly of Cathete. They'd fixed *him* all right! Sam would have loved to use his most murderous giggle, but he craftily decided to restrain himself. No need to upset Avis now.

Avis had her other hand down there. She reached inside the robe. The touch of her fingers on him was electrifying.

Sam groaned in anticipation of the pleasure to come.

Avis slipped an arm around his shoulders and eased herself against him. He could feel the firm weight of her against his robe.

She looked as if she really wanted to kiss him.

And then her hand tightened hard on his testicles and jerked them hard, and her other hand slipped up and knocked the Helmet off his head, sending it rolling across the smooth ceramic floor.

She was free and diving for the helmet in the next instant, and she would have had it too if in his agony Sam had not brought up both legs instinctively and caught her foot, tripping her.

He rolled off the couch and swung a fist at her, striking her between the shoulder blades and driving her to the floor. "Damn you, bitch!" he screamed through the nausea, and surged for the helmet himself.

But Avis was not finished yet. She swung her weight into him, dislodging him and sending him onto his side. She reached for the helmet, but he grabbed her arm and pulled her back, and she lashed out with a foot and kicked the helmet, like a soccer ball, so that it *thwack*ed into the wall and rolled out of sight behind the huge iulliin armoire.

Sam pulled her back and aimed a terrible blow at her head which she partly deflected.

Then he lost his grip on her and fell on his belly with a curse. She got to her feet, but he rolled too quickly for her and got between her and the helmet. He had brought no other weapons with him this time, not wishing to repeat the risk he'd run before.

Avis prepared to try to jump over him, but Sam got to his knees too quickly.

She couldn't get to the helmet. But the door lay in the other direction, and it was unlocked.

Avis ran for it, pulled it open, and dashed out into the corridor, Sam was close on her heels, without the helmet. The sword lay propped against the wall out on the balcony. If she killed herself he would have no one except Rilla.

Heart pounding, he pursued her across the gallery, past the startled gaze of poor Folo.

Avis missed the sword and came to bay, trapped by the parapet. Sam closed in. She could not be allowed to jump, she was much too valuable to him.

He tried to tackle her around the waist, but she kicked him and evaded his arms and ran to the air barque.

She leapt up the few stairs and onto the barque.

"No!" bellowed Sam in his fury. He pursued her. She kicked at him from the top of the steps until he caught one of her feet and she fell heavily on her back. He climbed the stairs, face purple from the exertion. Avis ran to the prow of the barque, and Sam came after her, leering. There was no escape.

"This time I will not be so gentle," he promised.

Avis prepared herself, fists raised. How could she ever hit Sam hard enough to gain the upper hand? It seemed impossible.

And then Sam's leer vanished, replaced by an expression of total astonishment.

The sunlight was cut off, there was a noise like a giant's hand clap, and a quick gust of wind stirred the vines on the walls.

"What?" gurgled Sam.

Avis turned and saw an enormous creature folding huge wings across its back. Its wide, blunt face was topped with a crest of gray fur; two enormous flippers and a wide fat tail supported the body. Its gaze raked across her from dark, intelligent eyes.

And jumping from the creature's back was a muscular man with a mane of gold-blond hair. He wore a loincloth and some belts, plus a helmet with a curving horn on top. On his hips he bore weapons—a short, scabbarded sword, an ax, a knife, a slingshot.

He looked up at them for a moment. Avis felt a stark gaze sweep across her, and then the man jumped the steps

in two bounds and cannoned into Sam, knocking him flat
to the deck.

Sam curled into a fetal position with a wail of despair.

The barbarian allowed himself a single bark of laughter,
then turned to Avis. He took her by the wrist, pulled her to
him, and hoisted her over his shoulder. He then bounded
down the stairs and over to the side of the huge flying
creature.

On its barrellike neck was strapped a large, ornate double saddle. Big hands seized Avis and swung her up and
into the back saddle. The blond vaulted into the front saddle, seized a set of reins that had been wrapped around a
hooking pommel, and gave a great shout.

The creature unsheathed enormous wings and flung itself backward from the balcony into the air.

Avis almost fell out of the saddle in shock. Empty air all
around her, nothing but sky, clouds, and vertigo. But instinctively she gripped the beast beneath her with her knees
and clung to the blond barbarian ahead of her.

The flying creature slipped sideways through the air for
a second and then flapped the enormous wings a couple of
times, grabbing air and hurling them skyward.

Behind them the massive tower diminished swiftly.

■ CHAPTER THIRTY-SIX

The humid vapor overlaying Balutnor Ganga intensified
through the next balaast. The light grew dim as the clouds
continued to build. Dagbabi work parties went out to lay in
protective covers on fields with ripe crops.

Cracka and Shay examined the aircraft, leaving Bat to continue his inventory of the interior of the tower and halls of the great house. They soon came to the conclusion that Wealo's V-wing was the better choice for them. It was built for distance travel, at moderate high speed. It had capacious fuel tanks, and yet there was considerable passenger room.

The interiors were covered in a pale blue polymer. The cabin doors, the window surrounds, and the lamp sconces were all done in plates of golden beepane, highly worked in an abstract style of smooth planes and triangles. The floor was carpeted in an ochre fabric with finely worked abstract detailing on the margins.

There were baths, lounges, and six cabins on the upper floor. Below those were empty quarters for dagbabi, the galley, and some storage space.

The controls were in a blister-topped cockpit that was a nest of dials and meters and iulliin switches, long stalks of purple and green glass.

Wealo would have to get them into the air. Cracka didn't think any of the rangers would master all the gauges and switches before he wanted to leave.

A check of the fuel tanks showed that they were near empty. They would have to get Wealo and Rukbhat and insure that the plane was properly refueled. They returned to the central part of the palace, beneath the great red tower, in one of the heavy ceramic automobiles that were maintained carefully by garage dagbabi.

As they came to a halt, Bat Maroon bounded out to greet them, eyes dancing with excitement. He dragged them down a long corridor into a musty room piled with dusty equipment and ancient weapons, like some medieval armory.

Bat brandished a sword, a heavy saber with a massive hilt and pommel. The blade was a pale green ceramic, the hilt a dark blue polymer, with wires of beeble forming the protective cup.

"Rukbhat says all this stuff was for dueling. They used to be hot duelists, the iulliin. A long time ago. He's been filling me in on the glories of the past. Did you know they used to ride a flying animal called punga."

"They're those big things painted on the wall."

"Yeah, they used to go out and hunt on them. A long time ago."

"Yeah, a *very* long time ago," Cracka said with disgust. "The iulliin haven't done much of anything for themselves in a hell of a long time."

Bat had discovered heavy hand weapons that used an explosive powder to fire small ceramic balls. "Look, I found some dueling pistols. They were serious about this stuff. Rukbhat knows all about it."

"Mmm." Cracka looked one of the pistols over. It was very large and fancifully made, but not heavy. "Looks like something out of the ancient times on Earth."

Bat had selected several swords with especially fancy hilts. He thrust one through his belt and assumed a piratical air. Cracka noted that a little set of knives was already strapped under his right shoulder.

"Knives?"

Bat flipped one out, let it spin, and then gave it to him. "Isn't it lovely? They're beautifully weighted—you could split a tronch boll at twenty paces with the biggest one."

Bat tried to interest them in swords of their own. He'd pulled out several, dusted them off, and set them aside. The blades were always of the pale green material, very sharp and heavy. The pommels were of darker green beeble, and the favorite type of sword was a saber-type slashing weapon. The iulliin did not seem to have favored foils, épées, or the other pointed dueling weapons of Old Earth. Cracka tried to imagine two of the tall, bony iulliin hacking at each other with the swords. It was difficult. The iulliin he'd met were not active, battle-worthy types, not even Wealo.

Cracka patted the iulliin energy weapon he carried on his hips. "I'll stick with this little heater, I think, Bat. I got a knife, and I can't see what use a sword is going to be."

Shay likewise decided not to encumber himself.

They left Bat to rummage in the remains of the iulliin golden past and went up and collected Wealo and Rukbhat and brought them down and drove them back to the airstrip.

The clouds had thickened considerably. They drove in a gray twilight down the access road, past the dark green trees. Balloon leaves were collapsing with a soft popping; hand palms were folding. The heat had become truly oppressive, tropical, sticky.

At the airstrip they drove up to the V-wing. Wealo called up the dagbabi ground crew and oversaw the refueling operation. Rukbhat served as translator for Cracka, who had many questions about the V-wing.

Cracka had made the learning of the iulliin language a new priority for the Prench Tronch ranger force. Cracka himself found it tough going. It had been a long time since Cracka had learned the French he took in Landing Site Meta-Catholic High.

Even Shay seemed to get the hang of it more easily than he did, and Bat was already semiconversant.

The amazing Maroon. As Cracka knew only too well, whenever Bat Maroon really took an interest in something, he mastered it almost effortlessly. The universe was perhaps fortunate that for the bulk of his life Bat had contented himself with only a small number of interests—gambling, intoxication, the opposite sex, and guns.

The fuel itself came in the form of a silvery, hydrogen-rich powder. In the engines the hydrogen was released, mixed with oxygen, and burned in either turbojet engines or ram jets.

But refueling was a slow process. The equipment at Balutnor Ganga was extremely antiquated. It was used normally only to fuel Rukbhat's personal jet, a much smaller craft than the V-wing.

Wealo was soon cursing the stupid dagbabi for fitting the wrong nozzles into the intake valves. Creatures of habit, they had always fitted the small nozzles in the intakes on Rukbhat's craft, which was ancestral to Balutnor Ganga itself.

With the troupe of maintenance dagbabi standing around him silently, Wealo changed the nozzles himself. The big reptile eyes followed every movement and recorded it precisely in the dagbab backbrain. From that moment, those dagbabi and their descendants would always know to use the nozzle for the big V-wings.

Finally the refueling was begun. The process promised to take time. Cracka and Shay put the two iulliin into a cabin aboard the V-wing.

Before he'd closed the door, Rukbhat turned a plaintive face to him. "What are you doing, siffile? Why do you fuel the V-wing?"

Cracka stared at him for a moment. "We'll be leaving this place soon. We're going to fly outward for a while, a good long while, and get away from Meninrud Lors."

"You will not take us with you, will you? We would prefer to stay here, in Balutnor Ganga."

Cracka shook his head. "I'm afraid your preferences don't matter much anymore. You'll be coming with us. We need you as hostages, and we also need to learn to speak your language. *You* especially will help us learn."

The iulliin shuddered. His imprisonment would continue. Even worse, he would be abducted into the depths of the clanth. Vast reaches out there paid only nominal allegiance to Meninrud Lors, great regions were virtually unknown.

Cracka and Shay turned their attention to victuals. They locked the V-wing and drove back to the tower and headed into the kitchens. Their action was unheard of. Nothing like it had ever happened before in living memory.

Hundreds of dagbabi scattered at their approach, a living frieze of heads, staring at the humans from the edges of the doors, tables, cabinets.

With gestures toward the big doors of the larders, Cracka tried to get the dagbabi to help. It was as if he spoke to a row of jewels; he received only rigid stares of shocked bafflement.

Cracka gave up on the dagbabi and yanked open the first of the big doors. He and Shay pulled out sacks and loaded them on a trolley and pushed the trolley out the door.

Goggling dagbabi stared after them in astonishment.

While they were loading the automobile, one sack burst and coated them both with white, powdered bokka.

They went back and searched the other larders. The dagbabi were stunned anew. The siffile did things that were inexplicable. They brought forth the food and broke it upon themselves! They came back for more!

In these times, dagbabi had few instructions concerning siffile, since there were no siffile at Balutnor Ganga. But dagbabi had never adjusted well to the presence of siffile. Siffile were too inexplicable, too fey and undisciplined. They could drive dagbabi to musht. And now there were siffile at Balutnor Ganga, and there was no code for the proper behavior norms in the brains of the poor dagbabi.

For their part, Cracka and Shay tried to ignore the reptile people as much as possible. Outside, the weather continued to indicate that a storm of some kind was building. A warm wind had begun to gust. Faraway lightning flickered again and again, forming nimbus glows in the murk.

They returned for another load. In one larder they found

chests filled with boltak, and in another, heavy-duty clear plastic bags filled with preserved airfish. They loaded the trolley with those, as well, and took that out to the car. The dagbabi watched them come and go and froze while in the presence of such ferality, such wildness and unpredictability.

Back at the airstrip the refueling continued. They unlocked the V-wing again and loaded the food supplies aboard. The little galley, set amidships on the lower level, had capacious storage sections, but they were soon filled with the sacks and chests. The overload they placed in an otherwise empty cabin, set forward of the galley, before the spiral stairs leading to the luxurious upper level.

They stopped for a few breaths, standing outside the V-wing. The refueling dagbabi continued to stand in a rigid little group, watching the dials on the pump gauges as they moved incrementally up the scales.

Cracka shook his head. "Strange little people. I don't know what to make of them."

Shay nodded. "Dagbabi?"

"Yeah."

"Give me the shivers," Shay rumbled.

Cracka looked off to the fabulous towers and gabled roofs of Balutnor Ganga, dim masses jutting beneath the dark clouds. "I think we'll have to carry the girl down to the car. I don't think she can really walk straight yet."

Shay's face darkened. "That filthy stuff. Make me sick to think what they done."

"Yes, it makes me sick too. We need to get the Homeworlds High Fleet to come in here and make some changes."

The wind gusted furiously.

Something made Cracka turn his head just then. Away in the clouds inward a bright little sun had blossomed.

"What is that?" Shay said uneasily.

A few seconds later a big, ugly hum ripped the air.

Cracka's heart sank. "We got company."

They ran for the automobile.

"No time to get Bat."

"No time to do anything."

They drove into the hangar, jumped out, and took up positions at either side of the main entrance, looking out.

The bright new sun increased in size rapidly. The hum grew as well, and then a sphere ship, one of the hunter-gatherer ships from the mother ship, dropped upon the air-strip on fiery booster jets.

It took several seconds for the thunder of the ship's landing to dissipate. Hatches popped open. Stairs extended to the ground. Several tall stick figures in black uniforms appeared. A squad of yashi assembled in front of them.

"Damn, they got yashi!" grumbled Shay.

Cracka eyed them uneasily. The high military had arrived. There were seven yashi, all armed with projectile-firing automatics. "Let them pass, then take them from behind."

The yashi marched forward as if on a parade ground, in a line ahead of the iulliin.

When they passed the hangar, Cracka and Shay stepped out behind them and leveled their energy weapons.

"Stop!" shouted Cracka.

They whirled, iulliin faces wide in shock.

Crack had the energy pistol extended.

He indicated that the yashi should drop their weapons, but they ignored his gestures, waiting for the order to fire on the siffile.

Instead Lord Xaapt touched a button on his wrist module and deactivated the energy pistols using the ship's computer control, via the communications interface built into the ancient weapons.

The little lights at the butt end of the weapons went out.

Xaapt ordered the yashi to capture the siffile and bind them and bring them along behind them to Balutnor Ganga.

The yashi loped forward with the grace and power of big cats. Cracka and Shay pressed the firing studs, but no hot green energy sprang forth. Cracka cursed, pressed again and again. It was no use.

The yashi closed. One sprang straight upon Cracka, who swung the energy pistol at the last moment and clubbed it in the face, which put it off its aim. It slipped to its knees, and he pushed it away with his boot. But the second one was too fast, and it crashed into him with all the power in its big body.

Cracka landed hard, and the thing was already swinging. A big lazy slap rang his head on the ground. The yashi was as strong as two men, and there was no escape from its embrace.

He saw them swarm over Shay, four of them holding down the big troncher, who cursed and kicked to no avail. Cracka was turned over and his hands were bound. He was jerked to his feet.

The iulliin stared at him coldly. In their eyes he saw nothing but extermination.

Leashes were set about the necks of the siffile while the iulliin spoke hurriedly among themselves for a moment and then turned and started walking toward Balutnor Ganga.

Lord Xaapt held forth on the danger and disgrace of what they had discovered. Feral siffile had been adopted by the Urtisim and given energy weapons and allowed to fire on iulliin.

All were capital offenses. The House of Urtisim would have to be put on trial, pulled down, and destroyed. Perhaps even the name expunged, the members disinherited and forced to serve among the dagbabi.

"It is indeed fortunate that you urged us to investigate

this matter, Xaapt," said Lord Meshama, chief of the investigative branch of the military police.

"There are many serious infractions here, that is plain," said Lord Gadulph. "Urtisim will have to be taken before the peers."

They walked forward, nodding among themselves, yashi before and behind, pulling along the captive siffile.

The unusual coincidence of Rukbhat Urtisim's being involved in an incident involving feral siffile on the Aplanga Front, and the incident involving Lady Weanda Urtisim, had provided the motivation for the investigative effort.

Lord Rukbhat dal Vnego Urtisim knew too much of the real picture to be allowed to defect to the Heads-in-the-Sand party. If such defection were discovered, then Rukbhat would have to be terminated immediately, without trial.

Lady Weanda, with her Heads-in-the-Sand connections, had come here, Rukbhat had allowed her to land, with that young hothead Wealo of Gors. The suggestion was ominously clear. Rukbhat dal Vnego Urtisim was betraying the high military.

Crack and Shay staggered along behind the yashi, leashed and bound. Cracka had a loose tooth, and the left side of his face was swelling. His nose was bleeding too, and in his heart was a feeling as hard as stone.

Raindrops began to fall, big heavy ones. Then hailstones, both big and small, began to clatter on the road. The iulliin produced compact umbrellas that expanded to protect them from the storm.

The yashi and the captives were left to get wet.

The wind lashed the hand palms. Debris and foliage flew past. Lightning forked the sky, and there was an immediate crack of thunder. The red tower loomed above, a dim mass in the now driving rain.

They emerged from the palm grove and came into sight of the main entrance to Balutnor Ganga, framed in great gray columns, with wide steps of faded weft. Tall oval windows looked down on either side.

The iulliin drew carefully to one side of the road, beneath a clump of palms, and surveyed the situation. The yashi were sent forward through the downpour toward the steps. Their fur was soaked, their weapons and webbing beaded, the water catching the lightning that flashed more or less continuously behind them.

Cracka and Shay were watched by a single yashi guard.

The yashi advanced up the stairs.

Suddenly there was a little whistling sound and a *thump* and the yashi guarding Cracka and Shay sprouted a big knife hilt in the center of his back.

He spun around and received another knife, in the chest, which toppled him backward. Bat Maroon appeared like magic out of the shrubbery to one side of the roadway.

He held a pair of antique iulliin dueling pistols, and he stepped in and swung them up under the umbrellas and right into the faces of Lords Meshama and Xaapt.

Lords Xaapt, Meshama, and Gadulph stared back at him, frozen in horror.

In broken Iullas, Bat threatened to kill them unless they ordered the yashi to surrender and turn over their weapons.

Lord Meshama bridled with rage at the suggestion.

The yashi had turned. They sprang toward the scene uttering bloodcurdling little growls.

Bat didn't hesitate. The pistol in his right hand boomed, and Lord Meshama was hurled to the ground by the short-range impact of the heavy ceramic shot.

His body twitched once in spasm, the legs jerking about, then lay still.

Everyone froze.

Bat held the other pistol to Lord Xaapt's head. The yashi were close now. Bat's finger tightened on the trigger.

Xaapt quailed. He could not afford to be killed. The war

effort needed him. Curtly he called to the yashi to lay down their weapons.

Bat pulled Lord Xaapt with him to stand beside Cracka, the gun never wavering from Xaapt's temple. Bat worked a small knife back and forth on the tough polymer cord that bound Cracka's wrists. It did not part easily; Bat had to saw away at it, keeping concentration on several fronts at once.

Lord Xaapt waited for his chance to jump away, to let the yashi mow down the impious siffile, feral creatures, as deadly as water-dogs and more intelligent. A contaminating species that had brought more grief than pleasure to the master race.

Suddenly Shay shouted, "Behind you, Bat!"

A yashi had crept up to springing range, through the trees and shrubs.

Bat rammed the gun against Xaapt's head. "Stop it or die!"

Xaapt screamed at the yashi to stop and it did, although it twitched and wriggled in visible frustration.

"Send it away!" screamed Bat in a strangled voice.

Xaapt swallowed and ordered it away.

The other yashi looked on intently.

At last the polymer parted and Cracka's hands were free. He took the knife and cut Shay's bonds. They scooped up the automatics dropped by the yashi.

Shay fired an experimental burst into the bushes. Bullets exploded with hot violet flashes among the foliage. The sound echoed back through the muffling mist.

The yashi ears twitched at the sound of the gun. They came up on the balls of their feet, prepared to fight or flee.

"What do we do with them?" Shay asked.

"I don't want to kill them unless we have to," said Cracka. He gestured to the yashi to sit on the ground in a group. Bat tried to tell Lord Xaapt to give the necessary orders and managed to get across enough of the idea. Xaapt ordered the yashi to squat down, and they did.

Bat breathed a big sigh of relief. Cracka turned and they clasped hands. "Ranger Maroon reporting, sir!" Bat shouted. A terrific peal of thunder cracked across the sky, more rain pelted down.

Cracka and Shay burst into laughter.

▓ CHAPTER THIRTY-SEVEN

Avis Prench sat on the Throne of Bones of the First Mothers, surrounded by the tribe of blond people that called themselves the Milk of the Zeit. She sat amid a potlatch of tribal wealth as the ruling mothers competed with each other for her favor. She was a goddess, a living goddess, and they, the people of the Milk, had found her. They vied for the favor of her genes.

Hongath, the mighty son of Mala, had not only found her, he had rescued her from a demon, as he boasted frequently during the toasting and drinking of zeit beer that had gone on nonstop since his return.

Hongath had flown to the forbidden, deadly places because of the tainted dreams. The dreams had been foretold, as warning of the proximity of a place of the old ones. It was all the fulfillment of an ancient, terrible prophecy:

The olden ones will come, out of their dreadful places, and take the Milk of the Zeit back to the doom of the dark. When the time is ripe the dreams will begin. This will be the first warning to the Milk of the Zeit. Then the eater must be turned and directed back the way it has come. Then must the punga riders watch for the return of the olden ones.

Now Mala produced a pair of goblets fashioned from the skulls of warriors, with jewel-quality molded bee-squeeze for stems and bases.

The other ruling mothers gasped at such display. The goblets were famous. Mala was emptying her hut of treasure to buy the first favor of the goddess.

Avis struggled to smile through the ordeal. The mothers gabbled furiously among themselves, but she could not understand a word. When Hongath had first brought her to the village, in the parasitic jungle that grew on the brow atop the great rogue eater, the chanting crowd had thrown themselves down en masse and rubbed their foreheads on the skin of the eater.

They had immediately seen that she was not of them, not of the tribe, for her hair was dark and her features were different.

By then, of course, she was hundreds of miles from Fanthenai. Behind Hongath, she had flown over seemingly endless dark forests and occasional crescent-shaped eaters. And then, to her surprise, they had suddenly left the green forest behind and entered a region that had received less rainfall in recent times. The forest had been replaced by zeit, becoming a prairie of brown and green tipped with pink. It waved, it shimmered, undulating under the winds.

Occasionally they had flown over green strips that marked canals, and there were lakes, usually round and ringed with forest, perhaps large craters filled with water. Near the water she often spied the white spirals of bee towers.

The punga was no passive flier, although it did glide most of the way. But whenever it had to, it powered itself

forward with enough force to push them down in their saddles. The muscles that drove its wings were immense; the
bone structure was polymeric, with tremendous strength
and flexibility.

For a lot of the time, however, it soared among the
clouds, gliding from one updraft to the next, angling along
weather fronts, racing on a cold wind blowing outward,
where a cell of chilled air was returning from the top of the
atmosphere, forming frontal systems all along its line of
approach as it spread out slowly, seeping into the lowest
pressure zones around.

A rippled plain of zeit was beneath them and the vault
of blue laced with gold cirrus high above, and hours went
by that way. Many hours. Avis had to fight to stay awake.
Asleep she feared she was sure to be dislodged. Yet there
was nothing but monotonous zeit below. Several times she
caught herself with her eyelids closed, dozing off into
dreams. Once she snapped awake as she was actually slipping out of the saddle.

And then at last they came upon the Great Eater.

Like a single sand dune that had swept up all the other
dunes on a beach into itself, it stood alone, five hundred
meters high, three kilometers across from one horn tip to
the other, two kilometers deep from mouth to vent. To that
monster from the depths of the vast steppes swooped the
punga, spiraling down past other, smaller pungas, some
with blond-haired children astride their necks.

In the lee of the eater's crest was a slight dip or depression, and there was the punga rookery.

Dozens of great punga nested here and brooded over the
young. The nests were untidy piles of dendrons and zeit
stalks. Carrion bees and other insects buzzed around the
scene.

The punga landed hard, an impact that it was prepared
for, with its powerful rear limbs bunched beneath it. Avis,

however, was almost thrown from the saddle, but Hongath put an arm out and held her fast to him. A good thing, because when the punga rose back on its legs, she would have fallen off.

The punga folded the immense wings across its back and pumped the stiffening fluids into the big sac that swelled its chest.

Hongath pulled her free of the saddle and then let go and they slid down together along the edge of the wing and then dropped the last meter or so to the surface, which was both the color and texture of bone. Small black plants grew from cracks and holes in the surface. Above their heads the punga gave a series of cheerful hoots, glad to be home once more, impatient to be free of harness.

They stood near the lip of the depression that held the punga roost. Hongath pulled free the punga's saddle and the complex bit and mouth harness.

Freed, the punga waddled to its nest, where a mate squatted over a single leathery brown egg. Both creatures raised their heads, their mouth flaps flew up and unfurled, and they brayed a giant greeting at one another.

Hongath touched her shoulder, bowed low, and waved her up the slope.

She stepped over the lip of the depression and into a forest of fantastic forms, bubble-leaved plants with trunks of glistening black and scarlet.

Then the people had appeared. Swarming out of a village of low structures set in clearings through the forest of bubble trees. They wore skirts and halters of hide worked with bright beads. The women had their hair in braids, the men, like Hongath, wore theirs shoulder length.

When they were about ten feet from her, the blond people had suddenly dropped on their knees. A number of heavyset women with long braids raised their arms to her in apparent prayer and begged her passionately to stay and bless them with a son. They promised to give until they could give no more, in order to win this privilege. Each had a son who was young and full of seed.

They scattered flower petals and scented jujubes made from the tears of hoppers. They sang soft songs of welcome, and danced before her.

They brought her to a hut where a bath was poured. The bath was made of beepane, stiffened by the rib cage of a punga. As they bathed her, the mothers of the tribe vied with one another for the honors of her attention, words, and gestures.

Among them all burned the wonder of prophecy fulfilled. The goddess was like them but not of that world. She wore the clothing of a technological culture. She had been rescued from a tower of the old ones, deep in the mysterious forest zones where few riders took the punga.

When she had bathed in water brought in by strapping youths and poured by smiling girls, they conducted her to the Throne of Bones and the ceremonies began in earnest. Avis sat, baffled, apprehensive, not understanding much of what was going on around her, her thoughts constantly returning to Fanthenai and her son.

The potlatch was finally concluded. Mala, mother of Hongath, had won. She ordered the young daughters to collect the wealth she had arrayed before the goddess and to put it in chests of fine beepane and place it all in the hut that was now made ready for the goddess.

Avis was finally allowed to get up from the Throne of Bones and was led to the hut and showed the fine bedding, futons of bubble fluff, tables and chairs of bone and beeble, that had been placed within.

She tried to thank them in Interlingua, but none of them understood. She blew them kisses, and they gasped and fell down on their knees again and then blew kisses back to her over and over.

At last the door closed and she was alone. She sank down on the futons and wept herself to sleep.

She was awakened by a gentle touch on her foot. She stirred and sat up. Hongath was there, kneeling before her, staring raptly into her face.

Hongath prayed to her, and begged the goddess to accept his seed.

She was silent, and Hongath knew it was that she did not speak the tongue of the Milk, for she was of the heaven place, where there was night as well as sun.

He pointed to himself and said, "Ko, yohut Hongath."

He repeated this.

Avis pointed to her chest and said, "Avis."

Hongath stared at her incredulously. Did the goddess wish him to kiss her breast? He would happily die for the privilege!

Perhaps he could show her, and then she would understand. He stood up slowly and pulled aside his robe. He was naked beneath it.

Avis gave a little scream and fainted.

CHAPTER THIRTY-EIGHT

With poor Rukbhat of Urtisim to translate the computer's messages, it didn't take very long for Cracka and Bat to get the hang of the spaceship's controls. Then they ordered the elevator door opened and explored the rest of the vessel. They found a number of small, neat cabins, a floor with an empty dagbabi room and a galley and some storage chambers, and then beneath that, three enormous storage chambers.

Automatic pallet loaders and docking equipment were stacked neatly beside enormous hatches. Equipment with tanks, compressors, and hoses was set on the floor. From one nozzle there had dripped a small puddle of a clear plastic material. Cracka touched it, picked it up. It was soft and pliable and stretched easily. He felt the hair on his neck rise.

He became more eager than ever to be gone.

They put the iulliin in separate cabins and locked them in, except for Rukbhat, who they kept to help interface with the alien ship's computer.

Then they brought Martherer Boan to the ship. She was still barely conscious; she had the bad shakes of the latter throes of addiction to the Rooms.

Finally they shifted the supplies from the V-wing to the sphere ship, carrying the heavy sacks of bokka up the long extension stairs themselves, something that caused Rukbhat considerable consternation. Why did the siffile not employ the dagbabi for manual labor? Siffile were hard to understand sometimes; feral siffile were impossible!

At last they were done. Shortly afterward, the ship's engines ignited and the angry hum erupted once more into the air around Balutnor Ganga.

They rose slowly into a clearing sky, a vault of pale cerulean in which the golden sun sat slightly inward of the zenith. The clouds of the recent storm were still visible, a great bank of gray and black, swirling slowly in the direction of Or and inward.

Once they were in the upper atmosphere, the main drives engaged. The ship accelerated and left the Sun Clanth for outer space. On the main view screen they were presented with a meager sky bearing nothing but the thin curving line of small red suns, regularly spaced, that made up the entire complement of stellar material in the Plowl. In a corner window of the screen was the complete spherical map of the Plowl, a sphere the size of an elliptic galaxy, smoothly patterned with stellar dots.

The ship put itself into a solar orbit on command, and Cracka convened a meeting to discuss strategy. "We have a ship, with supplies for several months, and we have some pretty important hostages. What next?"

"The mother ship?" Bat said.

"I don't know. Rukbhat assures us that the high military will be galvanized into a serious effort to destroy us. We represent something like the worst-case scenario in siffile management, it seems."

"They damn well right," said Shay with a big cluck.

"The high military will have a lot of ships, then." Bat immediately voiced their greatest potential problem.

"It gonna be hard to break in and get that mother ship," said Shay.

Cracka shook his head. "It's too soon for that. We have to think this through carefully. We can't afford to fail. We're the only hope for freedom for all the Calabels, and maybe all the rest of the humans they have in here."

"That's a helluva lot of people," said Bat. "They've had the Lemall's for thousands of years. Could be hundreds of millions, could be billions."

Shay groaned. "We never gonna get them all out."

Cracka had a grim expression on his face. "A lot of them are probably going to have to stay here, but we've got to make sure that we end this sickening slavery, the slaughter in their stupid war, and all the rest of it. We have to get a message out, into the real universe. Get a message to the Homeworld High Fleet."

Bat nodded.

"Meanwhile, we need a place to hide out," Cracka continued. "We stopped the indicator signal from the computer, unless Rukbhat has been unusually clever."

Rukbhat's long ears twitched at the sound of his name. The siffile spoke rapidly among themselves, and he could scarcely understand them, although he knew they were hatching a plot of some terrible kind. That was what feral siffile were bound to do.

"I don't think we missed anything. As long as we make him keep talking very slowly, we can work out pretty much what he's saying."

"So the high military can't track us now."

"As far as we know."

"Then we can just go to another Sun Clanth and find a place that's not too densely populated with goddamn iulliin."

"Exactly," said Cracka.

"We need somewhere kind of sleepy," said Bat. "Somewhere that's not going to notice a spaceship landing."

Cracka had a suggestion. "I want to find Nathan Prench —that kid is a genius. If anyone can work out a plan to get us out of here, he can."

"But he has one of these ships. He could be anywhere."

"Well, maybe." Cracka turned to Rukbhat and spoke slowly. "Is there any way of tracing a ship like this one that left the mother ship during its flight within the Plowl."

Rukbhat sighed and nodded. "There was a ship that left the mother ship. It was traced to a landing site in the Sun Clanth of Planggi. It is a long way away."

"By the Moth!" snorted Shay. "That's where Kid Folo be, then."

Cracka continued. "What are conditions like in this other place?"

Rukbhat shook his head ruefully. "It is difficult to say. There has been no communication with Planggi in a thousand zeem or more."

"No contact? You mean no radio contact, no ships, nothing?"

"Yes."

"Have they been overrun by your enemy?"

Rukbhat shrugged. "It is unlikely. Xaaca lies in the other direction. The Xaacans are slow but steady. They expand by attacking us a few clanths at a time. They attack the next only when the last is completely subdued."

"Has there been any communication with the ship?"

"No. It landed under computer control. The hatch was opened and the occupants escaped. The ship is still there. Our attempts to restart the computer so far have been unsuccessful. There is some concern that the siffile may have damaged it after the landing."

"So we know that they got out, and they're somewhere in that Sun Clanth."

"Oh boy, they got lotsa room to get lost," said Shay.

Cracka sucked in a breath. "How long will it take for us to reach this place."

Rukbhat shrugged.

"I will have to ask the computer."

"Go ahead. But remember, we're learning your language, and if you try and trick us, we'll be forced to eject you from the airlock." And into the biting vacuum of outer space, there to boil and explode. Rukbhat could visualize it all too easily. He wanted to live, very badly.

With little shudders, speaking very slowly indeed, he gave the computer the necessary orders. The reply came almost immediately. He turned to Cracka.

"At maximum acceleration-deceleration levels, we will need two balaast, but it will be an uncomfortable journey."

"But a relatively quick one, right?"

"Yes."

They pondered the situation. Cracka raised a finger. "Has any message been received from Planggi? Check that for me."

A few moments later the computer played a brief Mayday signal, picked up and stored, according to iulliin spaceflight regulations, in the flight file.

"Where are those coordinates?"

"In the Sun Clanth of Planggi."

Cracka rubbed his nose. "What are the chances the high military will investigate the source of this message?"

Rukbhat considered the question for a moment. "Well, until recently, it was unlikely to have been investigated. Planggi is backward and far away. No one has gone there in aeons. But your escape and the capture of myself and Lord Xaapt might prompt a more vigorous inspection. However, it must be noted that Lord Xaapt is intensely unpopular. Few will be troubled by his disappearance. As for myself, you already know how much the high military dislikes my activities. Indeed, it may well be that it is my giddy sister Weanda who will bring on your doom. Her absence will be bitterly resented by a great many diehards of her political faction. They it will be who will demand action against you, and possibly against this other group of wild siffile as well."

"I guess that makes you and Xaapt pretty poor hostage material, then. But at least we've got Lady Weanda to bargain with."

Bat gave a low whistle. "So they know where Nathan is, and when they work out what's happened to these iulliin they'll investigate the coordinates in the signal."

Cracka nodded. "If we're going to get that kid, we'd better get moving. We're ahead of them, we'll just have to stay that way."

They exchanged a grim look. The situation seemed no less hazardous than before.

Cracka gave the necessary orders, and the ship computer bade them take positions in the acceleration couches. The warnings were also given in the cabins below.

The ship turned, the engines reignited, and they moved away from the sun of Meninrud Lors, heading between other stars for the distant Sun Clanth of Planggi.

On the great steppes of Kan, Hongath, son of Mala, worked with the other men to turn the Great Eater.

They flew inward along the forest margin until they spied a herd of hoppers, whereupon they swooped down upon the hoppers and fired poisoned darts into a half dozen of the beasts.

These hoppers soon fell behind the herd and then collapsed, jerking in the last paroxysms.

Working quickly to avoid bee bites, the men butchered the hoppers and loaded them onto the pack pungas they had brought with them. For this purpose they used primarily the females, who could always be counted on to return to the eater and the nest.

Bees were beginning to appear by the time they were done, and soon they were running through clouds of hungry insects for their pungas. All pungas had a horror of bees and bee bites, so it was important to let them escape as quickly as possible.

Now the men spread the pieces of hopper on the zeit, with a few near the eater, and the rest dropped at calculated distances away, all in a line heading back into the deep steppes, lying inward.

The Great Eater had the usual love of dead hopper, a rare delicacy in the menu of monotonous zeit. But it was rare indeed for a hopper to lie around dead long enough for an eater to find one. Usually the bees got to it, and it was soon gone.

The Great Eater began to shift its lip in the direction of the scent. There was taste! There was hopper juice right there on the zeit!

The lip, a long flexible structure that rode just in front of the leading edge of the hard endoskeleton of the eater, began to tug in the direction of the taste.

Now the men flew past and dropped chunks of hopper close to the edge of the lip. Where the lip roved, it gathered everything in its path into the maw. Indeed, when the old members of the tribe died they were brought down and fed under the lip of the eater, renewing the tribe's right to live upon this Great Eater, which they had colonized in the days of the First Mothers, long ago.

As he flew low along the lip, Hongath fought the urge to slip from his saddle and cast himself to his death below, right in the path of the lip, so that his worthless carcass could be consumed immediately by the eater. Ground between the eater's huge flat teeth, he would be quickly dispatched to the peace of the heaven place.

The agony of living in the disfavor of the goddess and his mother Mala would be over.

He scattered chunks of hopper.

Bees were pouring in from a nearby nest, covering the chunks of hopper. But, feed as they might, they could not devour much of it before the eater would accelerate its mass on the great single foot and flow forward to engulf the tasty bits spread before it.

They circled their pungas above the eater's brow.

Yoragth, leader of the feeders of the eater, immediately proposed that they raid the bee nest. "This nest is greedy, it weakens itself foolishly. We should take advantage of it now and restock our sugar pots."

The Great Eater was turning very quickly now. The upper lip's underside was a furl of dark skin, stained with the juice of the zeit.

The Great Eater surged forward, eager for more.

Several men landed and put on protective clothing and thick hopper grease. Others dug out their bee attack equipment, including the waxy explosive made from a bees-queeze polymer activated by an organic acid. The wax would be used to blow holes in the nest shell.

Then they took to the air once more and flew toward the nearby bee nest that was attempting to rob the Great Eater of its treat.

Hongath was glad of the work. It was something to take his mind off the disastrous failure of his efforts to woo the goddess.

In the meantime, the goddess sat in her hut and continued her attempts to learn the language of the Milk of the Zeit. The work was exhausting. A young language, like the tribe itself, descendants of a small group of escaped slave women from an aerial human empire forty thousand kilometers away in the deep steppes of Kan. There were endless irregularities, vital nuances, and accentuation of the vowel sounds.

But Avis had to become proficient enough to make herself understood. She had to try to persuade them to go back and rescue her son and Folo, if they still lived.

■ CHAPTER THIRTY-NINE

In Fanthenai it had been humid and still for much of the balaast, but now it was lifting, the sky was covered with small salmon-pink, hounds tooth clouds, drifting outward in an unbroken stream. The sun was invisible behind them. A cool breeze had sprung up, displacing the humid air.

Sam Boan lolled upon his couch, close to the balcony rail. The dagbabi had brought him a sumptuous dinner—several filets of seared wita, bowls of bokka, fruits and berries to taste. Cup after cup of aged varmils had been poured.

For the first hour or so after gorging, Sam was content to float complacently on his couch. Then, as the alcohol wore off, Sam turned ugly. He threw his empty cup petulantly at the nearest dagbab and fumbled around for his helmet, but unable to find it momentarily, he turned and screamed at the Sun Mel. "Varmils. More, more. Now!"

The Sun Mel, the rope around his neck tied to the leg of Sam's couch, quickly ordered the dagbabi to fetch more varmils.

They stared at him for a moment. They trembled. They sensed complete wrongness. The master was forced to crouch on the floor, hands tied, neck leashed. The siffile lay drunk upon the couch. Then the moment passed and the dagbabi scurried to obey.

The Sun Mel turned worried eyes back to the mad, intoxicated siffile. The dagbabi had almost reached the point of musht. The Sun Mel could feel it, a palpable force, crawling with power through the minds of the hundreds of thousands of dagbabi that lived in the sprawling city of beesqueezers that lay beyond the tower.

How could he get the feral siffile to stop? He knew nothing of the siffile tongues. The creature was far too inebriated to understand Iullas. But if it carried on the way it had been, it was sure to arouse an outbreak of feral musht.

Unfortunately Sam's bloodshot eyes had already swung around to focus on the dagbabi still on the terrace, three of them, all wearing the small white smocks and hats of the kitchen staff. At the sight of the little hats, perched on the ridiculous lizardlike heads, Sam laughed. An ominous sound, his laugh. He groped around for his helmet.

"I want to watch their hats go floating down . . ." he burbled. Then he had the helmet in his hands, and he slipped it on and pressed the button. The dagbab control field came on. Under its direction, at this range, the dagbab was no more than an automaton, a fact that had brought Sam endless amusement since his discovery of it.

He fastened the field over the hapless dagbabi and seized control of their minds. He sent them to the rail of the terrace. Before them was a two-hundred-meter drop to the main setback of the tower. They teetered on the edge. Sam had them loosen the little square white hats, and then sent the first one over the edge. It vanished with a little shriek, the hat separating perfectly and then floating down more slowly, drifting in spirals out of sight into the city of dagbab tenements. The dagbab itself was no more than a blotch on the distant setback.

The next one's hat failed to separate properly; not until the body began tumbling did the small white shape split away and whirl off, to catch on a window ledge halfway down. Sam raved curses after the miserable creature for such a poor performance.

The third, however, was perfect once more, the ugly little lizard body sinking with a yelp while the hat floated.

Sam fell back on the couch and had a long, loud giggling fit.

Waves of hysteria pulsed through the tower and the surrounding buildings. The dagbabi had retrieved dozens of bodies from the setback. Sam's bored cruelty was straining the bonds of millions of years of servitude.

The sound of dagbabi fists being driven into dagbabi palms caused the Sun Mel to look up. A line of dagbabi chieftains, the Melga, had formed. They wore the ornamental bibs of office, with hats of soft beesilk in brilliant shades of pink and orange.

The Sun Mel groaned. "No, go back, you are in great danger!"

But the Melga hesitated; the master was not in control of the situation. The fat, bloated siffile was the cause of the problem. The Melga stepped forward to remonstrate with him.

Sam spotted them. "Oh ho!" He roared in delight and promptly clapped the control field down upon them.

They jumped in pairs, their hats fluttering after them, their eyes filled with astonished outrage.

Laughing uproariously, Sam squirmed around on his couch. The helmet fell off and rolled a few feet away.

An awful, ominous silence had descended on the city. The Sun Mel stared anxiously at the rope that bound him to the chair. Was there some way he could bite through it? He knew that was very unlikely. The rope, a length of high-quality beesqueeze, would outlast his teeth.

Meanwhile, Sam gazed out upon the endless beautiful land under the golden haze. Green forest, dark distant hills, a world of promise. "It will be mine!" he growled softly. "All this, it will be mine!" Now he knew other humans were in this clanth, humans that rode immense aerial beasts. Humans that had dared to interfere with his rule! He'd have them! He'd find those flying humans, and then he would begin to build his empire. He daydreamed pleasantly upon some of the details of the rule of Emperor Sam.

He had the airboat, and he knew how to fly that. He needed some of the lionlike aliens; they'd make good troops. And he had Nathan Prench to interpret the alien technology. And of course he had the little tronch pig Folo, with which to control Nathan Prench.

Then a frown crossed his befuddled brow. He was getting rather tired of his sister Rilla. He had never really liked her. But for now she was the only sexual outlet, so she had to be spared. But sometime *she* would stand on that rail and gaze down upon the setback. He'd keep her there for a while, too, to let her contemplate the end.

Maybe he'd have her wear one of those cute little white hats.

He whirled around suddenly. The dagbabi had failed to bring him more varmils. Sam bellowed for more. A chill silence followed. The breeze blew, moaning softly around the worn weft of the roof.

"What?" He roared. He lurched across the tiled floor of the gallery and peered into the service corridor. There were no dagbabi to be seen, and there was no varmils either. "Varmils!" he bellowed.

There was no response.

Sam shouldered into the service corridor. A dagbabi place, it was narrow and bare. Small, dimly lit rooms lay on either side. There weren't even any doors. Dagbabi lived without privacy.

Sam lifted his head. He heard something, out in the city, an enormous stirring. Then a sudden screaming broke out and a dozen dagbabi emerged into the service corridor. They ran toward him, leaping into the air and clacking their hard, toothless little jaws. It was an unnerving sight.

Sam turned and bolted for the gallery.

One of the creatures landed on his back. It snapped at his neck, tore at his shoulders. He screamed and tried to rub it off on the wall, but another was there, and another, and they cannoned into him and drove him out of the narrow corridor like a shell from the breech, staggering into the hallway and bouncing off the wall.

They flung themselves at him, jaws snapping like toothless hounds. Sam screamed and kicked and lashed out with his fists, clearing them out of his way momentarily, whereupon he ran for the doors to the balcony. He managed to slam them shut in the dagbabi's faces, and then he raced for the helmet.

But the doors burst open behind him, and the lizard men were only a few paces behind. They caught up by the couch, a pair leaping, crashing into Sam's shoulders, whirling him around. Another came right behind, taking him in the chest, pushing him backward, over the couch, landing heavily on the tiled floor, dagbabi rolling this way and that.

Sam twisted to his knees and screamed in mortal terror as he crawled for the helmet. The dagbabi leaped to their feet and rushed him, but by then he had it in his hands and they could not prevent his placing it on his head. It was still activated, pulsing on the dagbab control level.

He hammered the field down upon them and they squealed to a halt with gasps like the sound of steam escaping from a row of kettles.

They struggled with the field, but soon they were standing in a helpless row on the balcony rail. He sent them over the edge together.

But more were coming, an army was massing. Sam frowned.

He got to his feet. The dagbabi hadn't brought him any more varmils, and the effects were wearing off. In fact he felt distinctly ill. He was gasping for air. He was scratched and bitten and bruised.

He stumbled across the gallery and into the suite. He slammed the main doors shut and bolted them. "Need more arms," he mumbled.

Sam opened the door to the servants quarters and ordered Nathan and Rilla out. They stared around with wide eyes. Sam waved his arms wildly. "Dagbabi have gone crazy, we gotta fight them back."

Sam staggered a little. He stank of rotten fruit varmils.

"Where's the Sun Mel, Sam?"

"What d'ya want to know about him for?"

"He'll know what's going on."

Sam thought that over. It seemed to make sense. He was feeling very tired, and a little sick. "Well, all right, he's on the balcony."

Nathan went to the Sun Mel and untied the rope from the chair leg. The Sun Mel was pale with fright. "It is musht, as I warned you. The dagbabi have been pushed too far. They are accustomed to service, to occasional needful sacrifices, but not to suicide. He has been making them jump the rail, dozens of them."

"Oh, no." Nathan looked over the rail. Bodies littered the setback.

"What happens now?"

"The dagbabi will kill us all, destroy the tower, form themselves into an army and march off into the clanth. They will destroy everything in their path until they succumb to factional disputes and divide and die."

There was a sudden heavy thud on the outer doors. It came again and again.

"They will batter the doors down and then come in and slay us. They will chew us down to the last shreds of bone. There will be nothing left for posterity."

Sam ran to the door, bellowing, "Stop that! Stop!" He lashed out with the field. The dagbabi outside either froze and fell over or, if they were far enough away, merely ran away and crouched with their faces to the wall. Sam continued to project the field out through the door.

This bought them a period of respite, but after ten minutes the sounds of dagbabi scrabbling at the door returned.

Sam was forced to hurl the field at them again.

Soon Sam found himself weakening. The field was tiring to project, over and over, at full strength. His stomach felt distinctly queasy. His tumble over the couch had definitely put his back out, there was an ominous twinge in the lumbar region.

Now the dagbabi were hurling themselves at the door, smashing at it with a heavy bench brought up from below.

Sam was breathing hard. He whirled around. Nathan and Rilla were standing beside the Sun Mel, staring in horror at the doors, which shook repeatedly.

"The spear, and the sword!" shouted Sam. "They're in my room. Go and get them, you will have to defend yourselves."

They ran down the corridor to the room. Nathan looked back. Sam was out of sight. The booming on the door was louder.

Inside Sam's room they found the spear and the sword, leaning in one corner. Nathan looked around frantically for the other helmet but failed to find it. Sam had hidden it somewhere. Without it they were helpless in the sheriff's grip.

Rilla took the spear. She started back and called, "Come on, Nathan, before he gets angry!" Rilla had had to bear a lot of Sam's anger; she had become sensitized to it.

They ran back to the gallery—in time to see Sam pull up the stairs to the air barque, which he had freed from its moorings. "What about us?" Nathan yelled.

"You can fight the damn dagbabi, I need to rest. Don't feel good."

"Fight them with what? A sword and half a spear?"

"Yes. Exactly."

"Give me one of the helmets, Sam, at least give us a chance."

But Sam simply laughed. The air barque began to turn, to move away, stately and slow on its repeller fields.

Nathan and Rilla exchanged a long stare, then they looked back to the door.

The Sun Mel begged Nathan to cut his bonds, and Nathan did, sawing through the tough polymer with the sword. An awkward job, and he nicked the Sun Mel a couple of times. Each time the iulliin gave an exaggerated shriek of terror.

Then he ran to release Folo from the prison cage. Folo staggered to his feet. His wounds from the beatings by Sam were still unhealed. He was weak and feverish, but he professed himself ready to fight.

Rilla snorted in disbelief. "You look as weak as a kitten. We're all going to be dagbab food pretty soon, if you ask me."

"What can we do?" Folo said.

"Come on," said Nathan. "There's an access stairway inside the dagbab service corridor. It leads to an attic, and there's a door there that lets you up the last set of stairs to the roof. If we can get there we can hold an army off, because it's too narrow for them to come at us more than two at a time."

They stuck their heads in the dagbab corridor. A bare hall, small empty rooms. They ran down it and turned a corner. A single dagbab was waiting. It screamed and hurled itself at Nathan.

He barely had time to fend it off with the sword, then it came back and tumbled Folo to the floor. Its jaws were tight around Folo's neck and choked off his cries.

Nathan gasped, hesitated a moment, and then hewed down with the sword and cut the dagbab in half at the waist. The Sun Mel gave a shriek and fainted.

Folo tore the dying top half away from himself. Pale orange dagbab blood covered both of them. A sickening, sour metal stink arose.

The Sun Mel was brought round. He staggered back to his feet. His eyes went wide at the sight of the dagbab corpse.

They ran on and climbed the circular stair that rose to the uppermost floors of the tower. Here they entered Nathan's realm of exploration, and he quickly led them through low-ceilinged rooms filled with the junk of past aeons, into a corridor walled with ancient worn panels of weft turned brown by time.

At last there was a narrow stair that mounted to a single landing, it turned once more and came to a small door. This opened onto the topmost crown of the tower. A mini-

mal service platform, badly eroded by bees and time, was
set beneath the door and circled the crown of the tower
above the spiral-patterned roof.

"This is it?" said Folo, staring back down the narrow
stairs. They were trapped.

Nathan stared around them. "This is it. Last stand,
Folo."

"Unless Sam comes back with the air barque."

Rilla was pointing sunward. They saw the air barque,
hovering on its repellers. Sam was a visible blob by the rail
in the prow. He appeared to be watching the dagbabi down
below as they raged and wailed.

The chittering of enraged dagbabi arose beneath them
on the landing. Dagbabi suddenly appeared in the stairwell, running up lightly, snapping their jaws. The Sun Mel
gave a scream and, with a low keening cry, crouched on
the outside platform.

Nathan menaced them with a flourish of the sword, but
they ignored the danger and flung themselves up, their
screaming loud and terrible.

Nathan swung, and the sword bit deep in the leading
dagbab. Rilla pushed the spear into the one behind.

They collapsed together, their pale blood spouting furiously. Others scrambled up behind. They too were dispatched and fell on the bodies of the first. More came.
Nathan had to hack one of them several times before it was
subdued. Rilla had the spear wrenched from her momentarily, but Folo dived through and tore it free from the
dying dagbab in whose breast it was lodged before the
creature tumbled back down the stairs. Another was on
Folo's back at once, and Nathan had to cut it through before it could be dislodged.

Finally they stopped. Ten corpses were heaped on the
stairs. The reek of sour metal dagbab blood was very
strong.

Rilla collapsed outside on the platform, shuddering, and

sat with her back against the wall, staring bleakly at the Sun Mel where he cowered.

Folo was wary of the platform and stayed on the stairs, pushing the dagbab corpses away. They piled up on the landing in hideous profusion.

Nathan squatted down in the doorway.

"Doesn't look good, Nathan," Folo said through thick lips. It had been hours since he had water, and his lips felt rubbery.

"How can we get Sam to pick us up in the air barque? That's our only way out."

"It's no way out for me, Nathan. The fat man intends to kill me."

"But he isn't going to kill you as soon as the dagbabi will."

A sound down below caused them to sit up.

Rilla groaned, "Oh no, I can't take much more of this."

Dagbabi appeared on the landing, but they did not attack. Instead they merely pulled the bodies of the fallen away, jerking them one by one out of sight.

The stillness returned. Not a sound could be heard.

"What do you think they're doing?" Nathan asked the Sun Mel.

The Sun Mel, sunk in catatonic horror, did not reply.

Angrily, Rilla nudged him with her foot.

He fixed bleary eyes on the siffile.

Nathan repeated his question.

The Sun Mel shrugged; he worried his long fingers together. "They are returning to the primal state, without conditioning. Their society is being reorganized on the ancient warlike lines. Soon they will burn everything here and march off, probably in the direction of the sun. Dagbabi crave heat and rarely get enough of it in the temperate sectors of the clanth."

Nathan translated for the others.

"They haven't finished with us, then?" said Folo. "I was afraid of that."

Not long afterward they heard a distant commotion. The roar of a great crowd. Drums began to throb slowly and ominously. The roar grew closer. Rilla suddenly screamed and pointed down, past the broad sweep of the roof.

A vast dark mass of dagbabi was pouring through the streets and alleys toward the tower. Soon they could hear the rumble of the horde approaching from below. Louder and louder grew the drums, the cries, the mass chants of the dagbabi.

At last they turned onto the landing just below the roof-top door. Burly males, armed with clubs and small knives, ran screaming toward them.

Once more they raised their weapons. Nathan stabbed and hacked with the sword. Folo took the spear, seeking to finish any that got past the sweeps of the sword.

One especially burly specimen got past both of them, whirling, bleeding, onto the little inspection gallery. Rilla gave it a hard shove and it fell over the edge and slid down the roof a ways. Then it caught itself on a damaged section. Slowly, implacably, it began crawling back toward them.

Dead and wounded dagbabi had piled up now, almost blocking the door.

Suddenly Folo detected a different smell, one that cut through the reek of dagbab blood in the stairwell. "Smoke!"

A second later Nathan smelled it too. The stench grew in strength. The smell of burning beesqueeze.

"The dagbabi have fired the tower!" said the Sun Mel.

Rilla screamed once more and pointed to where small billows of black smoke were rising past the lip of the striped mushroom cap roof.

The smoke thickened rapidly.

Nathan and Folo desperately pushed bodies out of the way and started down the stairs.

Drums sounded with maniacal fervor. More dagbabi

came around the landing waving clubs and knives. They waded through the mound of the dead and started climbing upward.

"No way out," said Nathan.

Folo stood irresolute. "I think I'd rather jump than burn to death. What do you say, Nathan?"

Nathan contemplated the end. He felt cheated somehow, a life spent exploring the vastness of the Sun Clanth would have suited him fine. "I guess . . ."

The dagbabi suddenly stopped. Everywhere. Stillness returned to the tower, except for the now audible roar of the flames.

They looked at each other.

And then they heard it, a distant hum, a sharp sound cutting the sudden quiet. The Sun Mel gave a little shriek and pointed up into the cloud cover. A bright light was growing there, and then the light emerged from the clouds, bearing a thick gray sphere. The hum grew to a savage intensity while the sphere slowly lowered itself to a landing at the edge of the dagbab town.

"Another ship," breathed Nathan, scarcely daring to believe his eyes.

◼ CHAPTER FORTY

Sam Boan stared up at the descending light with an uneasy mix of emotions. Terror of the iulliin had sent him to the controls at once, and he'd put the air barque into forward drive at top speed, away from the tower. Sweat ran down his forehead.

Then he began to wonder if he was not foolish to be running away. Perhaps it would be wisest to go back and seize control of the ship and the iulliin. He could have them jump off the tower or something.

His hand strayed to the controls; he slowed the flight of the barque. But what if the iulliin were different? And when he thought about it a moment, he realized that they had to be. They had to have control of their own technology if they were flying one of those ships. That meant they might, they *must*, have defenses against the helmets.

That thought sent his finger to the switch again, and he increased speed once more to the maximum. He looked back nervously. The huge gray sphere floated down in a blaze of light on the outskirts of the city of beesqueezers. Clouds of dust and vapor obscured the scene.

Had they seen him? He dared to hope that they had not. He kept the craft on a straight heading, flying directly inward, toward the warmer heart of the Sunland.

In the large hut on the crest of the Great Eater, Avis Prench attempted to beg for the rescue of her son, and the others, from the grip of Sam Boan. She was hampered by her extremely inexpert command of the language of the tribe, called Hu-huginag, literally, "our way of speaking."

Mala and the other mothers of the Milk of the Zeit listened attentively to the goddess. She had already learned some Hu-huginag; clearly she was not dim-witted. Her genes would be a good addition.

"She didn't refuse your son because of a lack of brains," whispered Gana maliciously in her ear.

"Thank you, Gana," Mala hissed back.

Avis had paused. Did they understand her? Could she get through to them?

"Will you make-effort, friends my," she said haltingly.

Woonamala, the gray-haired eldest active mother, spoke up in her quiet but determined way. "The goddess must give us her genes. We are in desperate need of fresh genes. The Milk of the Zeit curdles because of the lack of new blood. Nine generations have we gone without contact. We are alone under the golden sun on the green zeit. Mental dwarfs and cretins we are becoming as a result."

When she finished they remained hushed.

Then Mala spoke. "What of this tale the goddess is trying to tell us? There is a mad god, a god of evil purpose. He enslaves the other gods in the tower from where my son rescued the goddess."

"Better to leave the mad gods behind," replied Woonamala. "They can only bring us trouble. We are blessed indeed by the goddess and her great gift of genes, but she must be made with child soon. We need fresh genes in this tribe, or we will be reduced to cretinism in a few more generations."

The younger mothers nodded; they all knew this. They were just too closely related, too far back.

Avis tried her appeal once more. "My son. Danger very great at tower. Please help."

Speaking slowly, Mala tried to reply.

Gradually Avis understood. It was not encouraging. The Milk of the Zeit was eager to have fresh genetic input. In fact, Avis now understood that she was supposed to have a child for them. That was why the young man that had rescued her had appeared undressed before her.

But while they needed fresh genes, they could not accept an outside male and allow him to live. An outside female was acceptable, she could even become one of the mothers of the tribe, but a male would be allowed to live only long enough to lie with all the available females and then he would be fed under the lip to the Great Eater.

"Better your son stay tower!" said the one called Mala,

a plump-faced cow of a woman with huge breasts, fat cheeks, and long gray-blond hair.

Avis wanted to weep but did not dare. It was apparent that her divinity did not give her much power over her own life among the Milk of the Zeit. She was expected to perform, not to rule.

"Goddess now see Hongath?" said Mala brightly. "Hongath can be made ready. Or if prefer I have good second son, Runga."

Avis stared at them.

The mother to Mala's right, Gana, now spoke up. "Goddess, you must have child. Else you demon!"

All the mothers gave a little shriek.

"If demon then you feed the eater!"

Avis shuddered. There was no choice, then. Either she had a child for them or she would die.

Mala then suggested that if Avis gave them a son, the goddess would be free to return to the heaven place and find her first son, if that was what she wanted to do.

Mala also told her, in a cheerful voice, that hostile demons that pretended to be goddesses were usually whipped severely before being fed under the lip to become fuel to drive the Milk of the Zeit across the steppe and away from the evil place she came from.

The mothers arose and left, big, plump women, successful in childbirth but inbred nine generations, the descendants of the very small group of women, one of them pregnant with a son, two of them with daughters, that had founded the tribe.

Avis went out and walked through the village of low-slung huts and out to a promontory on the crest of the Great Eater. She stared back the way they had come. An intermittent line of black dung marked their passage. Closer to the eater the ground was nearly bare, with all vegetation cropped off and devoured.

They were traveling at a remorseless two kilometers an

hour. By the time she'd conceived a baby and brought it to
term and survived giving birth *au naturel*, there among a
tribe of nontechnological blond savages, she'd be thousands of kilometers away from Fanthenai.

But to refuse Mala meant only death, and Avis didn't
feel like dying.

Avis watched the pungas, with and without riders,
swooping and soaring downwind from the eater. Tribe
children were examined when they were fully formed
youngsters, at about the age of six years terrestrial. At that
stage the cretins and retards were weeded out. At puberty,
retarded males were castrated, the females made barren
with the bitter juice of the yawale plant.

Those who passed the test administered by all the active
mothers of the tribe became flyers—the girls to fly until
they were first pregnant, the males to fly until claimed by
death. Life aboard the punga was dangerous if exhilara-
ting. Few males lived past the age of thirty. If they did,
however, the mothers soon poisoned them, for older males
were a great nuisance, and had been found to be bother-
some and rebellious.

She turned at last and went to Mala's hut. "Send your
son to me. He is a good man, I will have your baby if I
must."

And the Milk of the Zeit rose up in joy and celebration.
Hongath was summoned from the eater's cloaca, where he
was engaged in the work of castrated cretins, making dung
patties to fuel the cooking fires.

Mala greeted him with a wide smile. She clapped her
hands.

"Clean yourself, my son. I have won renewed favor
with the goddess for you. You will be given a second
chance."

The vapor and smoke gradually cleared, and Cracka had
the landing steps extended. The airlock opened. Cracka

and Shay went down to the ground. Rukbhat was urged out
by Maroon.

"C'mon, Mr. Rukhbat, down you go. You're our translator, you know."

Rukbhat felt the hatred from this siffile. It was strong
and sharp. He scurried quickly down the steps. Immediately he could tell that something was wrong, very
wrong.

The wide radial avenue leading into the dagbab town of
weft tenements was empty and still. Clouds of angry bees
buzzed over the empty beetables. No dagbabi were to be
seen.

In the center of the town, casting a giant shadow
through the dagbab world, was the tower of the iulliin, a
fairyland phallus of reddish material capped by a toadstool
roof that bore a white spiral pattern.

"Smoke!" said Shay, pointing to the tower. Wisps of
black could be seen rising on the far side.

Rukbhat felt the hair stand upon the back of his neck.
Uneasily he looked around him. There was no doubting it,
this was a case of musht. Something exceptionally griev-
ous had gone wrong.

"Where is everybody?" Cracka said.

Rukbhat shrugged. Could they not feel the eyes upon
them, thousands of ferocious little black beams, skewer-
ing them from the city. "I—I do not know. This is highly unusual." Rukbhat restrained himself from turning
and running back to the space ship. The thought of
the danger he was in made him almost faint from sheer
anxiety.

He must not warn the siffile, though, that was his duty.
It was plain to him. If the dagbabi devoured the rebel siffile, a grave peril would be cleansed from the Plowl.

Perhaps he could outrun them when they came? But if
he broke too soon he would warn the siffile. At all costs he

must not warn the siffile. Something in his brain hammered away with the fear.

They began to walk slowly toward the tower, down the avenue.

Bat Maroon sensed something awful in the air. "Hey, I don't like this!" He called down to them.

They heard something, a shout from far away. Bat looked up; he had it in a moment. "At the top of the tower —someone's waving."

Cracka and Shay studied the tower. It was true, there were tiny figures up there, a thousand feet or more, waving and yelling.

"What's wrong? Something is definitely wrong."

"I feel it too," said Shay. "I feel I'm being watched."

Cracka spun Rukbhat around and seized the alien by his long, scraggly throat. "Something is going on here. What is it? I don't believe you've been telling me all you know."

Rukbhat gasped. The siffile held up that long knife. One slip and it would slice into Rukbhat dal Vnego Urtisim and end his life forever. The thought was simply too appalling. "The dagbabi must have turned feral. It can happen, but it is very rare, I have never—"

Cracka choked off the rest. "Yeah, I bet."

There was a long troncher hoot in the distance.

"That's Kid Folo! I'd know it anywhere."

"Yeah, I'm convinced too. Let's head back to the ship real slow."

They started back, and suddenly a massive sobbing ululation sounded from fifty thousand throats and the tenement alleys swarmed with dagbabi, their jaws clacking, their legs pumping.

Cracka, Shay, and Rukbhat sprinted for the ship. The steps were sixty meters away. Behind them came a multitude of dagbabi, howling with the passion of musht. The clacking of jaws was a roaring sound, like a waterfall of mastication.

As they reached the steps, Bat Maroon loosed a burst of fire from his yashi automatic into the onrushing hordes. Three or four dagbabi hit the dirt. They vanished instantly beneath the rest.

Cracka in the lead, they sprinted up the steps, gasping for breath, the dagbabi right behind. "Start the airlock mechanism," Cracka yelled to Bat.

They reached the airlock and flung themselves through it as it whined shut in the faces of the dagbabi.

Frustrated, the reptiles beat on the outer airlock with their knobby little fists and howled in rage. Inside Cracka turned to the others. "I would say they're pretty upset."

Bat gave a harsh bark of laughter and continued reloading. Bony fists drummed on the hull.

Shay wiped his brow. "First time I ever thought I'd wind up as dinner for lizards."

Cracka ordered the ship's steps to be retracted, slowly. "Give them a chance to get off, we don't have any real quarrel with them."

CHAPTER FORTY-ONE

The ship's warning signal blared loud and clear across Fanthenai. But the dagbabi were beyond warnings. They clacked their jaws in fury and pressed close to the hated ship.

The steps had retracted into the ship, shaking off the last

one or two holdouts. On the screen the computer was showing the top of the tower. The smoke was boiling up around it.

"That fire is taking hold, Cracka. Looks like the whole place is gonna go up in flames."

"And we're sure the kids are up on top there?"

Bat nodded. "That's them all right."

"Know that Kid Folo's hoot anywhere," Shay said.

"Then we've got to move the ship."

Outside, thousands of dagbabi swarmed around the ship, their rage vented in mass chants and the shaking of fists.

"You'll kill a helluva lot of them if you do," Bat pointed out.

"Not unless we absolutely have to, Maroon. Let's see . . ."

Cracka ordered the computer to turn the engines on for a fraction of a second and then to dampen them down again.

After a delay of a second or two, there was a tremendous whipcrack and a flash of light and heat pulsed from the engines. The echo rattled off the walls and roofs.

A number of dagbabi were crisped in the flash, but a great many more were sent scurrying for their lives, self-preservation winning out over the fanaticism of musht. They turned en masse and ran back up the avenues, into the warrens of brown-yellow weft.

As soon as most were clear, Cracka had the engines on again and the ship rose steadily to a height even with the top of the tower.

Cracka ordered the computer to ease the ship over to the tower. "Get the airlock open," he yelled to Shay, who scrambled down from the control chamber to the entrance level. The outer door swung open shortly afterward.

The ship drifted slowly toward the tower, engines roaring.

Cracka had the steps extended, and raised to a point almost horizontal with the airlock, at which point the individual stairs had swiveled down to present a flat walking surface, fringed by the bars of the guide mechanism that supported the handrails on both sides. At the far end was the fan-shaped, two-meter-wide landing platform.

With the airlock open, the brutal roaring hum of the drives filled the ship. With it came smoke; the tower was ablaze at the bottom. The extension steps seemed to float, ever so slowly, toward the small group huddled together around the topmost crown of the tower. Smoke was pouring from the open doorway, and a solid wall of black smoke was rising on the far side.

The end of the platform trailed past the crown, the ship drifting slightly in the heat from below.

Cracka ordered the ship to stop, to backtrack. As it did, there was a sudden eruption of noise right underneath them, where the emission from the ship's engines had ignited the roof weft. More smoke billowed up, obscuring the extension stairs, pouring into the airlock. It even reached the control chamber, a harsh choking stink that had their eyes watering and their lungs aching.

The ship brought the extension steps back, in front of the high crown and its gallery. A pair of figures jumped for the steps. One seemed to miss. There was more smoke right across the screen, but then it cleared and both figures could be seen hanging from the end of the steps, holding on to a control rod that ran across the bottom of the platform.

The figures wriggled. Cracka was immediately certain that one of them wasn't human.

The steps moved back again and another figure jumped across to them safely, and then black smoke blew across the scene in ever increasing amounts.

Through Rukbhat, Cracka ordered the computer to get some close-ups of the people on the tower. The cameras probed the smoke, and a few moments later he found himself examining the Sun Mel of Planggi. "What the hell?" Cracka muttered. Then he saw Rilla Boan, her hair whipping around her in the wind raised by the fire. Behind her was a dagbab.

The computer announced that the ship's engines were overheating due to an exterior source of heat.

Cracka peered through the murk on the screen. Four figures were aboard the platform. He ordered the computer to shift the ship away.

The ship used attitude jets to swing itself a hundred meters or more distant from the burning tower. The extension steps wobbled a little; they were skillfully made, and very strong, but they had not been designed to hold such a weight unsupported.

Two figures were crawling along the steps toward the airlock. The one in front gave out little screams every time the steps shook underneath her.

Two figures were struggling, hanging from the control rod. With another pair crouched on the platform above them. One of the dangling figures was Nathan Prench.

In the close-up they could see the problem. On the platform were Folo and an iulliin. But they could not reach down far enough under the platform to get within a hand-clasp of the pair trapped below.

Of which one was a dagbab. Its eyes were bulging in fear as it clung to the half-inch-thick control rod.

Cracka jumped from his seat. "Watch Rukbhat!" he yelled to Bat, and he ran for the airlock, jumping past Shay Kroppa and starting out into thin air, on the steps.

The smoke swirled past, and huge flames were visible at the base of the tower. The town was sliding past dizzyingly, hundreds of feet below. The steps shuddered ominously with every step he took. Cracka did his best not to look down, not even to think about down. And he soon came to Rilla Boan, covered in soot, shuffling forward slowly along the steps, her hands gripping the rails so tightly her knuckles were white. Following her was a dagbab.

Her eyes went wide, white saucers in the smoke black, as she saw him. She tried to say something, but all that came out was a squeaky little scream. Her voice was gone.

Cracka shifted around her. The whole extension step array shivered in a gust of wind, and he faced the dagbab, which delicately moved to one side to let him pass.

He approached the platform, an iulliin was there lying flat out beside Folo, trying to reach underneath to Nathan.

"Out of the way!" yelled Cracka.

Folo looked up and stared at him in stupefaction.

"I—" he began, but Cracka got down and worked himself to the edge of the platform.

"Folo, hold my legs, I'm going to try and reach Nathan."

He swung out. Folo gripped his thighs. The iulliin held his ankles.

Below was a whirling cityscape of dagbab tenements.

And underneath the platform, hanging from the narrow rod, was Nathan Prench.

"Nathan!" shouted Cracka.

Nathan's grip was fading.

"Hang on, kid!" Cracka began swinging himself closer.

As he did so, the dagbab moved hand over hand, closer to Nathan.

He swung again but came up still six inches short. Nathan was almost gone, his hands losing all strength. The dagbab was right behind.

Cracka saw the dagbab get to Nathan, saw the bony little reptile hand curl around Nathan's right wrist.

The boy's left hand came loose, all strength gone. But the dagbab clutched his wrist and clung on with one arm.

Cracka swung himself again, pushing hard in desperation. For a sickening moment he felt Folo almost let go of his knees, and then he'd reached far enough to grab Nathan's outflung left arm by the wrist.

As he swung back, the dagbab released the boy and they swung back together and then, very slowly, were hauled back up onto the platform above.

They crouched there briefly on the platform.

Nathan's face was drawn and smoke-blackened, but he broke into an enormous smile. "The ranger! I should have known it would be you!"

Cracka grinned back and gestured to the ship. "Get over to that airlock before this thing collapses."

Nathan got.

Cracka turned back to the others.

"One more time, fellows. There's a dagbab down there. He just saved Nathan's life. We have to get him."

Folo stared at him. "A dagbab?"

"Yeah, come on."

Once more he swung beneath the platform, with Folo and the Sun Mel holding his legs.

The dagbab clung forlornly to the rod. The black reptile eyes were unreadable. Strength was fading, death approaching.

Cracka reached out a hand. For a moment the dagbab stared at him, then it swung itself toward him and he caught its wrist and together they were hauled up to the platform.

They scrambled across to the airlock, where Shay Kroppa hauled them in, pausing only a moment to exclaim "By the Moth!" at the presence of the dagbab.

Inside the airlock a wild scene of celebration broke out. Folo hugged Shay and Bat. Nathan tried to introduce the

Sun Mel to Cracka, Rilla wept with her arms extended to the ceiling, but whether out of relief, joy, terror, she knew not exactly which.

The dagbabs stared at them all with fixed, hypnotic eyes. The fires of musht were extinguished, but the bizarreness of siffile behavior still caused a tingling sensation in the dagbab brains.

The humans poured through the ship, up the access tube and into the control chamber.

Tied to his chair, Rukbhat watched them with open loathing.

Then he caught sight of the Sun Mel, an iulliin, clad in filthy rags, covered in soot.

The Sun Mel heard Rukbhat's cry and turned and almost fainted. There, at last, was what he had dreamed of finding all his life. There, dressed in the clothing of the ancients, was someone from a Sun Clanth that had retained its science.

"Who are you?" said the iulliin in the chair, at home amidst all the technology. His accent was strange, clipped, nasal.

"I? I am the unworthy Sun Mel of Planggi. Shazzeul ab vil Planggi, to be precise."

"Sun Mel!" Rukbhat exclaimed. The fellow spoke a strange, antiquated Iullas, and his title was a bizarre atavism from the distant past.

"Precisely, Lord, and that I am." The Sun Mel smiled and nodded, happy beyond dreams.

■ CHAPTER FORTY-TWO

They'd flown thousands of kilometers outward when Cracka finally decided to take them down and land in a forest of bright green hand palms.

They selected a good-looking clearing near a canal, and the ship computer did the rest.

When the smoke cleared they opened the airlock and extended the steps once more.

Cracka showed the forest to Ump and Illi, the two dagbabi. "You are free to leave if you wish," he growled in rough-hewn Iullas.

The dagbabi stared in silence at the forest. Then Ump replied, speaking very slowly so the siffile might understand. "We stay, if allowed. We feel better to be free with you than alone in forest."

After a few repeats, Cracka understood. Solemnly he shook each of the little aliens by the hand. Then he saluted. After a second's hesitation, they returned the salute flawlessly.

Bat Maroon fought hard to stifle the giggles, especially when Cracka fed him a freezing glare.

"Now I seen everything," said Shay Kroppa with admiration as the dagbabi headed for the stairs.

"Time for a conference, I think." Cracka led them back to the control chamber.

Cracka found Nathan talking with Rukbhat, the Sun Mel

beside them, adding to Rukbhat's confusion. Never had Rukbhat imagined anything more deadly than the Buckshore siffile. Now he was confronted with a youth who spoke fluent Iullas and who already understood far too much about the desperate situation the iulliin now faced.

"We have two more volunteers for the liberation forces," Cracka announced.

"Ump and Illi?" Nathan said.

"They wouldn't leave."

Nathan smiled. "Our friend Rukbhat here, on the other hand, would love to leave, wouldn't you Rukbhat?"

Rukbhat stared at them dully. The nightmare had become endless. He was lost in captivity to feral siffile.

"Anyway, Rukbhat seems to think that there's little likelihood of any pursuit. If they didn't come while I was transmitting from the tower, they won't make the effort now."

Rukbhat pursed his lips and stared down at his bony knees.

Bat sat down opposite the defeated iulliin lord. "From what he told us before, it sounded as if getting rid of him and Lady Weanda was going to make a lot of people real happy. I guess nobody wanted them back all that bad." Bat crossed his legs and picked at his nails.

"So what are we going to do next?" Nathan asked.

Cracka rubbed his chin and exchanged glances with Shay and Bat. "Well, that's what we have to work out. The Calabel people are all in the Meninrud Lors Sun Clanth. Maybe if we can get this ship back to the normal galaxy we can send out a call for help. Get the Homeworld Fleet in here."

Nathan shook his head. "I asked Rukbhat about that. He says these little ships aren't built to take the stress of the transition between the two universes. He says we need the mother ship to go back."

"That's what I was afraid of," Cracka said in a grim voice.

"What about Sam?" Rilla Boan suddenly said.

Nathan shivered. Cracka turned to Rilla. This was one problem he really wished he didn't have. "From what you tell me it sounds like we ought to find him, stop him from creating any more havoc."

"We should have finished him long ago," Bat said firmly.

"He's dangerous! With those helmets he's capable of anything." Rilla's eyes were wide.

"Well, he's not our only concern," said Cracka. "There's still Nathan's mother. We ought to try to find her, don't you think?"

"Find Avis?" Rilla rolled her eyes. "Forget it. You don't know if she's even still alive. You could search forever and not find her."

Glumly Nathan nodded. Finding his mother would be a tremendous task. The flying creature and its master might have carried Avis away in any direction, for an unknown distance. She was lost in the vastness of the Sun Clanth.

"Any ideas, Nathan?"

He shrugged. "We know the top speed of the air barque, and can therefore chart a circle for the possible area in which the sheriff might now be located—a radius of a few hundred kilometers by now."

He swallowed.

"But my mother was taken away many days ago. The flying creature was a punga. They can cover thousands of kilometers, if I understand the Sun Mel correctly, and if he knows what he's talking about. If that's true, then already the area we might have to search for her is pretty big—maybe too big."

"Lot of ifs in all that," Shay said.

"Yeah," Nathan said bleakly.

Eventually the meeting broke up. Bat and Shay went out

to explore the surrounding forest. Nathan stood in the rim of the airlock and watched them stride purposefully into the hand-palm stands.

The sun beamed down through the enormous blue sky. Cloud ramparts marched across the distance. Most of the palms were closed up, protecting themselves from water loss.

Out in the forest, by the canal, Folo and Martherer were walking, slowly, for Martherer was still very weak, although her heart felt so buoyant she thought she might float off the ground at any moment.

They didn't say much. Both were too filled with emotion for words. But they knew there was a lot to be said and that the time would be given them to say it. Neither could think of anything better right then than to be alive and in each other's arms.

Across the canal the hand palms waved in a slight breeze. Up in the sky cumulus clouds were gathering in the distance, the golden sunlight playing on their upper ramparts.

ABOUT THE AUTHOR

CHRISTOPHER ROWLEY was born in Massachusetts in 1948 to an American mother and an English father. Soon afterward he began traversing the Atlantic Ocean, a practice that has continued relentlessly ever since. Educated in the U.S., Canada, and for the most part at Brentwood School, Essex, England, he became a London-based journalist in the 1970s. In 1977 he moved to New York and began work on *The War For Eternity*, his first science-fiction novel. Published by Del Rey Books in 1983, it won him the Compton Crook/Stephen Tall Memorial Award for best first novel. A sequel, *The Black Ship*, followed. *Golden Sunlands* is Rowley's fourth novel.

By the year 2000, 2 out of 3 Americans could be illiterate.

It's true.

Today, 75 million adults...about one American in three, can't read adequately. And by the year 2000, U.S. News & World Report envisions an America with a literacy rate of only 30%.

Before that America comes to be, you can stop it...by joining the fight against illiteracy today.

Call the Coalition for Literacy at toll-free **1-800-228-8813** and volunteer.

**Volunteer
Against Illiteracy.
The only degree you need
is a degree of caring.**

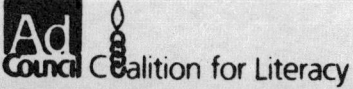

Ad Council Coalition for Literacy

LV-2

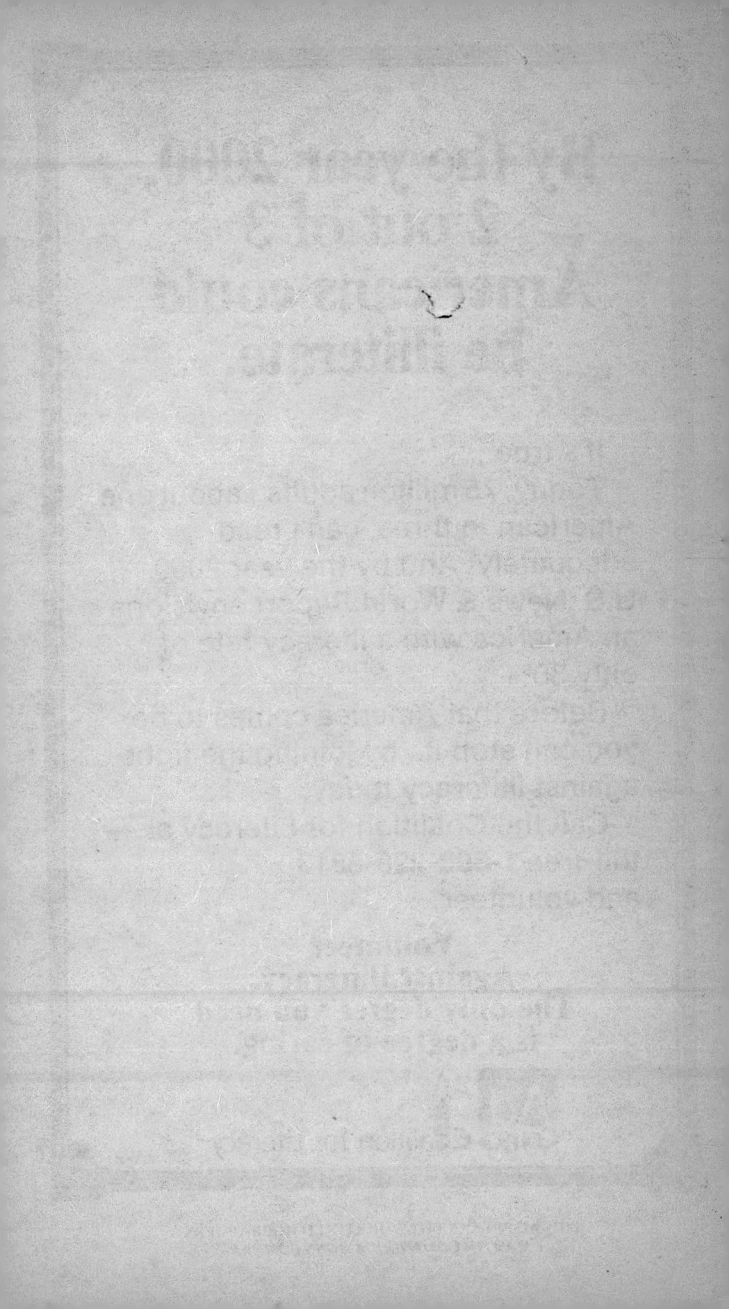